SPECIAL MESSAGE TO READERS

THE ULVERSCROFT FOUNDATION
(registered UK charity number 264873)
was established in 1972 to provide funds for
research, diagnosis and treatment of eye diseases.
Examples of major projects funded by
the Ulverscroft Foundation are:-

- The Children's Eye Unit at Moorfields Eye Hospital, London
- The Ulverscroft Children's Eye Unit at Great Ormond Street Hospital for Sick Children
- Funding research into eye diseases and treatment at the Department of Ophthalmology, University of Leicester
- The Ulverscroft Vision Research Group, Institute of Child Health
- Twin operating theatres at the Western Ophthalmic Hospital, London
- The Chair of Ophthalmology at the Royal Australian College of Ophthalmologists

You can help further the work of the Foundation
by making a donation or leaving a legacy.
Every contribution is gratefully received. If you
would like to help support the Foundation or
require further information, please contact:

THE ULVERSCROFT FOUNDATION
The Green, Bradgate Road, Anstey
Leicester LE7 7FU, England
Tel: (0116) 236 4325

website: \ ...erscroft.com

D1144056

After spending her early years in Lesotho, Beverley Eikli emigrated with her family to Adelaide, Australia, but was lured back to Africa after reading the diaries of her grandfather. There, she found work as a safari camp manager and met a bush pilot, whom she married after a whirlwind romance. Her husband's aviation career has taken them around the globe. Eikli now lives in Gisborne, a small town near Melbourne, with her husband and two daughters.

You can find out more about Beverley Eikli at her website: www.beverleyeikli.com

A LITTLE DECEPTION

When she embarks on a charade of exchanged identities one night to save the family tea plantation, spirited Rose Chesterfield gets more than she bargained for: marriage to the deliciously notorious rake, Viscount Rampton. Unwittingly implicated in a series of high-profile jewel robberies, Rose must outwit a jealous adversary in order to clear her blackened name. But can she regain the love and respect of her husband?

Books by Beverley Eikli
Published by The House of Ulverscroft:

LADY FARQUHAR'S BUTTERFLY
LADY SARAH'S REDEMPTION

BEVERLEY EIKLI

◆

A LITTLE DECEPTION

Complete and Unabridged

ULVERSCROFT
Leicester

First published in Great Britain in 2009

First Large Print Edition
published 2014

Revised 2013 by Beverley Eikli

A catalogue record for this book is available
from the British Library.

ISBN 978–1–4448–2216–8

Published by
F. A. Thorpe (Publishing)
Anstey, Leicestershire

Set by Words & Graphics Ltd.
Anstey, Leicestershire
Printed and bound in Great Britain by
T. J. International Ltd., Padstow, Cornwall

This book is printed on acid-free paper

For my beautiful, talented girls,
Dagny and Sophie.

The Deception

1

London 1818

'The only way we can honour Helena's debt is by giving Lord Rampton the deeds to the plantation, Charles.' Reining in her frustration, Rose cast a withering look at the comatose young woman upon the bed before transferring her contempt to her brother. She couldn't remember when she'd last been so angry. 'Clearly, Helena is in no state to petition his lordship for clemency.'

Charles stroked the limp, elegant hand that rested upon his wife's chest as he knelt at her bedside, his mulish stare focused on the dome of St Paul's through the dirty windowpane rather than at his sister's flushed and angry face. Sweat bathed his brow, hinting at the pressure he was under, but still he came up with the usual excuses. 'Helena's been unwell but she will soon recover her strength. We can delay tonight's dinner . . . play for time,' he muttered. 'More time will allow us to explore other options.' Though still a young man, the lines around his mouth and the furrows across his brow were deeply etched.

He'd been handsome and carefree when he'd married Helena five years before, Rose reflected as she knelt on the threadbare rug to reach beneath the bed for the blue glass vial, now empty, which had rolled there. Sighing, she held it out as she straightened. 'Helena promised to wean herself off this,' she tapped the bottle with fingers noticeably more workworn than those of the West Indies beauty whose gambling and laudanum addictions threatened their futures, 'if you promised to take her to England. You fulfilled your part of the bargain.' She studied the label, adding with a sigh, 'Perhaps it's just as well Helena can't attend Lord Rampton's dinner tonight. Who knows how she might conduct herself given the delicacy of the situation.' She moved to the door, her voice mocking as she dropped the laudanum bottle into her apron pocket. 'At least I can be relied upon to be decorous and obedient. Perhaps I should accompany you.'

Charles jerked his head up. 'You can't possibly go, Rose . . . though I appreciate your offer.' He looked more horrified than he had when he'd set eyes on his unconscious wife minutes before, and Rose almost laughed at the black humour of their predicament. Charles had status, Helena had beauty but Rose had wit and brains. Had she been the one orchestrating their precarious lives, she had no doubt they'd be in a vastly better situation. They'd certainly not be in danger of losing their only home.

Still jesting, she tilted her head and challenged with an arch smile, 'Surely, Charles, you don't subscribe to the notion that marriage confers some kind of magical status which I do not have, simply as your unmarried sister?'

He did not reply as he tenderly contoured the face of the unconscious woman who'd held him in thrall since the moment she'd fluttered her eyelashes at him so many years before. Meanwhile as Rose prepared to quit the room, her suggestion, preposterous a moment ago, took root and flourished.

She paused, her hand on the doorknob. Charles would allow Helena to ruin them all if Rose did not act in their defence. Watching her brother, she said carefully, 'Lord Rampton is due to set sail for the Continent before the week is up and our visit here is for less than three months. We'll have returned to the plantation before he's back in England. He'll never know I'm not Helena.' His opposition cemented her determination. Charles was weak and indecisive. Lord Rampton would almost certainly dictate terms that would be to their detriment and Charles would buckle. Suddenly her idea seemed their only salvation.

She moved back into the room and stroked her brother's arm, her tone wheedling. 'As you've said, I can perform no useful role as your unmarried sister, Charles, but why should you dine with Lord Rampton, alone, when at least *I* can get the measure of him? It's what we must do if we're to get the extension we need to repay Helena's debt.'

Bending, she whispered in his ear. 'Time, Charles, is what we need. I'm certain poor Mama and Papa have a few relatives mouldering in the wings who could help. But Lord Rampton is quite within his rights to demand an immediate settlement,' she caressed his cheek, 'and surely I'd be far more successful at playing on Lord Rampton's heartstrings than you.'

Rose could see Charles was wavering. His stubborn streak was always the final hurdle to overcome. To give in without a fight compromised the feeling that he was in charge, the young baronet, head of his household: his wife and two sisters.

'If I went as Helena — '

'No! Good God, Rose, are you out of your mind?'

Rose drew herself up proudly, more

6

determined than ever. Striving to remain calm, she said, 'Lord Rampton has met none of us and Helena was in masquerade when she lost to this other man who's transferred the debt to his lordship. How's Lord Rampton to know the difference when it's just for one evening? I'm sure I could persuade him to alter the terms — '

'No, Rose.' Shrugging off her hand, Charles shook his head emphatically. 'As Helena's husband I'm responsible for her debts and as your brother I'm responsible for your welfare. It would not be right to expose you to this . . . well, we don't know what kind of man Lord Rampton is. Ruthless. Calculating. Those are just some of the descriptions I've heard bandied about my club. I admit it's because of Helena we're in danger of losing the plantation but you had nothing to do with,' he looked pained, 'the sordid business that night.'

'With due respect, Charles,' Rose cut in sharply, 'I've had to contend with Helena's dangerous vices for the past five years and I think I can claim some credit for the fact that we still have a plantation!' She'd allowed her anger to get the better of her. Charles did not react well to anger. Changing tack, she added softly, 'I shan't disgrace you, I promise. I'll simply be there as Lady Chesterfield instead of Miss Chesterfield. It's not such a terribly wicked lie.'

★ ★ ★

'You will not attend Lord Rampton's dinner dressed like that!'

Edith, the loyal family retainer who had mothered the family for as long as Rose could remember, raked her charge with disapproving eyes before bundling Rose upstairs, pressing her down before her dressing-table. No further description was needed as to what she thought of Rose's drab grey velvet gown.

'It's the best I have,' argued Rose.

'And has been since you developed a chest and were out of short clothes. Miss Arabella! There you are! Tell me, what do you think of your sister's gown? Would you wear it in fine company?'

Arabella, combing out her long, white-gold hair as she perched on the edge of Rose's bed, regarded her gravely. 'Of course not, but Rose doesn't have any fine clothes. If I knew her ankles wouldn't show I'd lend her something of mine . . . which would still be preferable to that old rag she has on.'

Watching as Edith went about her task with deft fingers, smoothing her sister's glossy chestnut hair back from her high forehead,

8

coaxing the curls from a fashionably high topknot, she asked, 'Does this mean you plan on going about in fine company, after all, Rose? I thought you said the season was a lot of nonsense and you wouldn't be caught dead at anyone's 'drawing room'?'

'Your sister only says such things because there's no money to launch both of you, my girl. And does she look twenty-six with those fine eyes and glowing skin? Why, she'll always be a beauty.' Edith looked severely at her younger charge. 'Just bear in mind, Miss Arabella, that you have your sister to thank for the fact that you're to have a season at all.'

'Perhaps Rose could wear something of Helena's,' Arabella suggested, chastened.

'I couldn't possibly!'

'Well, you're exactly the same height as Helena and I'm sure she wouldn't mind, since you're going in her stead.'

Rose looked grim. 'That was not what I was worried about.' An image of Helena with her languid self-possession and love of finery flashed through her mind and for a moment the magnitude of what she was about to do threatened to engulf Rose. Could she carry it off? After all, compared with the worldly Helena she was a greenhorn, an unsophisticated Colonial. Cleverer than Helena, certainly, but by no means as self-assured in the company of men. Nor as beautiful. Without these attributes was she not as good as throwing herself to the lions and making fools of them all in the process?

She took a deep breath and cast all doubts from her mind. It was the only way. She had a role to play, and play it she would. To perfection.

'One of Helena's gowns,' she murmured, thoughtfully. Then, twisting her head to look at Arabella she said, wryly, 'You're right, dearest. Find me something . . . not too revealing. But don't tell Charles. Helena is still sleeping so I can't ask her, but it's for her benefit. Dear Lord,' she muttered, putting her hand to her chest and stroking the comforting drab grey velvet. It had been so long since she'd been in sophisticated company she'd never been told whether she had a cleavage worth showing, or not.

★ ★ ★

Ashley Delacroix, Viscount Rampton, eyed his dinner guest appreciatively across the table. Babbage had not lied when he had called Lady Chesterfield a beauty. His use of the term 'exotic' was, perhaps, a little off the mark. 'Classic English rose' was a more apt description; although perhaps Babbage had been referring to the young lady's unusually sun-kissed complexion and taste in attire, for the gown that barely clothed Lady Chesterfield this evening was considerably less modestly cut than the type of evening gown most English women favoured. Not that Rampton was complaining. It was always a pleasure to dine with a beautiful woman, especially one not too shy to display her ample charms to best advantage. It might explain, too, the reason for her husband not looking very happy, although that could, just as likely, be due to the nature of the business which had brought them together.

Rampton raised his glass to his guests and fixed Lady Chesterfield with an appreciative look as he proposed the toast.

'To a pleasant evening and the satisfactory completion of our business.'

It was unlike him to mix business with pleasure. Boredom had been to blame. When his friend Babbage had sworn he would repay his loan to Rampton within the sennight, then reneged with the surprising excuse that he was reluctant to press the lady who owed him the necessary means to do so, Rampton had been unsympathetic. But when Babbage had elaborated upon the evening that he and the 'exotic' beauty had spent together, Rampton's curiosity had, despite himself, been aroused.

To his surprise he'd found himself absolving Babbage of his debt by taking on Lady Chesterfield's debt in lieu. For no better reason than that he wanted to see for himself whether this apparently fascinating young woman would enthral him as much as the notoriously difficult-to-impress Babbage.

'I hope you are enjoying your visit to London, Lady Chesterfield,' he said, conversationally. 'My friend, Adrian Babbage — whom you will no doubt recall,' he added, his smile sly, 'tells me you have spent your life in the West Indies and this is your first visit to your father's home. You must still be adjusting to the climate.'

'I daresay I will not be here long enough to get used to it, Lord Rampton,' said Rose, coolly. She disliked the way her host's eyes travelled languorously from her décolletage to her face when he spoke. Certainly they were very fine eyes: a piercing blue, but the supercilious arch of the eyebrows disconcerted her. And while his unconcealed admiration was certainly balm to her self-confidence, there was something in their depths that hinted at a whole world of which she knew nothing.

She forced a smile. It was important that he should not suspect any discomfiture in her. Indeed, discomfiture was rare for Rose and it was highly disconcerting to suspect she wouldn't be feeling this uncomfortable had Lord Rampton not been such an exquisite nonpareil. Indeed, she could never remember having met a gentleman who exuded such potent magnetism — and who was aware of it, she thought grimly.

Thick dark hair swept back from high cheekbones while intense dark blue eyes glittered with unconcealed interest in her above his beautiful, straight nose, a fine piece of physiognomy which she found herself admiring simply so she wouldn't be drawn by his mouth.

Yet she couldn't help herself. That mouth of his was the only part of him that seemed not constructed from marble, for it trembled just a little — from amusement? — and though the suspicion that he found Rose or her predicament amusing should have out-raged her, for a moment all Rose could think of was tracing those exquisitely shaped lips with her forefinger before touching her own experimentally against what seemed the only soft part of the man.

She jerked back. Where had such a thought come from? Blushing, she forced languor into her tone. She was, after all, playing Helena, the bored beauty.

'Once this unsavoury business has been

attended to, and my sister — ' She caught herself just in time. ' — in-law launched, we will return home.'

Fighting the urge to slump and hide as much of herself as possible beneath the table, Rose held herself proudly. Self-conscious though she felt in Helena's outrageously daring, diaphanous silver-and-white evening gown, she knew any attempts at appearing coy or modest would only look contrived and draw further attention to what she wished, heartily, was not quite so obviously on show. She must not look down and frighten herself with the sight of how much bosom was revealed, although the faint breeze that ruffled the curtains and caressed her bare skin was a constant reminder. Edith had assured her that although she looked every inch the seductress, she was not, actually, indecent. It was small consolation.

It was true that Rose was unaccustomed to male attention, and as a result by Lord Rampton's lazy, confident smile. Oh yes, he certainly looked like a man used to getting his own way.

Well, Rose knew how to get her own way too. And success — no, survival — depended upon managing Lord Rampton in the same artful manner she managed her stubborn brother and her volatile, unpredictable sister-in-law. She must play the seductress, as naturally and consummately as Helena, who was the reason behind, and inspiration for, this whole charade.

Leaning slightly across the table, she contrived a faintly seductive pout, surprised at how easily it came . . . and by how much she enjoyed the results.

Charles had tried, several times, to interject. Characteristically he had allowed himself to be quelled on each occasion by an impatient response from Lord Rampton. Rose felt vindicated. Of course she had had no choice but to have come this evening. Her brother was completely out of his depth.

And he looked it. But was he, Rose wondered, aware of the almost conspiratorial smiles that their host continued to direct at her? Her skin tingled.

Rose had always been surprised that Charles was not firmer with Helena on the subject of Helena's conduct and wardrobe, though until now she had never realized how much licence marriage gave one to behave as one chose, rather than as one ought.

Dropping her eyes beneath another of Lord Rampton's searing gazes, Rose encountered her reflection in the highly polished silver epergne that formed the table centrepiece.

Edith had worked wonders with her appearance. The plain creature she'd always thought herself had been transformed into a society beauty with her wide-set bright eyes, pert nose and creamy complexion: the equal of Arabella's pale innocent charm and Helena's lush allure.

With the kind of confidence that now buoyed her she felt capable of anything. Even armed combat with Lord Rampton. Well, she had his measure. He was rich, bored, careless of others, no doubt having never suffered a moment's angst or deprivation in his entire life.

On reflection, the thought was not bolstering. Charity or leniency were not likely characteristics, nor had Rampton been given any good reason to extend either to the struggling Chesterfields.

She resisted the urge to slump in defeat as she acknowledged the size of the debt owed to this man which would suck the lifeblood out of even their marginal existence. What was Rose doing, dreaming of gilded futures when it was not too extreme to say a life in debtor's prison or the workhouse was a distinct possibility if she could not win over this man?

She took a deep, sustaining breath, flicking her tongue over dry lips. Lord Rampton, she realized, was waiting for her to broach the subject which had brought them to his dinner table.

'I realize, Lord Rampton, that you are owed rather a lot of money. Mr Babbage, however, indicated that . . . '

The beautiful Lady Chesterfield's hesitation, and the sudden colour that flooded her cheeks piqued Rampton's curiosity. He waited for her to finish, recalling Babbage's colourful account of this young woman's conduct one wild night during the previous week. It was all the more intriguing for, while Lady Chesterfield, with her lustrous chestnut hair, pretty mouth and high cheekbones beneath intensely blue eyes, was as beautiful as she had been painted, her demeanour did not accord with Babbage's description. In surprising contrast with her gown there had been lapses in her mien, indicating that Lady Chesterfield's confidence was not as iron-clad as she would have him believe.

'What did Mr Babbage say he was prepared to be, Lady Chesterfield?' Rampton prompted, unconcerned that, to his own ears, he sounded condescending. His efforts were rewarded as he watched the blush deepen and noted the difficulty she had in responding. He had not expected such sport when he'd asked the beautiful Lady Chesterfield and her lily-livered husband to dinner.

'Patient, Lord Rampton.'

'Ah, but there we differ, Lady Chesterfield. You see, Mr Babbage is a very patient man. At least, he is where beautiful women are concerned.' Rampton took a sip of his wine, savouring it, and the moment. 'I, on the other hand, am not.'

With amusement he observed the way her fingers clenched the stem of her wine glass and the obvious effort with which she forced herself to relax. She toyed with her glass before glancing at him over the rim, flirtation in her tone as she murmured, 'Mr Babbage is a gentleman.'

His lips curled at the implied rebuke. 'Whereas I am not?'

The seductive gleam that lit up her large blue eyes, and the curve of her mouth — shaped more like a rosebud than the full, sensuous look he generally preferred — went a long way towards explaining the effect this young woman had had on Rampton's erstwhile debtor. He felt a moment's exultation as he held her gaze. He could read collusion in their depths. Yes, he thought with satisfaction, with the Chesterfields as hard pressed for ready funds as rumour had it, there would be no difficulty coming to some mutual agreement with the beautiful Lady

Chesterfield whereby no money need be exchanged. Unconsciously he ran the tip of his tongue over his top lip as he returned a somewhat wolfish smile, gesturing to the footman who hovered at the sideboard to bring more wine. Here was the return on his investment this evening, considering the other diversions he had sacrificed.

'A gentleman?' repeated his lovely guest with evident amusement. 'I am forced to reserve judgement, Lord Rampton. Time alone will tell.'

It could be an entertaining season, thought Rampton, anticipation surging through his loins. Admittedly he already had a mistress but the relationship was on the wane. He was ready for fresh excitement and Lady Chesterfield was an exquisite-looking creature, long married and clearly disenchanted with her husband who had no doubt been chosen for her.

'Yes,' he considered. 'But Mr Babbage has no head for business. Which is why he is perpetually in debt and I am not. Nevertheless, Lady Chesterfield,' he inclined his head, smiling, ignoring Charles, 'I am confident that we can come to some arrangement.'

Yes, he was sure of it. He would not call in the debt. Once Lady Chesterfield had launched her sister-in-law, she and her husband would return to the West Indies. All that differed from the original plan was that, between now and then, he and Lady Chesterfield would have enjoyed a little more pleasure than either of them had anticipated. One only had to spend five minutes in their company to see that neither Sir Charles nor the lovely Lady Chesterfield were likely to object.

The time had come, he decided, to give his current mistress, the fiery, exquisite, but no longer incomparable Lady Barbery, her congé.

★ ★ ★

'You missed a rum do at Baroness Esterhazy's this evening, Rampton.'

Hesitating on the threshold to the library, Rampton turned, narrowing his eyes in greeting. It was hard to tell whether his brother was foxed or not.

He waited as Felix was relieved of his outerwear by Lavery before preceding his brother into the library. 'I had dinner guests.'

'Important dinner guests for you to have refused the baroness's invitation.'

'I turned down three equally enticing invitations, I assure you, Felix.' Rampton's tone was dry as he went to the sideboard, asking carelessly, 'And did the baroness enjoy her evening?'

'Well, she did her best to appear unconcerned by your absence.' Felix waited while his brother poured them both a drink. 'But I wasn't fooled for a minute. Of course, at the first opportunity she holed me up in a dark corner to ask what you were doing.'

'Indeed?' Rampton handed his brother the tumbler half-full of amber liquid, then settled himself on the leather sofa, stretching his long legs in front of him to gain maximum benefit from the small coal fire that burned in the grate. He felt a little guilty that he had trouble visualizing the baroness's bounteous charms when she'd been out of his life for less than six months. She'd been replaced by Catherine Barbery, his very first lover, who had unexpectedly waltzed back into his life a few months ago.

Well, now it was time for Catherine to go, too, he reflected, conscious of a very potent surge of desire that made him cross and re-cross his legs. Since last night, all he could think of was Lady Chesterfield's fair and fragile beauty. And those eyes: clear and incisive, as if she knew exactly what was on his mind and was both intrigued and terrified. He must go about his wooing with care. So many of his mistresses had thrown themselves at him but Lady Chesterfield was an altogether different proposition. He was visited by the interesting thought that she might be sizing him up as her first conquest. Her lapses of self-confidence would attest to that. Also, five years married to that dandelion baronet who agreed with every-thing anyone said — if they said it with enough force or conviction — must mean poor Lady Chesterfield, who was clearly a spirited little thing, was panting for a forceful lover. Having been incarcerated on the West Indies most of her life she'd have little knowledge as to how to go about the whole business.

Amusement and anticipation flickered in his self-acknowledged carnal depths and he realised, unrepentant, that he was licking his lips, already relishing the sport to come. Indeed, there'd be much of that, and he was quite happy to lead the way.

'Come now, Rampton, don't assume that indifferent tone with me. Three months ago you were wild for the baroness.' Felix lowered himself into the wing chair opposite, his mouth curling in a boyish and far less cynical imitation of his brother's. 'I told her I had not the least idea what you were up to this evening but that I was there in your stead and hoped she could regard me with similar affection.' With a shrug, he added on a philosophical note, 'She was unmoved. Even flattery, far in excess of her merits, made no difference. And then the baron arrived, all husbandly solicitation, so that was the end of that. Such a shame you always fall for the married ones.'

'My dear boy, you cannot pretend to be so naïve!' Rampton gave a short laugh. This was not a topic he wished to entertain with his brother. 'I'd be a fool to do otherwise.'

'You can't shrug off your matrimonial duty for too much longer, surely?'

'I endured a tedious evening at Almack's last night, in case you had forgotten.' Almack's was bursting with debutantes at this time of year. Rampton decided not to add that he derived greater sport from the more comely chaperones than he did from their gauche young charges, fresh from the schoolroom.

Felix, however, was well aware of his elder brother's predilections, for he said, almost testily, 'You need a wife, not a mistress, Rampton. Soon you'll be considered even more ramshackle than our dissolute papa.'

The amused smile froze. Rampton drained his tumbler. 'Why, Felix, I do believe you are serious.' Collecting himself, he assumed a tone that was far more light-hearted than he felt as he pointed out, 'Ramshackle I would be indeed to saddle myself — and the rest of the family — with an unsuitable bride. I long ago learned that duty and pleasure are two very different matters. And matrimony, you would do well to remember the next time you find yourself in thrall to the latest goddess, does not fall within the latter category. Rest assured that in the meantime, unless some worthy contender for my affections drops from the sky into my lap, I intend to take my pleasure while I can.' Yawning, he added, 'I'm off to bed. Unlike some, I no longer have the advantage of youth.'

Felix pulled a face as he watched his brother rise. 'God forbid, I'd better make the most of the few good years left to me. Looking at you is like looking at myself in a mirror in five year's time, all craggy and going grey.' He grinned. 'But without the boyish charm. Little consolation that the women seem to find a viscount in his dotage a more enticing prospect than his younger, far handsomer brother.'

Rampton snorted as he headed for the door, tossing over his shoulder, 'I think my pocketbook accounts for that.'

'I understand your caution, Rampton.' Felix's tone grew serious. 'But are you so afraid of parson's mousetrap? Surely you'll confess to having been intrigued by just one unmarried miss tossed in your direction?'

Rampton turned slowly, forcing amusement to his lips. 'The short answer, little brother, is no.' He hesitated. 'I have never been in love and my desire is whipped up only when I am assured my quarry is safely unobtainable.'

'But don't you get fagged with Mama forever charging you with your neglect in securing the family line?'

'Mama will have to be satisfied another ten years for that is when I plan to retire quietly to the country and breed sheep,' he grinned, 'amongst other things. In ten years a pliant, suitable wife will fit nicely into my plans. So if these questions are on mama's behalf, you can tell her that the nursery will not need decorating for at least a decade.'

Felix looked unimpressed. 'You really are just like Papa. Still, it can't be too bad having all these designing mamas trying to entice you with their daughters. I wish I were so popular!' He sighed. 'At least you're more discerning and discreet than Papa and, lucky for you, it seems there's no shortage of pretty matrons panting for your attentions.'

Rampton shrugged as he stroked the doorknob. 'It's hardly surprising I'm not inclined to chase innocent virgins, given the astonishing number of bored, highly desirable married women who make plain their desire for a little dalliance with a viscount in his dotage — as you put it.'

Once again, his thoughts strayed to the enchanting Lady Chesterfield. The messages she had sent him that night might have been mixed but mutual attraction had charged the air. He couldn't wait until their next meeting.

Felix tossed back his drink, then rose to pour another, saying in falsely sympathetic tones, 'Poor Rampton, to be leg-shackled by such mistrust must be a terrible thing. As long as caution remains your mistress you'll never find a wife. Anyway, what are your plans for tomorrow that you have to be up with the birds?'

Rampton contemplated the question. 'My plans for tomorrow,' anticipation turned up the corners of his mouth, 'and perhaps those for the next few weeks, will be to mix a little business with pleasure.'

'But you said — '

'I never said,' Rampton grinned, 'that pleasure and duty were mutually exclusive. And it just so happens that tomorrow is one occasion when they are not.'

2

Arabella leant back against the threadbare squabs of their hackney carriage, facing Rose, her eyes wide. Despite her new clothes she looked much more the schoolgirl than the debutante who must make a good marriage before Rose could return to her beloved island, having discharged her duty towards her little sister.

'You flirted with Lord Rampton? Just like Helena?' She giggled, ignoring Helena's darkling look. 'Rose, I can't imagine it. When you're with a gentleman you're always so . . . ' She floundered for the right word. ' . . . prim.'

Helena was not in a similarly light-hearted frame of mind. Tossing her glossy dark head, her eyes flashed as she muttered, 'Well, when it came to my clothes, Rose was as careless of those as she was of my feelings regarding this ridiculous charade.'

'Edith noticed the tear in the skirt when she fetched it from your room. She made a beautiful job of mending it, didn't she?' responded Rose, smoothly. 'I believe you caught it on a rosebush during Mrs

Caversham's card party the other week.'

Helena turned her head away from the two sisters on the seat opposite, her normally sensuous mouth a rigid line. She watched the handsome Park Lane residences pass before them.

'I daresay I'll never be allowed to forget that night,' she said, bitterly. 'I knew how it would be. Charles has never reprimanded me. With his experience of the world he understood that I was in an impossible position. Everyone had a wager. People would have assumed that Charles keeps me on short rations had I not kept up; or would even have accused me of putting myself above the rest if I had offered my excuses.'

'A shame you didn't know what fast company you were keeping, Helena,' remarked Rose. 'Or that you slipped out of the house and left Charles sleeping without asking his permission, for he'd have explained that gaming in England is very different from gaming at home, where people were a little more understanding of your . . . vices.'

'Gambling is not a crime . . . unless an unmarried woman plays for stakes which can only be honoured by those upon whom she is dependent,' Helena muttered.

Rose forced back her anger. The implication was clear. When Helena married, her father had settled a modest sum upon her. When Rose's father had died he had been so deeply in debt there was no dowry to settle upon either her or Arabella. Unless Charles took care of them, or they could find husbands for whom fortune did not matter — a slim chance indeed — they were entirely at the mercy of their closest male relative: Charles, whose finances they knew little about, but who never seemed to reproach his feckless, beautiful wife.

'Yes, but back home you've been gambling with the same people since you were seven years old, when your father first encouraged you to place a wager. You've only ever gambled with friends. Until now.'

Rose was not going to concede anything. Helena had never been properly called to task for her behaviour. Charles had begged his sister not to labour the incident, despite its repercussions for the rest of the family, saying Helena was deeply upset and likely to dissolve into remorseful tears. Rose only wished she could see it.

'Did Lord Rampton laugh at you when you tried to flirt with him?' Helena asked, changing the subject.

'He flirted straight back at me,' Rose laughed, recalling the evening with a surprising jolt of pleasure.

'He would not have bothered if you'd been dressed the way you are now.'

All the pleasure drained out of Rose as she contemplated her drab apricot velvet walking-dress. Apricot was a colour that made her look horribly sallow. The dress had once belonged to her mother, who had been taller and, at the time she owned it, stouter. Rose, who was not naturally gifted with a needle, had made a gallant effort to remodel it, but it had never been a great success. Not that that had mattered . . . until now. Their social life had been limited in the last few years of her father's declining health. Rose made few calls and rarely received them. Besides, it was not as if there had been suitors for whom she must make an effort.

Rose glanced at Helena and was disconcerted by an unexpected wave of envy. Despite wearing a sprigged muslin that was demure by her standards, Helena still managed to look striking. Like Rose the night before, Helena would have had no compunction about flirting with Lord Rampton.

No, she would not! Rose's momentary doubt as to whether Helena would have been the better candidate in persuading Lord Rampton to extend the terms of their loan was swept away by righteous conviction. Helena could persuade a man to do most things she wanted but Helena's voracious appetite would have had her setting out to make him her slave. Rose could even imagine Charles discovering his wife — Heaven forbid — wrapped in Lord Rampton's arms in some dark corner, which of course Helena would find some way to justify.

Heat prickled Rose's skin and she crossed her legs, suddenly uncomfortable by the unfamiliar sensations raging through her body. She put it down to the fact that she couldn't bear Charles to have to suffer such disappointment. Charles loved Helena to distraction. Indeed, it was a good thing it was Rose who was trying to twist Lord Rampton round her little finger.

'I wish it would meet with some horrible accident,' said Arabella, referring to Rose's unbecoming dress. 'I'm always meaning to accidentally pour something dreadful on to it and quite ruin it. But then Rose has so few clothes.' Smiling, she added, 'Rose looked so beautiful wearing your white dress, Helena, and with her hair done so modishly. I couldn't believe it was her. Maybe you could lend her more of your clothes and then she could go about in society and find herself a rich husband. Isn't that what you've always said she should do?'

'Yes, but not in my clothes.' Helena

shuddered. 'Anyway, you said yourself, my wardrobe is hardly compatible with the kind of figure darling Rose chooses to cut.' She glanced from her high-waisted, low-fronted sprigged muslin to Rose's prim, unfashionable gown. 'Rose looks every inch the spinster she is at such pains to present to the world. I wouldn't dream of insulting her by offering her the loan of my clothes.'

Anger silenced Rose as Arabella asked, 'But what about when Rose meets Lord Rampton again? She has to pretend to be you, and she can only do that if you lend her something from your wardrobe. It would be terrible if he discovered her deception.'

'Lord Rampton is about to set sail in search of far more engaging females than your sister.' Helena's clipped pronouncement shouldn't have excited the kind of emotion that assailed Rose — she knew it. She certainly was used to Helena's careless disregard; however, it took a great deal of effort to remain on her seat and not lunge for Helena and slap her face. Rose closed her eyes for a moment and held her breath. Good Heavens, when had her temper nearly got the better of her? Rose was distinguished by her composure and good sense. She was the *antithesis* of Helena.

'Well, at least Rose managed to play for

more time. She was very clever and clearly captivated the viscount.'

'He must be a kind man.' Helena smiled sweetly at Rose. 'No doubt he'd have been equally receptive to any petitioning female, whether she was an ape leader in drab apricot velvet or a diamond of the first water.' Ignoring Arabella's outraged gasp she added, 'Rose knows a dose of smelling-salts would have had me up to the mark in no time but clearly the chance to go about in company pretending to be a married woman proved too tempting to resist. But Rose had her chance.'

There had been just the tiniest pause before uttering the last sentence. Rose glared at Helena. It was just like her to drag up the past to bolster her case, rubbing Rose's nose in her failure to secure the one splendid marital chance Rose had ever been offered.

'Sir Hector was Father's best friend.' Rose's voice was tight. 'I had known him all my life. How could I possibly have thrown myself into his arms and felt joy at being his wife when he was more like a kindly old uncle?'

'He had the means to give you everything you wanted.'

'Is that why you set your cap at him after Rose rejected him?' Arabella looked uncharacteristically confrontational.

'Hush, Arabella,' Rose admonished, though touched that her docile little sister would take such a risk on her behalf. Five years ago the whispers were that Helena had indeed set her cap at Sir Hector before she'd married Charles with almost unseemly haste after Sir Hector's rejection. 'Why look! There's Aunt Alice waving to us from the upstairs casement,' she said, relieved that they were at their destination. 'At least, she looks so like Mama it must be Aunt Alice.'

★　★　★

'I declare, it's like seeing my dead sister walk through that door!' With outstretched arms, Aunt Alice greeted Rose at the top of the portico steps before leading them into her fashionable townhouse. 'You must forgive me for being such a sentimental creature. I was always much more of a silly than Beatrice.' Dabbing at her eyes with a lace handkerchief, she ushered the girls towards a comfortable cluster of seats once they'd reached the over-decorated drawing room. 'And you are the exotic creature dear Charles married,' she added, turning to Helena who was ensconced on a blue and silver upholstered Egyptian sofa. 'I believe he'd been dangling after you since you were in short skirts. So now,

Arabella, we need to find you a fine husband before the end of the season,' she gushed. 'Just see if we don't!'

Rose had never met her aunt, who'd waved Rose's parents off to their new life after her father had inherited the plantation shortly after gambling away his English estate.

'We are so grateful for your offer to launch Arabella,' said Rose. 'And Helena, of course, is dying for a Season. This is the first time she has left the island.'

'But what about you, my dear Rose?' asked Aunt Alice.

'Rose will look after Charles,' said Helena, with a complacent smile. 'They prefer a quiet life. Rose was telling me only the other week how much she preferred the idea of curling up with a good book than attending Lady Glenton's soirée. Isn't that so, Rose?'

Rose hesitated. 'I did say that,' she conceded, adding silently that it was only so Charles needn't feel so inadequate that he had not the funds to clothe both his sisters sufficiently, given his wife's extravagance.

'But my dear Rose, you are only in London this one Season. It may be your last chance to find a husband.' Aunt Alice's expression was almost comical in its distress.

'I do not want one, Aunt Alice.' Rose forced a smile. 'I couldn't bear to be away from the plantation for too long.' This, at least, was true. Rose had no intention of remaining in England, which meant it would be unfair to spend money they did not have on a wardrobe for her. Arabella needed fine clothes to make a good match. The last thing on Rose's mind was attracting a husband when her heart longed for the heat and familiarity of her island home.

Her aunt regarded Rose as if she had just admitted to a penchant for robbing graves. 'Not want a husband?' she repeated. 'But, my dear, every woman needs a husband, whether they want one or not. I thought that was why you were in England.'

'That's why Arabella is in England, and why I am here, accompanying her.' Rose blushed, adding awkwardly, 'Did I not explain that in my letter?'

'Oh yes, you said Arabella was to be launched but that there were not the funds to launch you, also.' Aunt Alice cleared her throat. 'I realize you are quite a bit older; however, surely if the opportunity presented itself, you'd be amenable to the idea of marriage?'

'Rose declares she is too set in her ways,' said Arabella comfortably.

'She's right,' murmured Helena.

Aunt Alice's grey corkscrew curls bobbed

about her ears as she looked from one girl to the next, seemingly at a loss for words. At last she managed, 'Ah, well, that's as may be, but some of us have been known to change our minds.'

The sound of loud clattering in the hallway followed by raised voices made them turn, but the new arrival passed by the drawing room, distance muting his heavy tread upon the stairway that led to the bedrooms on the upper floor.

Rose glanced across at Aunt Alice, whose face blanched and who was now holding her chest. She was surprised. Was that fear she saw cross her face? Almost instantly Aunt Alice dropped her hand and gave a girlish laugh, saying, 'With so much to be done, let us discuss wardrobes, and invitations this very instant.'

But Rose had not missed the momentary uncertainty before her aunt launched into a spirited discourse on the aforementioned topics, with occasional interjections from Helena and Arabella.

Rose looked on. Unexpectedly, she was assailed by such an all-consuming spasm of envy she wanted to shake herself. Helena was quite right. Rose could have contracted an alliance with the most eligible bachelor in the whole of the West Indies. Then all of them would have had wardrobes full of fine clothes.

Too late to turn back the clock. Five years ago Rose had not known that her father was virtually bankrupt, that the alternative to marriage was to be all but completely dependent upon Charles and the cold and beautiful Helena whom he'd married shortly afterwards with such unseemly haste.

'Oh dear, it's raining. And you girls had planned to go walking in the park.' Aunt Alice eyed the falling rain with concern. 'I'm sure it's just a shower. You'll have to stay until it's — '

Her sentence was cut short as the door burst open and an angry voice cried, 'Gad's teeth, Mama, will you look at what Riley's done to my hessians!'

Four pairs of startled eyes turned towards the door as a tall, dark youth of about twenty years strode into the room.

Ignoring the three girls, he made his way towards Aunt Alice and, turning to face her, stamped one boot upon the coffee table. Four china tea cups shuddered.

'I'm sorry, Oswald. I'll speak to him again.' Aunt Alice's voice wavered.

'You'll give him his notice, Mama, and that's final. He's already been warned once.'

'But, Oswald, I can't . . . '

Without waiting for her to finish, the young man removed his foot from the table, glared at the girls, then strode from the room.

Crimson, Aunt Alice stammered, 'I'm so sorry for the intrusion, my dears. That was my stepson, Oswald. Sometimes, when he gets in one of his moods . . . ' She trailed off before beginning a new sentence with pathetic eagerness, 'But most of the time he's quite charming.'

'I couldn't see anything wrong with his boots,' said Helena.

Alice shrugged helplessly. 'He likes them polished so he can see his reflection.'

Rose changed the subject and, when a ray of sunshine lit up the room, declared brightly that now they had talked Aunt Alice's ear off it was time for the three of them to be on their way.

'It'll be lovely and fresh for a promenade in Hyde Park,' said Aunt Alice, as she accompanied them down the front steps to the pavement to wait for the carriage to be brought round. 'I declare, the three of you look as pretty as a picture.' She looked wistful. 'I remember the days when Beatrice and I used to promenade . . . '

A passing cooper's wagon drowned her words, but as it took the turn it lurched into a ditch, sending up a spray of muddy water before righting itself and continuing on its way.

'Rose! Your dress!' shrieked Aunt Alice.

Muddy droplets had disfigured the entire front of it. Dismayed, Rose said, 'I'll just stay in the carriage while Helena and Arabella take a stroll,' but her aunt wouldn't hear of it, insisting, 'You must borrow one of my pelisses. I have so many, I'll never miss it.'

After much resistance Rose eventually gave in and returned upstairs with her aunt to look through her wardrobe. When she presented herself to the girls her apricot velvet had all but disappeared beneath a smart white, fur-edged pelisse, with neat gold buttons from hem to neckline. In addition she carried over her arm three cast-off gowns, all the height of fashion.

'I so rarely go about these days, yet I can never resist when my dressmaker pays a visit,' Aunt Alice had assured her. Rose rather suspected that this was her aunt's way of dispensing charity, but saw how much she'd offend her if she refused to at least take them home to try on.

'That's certainly an improvement,' Helena remarked, casting her eye over Rose as they took their seats in the carriage.

'White suits you,' said Arabella. 'You should wear it more often.'

Rose smiled. White was not a very practical colour, given the amount of time she spent overseeing their sugar plantation.

Now that the sun was shining so brilliantly the crowds were out in full force, promenading or driving through the park. The moment the girls were handed down they were caught up in the spirit of the spectacle. Unconsciously they slowed their pace to match the languid saunter of the other promenaders.

Much of their conversation with Aunt Alice had been spent discussing the invitations she had received and from which they could, in turn, benefit. Helena had, at the time, appeared bored, but Rose noticed how her eyes lit up at the spectacle of the handsomely garbed crowd. She saw, too, the familiar glint of criticism and was not surprised when Helena, with a toss of her glossy dark head declared, 'English women have no style,' as she levelled an accusing look at Rose. 'If you had not insisted I wear my most missish gown so as not to scandalize your aunt, I'd have shown up these dull English ladies.'

Certainly, the gown she wore today was a great deal more respectable and modest than most of her clothes. Nevertheless her exotic looks did mark her out, Rose noticed, though Arabella certainly received her fair share of attention as she gazed about her, bright-eyed, fresh-complexioned, dimpling frequently in response to a doffed hat. What Rose did not notice were the admiring glances leveled at her.

She was so busy marvelling at the interest her companions were receiving that she failed to heed the gentlemen heading towards them, one of whom was directing a particularly wolfish smile in her direction. Instead, Rose was watching with growing concern the particularly seductive pout that Helena was concentrating upon some approaching stranger who was obviously not Charles. She raised her head, prepared to warn off the interloper with a frown.

'What an unexpected pleasure, Lady Chesterfield.'

Helena opened her mouth to speak, but her words were cut short as Rose blurted, much too hastily and with much too much enthusiasm in her attempt to block her, 'Why, Lord Rampton, what a pleasure, indeed! Lord Rampton, may I introduce to you my sister-in-law Miss Chesterfield and her sister, Miss Arabella. Rose and Arabella, pray meet Viscount Rampton, with whom we had the pleasure of dining several nights ago.'

Rose was aware that her furious blushes and rapid breathing might be misconstrued. What was vital at this point, however, was that Helena should play the role assigned to her.

'A pleasure, Lord Rampton.' Helena inclined her head, her voice a modest murmur, and Rose watched, amazed, as her sister-in-law adopted the unlikely persona of a blushing innocent, her manner mimicking exactly that of Arabella who had not yet been to her first ball and who was often tongue-tied in the company of gentlemen.

'The pleasure is all mine,' murmured the handsome viscount, his amusement evident as his gaze rested on the transparently discomfited Rose before suggesting that fate obviously intended them to enjoy an afternoon's stroll together.

Whether by accident or design, Rose found herself in alarmingly close proximity to their recent host, while Felix brought up the rear, flanked by Arabella and Helena.

'A happy coincidence to meet like this, Lady Chesterfield,' remarked Lord Rampton, lowering his voice which lent an unsettling degree of intimacy to their conversation. As an unmarried young woman, Rose was unused to such dealings with gentlemen, just as she was unused to the quickening of her pulse and unexpected self-consciousness. She felt heat burn her cheeks and a curious churning in the base of her stomach as she forced a half smile to her lips and stared straight ahead, taking the arm he offered.

Good Heavens! She almost leapt at the contact. She was being worse than a schoolroom miss.

'Yet I couldn't help but notice that our sudden and unexpected appearance seemed to throw you into some confusion. Would it be rude to ask whether that was because you did not wish to see me again after the other night?'

'Of course not, sir!' Rose tried to channel her discomfiture into irritation. Naturally Lord Rampton surmised that it was for exactly the opposite reason. What a vain and arrogant gentleman. If he knew the real reason for her agitation he'd not be so smugly conceited. A glance at the self-confidence radiating from his beautiful blue gaze made her realize that a man of such consequence must be used to every other unmarried young lady setting her cap at him. Well, she was not one of them!

Managing an air of far greater confidence than she felt, she said, 'Since you were so kind in allowing more time to repay your debt, how could that be?' She cocked her head, proud of the way she managed to smile almost lazily up at him, just as she had seen Helena do a thousand times.

While she didn't like to admit how relieved she was to be wearing her Aunt Alice's fashionable white pelisse, teamed with a pair of pearl earrings that her aunt insisted had once belonged to her mother, she was amazed at the confidence her new fine clothes gave her.

'I feel mortified that your obligations towards me have placed you in such a difficult situation,' murmured Rampton, whose smile did nothing to bear out such a sentiment. 'Perhaps a hand or two at the card table could reverse matters?'

Rose cast him a narrow-eyed glance, tinged with doubt. It was difficult to know whether his tone of enquiry suggested that his offer might be one of gallantry, whereby he'd allow her to win thus settling the debt, or whether he was playing with her, enticing her to be as reckless and as daring as the Lady Chesterfield described by his friend, Babbage. She suspected it was the latter.

'I may be a gambler, Lord Rampton, but I am a principled one,' she declared, virtuously. 'I will not be returning to the gaming table until my debt is cleared.'

'I am sure your husband would be very relieved to hear that.'

'It was he who stipulated it.'

'Indeed? Then I am sure you would not

dream of disobeying him and suffering the consequences of his displeasure.'

Rose bridled at his mocking tone. How dared he speak in such slighting, sarcastic tones about Charles? 'No, Lord Rampton, I would not dream of it.'

'Said like the most loyal and obedient of wives.' His tone was gently mocking.

'Besides,' muttered Rose, 'there will be little time for such an opportunity since I understand you are leaving within the week.'

'I've changed my plans, Lady Chesterfield.'

Rose nearly gasped aloud at his sardonic smile while his words struck terror into her heart.

His smile broadened as he placed his large hand over her fingertips which she'd been obliged by good manners to tuck into his arm. Was his amusement due to the fact he'd heard her small intake of breath? She certainly hoped he had not. Rose was a consummate actress and her role was to play the careless, self-contained Helena. She could do it. She had to do it.

Lord Rampton lowered his head so that his striking eyes were on a level with hers, and said in conspiratorial tones, 'I'm a jaded bachelor, Lady Chesterfield, who has already sampled the wares across the waters.' He squeezed her fingers. 'The evening I spent with you and your husband made me realize that London offers greater diversions than I had thought.'

Oh, Dear Lord, what had she got herself into? Rose had no response though she understood his subtext perfectly. What she didn't understand — and certainly didn't like — was the tumultuous churning in her breast. Was it gratification, excitement or horror? Lord Rampton was making clear his interest in her.

But she was a married woman. Unobtainable. She didn't understand.

They walked on in silence, listening to the other three chattering and laughing behind them. Rose was struck by the unaccustomed girlish ring to Helena's laugh. She tried to force her mind from the implications of Lord Rampton's declaration. Of course, she must tell Charles immediately they returned, she decided. And with the next breath immediately decided that she certainly must *not*.

They had nearly completed their circuit. Rose indicated that the waiting carriage ahead of them was theirs and would transport them home directly.

'Sadly, if we are not to meet at the gaming table, we may see little of each other this Season,' said Lord Rampton. 'In which case, we shall have to arrange some other venue to discuss our business dealings.'

Withdrawing her hand from the crook of his arm, Rose managed, 'I'm sure that won't be necessary.' No, it would be far too dangerous and besides, she was, to all intents and purposes, a married woman. He couldn't possibly expect to further his acquaintance with her when Charles was in the shadows.

The pressure of Lord Rampton's fingers upon her own hand, which she'd been in the process of clasping around her reticule, made her breath catch while the unexpected steel in his voice made her realize she had spoken rashly.

'Indeed, Lady Chesterfield, I think it will. You do not deny that I have been unusually lenient in this matter.' The lively conversation behind them as they waited by the carriage reassured Rose that they could not be overheard. Or observed, for she feared she was trembling like some pitiful debutante caught in the glare of a powerful man's interest, and certainly not immune to his magnetism. 'I am not usually so with my debtors. It is one of the reasons I am successful in my business dealings. However, most of my debtors are not as beautiful, nor so . . . ' he brought Rose's hand to his lips, 'desirable.'

48

Rose opened her mouth to speak but no words came. She was glad at the chance to step back as the jarvey let down the steps.

Undeterred, Lord Rampton moved closer. 'Call it my interest on the debt, Lady Chesterfield,' he murmured, his voice warning before becoming the consistency of rich treacle. 'I think my leniency entitles me to a little indulgence from you, do you not?'

Rose managed an uncertain smile. Was such blatant familiarity accepted with equanimity by married women? She felt as if she were on another planet where all the social rules had changed. And yet, disconcerting though that was, she had never felt so . . . alive.

As he swung round to greet the others Lord Rampton's smile transformed into one of expansive good humour. 'Ladies . . . ' He bowed before handing first a blushing Arabella, followed by Helena, into the carriage. 'And Lady Chesterfield . . . ' His smile was half-conspiratorial, half-mocking as he assisted Rose. ' . . . I await our next meeting with the most agreeable anticipation.'

Once settled in the carriage, Helena sent Rose a narrow-eyed look. 'So that was Lord Rampton.'

Rose realized that she had made a serious mistake in playing down the man's obvious attractiveness to Helena. Not even a blind woman would have been impervious to his charm.

'Now I understand why you've told me so little about him.' Helena's voice was cold.

Arabella's unawareness of the tension between the two women made her admiring declaration, 'He's so handsome!', sound a false note in the stony silence.

Rose was relieved that her sister had failed to register Helena's suspicion of Rose's motives. It gave her a moment in which to formulate a defence, while Arabella added, with a thoughtful frown, 'His brother was very charming, too — don't you think?'

Helena dismissed this with a toss of her head. 'Young master Felix? Why, he's just a greenhorn. But, my dear Rose,' her smile was curious, 'what I should like to know is why you would wish to hide from us the fact that Lord Rampton is such an attractive man? Generous, apparently; accommodating, certainly . . . but not, we would be forgiven for thinking, in view of your description of him the other night, attractive. Surely that is a telling omission?' She paused, and Rose, already feeling the heat, knew she was fuelling Helena's enjoyment with her fiery blushes. 'I understood,' Helena went on, 'only that he had agreed to give you more time in which to honour your debt.'

'Your debt, since you seem to have forgotten, Helena.' Rose managed a scornful look before transferring her gaze to the passing street traffic.

'I beg your pardon. My debt,' Helena amended, unrepentantly. She paused, and a sly look crossed her lovely face before she added, disingenuously, 'Thank you so much for reminding me. I think it's time for me to pay Lord Rampton a call and make clear I am the one guilty of misdemeanour.'

'You mustn't!' Instantly Rose knew she'd made another grave miscalculation.

'Rose, darling.' The honeyed tone was at odds with the expression in Helena's almond-shaped, green eyes, narrow with speculation as she added, 'I believe you are quite taken with the generous Lord Rampton.' She leaned across to pat Rose's knee and her voice dropped to a whisper. 'Just a word of caution: be careful. Without wishing to interfere, I don't think you realize what dangerous ground you're treading. Lord Rampton,' she uttered his name with relish, removing her hand from Rose's knee as she drew herself upright, 'is not the kind who likes to be deceived.'

'I thought he seemed very nice.' Arabella looked in puzzlement at the two women.

Rose hesitated. She did not want Arabella to be privy to the reasons for the undercurrents between her and Helena. Forging on, she responded with steely determination, 'Do not underrate me, Helena. I am not the young innocent you imagine.'

'I'm glad to hear it.' Helena feigned relief as she leaned back into the squabs. 'In which case, since dear, clever Rose is on a mission to undo the harm wicked Helena has wrought, I'm compelled to play the part you've assigned to me.' She gave a husky laugh, cleared her throat, then uttered a girlish trill. 'It'll be quite a novelty playing the unworldly schoolroom miss again.'

'If you ever knew how.' Stung into an uncharacteristically barbed response Rose was determined not to back down. 'You were not even out of the schoolroom before you were calculating how to make the most advantageous marriage possible.'

'Charles?' Helena's laugh was bitter, tinged with hysteria. 'I was never in the schoolroom, Rose. You know Father's thoughts on education for females. He considered my beauty a lure for a duke at least! What use was education? But you insult me by implying that I was always motivated by avarice. When I was seventeen I was prepared to sacrifice everything for love! Yes! I'd have run away with nothing but the clothes I had on, but he who had no prospects was too proud to condemn me to a life which, he said, would be one of unending struggle. You didn't know that about me . . . that I was so selfless . . . did you? Now I'm married to your brother . . . ' Her eyes glittered with angry, unshed tears. 'So don't you accuse me of not making sacrifices!'

As the carriage negotiated a deep rut in the road the silence inside was tense. Rose bit her lip, repenting her earlier accusations. Helena was as unhappy with her lot as she was.

'Rose,' said Helena at last, the familiar mocking tone returning as she fixed Rose with a level look, 'this uncharacteristically madcap charade is, I assume, motivated by the desire to save us all . . . and not, I trust, prompted by romantic folly?' Squeezing Arabella's shoulder in a motherly fashion, she went on, 'Perhaps you should talk some sense into your sister, my dear Arabella. She is taking a big gamble in her desire to be the confident woman of the world she imagines Lord Rampton would admire. And we all know that Rose is not a natural gambler.' She clicked her tongue. 'I fear what may happen if she pursues this dangerous charade.'

Arabella, out of her depth, remained silent.

'Lord Rampton and I have come to an

arrangement, Helena,' Rose said, trying to sound more confident than she felt. 'It's only for . . . ' she steeled herself, 'a few weeks.'

'A few weeks! You told us all he was leaving by week's end.' A slow smile curved Helena's lips. 'Ah, but he is taken with you, Rose. He believes Lady Chesterfield can offer him diversions sufficient to make him want to stay.' She burst out laughing. 'What an interesting situation, and I, who have been bored for so long, am now enthralled.' Her eyes glittered above the steeple she made of her gloved hands. 'How will sweet Rose play the dangerous Lord Rampton?' She looked thoughtful before adding, 'Meanwhile, I am only too happy to take my cue from Arabella so that I can convincingly play the ingenuous schoolroom miss.'

'You are?' It was all Rose could manage.

Helena leaned forward and tapped Rose playfully on the shoulder with her fan. 'Now that you have engaged the interest of London's most notorious rake, Rose, I shall have much more fun as an innocent with an eye to London's most eligible bachelors than I would as Charles's wife.' She sat back again. 'I shall enjoy watching you sink deeper into a mire of your own making.'

3

'He asked you to dance three times?' Helena repeated. Rose, conscious of Helena's dampening effect on Arabella's previously high spirits, looked up from her stitching and remarked, with a smile, 'Viscount Yarrowby was obviously very charming, dearest.'

She knew Helena was chagrined; that she'd wanted to attend the ball the previous night but instead had had to nurse Charles, who had come down with a mild fever. Aunt Alice had chaperoned Arabella while Rose had hastily summoned an imaginary megrim herself. She had no intention of nursing her brother, who was not a good invalid, when that was Helena's duty.

'He's lovely,' Arabella enthused, eyes shining as she held one of the blue drawing room cushions to her chest and executed a twirl in the middle of the room. 'He was so sweet and charming all evening. Of course, he couldn't take me into supper as Lady Belton had engaged him to take in Miss Mawks, but he was by my side the moment he'd executed his duties.'

Rose could see she was intoxicated by her

success. And why shouldn't she be? Arabella exuded a fresh, ingenuous charm.

Her gaze strayed from her admiring appraisal of Arabella to Helena and a wave of trepidation engulfed her. Helena had always been, undeniably, the most beautiful of them all. She had spent her life being fêted and admired. Now, suddenly, she had been eclipsed. Not only by Arabella, but by Rose too.

Helena had promised not to expose her. But could she behave with malice towards Arabella?

Last night, as neither Rose nor Helena had gone out in public, the charade over Rose's identity had not been an issue. But what of the next ball or masquerade? Aunt Alice had lent Rose sufficient items from her wardrobe so she could deport herself in reasonable style, and Helena had agreed to play the debutante out of malicious interest, but what of Charles's reaction? And that of Aunt Alice?

Rose had come to England with no intention of entering into the social whirligig. So why did her heart now thunder at the possibility of venturing forth into society? Thunder — not from trepidation, but anticipation?

She was saved from having to explore the

uncomfortable conclusion to these thoughts by Helena's dampening response, 'I believe Lord Yarrowby is quite a bit older than you.'

'What does that signify?' Arabella's eyes widened. 'Papa was twenty years older than Mama, don't forget. And Lord Yarrowby is only fifteen years older than me.'

'Oh, so you're well advanced with your calculations,' remarked Helena, apparently tiring of the conversation. She rose, her high heels clicking on the parquetry, her silk gown swishing around her ankles as she made her way towards the door. As she turned, her gaze travelled Arabella's length, as if assessing her worth.

Arabella's jaw dropped as she realized that Helena was mocking her, but the hurt look on her face only made her sister-in-law laugh. 'I was not insulting you, *ma chérie*,' she said, her tone more kindly now. 'Rather the contrary. It would have been simply too stupid of you not to have considered all matters pertaining to his eligibility. Ah, a letter!' she cried, gaily, snatching up the thick cream parchment sealed with wax as the maid entered with the morning's post. But her disappointment showed as she turned it over.

'Rose, your admirer,' she said, stonily, after she'd dismissed the maid. 'Although, by rights, any letter addressed to Lady Chester-field should be opened by me. Well?' she demanded, when Rose merely stared at the missive as if she didn't know what she should do.

Rose would have told her to mind her own business had Arabella not also begged with childlike enthusiasm, 'Yes, do tell, Rose. Is Lord Rampton your new admirer?'

'Lord Rampton merely wishes to meet me this afternoon,' replied Rose evenly, once she had scanned it, folded up the paper and placed it in the pocket of her skirt. 'No doubt something to do with the arrangement we have over the debt.'

But after being ushered into Lord Rampton's drawing room, then spending several minutes engaged in trivial chatter about the appalling traffic conditions occasioned by that afternoon's wet and windy weather, Rose realized that her debt was far from Lord Rampton's mind as he eventually got down to the real reason for his request to her.

'I understand it was Miss Arabella's debut into society,' he said, conversationally, regarding Rose from above the rim of his cut-glass tumbler.

'Yes.' For some reason Rose was wary. With little experience of men she found being alone with one both disconcerting and exhilarating — or was that because of the man himself? Her palms felt sweaty and her throat dry but she held her head high as she practised the self possession that had always served her well.

'She has a certain charming freshness,' he went on, seeming to observe her more acutely than the remark warranted. 'More sherry?' he asked, suddenly by her side, bending to relieve her of her half-empty glass.

Rose hoped that if she kept her eyes trained on the fire, and a polite but distant smile upon her lips, he would not notice the rapid rise and fall of her bosom and the heat that flamed in her cheeks.

'I couldn't help noticing that she appeared to catch the eye of Lord Yarrowby.' Surveying her with an assessing look as he returned to his seat, Lord Rampton raised his tumbler in salute, took a thoughtful sip, then smiled. It was an intimate smile, as if he had known her a long time, and was assured that each understood the relationship between them.

Rose felt both foolish and naïve. She should never have agreed to meet Lord Rampton alone, though Edith had accompanied her here, allaying any suspicions Charles might have had. 'You were, perhaps, expecting Arabella to comport herself like a country bumpkin?' she asked, cautiously.

Lord Rampton's shout of laughter gave but short-lived relief.

'Having met the other women in her family the thought never crossed my mind.' His eyes twinkled.

Rose felt her defences crumble. No man had ever looked at her like that: with such unreserved admiration. Her pulse quickened. Nor would such a look ever have been likely to breach her defences, had it come from another man. She had never lost her heart, or had it even slightly bruised; she would not have thought such a thing possible. But Lord Rampton, with his strong, angular face, his frank, direct gaze and the most beautiful mouth she had ever seen, was doing all that and more.

'No, indeed, I'd wager that with your sister-in-law's refreshing want of airs and her pretty face she'll be the toast of the town. Which is all the more reason to warn you — '

Foreboding and confusion coursed through her. 'Warn me?' Rose repeated faintly, her hand going to the low neckline of the pretty pale-mauve voile Helena had surprisingly insisted she must borrow for her unchaperoned visit.

'Lord Yarrowby is a rake.' He stated it baldly, with relish.

'And Arabella danced with him but three

times,' Rose replied. Clearly Lord Rampton had requested her company on false pretences. Now was time to show strength. Lord Rampton was dangerous territory. Dangerous . . . she had to remind herself. She must have as little to do with him as she could before discharging Helena's debt.

'If you . . . summoned me here,' she emphasized the word with disdain, though her heart felt like breaking, 'simply to tell me that, then I think you have perhaps overestimated the depth of our acquaintance, sir.' She rose and looked around for a repository for her barely touched sherry.

Lord Yarrowby was a remarkable catch. Everyone said so, and if Lord Rampton wanted to pretend concern over Yarrowby's suitability merely to draw Rose into his lair . . . well, it was simply too much of a sacrifice to make — on either Arabella's or her behalf.

Drawing in a breath that she hoped would replenish the sensible side of her, she was surprised by his obvious dismay. Surely she had not strayed so far from propriety that he wouldn't understand by now that she did not take kindly to his subterfuge? His next words, however, had the effect of shocking her so much that she dropped back into her seat.

'I beg your pardon, madam. I had thought

your apparent fondness for young Arabella betokened a certain regard for her personal happiness. I had not realized that you planned to honour your debt through her . . . success.'

'Of course I intend no such thing!' Rose declared. 'Only I thought you had requested me to come here on the pretext of — ' She stopped abruptly.

Lord Rampton watched her confusion with amusement. 'Yes?' he prompted, mildly.

She waved one hand through the air dismissively, then took another sustaining breath in order to gather her disordered wits. 'Naturally,' she said through clenched teeth, 'where my sister . . . er . . . sister-in-law is concerned, it is of far greater importance to me that Lord Yarrowby should be a man of decency and honour than that he has a fortune and a title.'

'Bravo.' Her host congratulated her with heavy irony. 'Being somewhat tender-hearted myself I hoped to elicit such a declaration.'

'I am not completely shameless,' Rose muttered. 'You will get your money, as promised, my lord, and I shall ensure that my sister-in-law makes a match that will secure her future happiness which, I hope, will be free from financial hardship.' She rose. 'Good day.'

Lord Rampton shadowed her as she navigated her way around the furniture towards the door. She could almost feel the radiation from his body and she turned, supporting herself with one hand on the back of the club sofa, looking up to find his generously curved mouth smiling down at her, his deep-blue eyes sparkling with amusement.

'Lady Chesterfield,' he said, taking her hand, his voice filled with remorse, 'I have offended you. Hardly the action of a gentleman, especially when I have just accused Yarrowby — who is, I must tell you, a former friend — of lacking the qualities required to be called one.'

Rose had no choice but to surrender her hand, which he bent over with a flourish. A rush of sensation whooshed to her lower belly and she drew in her breath sharply. What had caused that? Surely not the mere touch of his lips upon her suddenly sensitised skin as he murmured, 'Pray, forgive me.'

'Perhaps I overreacted a trifle, Lord Rampton.' Rose slanted a sideways look towards him as she'd seen Helena do in the company of attractive men. 'You see, my sister-in-law is very dear to me and her happiness is paramount. I was horrified at the charge you just levelled at me.'

'In that case, Lady Chesterfield, all the

more reason to heed my warning.'

'That Lord Yarrowby is a rake? But, my lord,' Rose smiled wickedly, 'I had not thought the charge such a terrible one. If we ladies were to be warned off every so-called rake in town, who would be left to marry?'

Instead of responding in like fashion to her flirtatious banter Lord Rampton lowered his head even further. In fact, for one tantalizingly terrifying moment Rose thought he was going to actually brush his lips against hers and she stiffened, every fibre of her being on full alert.

She was still wondering whether she was disappointed or otherwise that he had not, when he added ominously, 'Most rakes, I am pleased to report, have more respect for their womenfolk. Now,' his tone was matter-of-fact as he straightened and saw Rose to the door, 'when shall I have the pleasure of furthering our acquaintance, Lady Chesterfield? Perhaps at Lady Pendleton's soirée tomorrow night? You have my promise — as a rake and a gentleman — that when next we meet, we shall concern ourselves with matters that are altogether more . . . ' The wolfish smile was in place as he supplied suggestively, ' . . . diverting.'

★   ★   ★

Helena sighed as she twirled a cushion tassel round her middle finger and gazed through the grimy windows at the church spire. 'I can't decide whether it's more fun being fêted as the unworldly virgin, or watching you grapple with the subtleties of experience. Come now, Rose,' she laughed her husky laugh, 'I've already pledged to play the part you've assigned to me.'

Too absorbed in her own dilemma as to whether it was pure folly to attend Lady Pendleton's soirée, Rose did not notice how bright her sister-in-law's eyes were, and how out of character was her enthusiasm for a plan from which she did not, apparently, benefit directly. She was relieved when Aunt Alice was announced.

'We were just discussing Lady Pendleton's masquerade tomorrow night, Mrs Withers,' said Helena, ignoring Rose's imploring look and small shake of the head. 'Happily Rose has agreed to accompany us.'

'Delightful!' Aunt Alice beamed as she settled herself.

'No, Helena, I was just saying I had decided not to accompany you,' Rose corrected her.

Helena, looking disappointed, turned an appealing gaze upon the older woman. 'Don't you think it wrong that Rose should deny herself the pleasures of the Season when she has only this one chance to secure a husband, for all she insists she doesn't want one?'

'Indeed, yes! What is it, child?' asked her aunt directly, turning to Rose. 'Is it clothes?'

'Helena has kindly promised to lend me those.' Rose summoned inspiration for her excuse.

'Then what is it, dear? You're not . . . ' Aunt Alice's eyes widened as an idea dawned. ' . . . afraid, are you?'

'Of . . . men?' Rose shook her head in emphatic denial.

'Dear Rose thinks herself the equal of any man,' came a lazy-sounding voice from the doorway.

'My dear Charles, so good to see you!' Aunt Alice exclaimed as her nephew entered the room.

Taking a seat, Charles added, 'No, Rose continues to eschew the idea of marriage as she has not yet met a man she considers her equal.'

'Well, perhaps it is not quite right to consider ourselves equal to men, but it is most definitely a shame to allow fear to stand in the way of finding a good husband. How is the world to go on?' asked Aunt Alice with a definitive air, glancing about as if for corroboration.

'What wisdom, Mrs Withers,' said Helena

with no hint of irony. 'The problem Rose has is that she can't go out without being involved in a terrible deception.'

In response to the obvious stupefaction of the others, she elaborated with an artful smile, 'All right, I confess, it was all my fault to begin with.'

'My dear Helena,' Charles interjected, but Helena cut him off, saying, quickly, 'Dear Aunt Alice — you don't mind if I call you that? No? And perhaps you, too, enjoy a little intrigue. Yes?' She glanced at Charles and Rose as if challenging them to interrupt before launching into her version of the truth. 'You see, it all began when Charles had an important meeting with a rich and influential gentleman — perhaps you know of him? Lord Rampton.'

'Indeed, I do.' Aunt Alice's tone was almost reverential. 'A dashing rake but the catch of the season, nonetheless.'

Helena nodded. 'However, I was indisposed, and as Charles could not go alone Rose had a wild idea that she would go in my place . . . ' She broke off, silence giving greater effect to her next words. ' . . . masquerading as me!'

A small frown of incomprehension creased Aunt Alice's brow. 'I'm sure it would have been perfectly appropriate for her to have gone as herself with Charles as chaperone.'

'Of course it was,' Helena laughed. 'But Rose sometimes has these wild ideas and she doesn't think of the consequences until after she acts. Apparently she had nothing suitable of her own to wear, and it would seem that wearing my clothes filled her with some rather outrageous inspiration. Consequently,' she took a deep breath, 'it appears that Lord Rampton was quite taken with Rose, yet thinks she is . . . ' She looked around the room, her emerald eyes gleaming with amusement, and finished with a staccato, 'me!'

Rose was fuming. Wouldn't Aunt Alice be shocked to learn that her niece by marriage was a gambler who had all but ruined the family, and that Rose's actions had been prompted to save the plantation and only home they had?

Revealing the bald facts was too much of a risk. Aunt Alice was a gossip and any suggestion that the Chesterfields were at the mercy of creditors would severely curtail Arabella's chances.

Rose smiled almost sheepishly at her aunt. 'Lord Rampton was supposed to be leaving for the Continent by the end of the week, so it seemed a safe enough deception in view of the fact that I needed to petition him for a little extra time to meet a small debt we owe him.'

'You owe Lord Rampton money?'

Rose felt the heat in her cheeks. Unable to look her aunt in the face she murmured, 'Happily, he has given us until the end of the Season. I couldn't have asked for more.'

Aunt Alice clicked her tongue and said, as if Rose were the guilty party, 'Just like your father, and yet he was adored by so many . . . ' She broke off, as if a thought had occurred to her. 'You say you owe Lord Rampton money? Why, I may just be able to help you. Meanwhile, perhaps all this deception is not such a wicked thing after all.'

Even Helena looked taken aback at this.

Obviously relishing the intrigue Aunt Alice continued, 'From what little I know of Lord Rampton, I gather he is only interested in married ladies . . . ' She pursed her lips like a schoolgirl plotting a great surprise. 'Why, my dear Rose, I think you may have accidentally stumbled upon the only way to call Lord Rampton's bluff. So, as Arabella's chaperone tomorrow night and,' she directed a decidedly crafty glance at Helena, 'yours, Helena, I'll be able to assist in carrying off this perfectly wicked little charade while investigating other avenues for honouring this debt,' her blue eyes twinkled with excitement, 'if it is ever called in.'

4

Having taken leave of two satyrs and a wood nymph Rampton fingered the cutlass at his belt, slung low upon his hips, and scanned the crowd.

For a moment he regretted his choice of costume. With one eye covered by a black leather eye-patch it was even more difficult to find her amongst the sea of elaborately costumed guests. Surely, if Lady Chesterfield saw him first she would make her presence known?

A frisson of concern tempered his confidence. She had been angered by what she considered his underhand tactics in luring her to his drawing room the other night.

With a sigh of moral righteousness he drew himself up. Of course he had to warn Lady Chesterfield of the danger Yarrowby posed to her young sister-in-law, even if it had provided a convenient excuse to see her again.

As for the debt, well, he'd much rather absolve her from that in return for her sensual charms, though she seemed not as forthcoming with those as he'd been led to believe. He tested the blade of his weapon. Something did not sit right with the picture that Babbage had painted, though outwardly Lady Chesterfield lived up to every detail of his glowing description.

'One of the few villains here, I see.' Glancing down at the owner of the husky voice which had intruded upon his reverie, he smiled at the exquisite Helen of Troy who now swept a pair of stunning emerald eyes from his boots upwards, pausing as they encountered the triangle of chest revealed by the open linen shirt. The young woman tilted her face up to his. 'Most gentlemen, I note, have chosen to parade as their favourite hero.' The full lips curved into a slight smile as she purred, 'I, however, have always found villains much more exciting.'

Rampton returned her admiring look.

'As bold as you are beautiful, fair Helen of Troy,' he said gallantly, bowing over her outstretched hand. 'However, villain that I am, I adhere stringently to convention by never pursuing conversations with beautiful women to whom I have not been properly introduced.'

'We have been introduced, my lord,' the young woman said pertly, adding in response to his enquiring look, 'The other day in the park. You were with my sister-in-law — '

'Forgive me, Miss Chesterfield,' he cut her off, emphasizing her maiden title, 'but as you are a foreigner and apparently unaware of appropriate behaviour for debutantes in this town, I feel it my duty to escort you back to your chaperone. Please lead the way.'

Her look of outrage made him smile, however he had no intention of fostering false hopes. The young Miss Chesterfield was undeniably an exquisite creature. To judge by her knowing eyes she was of the kind who would singe a thousand admirers who worshipped at her flame before waltzing off with the prize catch of the season.

And that was not him.

No, Rampton was far more interested in her exquisite sister-in-law, the strangely alluring and quixotic Lady Chesterfield. The brazen beauty at his elbow, now looking more sulky than sultry, was just the one to assist him.

'Allow me to escort you back to your party. Ah, Lady Chesterfield.' He bowed, gratified by the faint blush that bloomed in the young woman's cheeks. Unless she were a master of deception she appeared genuinely discomfited by his presence. 'Your sister-in-law became separated from your group and lost in the crowd. Fortunately, I was on hand to return her,' he swept Helen of Troy a disapproving glance, adding, 'before any damage was done.'

Rose managed a slightly shaken smile, despite amusement at Helena's obvious chagrin, but for all that, she was seriously discomposed. Not just by Lord Rampton's sudden appearance — and what a fine figure he cut in his pirate's rig-out. Nor by the wonderfully disconcerting fact that he looked positively delighted to see her, but by the discovery that he clearly disapproved of young women wandering off alone without their chaperones.

'Thank you, my lord.' Rose directed a chastening frown at Helena, adding reprovingly, 'Take care next time, my dear. You are no longer a colonial hoyden amongst familiar society.'

As soon as Rampton had left, after claiming a waltz later in the evening from Rose, Lord Yarrowby appeared. Dimpling, Arabella graciously acceded to his request, before gushing excitedly, 'He wants to wait for the waltz. Like Lord Rampton. Oh, Rose, imagine! If we take the fancies of Lord Yarrowby and Lord Rampton, Helena can gamble to her heart's content.'

Helena, directing a singularly unimpressed look at her sister-in-law as Charles returned to her side, placed a graceful hand upon her husband's sleeve and coldly indicated that she wished him to lead her on to the dance floor.

'What Arabella says is entirely true,' declared Aunt Alice when Helena and Charles were out of hearing. 'Two perfect matches! How I wish your mother were here to have seen it.'

The pang of unease that assailed Rose was not prompted by her own behaviour. She glanced at Arabella, who was gazing happily in the direction of her new admirer. Before Rose voiced concern regarding Yarrowby she must investigate whether there was truth in Lord Rampton's allegations. And she must do so before Arabella's feelings progressed beyond youthful adulation.

Yet how could Lord Yarrowby be guilty as charged by Lord Rampton when she had heard not a whisper against him? Dressed as Julius Caesar, a laurel wreath topping his golden curls, Lord Yarrowby looked handsome and boyish, despite his more than thirty years. Rose watched as he turned and perceived Arabella's eyes on him, his own crinkling in response. His extravagant bow caused a blushing Arabella to turn away to collect her disordered wits. The face she presented to her sister shone with excitement.

It was too early to voice caution. Lord Rampton's summons the other afternoon had been nothing more than a ruse to see how willingly Rose would go to him — and believe him. Rampton was clearly conscious of his power over women.

It was time to take him to task.

Thus, when Rose found herself in that gentleman's arms on the dance floor, questioning him about Yarrowby was one way to alleviate the self-consciousness she felt at being in such close proximity, to counter the light-headed sensations that threatened to turn her into a fool, for the aroma of bergamot-scented soap, leather and fresh sweat were a powerfully erotic combination.

Watching an ecstatic Arabella whirl past in Lord Yarrowby's embrace, Rose remarked, 'I can't believe Lord Yarrowby is as bad as you say. He appears such a good-natured gentleman.'

Rampton, executing a tight manoeuvre past a couple who had stumbled, pressed Rose more tightly against his chest. For one wild moment she was possessed by the idea of touching her lips to the triangle of bare flesh revealed by his open pirate's shirt — pretending it an accident, of course — just to see what a man's bare skin actually felt like. Indeed, daring and excitement thrummed through her and she immediately berated herself for missing her opportunity as he resumed the former steady rhythm of the dancing and remarked, conversationally, 'Far more good-natured than I am, I daresay.'

'But the other day you said — '

He cut her off. 'With respect, my dear Lady Chesterfield, this is neither the time nor the place. Now,' he finished briskly, as the music slowed to a finish, 'perhaps you would care to admire our host's fine collection of Old Masters.'

A tantalizing offer she dare not accept. 'I can't possibly leave Aunt Alice on her own . . . '

'Your Aunt Alice looks very pleasantly diverted by that notorious gossip, Lady Rodham. She'll keep her entertained for hours. Now, if that's the best excuse you can come up with . . . ' Caging her hand on his arm, he led her off the dance floor as if he would countenance no refusal.

And why not? Rose thought, fearful and excited as she followed him, uncertain as to what she felt about the liberties he might take.

Heart pounding, she justified her lack of resistance. What could be the harm in taking a married woman to view a collection of old paintings in a house filled with hundreds of people?

Nevertheless, when they found themselves

in the annexe, Rose was concerned to discover no evidence of any of the hundreds of guests who had thronged the ballroom, as her lack of experience was brought home to her. She was an inexperienced, unmarried woman with a reputation to protect, after all.

She turned to leave but his grip on her upper arm was firm and, as he drew her almost languidly back to him, she felt her defences crumble amidst a myriad of other emotions, not least self-condemnation.

This lasted little more than a second. Now was no time to act the coy maiden. There was Lord Rampton's good will to retain, and the knowledge that discovery would render her a fool, not to mention endangering their good standing with the gentleman to whom they owed so much.

'Helena . . . ?' he murmured, as if savouring the sound of her name. Placing one finger under her chin he tilted her head so that she was gazing into his eyes, hooded as they lingered on her face. 'You don't mind if I call you that?' His voice was a sensuous whisper. Rose felt her insides turn to jelly, a sensation accompanied by all the other hallmarks of what she increasingly realised denoted melting desire.

She closed her eyes while she felt herself enslaved by sensation. His proximity was driving her wild. Heat prickled the surface of her skin and she was conscious of her ragged breathing. She sucked in air sharply at the disconcerting feeling of her nipples puckering beneath her stays, opening her eyes in time to see his beautifully shaped lips moving closer towards hers.

Sense prevailed. She stepped backwards and out of his grasp, affecting a polite, amused smile as she wandered over to stand before one of the paintings. She was a single young woman. Yes, she was mad with desire right now but she also had no desire to be married. Should someone who knew or discovered her real identity walk into this room to find them kissing, her reputation would be compromised and his lordship would be under an obligation to marry her.

It was as simple as that.

Oh, but how she longed to feel his arms around her and his lips pressed to hers. Never in all her twenty-six years had she felt like this.

'I daresay you can call a woman who owes you a thousand pounds anything you like,' she responded, relieved she managed to effect the mantle of cool experience. 'I have always admired Lely, haven't you?'

'I must confess to a preference for Van Dyck.' Dropping the intimate tone he appeared at her side to study the painting that had caught her apparent interest. 'A noble calling, don't you think? Committing the world as you see it to canvas, and preserving it for posterity.' He pointed to a portrait. 'The Duchess of Conway. Warts and all. To have painted her as a beauty would have made a mockery of the artist's talent. My brother paints, you know.' He fixed Rose with an appraising look. 'I feel sure that if I asked him he would paint your portrait.'

'And why would you do that, my lord?'

'Because, my dear Helena,' Lord Rampton extended a hand towards her and gently traced the line of her cheek with his forefinger, his words dripping with suggestiveness, 'apart from the fact that such a painting would add to your husband's consequence, it would mean I could spend a great deal more time with you.'

★　★　★

'Cousin Helena!'

Startled by the youth who stepped in front of her, blocking her progress, Helena's momentary confusion was replaced by derision as recognition dawned.

'Master Oswald, I did not recognize you. A common highwayman.' With a curt nod she made to brush past Aunt Alice's stepson, adding, 'And I am not your cousin Helena.' The lad was a spoilt brat, at least three years her junior, and here he was trying to play the swaggering sophisticate. She did not appreciate such forwardness.

Unless it came from a real man like — she licked her lips and felt desire tingling her nerve-endings at the thought of him — Lord Rampton.

'Ah yes, Mama told me! Nevertheless, you are married to my cousin, Charles.' Oswald took a step backwards, impeding her progress. 'Perhaps you would honour me — ' Slate-grey eyes glittered at her through the slits of his mask. ' — with the next dance?'

'I wouldn't dance with a highwayman if my life depended upon it.' Removing his gloved hand from her arm, Helena made no attempt to mask her distaste, but after a couple of steps she faltered, discovering to her dismay and irritation that her husband had disappeared, and there was no sign, either, of her sisters-in-law or Aunt Alice. Or, regrettably, his lordship.

'The lady is abandoned?' Oswald's voice sounded in her ear. 'Perhaps, indeed, it is an opportune moment for a dance. Ah, a waltz. Not too daring, I trust?'

He was a good dancer, she allowed him

that after he had led her on to the dance floor. After several more glasses of champagne Oswald didn't seem quite so insufferable, especially as he was so fulsome in his admiration of her.

Obviously he enjoyed talking about himself, like most puffed-up popinjays, and it amused her enormously when he suddenly burst out, irritated, 'What you are looking at?'

Raising her head to look into his eyes, she broke into a peal of laughter. 'My reflection in your hessians!'

Oswald, who had been about to respond angrily at the slight, found himself, instead, steadying Helena as she swayed on her feet. 'It would appear the lady is foxed. Come, Cousin Helena, we must find somewhere where you can sit down.'

With little show of gratitude she accepted the orgeat he procured for her as he led her to a small sofa in a secluded annexe between the card room and the ballroom.

'I'd rather have what you're having,' she complained.

'And I'd rather return you to the company at large without besmirching my reputation.'

She hiccupped. 'Your reputation is nothing to be proud of, if what your dear mama says is true.'

'Oh ho, tales from home.' Oswald sounded

more amused than angry. 'Incidentally, she's not my mother. She's some addle-brained fool my senile old father married before he jumped ship for the Far East, and now I'm stuck with her until Papa gets called up. Sadly, his Maker appears to be in no hurry.'

'Just as I'm stuck with that addle-headed fool I married until he slips off this mortal coil.' Helena studied the trompe l'oeil on the ceiling while Oswald regarded her with greater interest.

'So the novelty of becoming Lady Chesterfield has lost its lustre . . . ' He moved a little closer. 'You realize, madam, that there are other avenues for disillusioned married women to pursue?'

'It wasn't my idea not to be Lady Chesterfield,' said Helena petulantly, slapping away Oswald's hand which he had insinuated onto her thigh. 'Your cousin Rose hatched the ridiculous notion that she could do a better job than I of petitioning Lord Rampton for a little favour.' She gave another hiccup. 'Now he's decided not to go to the Continent after all and I'm stuck playing the innocent virgin. I'm sure your mama has exacted the promise of silence from you under pain of death.'

The champagne was having its effect and Oswald's persistent questioning soon ferreted out the details his mother had omitted.

Helena smoothed the silky folds of her diaphanous gown. 'Your mother hinted that she knows how to lay hands on the funds to repay Lord Rampton. I think we're just waiting for someone to die . . . though she said she's prepared to lend an advance if that takes too long — '

'Oh, she is, is she?'

'Well, it seems only fair, since your stepmama inherited a fortune while nothing went to Charles and Rose's mama — '

'Because of their late father's faro habit, I believe,' Oswald interjected drily.

'Anyway,' Helena bit back defensively, 'Aunt Alice has no children, for you don't count.'

'Though she has reared me since I was ten years old.' Oswald smiled. 'So Mama is aiding and abetting this wild charade with her usual childish enthusiasm.'

'Yes, although she doesn't quite know the size of the debt owed to Lord Rampton. She just thinks Rose has lost her head to him. Which of course she has. And while I don't care a fig about Rose's reputation, I do care about securing the funds.' She hesitated, then added, 'Charles says if Rose can find a way of absolving us of the debt, he'll buy me a diamond collar.'

The corners of Oswald's thin mouth curled up. 'A diamond collar,' he said, as if much impressed.

'Yes, a diamond collar,' repeated Helena, avarice making her eyes sparkle.

'Well, my dear, I would hate to stand between you and a diamond collar.' His gaze strayed from her face to her décolletage, then back again. He scratched his pointed chin, appearing to ponder the matter. 'In effect, you want to dash your sister-in-law's chances of making good out of this so-called ridiculous charade and win yourself a diamond collar.'

'Yes, and I can't decide which is more important to me.'

Daringly, Oswald plucked at the sheer fabric of Helena's costume, as if to smooth it, and gave a low chuckle. The lovely Helen of Troy was clearly lost in a reverie of sparkling diamonds and heady revenge. Putting his lips to her pretty, seashell ear, he murmured, 'Have you not considered that both might be possible?'

★ ★ ★

Rose returned to find Aunt Alice deep in conversation with Lady Rodham.

'Where's Arabella?' she asked.

The women jerked their heads up almost guiltily.

'She's in safe hands, dancing with Yarrowby,' Aunt Alice reassured her.

'Dancing with Lord Yarrowby — again?' The concern in Rose's voice caused the women to break off their enthusiastically resumed conversation.

'She's made a fine impression on him.' Aunt Alice looked smug.

Rose glanced across the floor and saw Arabella, a fairylike creature in palest pink, supported like a fragile flower in Lord Yarrowby's embrace as he waltzed her around the room.

'We really know very little about Lord Yarrowby, Aunt Alice,' Rose cautioned. 'He appears charming, but . . . '

'Only son, set to inherit a vast fortune, and a title that goes back to Henry the Eighth's time. Like Rampton, he'd be a catch of the season. What else do you need to know, my girl?' asked the Lady Rodham. 'A simple lass from the West Indies would struggle to do better.'

'Yes, but what about other . . . well, you know . . . other associations?' Rose floundered.

'Ay, there've been mistresses. Noble women and dancing girls, alike. What of it?'

Rose felt embarrassed for reacting like the

cloistered colonial she was. Of course, many married men of their rank kept mistresses; it wasn't as if Lord Yarrowby had a wife as well.

'Miss Celia Baxter was the most notorious,' Lady Rodham said thoughtfully. 'An opera dancer. Dark-haired, round, ripe and pretty. I saw her at Covent Garden the night London was buzzing over the famous altercation between Rampton and Yarrowby.'

Rose concealed her distress. 'Altercation?'

'Yarrowby was set upon by Lord Rampton in Regent's Park, of all places. In the middle of the afternoon. Quite a scandal it caused, I need not tell you! Pistols at dawn — now that wouldn't have raised an eyebrow. But common street brawling!'

Aunt Alice ventured a surreptitious glance at her niece before quizzing her friend in what was clearly intended to be a tone of no more than casual interest, 'I am shocked. I had heard only good reports of Lord Rampton.'

'Men are brutish by nature.' Lady Rodham made a noise of disgust. 'I'll wager it was over nothing and certainly nothing I'd be worried about if I was planning to throw my daughter Rampton's way.'

'Yes, but what about Lord Yarrowby?' Rose asked with an anxious glance at the gentleman in question, who was now leading

Arabella towards them. The thought of Lord Rampton being driven by strong passions for a woman made it hard to breathe.

'A charming man,' Lady Rodham assured her without qualification. 'What does it matter if their quarrel was over some common little opera dancer? If Yarrowby stole her from Rampton, I'm sure Rampton had fixed his interest elsewhere within a day or two. That's men for you.'

'Your Lord Rampton has a long and shady past,' Helena said brightly, as she swept up to Rose. 'There was even a rumour that he locked one of his mistresses in his tower for seven days before the fair lady's husband discovered her whereabouts. There was a duel over that little scandal, too.'

'Spurious gossip-mongering,' Rose muttered, though her voice lacked conviction. Of course Helena would blithely say the first thing that came to her if she knew it would rattle Rose. She did not like the tumultuous feelings that overcame her, however, when Lady Rodham replied, 'What your sister-in-law says is perfectly true, my dear. Not that it has done his lordship's reputation any harm.'

'Ah, Oswald,' said Aunt Alice, forestalling Rose's reply. 'I'm sure Rose would be delighted to partner you in this set.'

With an ironic bow to Helena, Oswald

offered Rose his arm, brushing suggestively against his raven-haired cousin before putting out his hand to steady her.

'Forgive me, Cousin Helena,' he apologized, his eyes raking her salaciously.

Helena tossed her head, only to catch the yearning look her husband sent her from where he was engaged in conversation a few feet away. As Charles took a step towards her Helena lanced him with a look of contempt before feigning sudden interest in Aunt Alice's description of her new bonnet. Tiring quickly of the discussion, and having successfully deflected Charles, she allowed her eyes to stray across the ballroom thronged with exquisitely garbed, rich and titled people who knew not a care in the world while she, Helena . . .

Oh, but she was wasted on a sugar plantation far from the world's real excitement with a husband who was as exciting as a yam supper. And oh, how Helena detested yams, though Rose claimed she missed the food of their island home.

Well, Rose was welcome to the West Indies — and Helena fully intended that that was exactly where her sister-in-law would be returning. As for herself . . . Helena was still working on the conundrum as to how she could engineer remaining in

England. Certainly for longer than the remaining several months scheduled.

It was in the midst of such ruminations, as she affected the right facial movements in response to Aunt Alice's puerile chatter, that the glimpse of a familiar sardonic leer sent her heart free-falling.

She spun round, her heart plummeting all the way to her slippers as, with a laugh, he excused himself from his portly companion, a clergyman, and stepped into clearer focus. For a moment Helena thought she might faint.

There he was.

William the Conqueror.

She sucked air into her lungs. Conqueror, indeed! After all these years.

She didn't know whether to be filled with joy or fury. Her vision blurred and she had to blink several times.

Geoffrey Albright stood alone by a stone plinth, broader and even more handsome than she remembered. His light-brown hair was a little longer than he used to wear it but his look was just as she remembered: confident, tinged with arrogance, as he surveyed the crowd.

He turned, shock and recognition flaring in the depths of his cool grey gaze. Geoffrey Albright, the man she loved and hated in equal measure, right here in this ballroom, exuding all the familiar dash and heady danger he had all those years ago.

Helena sucked in air as she gripped Rose to steady herself. And as her world spun out of control she swore that someone would pay for all she had sacrificed.

5

'You're what?' Rampton looked at his brother as if Felix had just announced a trip to Outer Mongolia.

'I said I'm spending a few days in Kent. With the Kenilworths.' Felix helped himself to more kippers at the sideboard. Returning to his seat, he smiled blandly at his brother. 'I take it you've no objection?'

'You've declined their last three invitations. I don't know why you suddenly choose to accept now. How long will you be out of town?'

Felix grinned. 'You must have noticed that sweet Cecily is no longer a child. I actually failed to recognize her at Lady March's masquerade.'

'You realize, of course, that if you accept this invitation, you'll be expected to have offered for sweet Cecily before the Season's over.' Rampton didn't know why he suddenly felt so angry. No, of course that wasn't true, he amended as he poured himself more coffee. He'd assumed Felix would be on hand to paint Lady Chesterfield's portrait and the fact he'd have to wait until his brother had

91

returned from his jaunt to the country was more than Rampton's already-tried patience could endure.

Felix scarcely paused as he shovelled the food into his mouth. 'No, I won't,' he mumbled between mouthfuls. 'Your problem, Rampton, is that you think that when you're handsome and titled, everyone is setting their cap at you. Sweet Cecily could do far better than me, and she knows it. But the glint in her eye told me she'd enjoy my little visit just as much as I would and for exactly the same reasons.' He dabbed delicately at his lips with his napkin and offered his brother a saccharine smile. 'Who knows, perhaps I will offer for her before the Season's over. I certainly don't want to wind up a miserable old bachelor like you. Anyway,' he added, 'I don't know when it's ever been of any concern of yours what I do.' He fixed his brother with a studious look. 'Why, what other plans had you in mind for me?'

'I had hoped you might feel inclined to do a bit of dabbling in oils for a few days.'

'As a matter of fact, the very idea had struck me,' Felix said, rising. 'I intend to preserve the fair Miss Cecily's foxy prettiness for posterity. I suspect her mama will be much too taken with the idea of her daughter's immortalization to object to the many hours we shall necessarily be closeted together.' From the doorway he asked, 'Whose portrait had you in mind that I should paint?'

Rampton shrugged, as if it were of no consequence. 'Obviously you're not going to be here, so it doesn't matter,' he said, rising also and following his brother out of the door.

'Perhaps the fair Helen of Troy whom I saw you manhandle at the masquerade?'

Rampton managed to sound cool though the thought that he'd been blatantly targeted by a calculating debutante was terrifying in the extreme. 'The shameless young woman positively threw herself at me.'

Felix made a pretence of being scandalized. 'No! And don't tell me. She isn't even married? Mark my words, Rampton, you'll get your fingers burned one of these days. However, I'll paint the fair Lady Chesterfield's portrait — as I assume that's what you want — when I return from the Kenilworths.'

Rampton frowned. 'No discussion over remuneration? Why do you accept so readily?'

Felix raised an eyebrow. 'Because, Rampton, your exploits are legion, and I am filled with envy and humility. And it just occurs to me that I have never properly seen you in action.'

Rampton allowed the corners of his mouth

to turn up but he remained silent as he contemplated the very delicious idea of being closeted alone with Lady Chesterfield for hours at a time. He was not about to admit the extent to which he'd been affected.

The little chit knew exactly what she was doing and was enjoying this game of cat and mouse, he thought with irritation. Quite clearly the lacklustre Lord Chesterfield was as unexciting as a wet rag and she'd singled out Rampton for more than just the benefits of absolving herself of her debt. The fact she'd chosen to pursue him using blushing innocence as her bait, was a novel change, he supposed, to the jaded sophistication employed by most married women.

His reverie was broken by Felix's laugh. 'Just make sure you're discreet when you finally succeed in bedding this fair creature with whom I can see you're entirely obsessed.'

'Oh, I don't think her husband is a concern.'

'It's not her husband I was referring to,' Felix said over his shoulder from half way up the stairs to his quarters. 'Jealous adversaries of the female variety can be far more dangerous.'

'Oh, you mean the baroness?'

'She's not the only one. I mean, Rampton,

you're the catch of the season.' Felix grinned. 'Just be careful.'

★ ★ ★

When Rose received a hastily scrawled note from her Aunt Alice after she'd dressed herself for the morning she had no idea as to the reason for the peremptory summons. Especially knowing her aunt was laid up in bed with a nasty head cold.

Alice was certainly playing the invalid to the hilt when Rose was announced. She was propped up in bed on pillows, a scented flannel upon her brow but her eyes were bright and her voice eager. Indicating a chair at her side she gushed, 'My dear girl, I am so glad you came so promptly. Now, tell me, what communication have you had with your father's family since he died?'

Rose tried to think. 'Why, none,' she replied. 'That is . . . not since the condolences.'

'Ah.' Alice smiled knowingly. 'Do you perhaps recall your father's Aunt Gwendolyn? An older half-sister of his mother?'

Rose looked blank, though she had an inkling as to where this was heading.

Aunt Alice sat up straighter, the sudden exertion causing a fit of coughing. Waving aside the glass of water Rose offered her she said, 'My dear, I've just heard the most wonderful news.'

'Yes?' Rose suspected that what Alice considered wonderful involved a corpse or two.

'Lady Rodham came to visit me last night. She mentioned the death of the son of a dear friend of hers, a certain Obediah Pike. At first I didn't take much notice, but the name sounded familiar. It wasn't until this morning that it struck me. Obediah was the only child of your father's Aunt Gwendolyn. Well,' Aunt Alice wrapped her shawl more tightly round her, warming to her theme, 'I had one of my lads make enquiries first thing, and I was right!' Falling back into the pillows, her expression was full of expectation as she searched her niece's face.

'Well?' she demanded in response to Rose's silence. 'Say something!'

Rose hesitated. 'Poor Mr Pike,' she said, lamely.

'Yes, yes, and pity his mother too,' Alice said impatiently. 'The thing is, it won't be long before Gwendolyn starts thinking about her heirs, now that her only son is dead and she an invalid. She never was very close to her natural brother and sister, but was quite attached to your father at one time. My dear

Rose,' she rubbed her hands together, 'the time has come to pay your Great-Aunt Gwendolyn a visit. But first I'll take you to my dressmaker!'

Rose chewed her thumb nail and contemplated the possibilities an unexpected windfall — whether it was from Great-Aunt Gwendolyn's quarter, or elsewhere — suggested.

If she were able to repay Lord Rampton's debt she'd have no reason to see him again. It was a dampening thought. The intensity with which he'd gazed into her eyes had quite clearly conveyed his interest in her. As for herself, simply conjuring up his image was enough to make her breath come fast and shallow and her body react in all manner of unexpected ways. She fanned herself with the book Aunt Alice had just asked her to read to her as she tried to master her emotions using her usual ally, common sense. Clearly, she must have misinterpreted his lordship. She was a married woman as far as he was concerned so there could obviously be no deeper association between them than existed now.

But it was disquieting to know what a slave she was becoming to her feelings for him. No, she decided, clearing her voice to begin a novel titled *Sense and Sensibility*, which surely preached the virtues she must uphold, there could be no future with the handsome viscount for so many reasons, meaning she should limit any contact she had with him.

★ ★ ★

Sitting in front of a small fire in the drawing room, Charles laid down the law. Reluctantly, Rose agreed that accompanying everyone to Almack's after dinner was unwise, telling herself for the thousandth time that she must avoid opportunities that would only inflame her dangerous infatuation with the gentleman to whom they owed so much. At Lord Rampton's dinner, which was to precede the outing to Almack's, she need only speak when spoken to directly, and allow Charles to speak whenever possible on her behalf.

Aunt Alice had nearly secured the funds that would enable them all to sail honourably home after Arabella had contracted a suitable match. She had no further reason to court the good offices of Lord Rampton.

She glanced across at her brother, who was still talking, his tone now fearful. 'Besides, why has Lord Rampton invited us to dine? You don't think he's changed his mind and is going to call in the debt immediately, do you?'

'I expect we'll just have to wait until the

turbot in chive sauce to find out, darling.' Helena's voice drifted across the room from where she sat playing cards. As usual, her sarcasm seemed not to faze Charles.

Raking his fingers through his thin pale hair he addressed Rose, who sat opposite him, with contrived firmness. 'Now, you're to behave yourself, Rose. Your conduct last time we dined with Rampton was scandalous and deeply embarrassing.'

'Well, I for one wouldn't miss it for the world,' interjected Helena. Rose bit her lip and forced herself to remain silent. She was usually good at wheedling her brother into doing things for which he had no enthusiasm, but she recognized that, in this matter, the least said the better. He could dig his heels in at any moment and state categorically that she should not be allowed to go and she couldn't bear that to happen, having decided that tonight's dinner must be the last time she enjoyed Lord Rampton's company.

'Watching Rose at the masquerade, anyone would think she was quite a woman of the world,' Helena added, appearing at her husband's side and resting a hand on his shoulder. 'With vast experience of men.'

Rose quelled the impulse to defend herself. 'Are you still put out that he rejected the advances of the fair Helen of Troy by bringing you back to your chaperone so smartly?'

'I was simply put out at being treated like a silly little debutante — all on account of your silly little deception,' Helena said, coolly.

If Rose felt angered by her sister-in-law's remark then, she was able to enjoy a sense of victory later that evening as their host gazed at her across the table with blatant admiration.

'You're not missing anything, Lady Chesterfield, if you elect not to accompany the rest of your family to Almack's.' Lord Rampton's tone was intimate; and of course Rose should have been embarrassed by the fact that he had eyes only for her and that dinner, as on the first occasion on which they had met, was almost a tête-à-tête between them. Charles was again rendered virtually mute by a mixture of awe and helpless indignation, while Helena contributed little because it seemed she was playing the debutante to the hilt.

Yes, Rose should have felt embarrassed. Instead, she felt exultant.

'Its reputation is quite undeserved.' Rampton's eyes were once more drawn to Rose as he added, 'I have never understood the lengths the public will go to be admitted. Desire will have people do extraordinary things.' His voice was like a caress. Rose plucked at the neckline of the gown Helena had lent her and wondered whether the others noticed the viscount's interest. It certainly could not have escaped Helena's attention.

'I'm told the strongest refreshment served is orgeat,' she said. 'Not even champagne punch. And that Lady Jersey and the other patronesses wield enormous power.'

'A mere whiff of scandal will have one banned from their hallowed precincts,' said Helena. 'Which is enough to destroy anyone who has social pretensions. Still,' she added, virtuously, 'scandal is only dangerous to those careless enough to get caught.'

Rampton gave a short laugh. 'Hypocrisy is alive and well, Miss Chesterfield.' He rubbed his jaw and added, with a disarmingly frank look at Rose, 'Alas, subterfuge is often the only defence when one is a slave to duty and one's family's dynastic ambitions.'

Rose felt herself blush to the roots of her hair. Of course he could know nothing of her own deception. Nevertheless, it was a wounding remark to make in any husband's hearing, and Rose sent an anxious glance across to Charles. It appeared that he'd not registered Rampton's words. He was gazing at Helena whose sharp eyes followed the exchange between Rose and Rampton.

'Phew!' Charles whistled once they were back in their carriage, relaxing into the squabs with apparent relief before glaring at Rose. 'This is madness! Why on earth do we persist with this ridiculous charade? When will Aunt Alice tell us whether we have the money to pay the man, or not? If we don't, I'd rather come clean with his lordship and to hell with the consequences.'

'It certainly was none of my idea,' Helena pointed out, self-righteously. 'But darling Rose swears her stalling tactics are necessary to give Aunt Alice time to lay her hands on the necessary funds, and that scandal and humiliation are in store for all of us if her fraud should be revealed.'

Rose didn't enter into the argument, only pushed aside the curtain to look into the darkened streets. The back of her neck prickled with a mixture of guilt and desire. Of course she should never have got themselves into such a mess, but revealing the truth was too dangerous and had the potential to cause a scandal that would damage Arabella's chances.

She had always prided herself on her sense of duty, yet nothing now seemed important when compared with the pleasure of Lord Rampton's company. It wasn't just that he was handsome and exuded a magnetism she'd never encountered before. No, for the first time she knew what it was like to be fêted as a beautiful and desirable woman, just as Helena was constantly fêted. And the feeling was irresistible.

She listened as the rain beat loudly on the carriage roof and felt the carriage jerk as the horses responded to the coachman's whip. Not only was she in love, she relished the freedom that her disguise as a married woman gave her. Longing tugged at her heart and she closed her eyes, despair curdling in her stomach as she reflected upon Lord Rampton's obvious desire: a desire she had no choice but to resist.

She was glad when the others deposited her at their town house before going out again to spend the rest of the evening at Almack's. She must wean herself off this dangerous man who made her feel things she should not, and want things she knew she could never have. Her heart was not important. As long as they repaid Rampton his debt they could return to their plantation after seeing Arabella contract a wonderful match . . .

Yarrowby?

She felt a moment's discomfort at the thought of Lord Rampton's warning but she rallied at the memory of Lady Rodham's description of two young men fighting in Regent's Park. Rampton and Yarrowby had clashed over a woman. Clearly, rivalry was at the root of Lord Rampton's caution.

'Miss Rose, you have a visitor.' Edith stood in the doorway, her grey hair hanging down her shoulder in one heavy plait, a thick shawl wrapped about her shoulders.

Rose put down the book she was reading and glanced, surprised, at the clock. 'It's nearly ten o clock.'

'It's Lord Rampton.' Closing the door quietly behind her, Edith crossed the room. 'Fortunately no one else saw him.' She spoke softly. 'I was able to leave him to wait in the library while I enquired as to whether you were receiving visitors at this late hour.'

Rose felt the colour flood her face. Lord Rampton? Did gentlemen really visit married ladies at such a late hour? But then, if no one but Edith and seen him . . .

She tossed the book to the floor, sat up straight. 'Oh, Edith,' she whispered urgently. 'What shall I do?'

'Do you want to see him or not?'

'Oh yes!' Embarrassed by such a heartfelt and spontaneous admission, she added, 'Well . . . I daresay I shouldn't, should I? I mean . . . what would Charles say?'

'We would never tell Sir Charles,' declared

Edith, as if Rose were mad. Her pale eyes shone. 'And what harm could there be in receiving a gentleman caller? I would be near by if you needed me.'

Rose blinked. Could Edith, who had always been such a stickler for proprieties, be encouraging her to do something which would cause any self-respecting mama to die of shame? Or would it? That is, if it were never made public? It did not require much persuasion.

'Lord Rampton is greatly taken with you, Miss Rose. He is not here on account of the debt he is owed.' Edith gripped her wrists, her meaning never clearer. She'd devoted her life to Rose and her siblings and was as vigilant as any designing mama. 'Make the most of your chances, Miss Rose.' The urgency in her tone infused Rose with daring. 'Chance does not knock at your door every day. You are unmarried and he is in need of a wife.'

Shocked and excited by Edith's approval, while ignoring the inherent conflict created by her deception, Rose tilted up her chin and took a deep breath. Then, like a woman of the world who was used to such requests, and not the green girl she really was, she said, 'Yes, tell him to come.'

The wave of anticipation that flooded her

as he was announced was nearly overwhelming but she managed to retain her composure with the observation that she'd discussed Byron with him over his dinner table, calmly and intelligently, not two hours since. Now he faced her, tall and broad-shouldered, his eyes impossible to read. He had come seeking her out. Her and her alone.

Not that his first words indicated this. 'I see you are unaccompanied, Lady Chesterfield,' he remarked casually, as if this surprised him.

'You know very well that I'm alone.' Her voice was low as she watched him carefully. Why had he come? What did he want? 'We discussed this evening's plans over your dinner table.'

'Ah yes,' he said in a low voice, taking a step forward and standing just a little to the right of the fire so that he did not block her heat. Not that there was any need for such a gesture. Rose's temperature was rising rapidly.

His eyes held hers and a smile curled the corners of his lips. This time Rose had no response. Her heart thudded so painfully she wondered whether he could hear it. She schooled herself to remain still, not to squirm with embarrassment or appear too eager. Nor to turn him away with a lack of enthusiasm.

'I looked in at Almack's briefly.' He

remained standing a few feet from her, his hands clasped behind his back. 'In case you had chosen to accompany your family, after all. When I saw you had not I was concerned . . . ' His voice trailed away and his intensely blue eyes bored into hers before he added softly, ' . . . that you might be lonely.'

Still Rose made no rejoinder. It was hard enough just forcing herself to breathe. Every nerve ending was like a taut violin string, heat prickled the surface of her skin and the most unbearable longing threatened to turn her into a fool. No, she had no choice but to wait, then act accordingly.

'Come here,' he said, softly, and Rose felt her body answer the summons before her mind had time to fully comprehend. Before she had registered what she was doing she had closed the distance between them and was abandoning good sense with the breath that left her body in a whoosh as she raised her lips to meet his.

There were no gentle preliminaries. Hot and demanding, his mouth covered hers as he cupped her face, almost drinking her in and she, seemingly boneless, wilted in his embrace.

His lips burned hers as he growled against them, 'I've looked forward to this moment since I first laid eyes on you,' before resuming his passionate assault, his hands roaming over her body, cupping her bottom as he drew her against him.

Dear Lord, it was terrifying, and it was wicked and oh, so exhilarating. She was an innocent. Inexperienced. She knew she should be shocked by the liberties and the jutting angles of his masculinity, but her body answered with equal ardour as her hands twined behind his neck and her tongue tangled with his in a dance of seduction that could have no happy resolution — but she could take what he offered, now, and she'd have that to sustain her for the rest of her days.

She squirmed at the disconcerting feeling of molten liquid pooling in her lower belly, but she only pressed herself closer, for in the drawing room she was still mistress of her own destiny and her reputation was pre-served. She could show him how much she desired him but when he released her, here it would end.

'You are wicked, my lord,' she told him, kissing his ear, running her palms over the roughness of his angular cheekbones and revelling in his caresses, arching into him as he contoured her body without shame, knowing that he would realise it could go no further since she was, in his eyes, a married woman, and that she was due to leave the country in a few short weeks.

'And you are a minx,' he muttered against her throat, drawing back at the sound of heavy footsteps in the passage, and adding, just before Edith made her presence known, 'but don't you think you've got the better of me.'

Rose widened her eyes and smiled into his face, still only inches from hers. 'Time will tell, my lord,' she said, with emphasised coquetry. She sighed as she stepped backwards and out of his embrace. 'I am mindful of the fact I am deeply in your debt.'

He reached out one hand to stroke her jawline. 'Yes, you'd do well to bear that in mind,' he murmured.

6

Rose was still tossing and turning with excitement when she heard the others return home. At the top of the stairs Arabella's voice sounded sleepy as she bade everyone good night but Helena's was sharp as she demanded of her husband, 'It's time to take your sister to task and demand that she have nothing more to do with Lord Rampton. He's dangerous.'

'You wish to expose the charade?' Charles sounded nervous, as well he might, and Rose cringed at the knowledge that she'd forced it upon all of them, without real thought for the consequences.

'How can we?' snapped Helena. 'No, I'll continue to play the innocent virgin but Rose is out of her depth. Do you not see how she turns into a blushing fool the moment he all but looks at her?'

The rest of the conversation was lost as the pair continued along the passageway and all of Rose's earlier excitement drained away.

Yes, she was being a fool. A fool to entertain any hopes that something might come of her association with a dashing, eligible man who clearly desired her and was in need of a wife.

So it was with resigned enthusiasm that she listened to her Aunt Alice expound upon the possibilities inherent in a recently-received invitation from their fabulously wealthy Great-Aunt Gwendolyn who was in need of an heir.

'She wishes you to call on her,' Aunt Alice told her as they took a turn about the rose bushes. 'She's very ill, you know. The end is expected daily.'

Rose stopped and stared at her aunt. 'But — ' she began.

'Yes, yes, I didn't waste time, my dear.' Aunt Alice beamed. 'And nor did she. This could make all the difference to your prospects, you know, Rose, if Lord Rampton considers a sizeable marriage portion a necessary part of the settlement.' She floundered for a second. 'Which is not to suggest that I doubt your ability to entrance him of your own accord.'

They resumed walking. 'In all good conscience,' sighed Rose, 'I can't visit Aunt Gwendolyn like some blood-sucking relative.' Nor, she added, silently, would a sizeable marriage portion make her desirable in Lord Rampton's eyes. Not once he discovered the extent of her charade.

'My dear Rose, you have far too many scruples.'

If only that were true, thought Rose, as her aunt continued, 'Your Aunt Gwendolyn is, if nothing else, pragmatic. Her fortune must be left to someone and she has little love for the other blood-sucking relatives who are suddenly offering their condolences.'

At Rose's continued silence she persisted, 'So, you will call on your Great-Aunt Gwendolyn soon? The poor soul would so enjoy the company. She is quite bereft.'

Rose was soon to discover this a lie on both counts.

'I don't know how many times I told that lazy good-for-nothing boy of mine that whist would be the death of him,' pronounced Aunt Gwendolyn in what Rose discovered was the old woman's characteristic hiss, and not the vestiges of a bad throat. 'Gaming! Were I prime minister it would be outlawed and punishable by transportation.' She drew in a laboured breath, exhaling on an even more venomous hiss. 'He was raking it in when his heart gave out and he landed with his nose in the middle of his pile of coin. Obediah never knew how to deport himself!'

'I'm so sorry,' Rose said in tones that she hoped sounded passably sympathetic. Not that the wizened old face which peeped from the starched frills of Great-Aunt Gwendolyn's white lace bonnet appeared in need of cosseting or sympathy.

'So.' She gave Rose a beady look, her eyes travelling from the top of the curling feather that adorned Rose's bonnet to the tips of her slippers. 'I see you favour your father. Now there was a notable rake, to be sure!' There was admiration in her tone. 'Broke a dozen hearts and kicked up a lot of dust before he married your mother — for love!' She made a noise indicating disgust. 'Worst mistake either of them ever made. He needed someone strong to keep his dangerous impulses in check. Not some whining, puling beauty who'd be the death of him. Make no mistake about that! Were you to have favoured her I'd have given you short shrift for sitting at my bedside with only one thing on your mind: my fortune.'

'With respect, ma'am, Aunt Alice insisted that I came. I have as little desire to be sitting at your bedside as you do to be entertaining me.'

'Miss Alice Wentworth! Addle-headed muttonhead who runs around in terror of that stepson of hers. Oswald! Now there's a nasty piece of goods. If the whisperings I've heard are true he should be sent packing to the Peninsula or transported.'

'Aunt Alice has been very good to me.'

The old woman shrugged and her small black eyes seemed to sink into the folds of her wrinkled flesh. 'Perhaps more so than you might suppose.' Her eyes flashed. 'The irony is I'll never see the reaction of those grasping relatives upon finding they'd been passed over in favour of the daughter of my disgraced half-nephew, eh? A girl who only turned up at my deathbed to inveigle her way into a fortune.' She pursed her lips and watched for Rose's reaction.

'Why would you do anything so addle-headed?' Rose knew she was being tested. 'When I am nothing to you?'

'Except the vehicle of my malicious pleasure.' The old woman gave a gusty sigh and turned her head. 'But you're not the first to whom I've intimated such intentions.' When Rose did not respond she swivelled a sidelong glance at her. 'I'm tired,' she said, petulantly. 'It's time for you to go, young lady. Rose? That was your name, wasn't it?'

★ ★ ★

At last. Rampton felt satisfaction course through him as he raked his eyes over lovely Lady Chesterfield whom he'd just ushered into Felix's studio. His brother was to do the

114

preliminary sketch of his subject in his artist's studio, a quaint circular room on the second floor of the tower.

It had not been easy. The lady really was determined to make him sweat over this protracted courtship, for she'd declined his offer to be painted twice until he'd approached her husband and stated, baldly, that his brother, a noted portraitist, had a week only in which to render her likeness; that her good fortune would inspire envy amongst the *ton*, inferring that this could only be a good thing.

Rampton increasingly got the impression that there was little of substance in the relationship between Sir Charles and the intoxicating little minx that was making Rampton's life hell.

Fortunately Sir Charles had waved one of his long-fingered, ineffectual hands in the air and muttered something about being honoured, whereupon Rampton had fixed a time, there and then.

Now she was here and he was aware of his urgency to have her almost as if it were a living thing co-existing within himself. If he couldn't orchestrate the necessary solitude so that he could begin to make the most of the few short weeks left to them he thought he'd go mad.

Watching the play of emotions across her mobile features, Rampton considered how unlike she was from the worldly women whose company he usually sought. His brother, a short distance away, was mixing paints, but he'd already been coached on what signals indicated he must leave them to it — and not return.

'What an inspirational view,' said the young woman, impressing him by her artless tone as she went to the large windows. Ha! As if she didn't know what game they were playing. 'I know your brother shall do a famous job in painting me.'

A stab of jealousy surprised Rampton. Wishing he were the one wielding a paintbrush, he replied, 'He'll have me to answer to if he fails to capture your perfection.'

Her shy laugh touched him, surprisingly, with something beyond the baseness of his intentions. Impulsively he moved towards her, hesitating at the last moment, for clearly she was not priming herself for passion. Good God, he was on the verge of asking permission for a kiss. When had he ever felt the need to ask permission? It was why he associated only with married women. The rules were established. Each knew exactly where they stood with one another. Conversation was sophisticated and entertaining and

116

expectations not unrealistic.

Mind you, there had been surprising exceptions, the most recent being Catherine Barbery, whom he had always considered the most aloof and detached of his paramours. She had exhibited an uncharacteristic show of jealousy when he had — with great tact and predictability, he'd thought at the time — severed their relationship the evening after he'd met Lady Chesterfield.

He was ashamed to recall that her tears had elicited in him a strong desire to put as much distance as possible between them.

The flicker of surprise in Lady Chesterfield's clear blue gaze as she realized what he was after, followed quickly by delight, nudged at some unrealized tenderness within him. She was enchanting. A quixotic mixture of intelligence, strength and disarming naïvety. Standing before her in the tower room he imagined himself the knight in shining armour who must once have stood at these very windows, wielding bow and arrow to protect his fair lady.

When was the last time he had thought like that? Had he ever? Certainly not in relation to the dozen or more beauties he'd taken as his mistress since he had graduated from the schoolroom. Rampton had not ever considered himself ready to pledge himself to a single woman and what he felt now was decidedly uncharacteristic.

'I prefer what's inside the tower room to the view outside,' he said, savouring the clean, fresh scent of orange blossom water as he enfolded her in his arms.

Her face tilted upwards. Gently he kissed the tip of her nose, preparing to signal to his brother to leave them . . . before the sounds of approaching girlish chatter made him freeze. Surely not?

Lady Chesterfield stepped back, her expression regretful as she ran her hand across his cheek and he said, through gritted teeth, 'Do not tell me, madam, that you have come with an army of attendants.'

The door was thrown open before she could answer and there was the admittedly beautiful but dangerously forward Miss Chesterfield, whose intimate smile only served to highlight why he was so wary of designing debutantes.

'I'm told you can see the dome of St Paul's. Ah, Lord Rampton, Mr Felix . . . ' This was delivered in a breathy gasp as Felix stepped forward while Rampton quickly dropped Lady Chesterfield's hands and felt his rising frustration assume monumental proportions.

'Mr Felix, how clever you must be to paint

my sister-in-law. How many sittings do you think you'll need?'

'Three,' said Felix at the same time as his brother nominated 'five', adding with a laugh, 'Although Lady Casterton needed seven to get the proportions of her monstrous nose right.'

'Well, Rose has a little nose — too little, really, for the proportions of her face,' said the young woman with a guileless smile, 'so I'm sure it won't take as long.'

Rampton felt his protective instincts rise to the fore. 'Perhaps you are envious, Miss Chesterfield, if you feel the need to criticize. Lady Chesterfield could not be improved upon. However,' he continued, softening, 'I'm sure if you asked my dear brother nicely enough he would paint your likeness, too.'

'I doubt that brothers are so appreciative of their sisters' likenesses staring down at them from the breakfast parlour wall,' responded the young woman with a sigh.

Briskly, Rampton said, 'If it is to be finished before the charming Chesterfields leave England, Felix will have to work hard — without interruptions.' With a meaningful look at Lady Chesterfield, he bowed over her hand, adding, 'Madam, what about Thursday, in the morning when the light is best, for your next sitting?'

Two days from now. It seemed to Rampton an eternity before he could spend time alone with her. In the meantime, though, he might manage an intimate moment conversation or two at Catherine Barbery's ball, an entertainment for which he had little enthusiasm but which he'd felt obliged to attend.

He levelled a challenging look at Helena and Arabella. 'My mother intends calling on me on Thursday. She has been quizzing me tirelessly about the West Indies and indicated that she wished to meet Lady Chesterfield most particularly.' He frowned at Helena. 'I understand you young ladies are committed to a dancing lesson.'

'As is my dear sister-in-law,' said Helena sweetly.

'Then it's just as well that she is already such an exquisite dancer.' He looked at the young woman whose unconventional behaviour had briefly aroused his interest before he'd realised she was just the reason he wanted nothing to do with unmarried misses, and said with a colluding look at Lady Chesterfield, 'So, Thursday morning it is.'

'Thursday morning I have made other arrangements,' said Felix, testily, when he finally put down his charcoal, having rendered a preliminary sketch after their visitors had gone.

Rampton grinned. 'Perfect.'

'Oh, look! A parcel!' Removing her bonnet as the three girls entered the drawing room Arabella darted towards the low table on which the small, beautifully wrapped item lay.

'It's addressed to Lady Chesterfield.' Edith's tone was uncertain as Arabella handed the cigar-shaped box to her sister-in-law, who frowned as she scanned the accompanying card before thrusting the parcel at Rose.

'A paean to Lady Chesterfield's golden tresses,' she said with disgust, 'which would suggest it was not intended for *this* Lady Chesterfield.'

Heart thumping, Rose lifted the lid, then gasped as she beheld the magnificent gift: a diamond necklace composed of alternating flowerheads and entwined oval links.

'Oh Rose, I've never seen anything so beautiful. Why, no man would give such a gift if he didn't intend to make an offer,' gabbled Arabella, who immediately put her hand to her mouth, blushing. 'But of course, Lord Rampton doesn't know he's free to make an offer. Why, you must tell him — '

Edith cut in sharply, 'Miss Rose will not be accepting the gift.'

One look at Edith's grim look stayed

Rose's objection, but it was Helena who said, frowning, 'I believe I've seen it before.'

All eyes turned upon her as she reached for the priceless article and studied it carefully. 'I don't believe it's paste, either,' she gasped. 'But why . . . ?' She shook her head and Rose, desperate to know what she was alluding to, asked, 'Are you sure? Where have you seen it?'

Slowly Helena handed it back, still frowning. 'You are very fortunate to have won the esteem of such a gentleman, Rose. You will indeed make all our fortunes.' Suddenly she smiled. 'As for where I've seen it, I believe it was displayed in the window of a jewellery shop. Yes, I'm sure of it.' She turned to Edith. 'And why must Rose not wear it? It is but a trinket compared with what Lord Rampton is owed, yet it would offend him if his gesture were refused . . . and Rose seems willing to go to any lengths to please our esteemed friend.'

Edith's voice was tight. 'I will not see Miss Rose compromised over this.'

In the tense silence Rose caressed the intricately fashioned gift while her insides churned. Was Lord Rampton in the habit of such generosity? Could he really admire her so greatly as to believe her worthy of such extravagance? She knew the answer already.

Lord Rampton considered her favours worthy of such extravagance, but Edith was right. She'd gone too far already and it was time to focus on Aunt Alice's avenues of repayment. However much her own body yearned for Lord Rampton's caresses and her mind considered the risks worth taking, she could not compromise herself and thus her family.

'You are harsh, Edith, when no Chester-field woman has received anything as fine as this,' Helena complained, fingering the thin gold chain around her neck.

The argument that followed was short and decisive. 'Miss Rose will not have her reputation besmirched in order to repay your debt, my lady,' Edith said, pointedly.

But it seemed that Helena was not too chagrined to make her own generous offer to Rose later that evening when visiting her in her dressing room.

'After all, you're on a mission to repair the damage I've caused so I must support you,' Helena said, offering Rose the diaphanous gold-and-green silk and net gown she'd not yet worn. 'Charles has said how important it is to keep Lord Rampton on side while Aunt Alice secures the funds to repay him.'

Rose took the gown Helena proffered and stroked the lustrous fabric while she waged an internal war between wanting to accept the loan while at the same time wondering at Helena's motives.

'You don't trust me, do you?' Helena asked after a silence. 'You can't believe I'd lend you my most fashionable gown and meekly accept the role you conferred upon me while you masquerade as me the entire season.'

Rose sat down on the bed, the gown across her knees. 'No.'

Helena never acted charitably without an ulterior motive. Helena hated Rose. Rose had known this deep within her since the day Helena had become Charles's wife. She wasn't certain why. Surely it wasn't that she was jealous of Rose. Helena was far more beautiful than Rose and Charles doted on Helena, lavishing clothes, jewellery and attention upon his wife while barely catering to Rose and Arabella's needs.

★ ★ ★

With disquiet, Rose donned the gold-and-green silk for the ball that evening before Edith arrived to fashion her thick chestnut-coloured hair into the graceful, flattering style which had won her such approval lately. Why had she never realized the difference clothes and hair made to a woman?

But inevitably this reflection was tainted by the thought that life would soon be very different once she was back in the West Indies. Tainted also by reflections over what Helena had said, though she tried hard to dismiss that, as she did most of what Helena said in order to make everyone else feel they were responsible for the bad hand she obviously felt life had dealt her.

No, Rose knew that when they returned to the plantation hard work would take precedence over all. As her mind turned to the next few weeks, the familiar knot of worry lodged in her throat. What was to be done about the debt to Lord Rampton?

Not for one moment could she happily assume her great-aunt would leave her a groat.

Lord Rampton himself refused to discuss the matter. She had tried to broach it on the dance floor but he just laughed that deep, sardonic laugh of his and changed the subject. Then he tightened his grip on her.

It left her confused. He seemed to be reading from a subtext she couldn't quite understand, though increasingly the thought of tomorrow's sitting to Mr Felix terrified and excited her. The wanton longings of her body reminded her she must be careful and that she should take comfort in the knowledge that Lord Rampton's brother and mother would be in attendance. Whatever happened, preserving her reputation and good name was just as important as repaying Helena's debt.

Later that night, with just an hour before they were due to depart for Lady Barbery's ball-assembly, Rose met Helena in the passage. Her exotic sister-in-law looked like an exquisite bird of paradise, dressed in celestial blue lutestring with gold trimmings, and for a brief moment Rose was filled with envy.

'Why aren't you wearing the necklace Lord Rampton gave you?' Helena's tone was sharp as her eyes skimmed Rose from head to toe. There was no approval in her look.

'You heard Edith. What she said was true.'

'Do you think Edith knows more about the rules of society than you — or me?'

She touched the modest chain that hung at Rose's throat. 'I would never have lent you such a beautiful gown if I'd known you'd insult it with such an inferior jewel. Who gave you that?'

Before Rose could express her anger — for Helena knew perfectly well that Charles had given the gold chain to her — her sister-in-law gripped her arm.

'Come!' She dragged Rose up the passage

to her own room and pushed her on to the bed before rummaging in the drawer of her dressing-table. Rose heard her muttering under her breath before she turned, brandishing a velvet pouch. 'For one terrible moment I thought Charles might have found it. There!' she said, triumphantly as out of the pouch tumbled an exquisite confection of gems linked by a gold chain.

'Where did you get this?'

'It was given to me.'

'Charles . . . ?'

'Of course not!' Helena's tone was impatient. 'You're not the only one to have admirers.'

'You should never have accepted it!' Anger replaced Rose's fear.

Helena tossed her head and began to pace the room. 'I wish you and your loyal retainers didn't share such outmoded scruples,' she said, before conceding with a sigh, 'Of course I can't. If I could, you'd no doubt insist I sell it to repay Lord Rampton . . . though it wouldn't go far. But I think you have an obligation to the rest of us to wear Lord Rampton's diamonds.'

When she brandished the velvet-lined box that had arrived earlier in the day, Rose reared back in anger. 'You heard Edith, how can I possibly wear a gift that — ?' But

Helena cut her off, her tone bitter. 'Oh yes, you have too much honour to accept a token which is nothing to the giver but which would go a long way to ensuring we all retain a roof over our heads.'

Rose heaved in a breath. Again, this argument had its roots in past history.

'I will not have you accuse me of ruining all our lives once more, just as I supposedly did when I refused Sir Hector's offer all those years ago.' Rose thrust the necklace at Helena.

'Don't be ridiculous!' Helena snapped. 'Do you think I blame you for refusing to sacrifice the rest of your life because your brother is too pathetic to provide properly for the rest of us? This is different. It's a piece of jewellery, a token of someone's esteem.'

'A married woman ought not accept gifts from admirers.'

'The woman Lord Rampton admires is not married.'

Rose gasped and Helena laughed, saying bitterly, 'Look at us. You've been given a gift that you can flaunt to the world to remind them that we Chesterfields are people of substance. If you don't wear your diamonds, then I shall wear my gems.'

'Of course you can't! What would Charles say?'

'Do you think me such a fool?' Helena snorted. 'Of course I can't possibly wear the thing, and this — ' again, she touched the simple thin gold chain at her neck, ' — is all I have to set off my gown.' Her bosom rose beneath her tight, lace-edged bodice. 'All I'll ever have,' she said, bitterly. 'Oh, I know you think I'm extravagant with my silks and laces, but at least I can make the most of my youth with some beautiful things, and I'm fortunate to have such a skilful seamstress . . . but beautiful jewels will always be beyond my reach. You, however, can wear this tonight. Put it on after Edith has finished attending to you and tell Charles you borrowed it from Aunt Alice. It will raise the tone of your ensemble and surely put our family on a better footing in the eyes of the *ton*.' Her shoulders slumped as she ran the back of her hand across the tassel fringing the faded curtains. 'While it is common knowledge that Arabella comes with little enough of a dowry we don't want to be distinguished by our penury.' Rallying, she draped the diamonds around Rose's throat and fastened the clasp.

Rose turned to the cheval mirror and gasped. The glittering diamonds set off her ensemble more exquisitely than she could ever have foreseen. The string of stones nestling against the creaminess of Rose's throat became an object of fire and brilliance and Rose felt the confidence of a queen course through her veins.

'Show Lord Rampton what you're made of.' Helena's whisper tickled her ear.

★　★　★

In the large marble-tiled hallway of Lord and Lady Barbery's London residence the Chesterfields were relieved of their outer wear, before mounting the stairs to the saloon, a magnificent room of stately proportions, decorated in rose and gilt and illuminated by hundreds of wax candles.

When Rose almost immediately spied Lord Rampton beneath a candle sconce on the other side of the room, deep in conversation with several soberly dressed gentlemen, her hand went unconsciously to her throat. Bolstered by the confidence of how well she looked, she was able to curtsy and smile with the regal possession of a queen when the viscount acknowledged her with a gracious half-bow.

Rose drifted from conversation to conversation, wending her way into the heart of the company and steadily closer to Lord Rampton. It was like a game. She knew he was acutely conscious of her. Several times she caught him watching her out of the corner of his eye. Instead of directly accosting her, however, it appeared they were destined literally to bump into one another.

But all her pleasure in the evening was about to come to an abrupt halt.

When several knots of revellers still separated them, Rose was surprised to be addressed in the familiar clipped tones of Lady Barbery, to whom she'd been introduced at the masquerade earlier in the week.

Rose turned, the icy glare directed at her very different from the gracious charm the lady had bestowed upon her when last they met.

And as Lady Barbery clawed at the diamonds at Rose's throat, her shrill words sent Rose reeling into a vortex of horror.

For no-one had ever called her a thief before.

7

Mute with embarrassment, Rose was unable to reply to Lady Barbery's hectoring questioning as she backed into a corner, the blood pounding in her head as she clutched the diamonds at her throat. 'It was a gift,' she managed, glad the gentleman closest to her appeared to be deaf and was addressing his companions in stentorian tones, which drowned out Lady Barbery.

Lady Barbery's nostrils flared. 'A thief *and* a liar!'

'Dear Lady Barbery, what appears to be the trouble?'

Rose froze at his nearness. Lord Rampton's quiet, authoritative tone was music to her ears.

'That woman,' Lady Barbery's words suggested Rose was beneath contempt, 'is wearing the diamond necklace given to me by my own husband . . . my diamond necklace which went missing three days ago.'

'Perhaps it is a copy,' murmured Lord Rampton. 'Imitation is, as you know, the sincerest form of flattery.'

'And, pray, tell me, my dear Rampton,

where is the craftsman who can fashion my necklace down to the last diamond in less than three days? Without the original to work from?' Lady Barbery sounded in no mood to be mollified.

The only advantage of being in this horrendous situation was that Lord Rampton was pressed tightly against Rose's side, a barrier to those who would have shown the prurient interest that would spell death to the Chesterfield's social aspirations.

'It would appear someone has played a very cruel or wicked joke on Lady Chesterfield.' Lord Rampton gave Rose's hand a surreptitious and reassuring squeeze. 'For I was in her drawing room when she received the gift from an unknown admirer.'

Rose and Lady Barbery gasped and the viscount went on, 'Perhaps we're looking for a light-fingered anonymous admirer who did not foresee the consequences of his actions and sought to impress Lady Chesterfield with his devotion. Perhaps the necklace changed hands several times before it was legitimately bought.'

'Someone must be called to account!'

'Someone will be.'

Rose was as conscious of the viscount's resolute tone as his hostess appeared to be. Lady Barbery placed an elegantly gloved hand upon his forearm and purred, 'You'll discover the thief, Rampton, won't you? If someone is wanting to make mischief, it is in all our interests to learn why.'

'Of course,' Rampton murmured. 'Meanwhile I suggest discretion is our ally. Lady Chesterfield can return the necklace in the morning.'

Who was the victim? Rampton wondered a little while later, as he gripped the railings of the small balcony off Lady Barbery's private rooms and gazed into the darkness. Someone wanted to make mischief but at whose expense? That of Lady Barbery or Lady Chesterfield?

'You were most gallant this evening, Lord Rampton.'

Startled by the low, husky voice, he turned, unable to place it as that of one of his female friends, as his companion went on, 'Lady Chesterfield is fortunate to once more find a protector who will defend her.'

Rampton summoned a quelling look to match his tone. 'What the devil are you doing out here, Miss Chesterfield, alone with me? Go back downstairs at once!'

'No need to act like an agitated mother hen.' Her amusement was evident. 'I'm not a child.'

'You are not yet presented. You have your

reputation to safeguard.'

'Where I come from debutantes are not as protected as their sisters in England.'

'If anyone should find us — '

'You'd have no choice but to marry me,' his bold companion supplied sweetly. 'Have no fear on that score, my lord. I've no intention of marrying an Englishman when I am simply counting the days until I return to the West Indies.'

Rampton stopped just short of placing his hands on her shoulders and pushing her away. If he were caught even touching her he hated to think of the possible consequences. 'I've no desire to be accused of ruining some gently reared young debutante and being saddled with a wife as a matter of honour,' he muttered.

Discomposed by her chuckle and proximity, he stepped back adding, 'But what charge is this? One might almost imagine you believed your sister-in-law guilty of the theft of Lady Barbery's necklace.'

'Of course she didn't steal it. Not like a cat burglar, creeping into this house in the middle of the night, or a common light-fingered thief who snatched it from Lady Barbery's neck when she wasn't looking.' The girl laughed again: a deep-throated, sensuous noise which Rampton found hard to reconcile with the debutante by his side.

'It's one of my sister-in-law's famous little games. Her way of relieving boredom.' Miss Chesterfield gave an eloquent shrug. 'She means no harm and would have returned it, but my sister-in-law considers the West Indies a virtual prison. She's too delicate for the harsh climate and she despises her husband; so she's developed her own ways of amusing herself. Of course, poor Charles is at his wits' end, and will be so grateful that you've saved her from yet another scandal.'

She dropped her eyes demurely. 'At the masquerade the other night she was with her cousin, Oswald, a nasty piece of work, let me tell you!' She shuddered. 'But they are in many ways of the same mould. I heard her dare Oswald to steal Lady Barbery's necklace — '

Rampton snorted. 'And parade the stolen gems without discovery?'

The girl shrugged. 'That was not the point. Lady Chesterfield's dare that Oswald could steal it was matched by his speculation that Lady Chesterfield would wear it . . . and be championed.'

Rampton stared. Her claim was outrageous.

Miss Chesterfield smiled. 'Each time my poor sister-in-law goes just that little bit further. It's like a disease and poor Charles can do nothing about it, short of locking her up.'

'You certainly are no friend of hers.'

'You think I don't speak the truth?' She laughed softly. 'Helena hasn't got this far in life without being a gifted liar, a consummate actress. After living such a limited social existence as we did in the West Indies her exploits are known and, to an extent, tolerated, but now she has a new audience. A multitude of new admirers.' After a long pause, she added in a whisper, 'Poor Charles.'

'Poor Charles, indeed,' he echoed, straightening and indicating the double doors that opened in to the rooms behind the balcony. 'Not only does he have the exploits of his wife to contend with, but his sister seems happy enough to excite the gossips also. It's time to leave, Miss Chesterfield.' Gripping her elbow, he steered her into Lady Barbery's boudoir, which was in darkness. 'Alone.'

Anger quickly replaced her surprise as she jerked her head up. For a minute he almost thought she was going to stamp her foot.

'It's been a pleasure, Miss Chesterfield.' He bowed, and was relieved, when he straightened, to find she had gone.

He turned back to the railings, thoughts of Lady Chesterfield churning in his mind. Lady

Chesterfield . . . masterminding the theft of Catherine's diamond necklace so that he would champion her? He rolled his shoulders as if his perfectly cut coat were too tight, and balled his fists.

She certainly knew how to tantalize a man, upping the ante with each innocent visit. Had he misread the signs? Each time she'd seemed to be holding him at bay, but was she really trying to convey to him that she was tired of waiting; that it was time for him to be more masterful?

Rampton was not a man who liked to be kept waiting too long, either. He exhaled into the crisp air, making a noise that was part sigh, part growl of anticipation. If the exquisite Lady Chesterfield was so bold that she'd go to the extremes Miss Chesterfield suggested, it was time Rampton took matters even more boldly into his own hands.

He shifted position, unable — nor wanting — to shed the heady desire he felt at the thought. What sweet relief it would be to finally tear off her clothes and tumble her on his expansive carved four-poster designed for such nefarious activities and located in his tower room.

Lady Chesterfield was clearly panting for his tender — or not so tender — ministrations.

Lady Chesterfield had been kept waiting long enough.

★   ★   ★

When Rose saw Helena emerge from the passageway into the ballroom she found the courage to launch into the throng of revellers and accost her sister-in-law, pulling her into a secluded corner.

'It was you, wasn't it?' she accused, fingering the hated jewellery at her throat which Lord Rampton had advised her to wear in order to save face. 'I don't know how you did it but you found a way to spirit this out of Lady Barbery's possession and around my neck in order to damn me in everyone's eyes.' She was nearly in tears and Helena's superciliously raised eyebrows did nothing to soothe her disordered nerves.

'Pray, calm yourself, my dear Rose . . . or should I say, Helena, and do not accuse me of underhand dealings.' With a self-righteous smoothing of her powder blue sash, she went on, 'Do you think I came to London to be dressed as an innocent while you parade around in the clothes Charles bought for *me*? Yet have I even once stamped my foot and told you I will no longer countenance the charade you forced me into?'

Rose drew in a shuddering breath. 'I'm forced to concede I acted rashly, and I'm sorry for it, but your actions tonight could have had me facing the hangman's noose. Do you not realise that?'

Helena clicked her tongue. 'Lord Rampton championed you, Rose. That's all that is important. I had no idea that such nefarious activities accounted for the fact your lovely necklace graces your neck — albeit temporarily — but now we know who it really belongs to you can return it while you redouble your efforts to ensnare the delectable Lord Rampton in order to leg-shackle him at the altar. I'd say this was a very happy state of affairs and you should be thanking me for insisting you wear it, not accusing me of — what? Stealing a necklace? The idea is preposterous.'

Rose glared at her. 'I'm not accusing you of stealing it but I am certain you know more than you're admitting. Furthermore,' she added, lowering her voice, 'as a supposedly married woman Lord Rampton is hardly about to offer for me. Oh, yes, I know you think I should play my hand. After all, a rich husband would benefit us all. And you say I should thank you for achieving tonight's outcome whereby he's championed me, but,' she drew herself up proudly, 'what joy would there be in a union with a man I'd tricked into marriage? You should know that as well as I, Helena.'

She'd struck a nerve. Tossing back the last of her champagne, Helena looked at her with loathing. 'I did not trick Charles into marriage,' she hissed. 'He'd been panting for me since long before I was out of short skirts. If you want the truth, I was forced into marriage with him when the man I loved left me. But that's a long-ago story. Let me just warn you now, my dear Rose, that I intend that you redress all the past ills you've visited upon the family — namely me. You will marry Lord Rampton and it won't be hard to achieve. I've seen the way his eyes follow you . . . the lust that consumes him.' She paused, snatching up another coupe of champagne from a passing waiter before continuing with studied sweetness, 'Arabella will receive an offer from Lord Yarrowby within the next six weeks, and you will ensnare your handsome Lord Rampton.' Raising one eyebrow she contoured the tip of Rose's breast with her fan and leant into her. 'You've kissed him, haven't you?' Her voice was low, sending fear and excited longing up Rose's spine. It mingled with the disquiet Rose felt at Helena's reference to the untested Lord Yarrowby and was swept away by shame when Helena whispered, 'And it made you want more, didn't it?'

Fiercely, Rose shook her head while she reined in her temper. In clipped tones she said, 'Honour dictates that I repay what is owed him, as promised, and Aunt Gwendolyn has all but promised — '

'Aunt Gwendolyn likes to play games and the only assurance you have that we will not all be forced to live like paupers is to play on the feelings of your handsome viscount.' Helena twirled the stem of her glass as she contemplated Rose over its rim. 'It is your duty. My hands are tied for I am already married to a man who has not the funds to pay the lease on our shabby little London abode for more than two months but you, Rose, have a duty to ensure that you and your pretty little sister make the matches that will liberate us all.' She gave a short laugh. 'I am limited by the narrow sphere to which you relegated me, Rose, but you can be sure I'll be doing all I can to achieve the happy outcome we all deserve.'

8

Rampton paced the tower room and watched the road, his agitation fuelled by frustrated desire.

In the days since Catherine's ball-assembly his enquiries had given vastly different perceptions of Lady Chesterfield. Of course, she had been in England for just a few weeks, but a member of his club who had spent time in the West Indies had some interesting *on-dits* about the enigmatic beauty. While these had made Rampton feel a dupe, they'd fuelled the fires of his desire.

Lady Chesterfield, from most accounts, had a decided penchant for money, mischief . . . and men.

His frustration had reached monumental proportions when, two days ago, she had come for her second sitting to Felix with her maid in tow. Yet surely the gleam in her eye hinted that she was as eager as Rampton was to graduate to the next stage of their relationship. Was there not a wicked, colluding glint when she asked him how investigations into the theft of Lady Barbery's necklace were proceeding? Dammit, what was the woman playing at? Did she want him to tie up the maid and bundle her in the antechamber so he could ravish the object of his lustful desires upon the hearthrug?

Actually, the thought had crossed his mind but the maid looked like she'd be a force to reckon with.

Now, though, he had reasonable grounds for thinking that his waiting was at an end. There was only so much cat and mouse a man could take and the surprised look the confounded woman had levelled at him when he'd told her so under his breath as he'd farewelled her during her last visit had been followed up by a colluding squeeze of his fingertips.

In the meantime Rampton had appeased his former mistress with the sop that hers was one of a curious spate of jewel thefts being investigated at higher levels. It was entirely possible, he'd suggested, that sensitive documents in the possession of Catherine's husband, who held an important government position, were the real target and the theft of jewels merely a ruse to deflect attention. It was fortuitous that another theft of a diamond necklace had come to his ears since Lady Barbery's ball.

Waiting for Lady Chesterfield now, Rampton realized how tense he was when the

144

ribbon of dust in the distance which heralded an approaching carriage made him literally sag with relief.

At last. So she hadn't reneged and made a fool of him.

Felix was in the opposite tower, now, mixing his paints, and would soon usher Lady Chesterfield to her seat for her final sitting. Casting his eye over the masculine appointments of his bedchamber Rampton focused his attention upon the panel behind the large, baronial four-poster in which he and his forebears had been born. The panel hid a secret staircase that connected each floor with the courtyard outside as well as a passageway to the opposite tower. It had been constructed during the time of the dissolution of the monasteries several centuries earlier, when the family had been devoutly Catholic. Many Catholic priests had sought refuge in the darkness before making their escape but now, in safer times, its use was limited to pursuits of a far more frivolous kind. He gave a low laugh. Lady Chesterfield, he felt sure, would be keen to view such a curiosity.

No woman had ever affected him like this one. She was fascinating. Intriguing. He loved her strange combination of coquetry and innocence. She was quite unlike any woman he'd ever wanted.

And he wanted her like he'd never wanted anything in his life.

★ ★ ★

With difficulty, Rose had succeeded in dispensing with Edith's services, slipping out of the house when Helena and Charles had taken Arabella to the Bullock's Museum. To avoid the outing, she had pleaded a megrim and although Helena had looked at her with scepticism, her sister-in-law said nothing. No, Helena must have no idea that Rose intended seeing Lord Rampton alone, for although Helena might feel Rose owed them all a glittering marriage to a moneyed peer, Rose knew the repercussions would not be worth it. She wanted his love, not his angry scorn, which is what would be inevitable should he find himself tricked.

But if nothing else, she was desperate enough to take a chance and at least enjoy being the object of his lust — to a degree.

Felix would be wielding his paintbrush, acting as chaperone, but she felt sure Lord Rampton would somehow engineer a few stolen moments where she could melt in his embrace and revel in the kisses he rained upon her, just as he had when he'd come to see her in her drawing room what seemed an age ago. Since Helena had spoken of 'wanting more' the phrase had assumed monumental proportions. The truth was, Rose wasn't entirely sure what that entailed. She was keenly aware of the extraordinary sensations his body whipped up in her own. They made her feel breathless and out of control. But surely a bout of passionate kissing would alleviate that? She knew she was risking her reputation in calling upon an unmarried gentleman, but he had as much desire of ruining her reputation as she did. Marriage was definitely on mind, she acknowledged. And besides, Master Felix would be nearby and possibly even his lordship's mother. All in all, she and her reputation would be safe.

Rose had no idea quite how much she was anticipating her rendezvous with his lordship until Felix, after greeting her warmly, said, 'Can't imagine where Rampton's got to.' He led Rose to her chair where he began to arrange the folds of her gown. Although his actions were intimate, moving an arm here, tucking in a lock of hair there, his manner was business-like.

Returning to the easel and picking up his paintbrush, he continued, unaware of the pain his words caused, 'There was some business with the overseer. They're out on the estate but I think Rampton was unsure whether he'd be back in time to see you.'

'Oh,' was all Rose could manage, thinking of the lengths to which she had gone to orchestrate this clandestine meeting with Rampton. She had an hour, at best, before Helena would demand that Charles must send out a search party. If she did, it would seem that Charles's anger would be over nothing.

Felix's tone was conversational. 'I hear you set sail in a little under four weeks.'

'A great loss, I'm sure you'll agree,' came a familiar drawl and Lord Rampton strode in.

As usual, he dominated the room, his broad shoulders filling out his perfectly cut riding-coat, his buckskin breeches tucked into highly polished hessians. He bowed deeply to Rose, taking her hand in his, caressing the sensitive skin with his lips. It was a blatantly provocative gesture and, embarrassed, Rose darted a look at Felix who was pretending great interest in mixing the burnt umber on his palette.

Lord Rampton stepped back and took up position at his brother's shoulder. 'A rose,' he murmured, transferring his gaze from the almost completed portrait to Rose who reclined on the velvet-draped chair.

She jerked forward, as if stung, then looked up to see him gazing into her face with an

148

expression of deep concern. Embarrassed, she gabbled the first words that came to mind. 'You have the most fascinating home, my lord. I've heard tales it was used to hide Catholic priests in fear of their lives.'

His eyes crinkled with amusement. 'I'll show you the secret passageway, if you like.'

'Very much.'

This seemed to please the viscount who, after peering over his brother's shoulder, remarked, 'Fine work, Felix, but do not take it amiss when I say that no painting could do justice to Lady Chesterfield.'

'The inevitable passing of time will ensure that it is a constant reminder to Sir Charles of his good fortune,' Felix murmured, which only added to Rose's discomposure.

'Where do you suppose it will hang, Lady Chesterfield?' asked Rampton.

'In the breakfast parlour, I daresay.' In truth, it would be consigned to the attic, she thought sadly.

'An ocean away,' Felix commiserated, 'and a terrible loss, though perhaps you'll be a more frequent visitor to our shores, now that you have tasted its delights.'

'I shall have to make the most of those delights while I am here,' replied Rose. 'I cannot see myself returning.'

She glanced at Rampton and was surprised

at the warmth of his smile. He did not appear to have taken account of what she had just said, or else she'd misunderstood the depth of his admiration, she thought with sudden dismay. Perhaps he was satisfied with a little flirtation for a few weeks and would feel no regret at saying goodbye.

She shifted in her seat, impatient for Felix to finish so that she and Rampton could be alone. Five minutes. No, fifteen. That was all she craved. The fifteen minutes during which she'd enjoyed Lord Rampton's passionate kisses when he'd found her at home alone had stoked the fires of a desire she had no idea she possessed, and banished her natural caution in her need to experience those sensations just once more. Surely it was not such a great sin to want a handsome man to make her feel beautiful and desired? After all, it was not as if either were otherwise attached. Still, she was keenly aware of how divisive her charade would be were he to discover it.

But he would not. If Aunt Alice's predictions came true, Rose would be able to raise the funds to pay Rampton's debt honourably, meaning that it would be her choice to be in Lord Rampton's arms through her own desire alone. He could never accuse her of inveigling her way into his affections as an underhand means of absolving her of the debt. The knowledge was liberating.

After what seemed an eternity Felix, with a great show of deliberation, put down his paintbrush and stepped back from his work, pronouncing his labours at an end.

Rampton seized Rose's hand to whisk her out of her chair and they crowded behind the portrait to admire his brother's work. Felix was grinning with well-deserved pride, for the portrait did Rose justice, highlighting her fragile paleness, imbuing her with a shining innocence that was far from wifely but strangely true to life.

Rampton pulled the velvet bell-rope and a footman entered with a silver tray bearing a bottle of vintage champagne and three crystal coupes.

'We must celebrate!' Pouring out the frothing liquid, he handed Felix and Rose a glass each.

Rose felt deliriously happy. She knew her brother would not be pleased, and that the portrait would never grace the walls of the public rooms of their house. However, when she was old and grey she would look at it and remember a fine and handsome gentleman had once thought her a great beauty.

Another bottle was poured to general light-heartedness during which Rampton caught her round the waist and declared her the beauty of the day, then Felix made his excuses and left. At long last Rose and Rampton were alone.

'I am honoured, Lord Rampton,' Rose said, only aware as she spoke that she was feeling as lightheaded as she felt light-hearted. She nodded towards the painting. 'And you have been patience itself.'

He took her glass and set it down on a little table beside the window. 'I have been patient, haven't I?'

The deep timbre and intent of his words resonated through her and she felt herself trembling as he pulled her closer against him within the circle of his arm while with his free hand he cupped her chin. Tilting up her face, he kissed her gently on the lips.

She felt the heat rise up through her body and stirred slightly. 'I don't mean about that,' she said, hearing the uncertainty in her laugh but loving the intensity in his look. She'd never felt this way; so deeply connected. 'I meant in my ability to repay the debt we owe you.'

'What?' His eyebrows arched over his blue eyes as if in faint censure for spoiling the moment. 'My dear, I assure you I have no intention of hounding you for such a trifle. Now, where were we?'

The pressure of his lips on hers increased, pushing away the faint concern she felt at his words. He must not think she'd trade . . . this . . . for what she owed him. She opened her mouth to speak and the tip of his tongue, which had contoured her lower lip, plunged in, deepening the kiss.

She gasped, feeling her legs buckle as he caught her fully in his arms, pulling her against him. There was no mistaking the all-consuming nature of his desire but what frightened her was the force of hers. Her head spun with wicked, unexpected thoughts while strange, intoxicating sensations coursed through her body, making her skin prickle and causing her to push her breasts against his seeking hands. It was behaviour she'd never imagined indulging in. It was wanton . . . She had plunged into dangerous territory. Uncharted territory.

'Not here,' she protested, her voice barely above a whisper.

Rampton looked down at her, saw the deep blush that had spread over her porcelain fine skin, and was impressed. The lady could even blush on demand. He glanced at the room, in which the only furniture was two large, but quite unsuitable, armchairs and a collection of occasional tables, and tried to master his ragged breathing.

'I think it's time to show you the secret passageway,' he suggested.

'I should be most interested.' She sounded breathless. Eager.

Smiling, he felt like the cat who had got the cream. Actually, he felt in physical pain at having to truncate these passionate proceedings. He offered his arm and, with courtly grace, led her out of the room. Obviously she could not wait for this moment, either. He glanced down at her and imagined her naked, writhing beneath him, eyes vacant with lust, skin flushed and covered with the moist sheen of their love-making labours. Oh, he would show her just what a wonderful lover he was. She'd not want to leave his bed until she was forced to do so in order to return to her island home.

He was surprised at the stab of disappointment he felt at the thought. Still, he was not a man who wasted time on the preoccupations of the heart. His was a remarkably resilient one, thank God. His mother had taught him there was no room for sentiment and he was not a man to pine for foolish fancies when the action of the present was all that mattered.

And the moment for action was upon him. He increased his pace. It had been thoughtless to have started proceedings in such a cold, bare room when he'd intended to shepherd her to his nice, big, comfortable bed; however, he'd found himself unable to exercise his usual restraint. He slanted a glance down at her wide-eyed look, focused on her kiss-swollen lips and felt a jolt that, extraordinarily, seemed to travel from his groin to the region of his heart.

She paused amidst their progress. 'Tell me some of the legends about the heroic Delacroix men,' prompted Lady Chesterfield — his soon-to-be-mistress, he thought with an even greater jolt of excitement as she pressed against his side and smiled up at him. He laughed, his mood expansive.

'Ah, so many of them. But not all Delacroix were men of honour.'

'Unlike you, my lord?' she suggested, upon a faint hiccup.

'You flatter me, madam,' he said, hoping his look was not too salacious. An English rose. He had said it before, but how apt was the description, for in the summer sunshine, her bonnet tied demurely under her pretty little chin.

Clearly she was an accomplished coquette. Good God, she'd kept him on the barest thread for longer than any mistress. Two thousand pounds and she was his. Indeed, he'd have absolved her of twice the amount and believed he'd got the bargain.

At the foot of the tower he lifted the latch and pushed open the door. It gave way, protesting on rusty hinges, and they stepped into the gloom. Closing the door behind them, they were plunged into darkness and immediately he felt her pull away.

'I don't think . . . ' she began, but her coyness seemed unnecessary now they'd come this far. He laughed again.

'My male vanity is wounded. I'd have imagined you'd draw closer to me for protection.'

'I'm sorry.' Rose chided herself for being foolish. Lord Rampton was taking her, at her request, to see the hidden passageway. Hadn't he already proved he was a gentleman of honour by pulling away at her first display of reluctance?

'If you're afraid of the dark we'll open the door to the outside and let in the light. I had thought to give you a sense of the authentic. Remember, these Catholic priests made their escape in the dead of night, their lives hanging by a thread.'

He pushed open the door to let through a weak shaft of sunlight; then, taking Rose's hand, he led her up the spiral stairs.

'What's in there?' Rose asked as they reached a room on the next level.

'You are impatient,' said Lord Rampton as if something amused him. 'It's nothing but a room full of dust sheets. It's the room on the next level that's of interest.'

'Where does the secret tunnel lead?'

'From behind the bed down a back staircase and under the courtyard to the park beyond.'

'From the bed,' Rose repeated faintly. Her light-headedness was beginning to give way to her natural caution. The heady desire she'd felt when he'd been kissing her was fast being replaced by concern. She should not be allowing a gentleman to lead her alone and into the dark, to an unknown destination. Her years of training, her innate common sense, should have her pulling her hand out of his and stumbling back down the stairs and into the sunshine. Her foreboding was growing. There was still time to save face. To save her reputation.

Lord Rampton continued to propel Rose forward. 'You did say you wanted to see the secret passageway.'

Was that the faintest note of exasperation she heard? She caught herself up. She was being foolish.

'Yes, of course.' She was finding it hard to breathe. Whether it was because of the many stairs or caused by his nearness, she had no idea. And now she was on the second landing and Lord Rampton was throwing open the doorway to a sumptuously decorated room. His bedchamber? she thought, in sudden horror, as she took in the intimate details: the dressing-table on which was laid out his brushes and combs, the shaving-stand, the brocade banyan draped casually across the end of the bed. And what a bed it was! Exquisitely carved with a headboard depicting a hunting scene, there was nothing fainthearted about the rest of it. Instead of the conventional brocade counterpane it was covered by what appeared to be an enormous bear skin.

'And so the secret passage begins here?' she said, hoping her voice didn't tremble as much as she feared it did.

'Yes, my love.'

Rose looked up, half in surprise, half in fear. The endearment was both music to her ears and an alarm bell. Lord Rampton closed the door behind them, catching her to him so suddenly that she stumbled and fell into his arms.

'Please — ' she began, but his mouth, hot with desire, drowned out anything else she might have said.

For a split second she thought to push him away but her simmering desire so clearly answered his own, combusting into desperate passion and the pulsing desire to push the boundaries of her sensual experience. Resistance wilted before it was even born.

His arms were strong and tight around her, and she sagged against him, another attempt at protest dying upon her lips as he lifted her and carried her to the bed.

She'd never felt a man move above her as he did now, covering her with his body and kissing her eyes, her nose and throat. In mere moments, of course, she'd return her two feet to the floor and profess her desire to end matters there. She'd tell him she wanted to take it slowly. Yes, that's what she'd . . .

Dear Lord, what was he doing? All thoughts of acting upon her good intentions evaporated as she gave herself up to these new sensations which threatened to drown her in a surfeit of pleasure. He'd somehow managed to undo the back of her dress and now his mouth was hot upon her exposed breast. What started as a cry of objection became a cry of pleasure as molten desire coursed through her, making her surely the most willing captive that ever existed.

'You are exquisite, Lady Chesterfield,' he murmured as he kissed the hollow of her throat.

Opening her eyes, she was reassured by the

intensity of his smile. No respectable woman would allow herself to be in such a position but she was prepared to take the chance. She was not just another conquest. He not only desired her, he wanted her for his . . .

Common sense returned.

What a fool she was! He'd forever hate her if he discovered the truth.

Struggling out from beneath him, she made an ineffectual attempt at restoring modesty, pulling her skirts back over her knees. How many women had been brought to ruin by such naïvety?

But with a deep chuckle and, as if she had no more strength than a butterfly, he pushed her onto her back once more. 'You've tried my patience long enough, you little minx, though I'll admit your merry little dance has nearly killed me with the need to have you.'

Only when he raised his eyes to hers did self-preservation kick in and she jerked herself into a sitting position.

His laugh drowned her small shriek as he threw her back onto the bed. One in which she would have been quite happy to flounder in captivity if there were not her future to think about.

Yes, she wanted him, but not like this. What kind of woman was she? Terror and mortification gripped her. She managed to twist her head away and with a gasp forced out, 'Please — !'

It was an ill chosen protest, for of course he interpreted is as a plea for more.

'You are a delightful enigma, Lady Chesterfield,' he rasped, between hot kisses. 'I don't think I've ever wanted anything more in my life.' He paused a moment to brush a lock of hair back from her face. She could feel her heart hammering. Surely he could feel it too. He would attribute it to desire, not panic, and she had only herself to blame.

She opened her mouth to speak. To tell him the truth, but a contradiction of emotions rendered her mute. Her body was willing him to continue his pleasuring, while her mind railed at her wickedness. She had been a fool. A naïve, innocent little fool, but would she ever experience such pleasure again? She was unlikely to have another chance at love. Why should she not simply succumb to enjoyment . . . just for once?

It was not worth the risk.

Lord Rampton's voice, husky with passion, made her pause. 'I wanted you from the moment I met you, my love.' He kissed her lips as he cupped her face. 'No woman has stirred my senses as you have.'

They were words she longed to hear but a

lifetime of training dictated that she should make her escape.

Now he was creating even more wicked sensations, and the words she'd been trained to say would not come. Her desire for this man was stronger than anything she had yet experienced.

She should galvanize every ounce of restraint in order to extricate herself from his irresistible embrace, but where was her will? She'd never known what love and desire were until now.

It was madness but she'd do it. Give herself to this man for this one time only, yes, take the chance for it would be the only chance of love she'd ever get and she had a lifetime of loneliness to fill with the sustaining memory of these burning few short moments.

She was ready to do this. With this one man only for she . . .

Loved him.

Loved him for making her feel what no other man on earth had ever made her feel. Loved the humour deep beneath his ironic, masterful façade.

He tilted his head and his words came out as a soft rasp. 'What did you say?'

Surely she'd not spoken of her love aloud? She opened her eyes to see his fleeting confusion but she shook her head, arching against him, not wanting to lose the moment now that she had steeled herself.

His breath was coming fast and shallow. Lust glazed his expression, twisting his lips into a wicked, colluding smile as he ground out, 'My God, Lady Chesterfield, but you are — '

On the periphery of her consciousness Rose registered the heavy footsteps upon the stair, growing louder as they approached. She tensed, momentarily, then cast concern from her mind as she moved beneath this man she loved and desired, blind to all but her own desire.

A grave error, she now realised, as she heard the door being wrenched open on creaking hinges, before gasping at the cry of rage that echoed through the room. 'What in God's name is this?'

She felt the momentary shock of the man above her before he pulled back and rolled off her, drawing her into his embrace to cover their nakedness. He needed almost no time to collect himself before he was demanding of the interloper in a low, accusing growl, 'I might ask you the same question, bursting into my bedchamber like this.'

She was impressed at Lord Rampton's ability, even under such duress, to play the cool, affronted party. Trembling, she ventured a quick look over his shoulder and saw Charles upon the threshold, his normally pale and placid face suffused with outrage.

Advancing to the centre of the bearskin rug that carpeted the floor, he stabbed a finger in their direction, struggling to force out his words. 'What are you doing?'

Rose buried her face in Lord Rampton's chest, her body burning with shame as she tried to soak up all the warmth of that moment, for it would be a cold place she was going to be living in, soon, she realised.

His lordship did not flinch as he continued to shield her. Her brother was visibly shaking. Charles's rages were few but unpredictable, so when he hissed, 'If I'd thought to bring a pistol I'd shoot you through the heart,' she exhaled in relief, silently endorsing Lord Rampton's rejoinder which he uttered in a tone of unconcern, 'I'm relieved at your lack of foresight,' before he added, 'Your wife might have taken exception to such over-excitement — though I would suggest a little more excitement in the marriage bed might not have seen her here.'

'Wife?' expostulated Charles, his pale face mottled purple with rage.

Rose swallowed and pressed her forehead against Lord Rampton's warm, hard chest, dread and weary acceptance swamping her as she felt his arms tighten when she tried to withdraw.

Charles could have only one response to this and the silence seemed an eternity as she awaited the inevitable unmasking. Waited for the moment when her hopes and dreams would be reduced to cinders and she was exposed for the fraud she was.

'That's not my wife.'

She groaned softly as she felt Lord Rampton stiffen in shock at Charles's next words: 'That's my sister!'

The Consequences

9

'Miss Chesterfield.' *Miss* Chesterfield. The name should have provoked rage; instead, Rampton was dismayed by a surge of feeling that was so far from rage as to render him no better than a slavering schoolboy when confronted with the object of his adolescent obsession.

'Show her in,' he said, struggling for the self-possession that had always been second nature to him and tossing aside the reading matter that had failed to engage his attention for the past hour.

So, she had come to state her terms.

Having been caught well and truly *in flagrante delicto*, he accepted he had no one but himself to blame. Experience with women had tuned his antennae finely when it came to sensing all manner of ruses calculated to inveigle him into matrimony. But Lady Chesterfield — *Miss* Chesterfield, as it turned out — had slipped entirely under his guard.

Stonily he faced the door while he waited for her to enter, the events of the past week flashing through his mind. For twenty-four hours after she'd been hauled off by her brother, Rampton had paced his study like a caged lion, fuelling his anger with the multiple lies and untruths she'd fed him as he tried to relive exactly the moment at which he should have become aware of her deception. Any half-intelligent man would have sensed that not all was as it seemed at the very outset, he told himself.

Cynically, he had waited for *Miss* Chesterfield to call and negotiate the terms of his matrimonial incarceration. He had practised all manner of snide and ironic responses, while his anticipation at seeing her again had grown steadily more unbearable.

He wanted only to tell her what he thought of her.

So he assumed.

But she had not come, and that had been worse.

After three days he had snapped. Arriving unannounced, he had confronted a pale and patently uncomfortable Sir Charles in his study and stonily dictated the terms of a marriage contract. He was a man of honour and he had compromised a lady. She was the clear victor in their final round. She had more than just pinked him. Now he must pay the price.

Rampton had been prepared for a rambling defence from Sir Charles of his sister's behaviour. And, if Sir Charles were in a robust mood, perhaps a healthy lashing of recrimination for Rampton.

But when the young baronet said only that his sister did not wish to marry him, Rampton was at last moved to anger.

'Doing it too brown, sir!' he declared. 'She engineered that little scene so that I'd have no choice but to suffer her joy as she leg-shackled me into following her triumphant progress to the altar!'

Sir Charles, looking white around the gills, concurred miserably, 'I know, I know. But she's made me tell you, expressly, my lord, that she has no intention of holding you to marriage. That, in fact, she does not desire it.'

'Does not desire it?'

He could not believe it. It was all part of the charade. There was a trick involved somewhere, though right now he could not see it.

Not want to marry him?

Why, every unmarried female participating in the social whirligig was there with only one thing on their minds. Most of them saw waltzing off with him as the ultimate feather in their caps.

Not want to marry him? When she'd gone to such pains to ensnare him?

The very notion was preposterous.

171

He would not believe it.

The sad truth was, he had not the words to respond. Naturally, he should hoist her on her own petard and take her at her word. He should simply leave town for the Continent as had been his initial plan, and that would be that; an end to the matter.

The problem was that while common sense dictated this as the correct course of action, his damnably errant heart started playing up to such a degree he needed to see her just one more time to conclude that he was as fortunate a man in escaping parson's mousetrap as any who'd been tricked by the feminine wiles of a calculating female. His parents' patently unhappy union was a reminder that a wife was a ball and chain for life; not an irritant that could be dispensed with when the desire took hold. Rampton had looked forward to many years during which he could sow his wild oats and indulge his predilections for a variety of women before he succumbed to the allure of the one extraordinary creature who would satisfy his needs for both wife and lover for his remaining years.

Clearly, a woman who had tricked him with such calculation did not answer the criteria, but he was determined to make the best of it.

Now, seven days since that fateful afternoon in the tower room, the scheming *Miss* Chesterfield was about to walk through that door. His stomach should be churning in anger at the prospect of coming face to face with her. Fury should be boiling in his veins.

Instead, he felt his heart hammering and his palms go clammy — even though he knew that the long delay in seeing him again must be attributed to the fact that she obviously had a particularly assiduous man of law looking into Rampton's assets and what might be demanded as a matter of honour.

At last the damnably alluring, deceiving Miss Chesterfield stood before him. She looked proud and defiant, that strange combination of strength and fragility piercing his armour, dissipating his anger and whipping up the desire to enfold her in his arms. Except that the look in her eye warned him to have a care.

'My brother conveyed to you my feelings about the idea of matrimony with you, my lord?'

He was silent while he tried to make sense of her barely suppressed anger. Her beautiful mouth was compressed, her breathing shallow, while her eyes bored into him with something that felt uncomfortably like recrimination.

As if she were the wronged party.

Nothing could have been more calculated to drive him to fury. The longing to hold her tenderly was replaced by an overwhelming urge to shake — no, kiss — some sense into her.

He reined in his anger. 'A pity, then, that you took matters to such extremes. Lady Barbery's diamond necklace? Was that to ascertain the level of my affections? You were testing me, weren't you, Miss Chesterfield? To see how easily I would dispense with common sense in order to come to your rescue?' Rampton snorted. 'A bold risk, but it paid off.'

She had been staring at her boots, still having refused his offer of a chair, but she raised her eyes at this. 'My sister-in-law . . . Helena . . . said she thought she recognised Lady Barbery's necklace in a parcel that arrived from an unknown admirer. I know nothing more than that.'

He saw her attempts at appearing discomposed: the slight tremble of her hand as it went to the thin gold chain she wore round her neck. He was not taken in.

She said, 'My Lord, do you not think it possible that Lady Barbery herself was behind this malicious act, designed to make me appear the culprit? I believe she was very upset when you gave her her congé . . . is that not the term?'

'Pah!' Rampton swung to face the window and balled his fists. The thought had occurred to him at the time but it had since been buried by Miss Rose Chesterfield's far greater treachery: her devious husband-hunting methods, which had caught him like a fool. 'Catherine and I parted amicably enough, though I'll concede she may have felt ill will towards you, having usurped her in my affections.'

She inclined her head. 'Then the theft of her necklace remains a mystery. It must have been motivated by jealousy but since no harm was done and I shall be returning to the West Indies next week there is perhaps no longer the imperative to solve it.'

'Good God, are you out of your mind?' The expletive was out before he could stop himself. He had not expected this. Without thought he acted on his overriding instinct which was to keep her here. She was so very appealing in her guise of distress and he had grudgingly to admit that he was finding this interview more diverting than he'd expected.

Trying to maintain his composure he asked through gritted teeth, 'Can you really suppose I am so devoid of honour that I would not insist on marriage between us?'

'My virtue remains intact, my lord, and my brother is the only witness to my want of propriety.' She raised her chin proudly. 'You remain a free man.'

His first impulse was to seize her, hold her tight her in his arms and — well — once again kiss some sense into her.

Then he realized that this was exactly what she intended he should do, so he restrained himself in order to call her bluff. Miss Chesterfield might be devilishly disarming, but she had used the vilest trickery to lure him to the altar and he'd be damned if he'd be saddled with such a cunning female for the rest of his days.

No, he would go to his club, take up where he left off before he ever met her, and banish her from his mind.

He had fully intended to do the honourable thing, but if she were going to play games in order to boost the terms of a proposed settlement then she would find that she had sorely miscalculated.

Yes, he would leave her dangling for a few days. She'd soon come to her senses. She wanted to marry him. That was what this was all about. Had been, from her perspective, since the day she had met him. And to tell the truth, he'd got used to the idea during the past seven days. Had even come to like the notion.

Though not at such cost to his pride. She would not fleece him into the bargain. He would marry Miss Chesterfield on his terms.

Before he'd formulated the right response she'd bowed, saying, 'Good day to you, my lord. My apologies for giving the impression that I tricked you; however, I stand by everything I said. We no longer have anything to discuss.'

★ ★ ★

He'd hoped the rallying company of a few chosen male friends and a visit to the opera would restore his spirits. It wouldn't be long before Sir Charles and his sister would resume their assault upon his conscience in order to persuade him to settle a ridiculous sum upon his dowerless and shameless bride-to-be. Of course he'd be generous, but he wouldn't be taken for a fool.

So he went to his club.

And waited.

Every evening for the next seven days he was on tenterhooks for some word from her.

When she did not come he returned to pacing his study like a caged lion, his anger increasing, while he mulled over what to do.

Clearly he had no choice but to marry the

wench he had defiled — not just in his tower room, but publicly, for the town was buzzing with the titillating story of Miss Chesterfield's daring. No doubt her lily-livered brother had spread the scandal, prepared to destroy his sister's reputation in the sly knowledge that honour would prompt the duped viscount to make Miss Chesterfield a viscountess.

As the silence stretched his anger grew.

So he waited another five days, growing ever more insufferable to those around him, until one day Felix shook his head and said in a tone of exasperation, 'I don't know what has got into you, Rampton, but if she has a fine head of chestnut curls and flashing blue eyes you'd better hasten to the docks because she sails on tonight's tide.' Savouring his after-dinner brandy, his brother added, thoughtfully, 'Thought, meself, that you'd already made her an offer she couldn't refuse.'

If Rampton imagined he'd harboured nothing more than grudging admiration for a pretty head and more than her share of guile, he realized in that moment he'd been deluding himself.

Irritation, anger, severe provocation — all the emotions against which he had been battling for more than two weeks — were swept away by dismay.

Clearly, his feelings were written all over his face for, with raised eyebrows, Felix gave a surprised laugh. 'Don't tell me you didn't know?'

Rampton shook his head.

'Well, don't that beat all? I was surprised you'd let her go, knowing how your feelings had got in the way this time. I say, Rampton, where are you going?'

Rampton had risen with such force that he'd knocked over his chair. Now he turned on Felix as if his brother himself were responsible for the current dire state of affairs.

'Where did you hear this? Why did you not tell me before?' he asked grimly.

'Good Lord, Rampton, the girl's free to do as she chooses. If she's already turned you down don't you think it a little on the brutish side to chase after her and drag her off the boat?'

'Brutish?' He snorted. 'I'm sure it's no more than she expects, playing her clever little games and waiting for me to come running.'

'Which — might I point out? — is exactly what you are proposing.'

Rampton glared. 'Don't you grin at me like that, little brother, unless you're after a hiding. You always were dashed provoking.'

'Not, it would appear, as provoking as the lady in question.'

Catching sight of her, alone on the docks, overseeing the stowing of her luggage, was like receiving a veritable knee in the solar plexus. After riding like the wind, now that Rampton had her in his sights he could afford to relax and feast his eyes on her a little while he tried to make sense of why he really was doing this.

It was dusk. A brisk wind tossed some escaped chestnut strands from beneath her bonnet and whipped her cloak and dress around her ankles. There was no sign of her brother, but she appeared entirely in charge of the situation, directing several porters who were carrying her trunks up the gangway.

'Mind your step,' she said, as one of them stumbled. 'Those are my worldly goods. Take care of them.'

Rampton focused on her rosebud lips and her pert little nose as she dispensed orders with all the confidence of one who was used to running a large estate. Another justification for making her his wife, he thought, pleased, for it went beyond his simple lust for her.

He stepped forward and raised his voice above the stiff breeze. 'I'd have thought you'd take better care of your reputation, Miss Chesterfield. What, in God's name, are you doing?' Rampton had to steel himself against the overpowering desire to approach her from behind and either whisk her, struggling, into his arms, or to press her against his chest and crush all resistance from her.

Battling not to display the full force of his feelings he said to the porters who had momentarily put down Rose's trunk, 'Carry it to my carriage. The lady will not be sailing, after all.'

'How dare you — '

'How dare you make off like a thief in the night with no word to me, Miss Chesterfield?'

She drew herself up indignantly. 'What concern is it of yours whether I stay or leave, my lord? No! Do not take that trunk over to that carriage,' she said, crisply. 'Despite what this gentleman says I *will* be sailing.'

Rampton gripped her wrist and jerked her round to face him. Blinking she stumbled and he was finally able to hold her.

'I forbid it!'

'My lord, what becomes of me is none of your concern. My reputation is ruined but that was not your fault.'

'Have you no concern for your sister, then?' Surprising himself with such creative logic, he went on, 'You once had me believe that Arabella's happiness was of more account than your own.'

'You know it is!' She seemed close to tears. 'I am entirely at fault and I deserve

181

everything that will no doubt be meted out to me for conceiving this outrageous deception.'

To his astonishment, he found himself stroking her cheek as she went on, 'Truly, my lord, I had no more thought when I took on Helena's identity than to salvage a situation which might see us lose our home.' She shuddered and his insides cleaved in sympathetic response — a very rare sentiment — as she said brokenly, 'I simply wanted to play for more time in which to repay our debt to you when Helena was unable to meet you. I never thought it would come to this.'

'Nor did I.' A great lump seemed to have lodged in his throat. Tilting up her chin so that she had to look at him, he was struck by the most extraordinary desire to protect her. Even more extraordinary was that he entirely believed her simple reason for continuing her charade. The sincerity in her limpid gaze found their mark, lacerating every doubt he'd harboured towards her. Suddenly his greatest challenge was to persuade her to stay and marry him.

He held her tighter, his beleaguered brain running through artful arguments while his heart thundered its encouragement. 'Think of poor Arabella. What chance does she have of a good marriage if you turn tail and run, given the rumours regarding your scandalous behaviour?'

Sliding her eyes away from him, Miss Chesterfield looked more mutinous than ashamed. Rampton couldn't believe it. He'd thought that by now she'd have cleaved to him, adding that she'd carried on her charade because the force of her feelings were too strong for her to relinquish him.

Considering the way she was behaving now, he was beginning to wonder whether she'd ever wanted him at all. For a moment doubt returned as to her motives. Quickly he cast it aside. Whatever the truth, the urge to make her want him was more powerful than anything he'd encountered in his life.

'If you have no concern for your reputation, at least consider your sister's,' he persisted grimly. 'You're condemning her to social pariah status if you simply leave her in the lurch like this — unless you're forcing the poor innocent to return home with you.'

She shook her head. 'Aunt Alice has kindly said she'll look after her. Arabella's kind nature and her loveliness will compensate for my deficiencies. I have released you from your obligation.'

She'd pulled away. Now Rampton gripped both her wrists and brought his face down to hers. 'I intend getting a special licence,' he tried for greater authority, 'unless you have a particularly strong aversion to becoming my wife.'

Good God! Still she resisted. He'd thought she'd be shedding tears of gratitude by now. It was not often that Rampton's confidence was shaken.

Holding her away from him so that he could look into her beautiful, fine-boned face he said what was in his heart before he had time to question his good sense in baring his soul so completely. He'd never felt like this: so completely stripped bare and vulnerable, totally dependant on another being for his happiness. A woman, at that. One who had deceived him.

Emotion made the words come out a low, rasp. 'If I asked you to marry me because I truly believe I couldn't live without you, would that alter your mind?' The ardour that injected his question surprised him. But then, he'd been consumed by it since he'd first met her. Now he felt himself dangling by a thread as he waited for her answer. Like a lovelorn schoolboy.

★　★　★

Rose's first instinct was to question whether she had heard him correctly. Lord Rampton had asked her, yet again, to marry him? Not just asked, but begged, the force of his feelings revealed not just in his emphatic tone but by the raw longing in his expression.

It was beyond her wildest imaginings.

She opened her mouth to respond. To bare her own heart and tell him she had never believed such happiness possible; that she had never sought to trick him. But as she did so a nearby shout demanded their attention.

'Lord Rampton! Good morning to you.' Her brother's head emerged from below decks where he'd been inspecting Rose's cabin, an uncertain smile of welcome on his face.

Rose saw there was no similar warmth on Helena's face though there was a certain sly satisfaction as she murmured with a smile, 'Lord Rampton, what a surprise.'

Helena might well have been referring to the fact that Lord Rampton had not relinquished his hold on Rose.

He saluted them both, squeezed Rose closer and announced in expansive tones, 'It may come as a greater surprise to you that Rose has just agreed to become my wife.'

The smile he directed at Helena was so imbued with pleasure and goodwill that Rose could not doubt that his decision to wed her stemmed from desire, pure and simple. She forced back the kernel of doubt that honour and coercion had had their roles to play.

'Isn't that right, my love?'

It must have been the dazed expression on her face that caused him to laugh out loud and kiss her quickly upon the lips before releasing her to the expected gestures of congratulation from her family.

'How very clever of you, my dear Rose,' her sister-in-law murmured as she touched her lips to Rose's cheek. 'And it is what I directed you to do. Just make sure you are not greedy with the benefits.' Her breath tickled Rose's ear. 'And that you remember those who facilitated your good fortune.'

'I'm afraid you'll be sailing without her,' said Rampton, stepping forward to reclaim his intended. He seemed unable to wipe the grin from his face.

'Rose was to travel alone,' Charles said, casting a troubled look at Helena. 'Our plans have changed, for we intend to remain some while longer in England. I had hoped to,' he looked nervous, 'find a means of securing the funds we need to repay you. We have expectations that an aunt of — '

Rampton cut him off. 'No need to lose sleep over such a trifle. This marriage obviously negates the debt.' He levelled a fond look at Rose. 'Though I hesitate to call it a trifle when it was the means of bringing your sister into my orbit.'

Rose felt as if *she* were in a different orbit. Lord Rampton . . . holding her as if he could not bear to let her go? Speaking as if their marriage were the most marvellous outcome?

Raising his hand to halt Charles's sputtering gratitude, Rampton went on, 'Let us return to town and tell Arabella and Felix the happy news.'

'Expect Arabella's congratulations to be more muted than you might have expected,' Helena said. As always, she managed to find a way to dampen Rose's happiness. 'Arabella is nursing a broken heart.'

'Yarrowby?'

Rose felt as much as saw Rampton's relief. All he said, though, was, 'My commiserations. Perhaps my alliance with her sister may aid her future prospects.'

Rose's heart leapt. Might Rampton really be generous to her family even after having been so thoroughly duped? She realized that any prospective suitor for Arabella would have withdrawn on account of the scandal Rose had caused. Indeed, her misery of the past week had been as much due to her guilt over Arabella's injured prospects as in accepting that Rampton was lost to her.

Now there were the legalities of their union

to be seen to, with Rampton declaring his intention to get a special licence so that they could be married without delay.

Rose opened her mouth to speak but Rampton squeezed her hand and went on, 'After that, I think a protracted bridal tour sounds in order. The world needs to know this is a love match.'

A love match. Rose existed in a state of euphoria that nothing Helena could say, and not even Arabella's unhappiness, could dampen.

Sadly, Rampton's mother put an end to their planning a protracted bridal tour by pleading a severe chest ailment that, she insisted, was mortal, but the wedding ceremony was held at St Mary's three days later with a sprinkling of well-wishers.

Rose had never been more nervous in her life. The last thing she had expected when she set out from the West Indies was a glittering match.

And while a glittering match was all very well, it was the man himself who set her pulses racing. Each time she glanced at him she had to pinch herself to realize that the fairy tale had come true.

Except that it wasn't all a fairy tale.

Scandal was inevitable.

But it need not be attached to her name

indefinitely. She would see to that. The gossip-mongers who asserted that the new Lady Rampton had deceived her husband into marriage would search in vain for signs that all was not well between them. He himself had called it a love match.

She smiled at her husband and her heart leapt as she saw her pleasure reflected in the gaze he returned as they stepped out of the church, now man and wife. Tenderly, he caressed her cheek as she rested it briefly against his shoulder.

'Try not to over-exert yourself at the wedding breakfast,' he whispered. Tipping her face up towards his, he added with his characteristic wolfish grin: 'You'll need all your reserves for tonight.'

Helena was the first to offer her congratulations after the ceremony, mustering an impressive display of sincerity as she kissed Rose. She was radiant in primrose silk, her dark hair caught up in an ivory comb in a simple style that accentuated her high cheekbones and dark, smouldering eyes.

'Brother-in-law,' she said, eyes dancing, holding out her hands, forcing Rampton to walk forward and take them. 'May your impulsive gamble on a wicked Chesterfield pay off.' It was a bold and familiar speech ameliorated fortunately by Rose's husband's obvious delight in his unexpected and hasty marriage.

'Congratulations are due to my clever wife for realizing before I did what a crotchety old bachelor like myself really needed,' he said.

Proudly he led Rose across the threshold and into the vast marble-floored hallway of her new London home. The household servants stood in two ordered lines from the foot of the sweeping staircase.

Having introduced them to the new Lady Rampton, the newly-weds preceded the guests into the saloon, where the sumptuous wedding breakfast was laid out.

'I didn't think you had it in you, Rose. You have triumphed.'

Helena had not wasted an opportunity. Finding Rose alone for the moment, the silken tones hid the unkind insinuation.

'My good fortune is all due to you, my dear Helena,' Rose responded. 'It was, after all, you who sent Charles looking for me the day the painting was finished, was it not?'

'I am always so conscious of your shining halo, my dear Rose, I had not anticipated that he would find you so compromised.' Helena's smile did not reach her eyes. 'A lucky thing for you that Lord Rampton is an honourable man, otherwise you'd be languishing, a lonely and maligned spinster in the West Indies for the rest of your days.'

'I'd have had company when Charles finally brought you home.' It was an effort to sound brighter than she felt. Helena could be depended upon to find her most vulnerable places. 'Tell me, Helena, what really keeps you in England? It wasn't the debt, was it? You'd have found some way of brushing that under the carpet, or otherwise appeasing Lord Rampton.' Rose was pleased to see that this found its mark.

A shadow crossed Helena's face before she resumed smoothly, 'Our overseer appears to be doing a better job than Charles, or you, ever did. The plantation is prospering and now that you've landed yourself such a catch, Rose, I no longer have to *pretend* to be someone I'm not. My enjoyment has just begun. Besides, if I play my cards right Charles might find his way to furnishing me with a diamond necklace.'

'Like Lady Barbery's?'

'Exactly. Only I don't mean one that's been stolen, my dear Rose. What a perplexing mystery that was.'

It was wrong to feel such vitriol for anyone on this most joyous of occasions. Five years of training enabled Rose to say with reasonable equanimity, 'You achieved nothing, Helena. Rampton knows I am innocent.'

Helena's eyes widened with mock concern. 'Rose, you surely didn't imagine that my insistence that you should wear the necklace — though I admit, I was uncertain as to its origins — was prompted by malice? Why, I wanted to test Lord Rampton, see how he'd champion you if indeed there were something havey-cavey about the gift.'

This was too much. Fighting the urge to hustle her sister-in-law into a nearby antechamber and simply have it out with her, Rose said in a low voice, 'You really think me so credulous? That I'll believe whatever you choose to tell me? What about the timing of Charles's visit to Rampton's tower room? You orchestrated that, too. Tell me the truth, Helena.'

Helena put her head on one side as she said, brightly, 'The truth, Rose, is that it's entirely due to me that you and your handsome, *rich* bridegroom are here today and I'd like a little credit. My, what a lovely bride you make.' Dropping her voice she skimmed her gloved hand along the length of Rose's forearm, feigning affection. 'Of course, marrying your viscount was the easy part.' She drew back and her smile faded as she added, almost as if it were a vow, 'And may you be as happy as I've been the past five years.'

Before her spirits had quite plummeted to her toes, Rose was relieved to see Rampton advancing, wearing the well-satisfied smile that filled her with happiness and banished her fears regarding their future together. Helena had not seen him. She was still eyeing Rose with a distinct lack of felicity. It was this which enabled Rose to feel charitable. She must remember, she told herself, that dissatisfaction was not a crime and nor had Helena committed anything beyond achieving, in fact, Rose's happiness. Helena's discontent with Charles did not mean she was a disloyal wife in more than thought, and if she could find happiness as the feted Lady Chesterfield in London's drawing rooms, Rose would be glad.

'Rampton . . . darling.' What power Rose felt to purr those words and have her husband respond — in front of her jealous sister-in-law.

'My clever wife has brought me to heel, Helena, and not long before time, too. Now, my dear . . . ' He put an arm around Rose's waist and was about to draw her away before good manners intervened as he glanced at Helena's empty hand. 'Shall I fetch you an orgeat, in case you've developed a taste for the sickly liquid, sister-in-law?' He smiled wickedly. 'Or should it be champagne? I keep forgetting that you are the worldly, married Lady Chesterfield.'

'Just as long as you remember that dear Rose is your innocent and unworldly wife.' Helena's eyes glittered, but her laugh was mirthless. 'Though for someone so innocent and unworldly she has done a fine job achieving what a great deal more designing misses have failed to achieve, I must say.'

★ ★ ★

Rampton assigned his housekeeper, Mrs Hopkins, to show Rose the house of which she was now mistress. The wedding had been conducted in such haste that Rose had only seen the entertaining rooms.

Now, while Rampton was ensconced in his library with his man of business, preparing to leave for Larchwood, his country estate, a few days later, Rose trailed after Mrs Hopkins as the venerable retainer flung open the doors to Rose's private apartments.

Her bedchamber was decorated in green and gold. Once sumptuous, it now had a faded charm about it.

'This used to be her ladyship's room, but his lordship says it is to be redecorated to your liking.' Mrs Hopkins did not look encouraged by the prospect.

Rose was about to ask what her ladyship, languishing apparently on the point of death in the country just now, might have to say about that, but then thought better of it.

Mrs Hopkins, cold and erect, nodded stiffly as Rose dismissed her. Was she one enemy in a houseful of hornets? Did the minions downstairs make malicious remarks about their mistress's dubious claims to her new title? Had they heard the rumours surrounding the new Lady Rampton's wicked deception? Did they know she had been implicated by Lady Barbery in the theft of that lady's diamond necklace?

As Edith had decided to remain with Arabella, a plain, sour-faced young girl called Beth had been assigned as Rose's lady's maid. Though Rose would rather have had Edith as an ally in her new home she feared for Arabella's welfare with Helena as her protector. Her younger sister's happiness was now Rose's chief concern. Once the scandal Rose had created had subsided — as Rampton had assured her it soon would with him by her side — she hoped the girl would be settled before too long.

'What does my lady wish to wear for dinner?' Beth's tone was courteous but, as she awaited instruction, Rose saw no warmth, no desire to do more than simply her job.

She was disappointed. Having the respect of one's lady's maid was important to bridge the divide between upstairs and downstairs. Rose would have hired a girl herself, except that the dowager had assigned Beth to Rose specifically after hearing that Rose's old nurse would not join her in her new home. Rose wondered whether the act had been kindly motivated, or the opposite. Judging by her new maid's sharp features and thin mouth, young Beth had an uncertain temperament.

10

Rose wasn't sure whether she was sorry or otherwise that the Dowager Lady Rampton was not present to observe her son's obvious self-satisfaction — and satisfaction with his new wife — at breakfast the following morning.

Any qualms she'd had regarding her ability to please her husband in the bedroom as his legal wife, as opposed to the woman he had obviously intended to take for his mistress, had not been realized.

Not only were they not realized, they were well and truly quashed.

She had woken to find him looking down at her, admiration and desire brightening his gaze.

'Do you know,' he'd said, running an appreciative hand along the curves of her body as she lay on her side, 'that you are the first woman I've woken up next to who has filled me with the insatiable desire to repeat in every detail the events of the past eight hours.' Collapsing on his back and looking ruefully at the ceiling, he murmured, 'But I must not be a brute. You're an innocent and must be feeling very tender.'

'Yes,' agreed Rose, reaching across to kiss him on his beautifully shaped mouth. 'Very tender towards you, my love.'

She squealed as he flipped her onto her back.

'You must know the penalties for your trickery include a great deal of close contact with the man you set out to deceive,' he chuckled, straddling her. 'You're a clever woman for knowing before I did exactly what I needed, dear heart,' he reassured her, kissing her neck, tenderly.

'Surely a man who has no intention of being leg-shackled has good reasons for not wanting a wife,' she responded. 'Helena tells me you tire quickly of your mistresses.'

'A good friend, isn't she?' he responded drily. With a sigh, he conceded between kisses, 'My thirst for novelty does not reflect well on me, I'll admit.'

'Will you take a mistress when you tire of me?' She cupped his face. 'After all, albeit unwittingly — or at least for noble reasons — I deceived you, Rampton. What happens after the novelty of having a wife wears off?'

Raising himself on one elbow he looked down at her, his expression serious. With his forefinger, he gently traced the contours of her nose and cheeks as he said in a low murmur which resonated with sincerity, 'The reason I have not wanted a wife before now is that I truly believe that wives and mistresses are not a happy mix.'

Rose bit her lip and felt a surge of hope at his tone. Conviction burned in the depths of his eyes and the expression he focused upon her sent tendrils of the deepest love and communion curling about her heart.

He kissed each eye in turn, almost reverently, before resuming. 'My father found it exhausting while my mother became a bitter creature obsessed with finding endorsement of her charms as a result of the disregard she received at home.' Stroking her cheek, he added, 'To tell you the truth, I'm delighted that I was led into a union which I heartily believe will satisfy me on all levels. Now, are *you* satisfied?' With a wicked grin he seized her by the hips and raised her so that she was lying the length of him. 'No, there's no need to tell me in so many words. Actions will do just as well.'

★ ★ ★

Rampton showed every sign of being entirely satisfied with his new wife. Unfortunately, Rose's meeting with her mother-in-law in the country the following week suggested that her every fear about this lady's feelings towards her were right on the mark. She was glad to be bolstered by having Rampton at her side, making clear his obvious pleasure in his sudden and unexpectedly changed circumstances.

'So glad your health has improved, Mama,' he remarked, drily, as he kissed the dowager upon her powdered cheek.

The newlyweds had travelled together by carriage, breaking their journey for the night at an inn some hours away, arriving at Larchwood around noon the following day. The dowager viscountess received them at the top of the shallow stone steps of Rampton's magnificent home and had, with a great show of fondness, embraced Rampton, and with a great deal of reserve, stooped to plant a cool kiss upon her daughter-in-law's brow.

'Rampton never told me you were so small,' she said in greeting, turning to lead them into the house.

'I'm sure I never neglected to mention any one of her many virtues,' said Rampton, smoothly, giving Rose's hand a reassuring squeeze.

He reassured her again when he put his head around the door of her dressing-room where she was seated in front of her looking-glass in her own sumptuous apartments a little later.

'Mama may appear a gorgon, and I'll admit she'll need time to come round. Just remember, my love, no woman would ever have been good enough for her son. Soon she won't be able to help loving you.'

It didn't take long for Rose to be quite certain that loving her daughter-in-law was something his mother would never do. Not only was Rose inferior in birth and address to the wife Lady Rampton had desired for her son, she was clearly a fortune hunter with a past mired in deceit and scandal. In the drawing room later that afternoon the older woman's feelings became clear as Lady Rampton recounted her difficulty in making up a party of ten, which was to serve as Rose's introduction into local society.

'I had more refusals than acceptances, I wasn't sure whether to cancel the whole thing.' The dowager looked at her son severely, as if to suggest it were his fault for marrying a woman no one wished to be obliged to receive, much less recognize as his wife.

Rampton pretended nothing was amiss as he reached for a spiced biscuit. 'Lord and Lady Albright?'

'They accepted, yes.'

'What about Geoffrey?'

'He returned from London yesterday, so he has been included,' his mother replied, referring to the Albrights' son.

'You were not obliged, Mother,' Rampton said in clipped tones, before asking, 'The Colonel and Mrs Carstairs?'

'Declined, I'm afraid. As expected. The trouble is, half the county have drawn their own conclusions about such a hastily conducted marriage.' She took up her dainty teacup and added, over its rim, 'You must have expected this.'

There was an awkward silence. Rose, out of the corner of her eye, saw her husband tense.

'How could there not be?' Rose said, smiling. Rampton had been about to defend her, but she must not pit him against his mother. She had not lived five years in the same household with Helena without learning how to defuse a potentially explosive situation. 'Our courtship was highly irregular and I'd be surprised if I were not branded a scheming fortune hunter.'

'Who vehemently opposed the notion of marriage to me until I wore her down,' added Rampton, with a bolstering smile at Rose.

The dowager sniffed. 'Rampton never could resist a pretty face.' She glanced up at the enormous portrait that hung above the fireplace. It was of the dowager, painted when she was a young girl. She had been beautiful, if the artist were to be believed, and had obviously been conscious of it, judging by the complacent little smile. She was smiling at Rose just like that now. Only youthful complacency had, with age, turned to malevolent smugness.

'At least you don't disgrace the family line with your appearance, though that's hardly the first consideration.'

'The first Lady Rampton was mistress to Charles II,' explained Rampton. 'Nor can it be forgotten that my own dear mama had the honour of turning down our good King George.'

'Rampton, this is not a competition,' said his mother with almost grotesque playfulness. But when she turned her gaze once more upon Rose her eyes were cold and her words held a warning. 'Rose, I've no doubt, is well aware of her obligations. She knows she'll have to tread warily to avoid being branded the scheming fortune hunter she has just described herself.'

★ ★ ★

Rampton was clearly pleased by Rose's enthusiasm for going riding that afternoon.

'Another surprise. I did not know that you could ride,' he said as they wandered over to the stables.

'How do you suppose I oversee the estate back at home?'

'Your home is here now.' She smiled.

'I hope you don't plan to mount me on some docile little mare with absolutely no spirit.'

'That's exactly what I plan to do. Until I've satisfied myself you're not going to break your neck within a month of marriage I'll decide what's best for you.'

Rose dropped her voice to a murmur and said, provocatively, 'Perhaps the neighbours would think that a little drastic in order to rid yourself of the wife you were forced to marry in haste.'

'Madam, if we were not in public your inflammatory suggestion might be met by a sturdier response.' Smiling wickedly as the groom led a docile grey mare across the yard, he gave Rose's bottom a small spank.

She was not expecting it and blushed as the groom raised his eyebrows at her squeal.

'Fraid she's the littlest, most docile one we 'ave, miss. But if you's afraid of 'orses — ' he said, misinterpreting her response.

'No need to worry, Briggs,' replied Rampton, leading Rose across the cobbles. 'I believe it was you who once remarked I'd as sure a touch with the ladies as I have with the horses. Now Rose, as you can see, this is the horse. Over here is what's called a mounting block. I shall assist you to get onto this creature's back but you mustn't scream. It only looks a long way down.'

Ignoring Brigg's mumbled response and fierce reddening, and his wife's indignation, Rampton encircled her waist.

'In answer to your previous question, my love,' he murmured, his breath tickling her ear, 'the neighbours will soon be in no doubt as to exactly why I was so eager to wed you.' He glanced behind to make sure he was unobserved, then skimmed Rose's shapely contours before hoisting her on to the horse. 'Because I can't keep my hands off you.'

Unexpectedly he found himself hoping they would be observed by all and sundry as they traversed the country lanes and tracks. Rose would certainly be seen to advantage here and he was just as anxious to dispel any speculation that this had not been a marriage of his choosing.

To think he had nearly thrown away this chance of happiness.

★ ★ ★

By the time they headed for home Rose was feeling a great deal better. That is, until there came an uncomfortable and somewhat perplexing encounter along the way.

'I say, the bridegroom returns.' From around a bend in the rutted lane appeared a tall young man on horseback. Judging by his attire and the way his hair was curled Rose could tell he was a Corinthian. Rose was conscious of her husband stiffening in the saddle.

'And you, Geoffrey, I hear, managed to slither free of your obligations.'

Rose hid her surprise. It was not often Rampton failed to dress up his disapproval with jest.

'Not without honour, my dear Rampton,' replied the young man with a graceful bow from the waist, smiling, despite his hostile reception. 'If your own wife were not herself such a beauty you might well have benefited from my advice on such matters.' He nodded at Rose, adding, 'No disrespect intended, Lady Rampton. Your husband and I are old friends.' He paused. 'But as he appears to have forgotten his manners allow me to introduce myself. Your neighbour, Geoffrey Albright, at your service.' He gave another half-bow in the saddle, his eyes lingering on Rose.

With a curt nod, Rampton prepared to move on. 'Good day to you, Geoffrey. I believe we expect the pleasure of your company at dinner.'

'You must dislike him very much,' Rose remarked glancing back at the young man's departing figure. 'Your reception somewhat belied his assertion that you are old friends. How long have you known one another?'

'All our lives.'

★ ★ ★

With the last-minute cancellation of Mr and Mrs Brierly the dinner party was reduced to eight. Rose learnt this by arriving at the drawing room just before the event in time to hear the dowager mutter, 'I don't see why you appear so surprised, let alone put out, Rampton. Frankly, I'm surprised the Brierlys are the only ones to have offered their apologies at the last minute. It's only because the rest of them thrive on salacious gossip that they can't bear to refuse an invitation to see the woman who has — Ah, Rose, there you are,' she broke off as she noticed Rose framed in the doorway. Lady Rampton did not even blush.

'The woman who has stolen my heart,' said Rampton, softly, warningly. Sweeping his mother with cold eyes, he moved to Rose and put an arm about her shoulders. 'Rose is the woman I love and that is the reason I married her.' He looked as though he was making an effort to keep his anger in check and Rose was half-afraid, half-gratified by the expressions that flitted across the dowager's face: surprise, indignation and . . . apprehension. No doubt she knew she had gone too far.

'Rose, my love, shall we greet our guests?'

Despite Rampton's earlier chilly reception of his old companion, Geoffrey, he was cordial as he greeted him now, this time in company with the young man's parents.

Although Geoffrey's starched shirt points weren't so high as entirely to obscure his cheekbones, it was apparent by his elaborately tied cravat that Mr Albright aspired to high fashion. He was handsome in an affected way, but Rose far preferred her husband's understated elegance.

'I hadn't thought to see you returned so soon, Geoffrey.' The dowager Lady Rampton greeted the young man with a certain reserve. 'Rumour had it you'd be gone another month.'

'That's why it was just a rumour,' he replied, smiling as he bent over her hand. 'They're simply buzzing around me at the moment.'

'Yes, aren't they,' she replied drily, and again Rose wondered at his crime, if that was what it was.

Then the dowager was smiling almost coyly as she quizzed him on his latest exploits. Obviously his crimes did not really matter. People would never snub him by declining his dinner invitations. He was a man.

A man who certainly knew how to charm, for not a minute after his frosty reception he was enjoying a tête-à-tête with his hostess who seemed to be murmuring in a decidedly intimate manner, and whose reference to the West Indies had Rose twisting back from her stilted conversation with Geoffrey's unforthcoming step-father.

'You look absolutely gorgeous, darling.'

Rampton's murmured praise as he brushed past her enabled Rose to muster a dazzling smile. She had won over her husband against the odds. Now she must do the same with the neighbours she decided, as they all seated themselves.

Taking comfort in her appearance was a novelty. In the West Indies she had barely made the effort to dress her hair in anything but the most rudimentary twist, nor had she worried about complexion enhancers. What was the point when she owned no fine clothes? Or when there was no-one who held the least interest for her?

But while it bolstered her confidence to be so openly admired by her husband and at least several of the gentlemen there, she wished she'd not been seated next to Geoffrey, whose bold and piercing looks made her distinctly uncomfortable.

'Lady Rampton, it is an honour to meet one of the ravishing Chesterfields at last,' he said, turning to address Rose now that his neighbour had been engaged by the gentleman on her other side. 'I believe the three of you have taken London by storm this season.'

Glancing up from spearing her pigeon breast, Rose had half anticipated the predictable gallant admiration, but his gaze was peculiarly intense, frankly appraising, and distinctly unnerving. She licked dry lips, uncertain how to answer, but certainly wary of appearing too cool, or too encouraging. Certainly not until she knew better what kind of man Geoffrey Albright was. She was saved from having to respond when he asked, unexpectedly, 'Do you suppose we have met before?'

She drew back, startled. 'I've only been in the country a couple of months.'

Geoffrey leaned a little closer. His long, contemplative silence was unsettling. At last he said, with a little laugh, 'Perhaps in another life, madam. I am sure that in another life we were once . . . ' he drew back, his gaze flicking over her as if she were a prime article, ' . . . very close.'

Before Rose could voice her indignation Geoffrey resumed, 'I hear you sat to your brother-in-law, a noted portraitist.'

'I hear you've been out of the neighbourhood,' responded Rose, coolly, though she was churning with disquiet inside.

'Just in the neighbouring county, staying with friends.' His smile was bland before he turned the conversation back to her. 'Of course, all the talk was of the unexpected speed of your nuptials. You can imagine how many fair noses were put out of joint when it was learned that the beautiful but obscure Lady Chesterfield — I beg your pardon, Miss Chesterfield — had no sooner stepped ashore from the colonies than she'd snared one of the country's most eligible and elusive bachelors. So, ma'am, having known Rampton all my life, and of his resistance to marriage, you understand why I have been excessively keen to meet you.'

'It's as well, then, that you're such close neighbours, since I'd hate to think you might have travelled a great distance only to be disappointed,' said Rose, leaning aside so she could be served from a platter of beef.

'I would not have been disappointed had you been cross-eyed and hare-lipped. It was my curiosity that needed satisfying.' Geoffrey's eyes reminded her in that moment of those of a well-fed cat, confident of itself and its quarry. 'Rampton's idea of the perfect wife is a plain, docile girl who will leave him to his own devices,' Geoffrey went on, cruelly. 'From what I have heard, you are far from docile, and you most certainly are not plain. Already you've led him quite a dance.'

Rose acknowledged his words with the barest of smiles, forbearing to reply as she picked up her knife and fork. She felt embarrassed and trapped. Mr Albright, senior, on her other side, was deep in conversation with Rampton's mother. Glancing across the table she caught her husband's eye, and he, reading the desperation he saw there, went so far as to breach good manners by leaning across the table to say, 'I believe you've been a guest of the Huntingdons this past fortnight, Geoffrey. Weren't you supposed to stay a month?'

Geoffrey gave a careless shrug but a faint blush belied his assumed indifference. 'A week would have been sufficient in such dull company,' he said. 'Naturally I had no desire to cause offence, so I invented the excuse that Mama was poorly and wanted me home. If you've heard anything else then it's been invented.'

'Ah,' Rampton, nodded, as if satisfied. Rose tried to recall if she'd seen Geoffrey Albright before.

'Knowing you, Geoffrey, as I do, I was unable to give credence to the rumours that have been circulating. I see you've been admiring my new bride.' Rampton changed the subject. 'I had to act quickly to secure her consent before she set sail for the West Indies. She was on the point of embarking, in fact, when I waylaid her,' he sent Rose a smouldering look, careless of the interest of the rest of the table, 'and finally overcame her resistance to the idea.'

When the guests had left and they were alone, Rose looked up from her dressing-table and asked, 'Does Geoffrey Albright have a sister whose aspirations towards marriage with you I might have blighted?'

Rampton, stroking her shoulders, looked perplexed. 'He has no sister.'

'Well, he certainly made it plain that his attendance here was more in the nature of a visit to the zoo to see what sort of creature I really was than a genuine desire for our society.' She bit her lip, watching him in the looking-glass, close to tears. 'I wonder how many others felt the same?'

'Geoffrey — my friend as you erroneously term him — would not have been invited here at all if I had had anything to do with the guest list.' Rampton leant down and put his cheek against hers, smiling at her reflection. 'Rest assured that you were mightily admired tonight. By Geoffrey too, who, I must warn you, is very much in the petticoat line. I do not care for his society but for some reason my mother has had a fondness for him since we were brats together.'

'Were you not even friends as schoolboys?'

'Age and proximity were all we had in common.' Rampton gave a grim laugh. 'You'll have heard, no doubt, several sly references to his recent house visit to Colonel and Mrs Huntingdon. They have a son and two daughters, the younger a pretty enough creature just out of the schoolroom but too giddy, it was thought, to unleash on society this year. In usual fashion it seems Geoffrey played fast and loose with the young girl and she, knowing no better, her head doubtless turned by his pretty compliments, has become in consequence the talk of the town, to her detriment.'

'You mean he's compromised her reputation and won't behave in good part?'

'My dear, the man is married with an invalid wife. Not that you'd know it from the way he comports himself about the country-side like a gay young blade.'

He drew Rose up to stand beside him and continued, as he led her to the bed, 'But no, he prefers to brag about his involvement with Miss Huntingdon, suggesting it was she who led him into all sorts of disgraceful scrapes.'

He had Rose trapped against the bed. Leisurely he began to nuzzle her neck while loosening her silk peignoir. Beth had performed her duties and been dismissed for the night.

'A wife!' Rose was shocked. She arched against him. 'He never mentioned her during our conversation and I quizzed him all about his family.' For once she felt little answering response to Rampton's obvious desire. All her plans of dazzling the company and gainsaying the gossips who said she'd trapped her husband lay in ruins. If Geoffrey, with his obvious penchant for female company, could make her feel this unworthy, how would she fare when confronted with the more virtuous element of her neighbours?

'Yes, scandalizing, isn't it?' Rampton sounded amused. 'I blame his pea-goose of a mother,' he went on, conversationally. 'She dotes on him. Takes his part and always has done, whatever mischief he's engaged upon.'

Rampton bent to nibble Rose's earlobe.

Normally Rose would have been in thrall. Now all she could think of were Geoffrey's insults and hurtful insinuations. Rampton had sat across the table and observed the conversation, yet he had no idea just how insulting Geoffrey had been.

Tonight's dinner with its declined invitations and Geoffrey's brazen curiosity, and his cruelty in dealing in home truths, made Rose realize how compromised she really was. And how much it affected Rampton's standing in the community.

'He's been horribly indulged by his stepfather, too. His mother was a poor widow and Geoffrey just an infant when she married Albright. She believes her precious Geoffrey was inveigled into marriage. But the girl's a simpleton. A very comely simpleton, I grant you. Geoffrey was loath to do his duty until forced.'

Rose pulled away again and closed her eyes. His words scorched her soul. Perhaps Rampton would think her in the throes of ecstasy. But for that moment she could not bear his touch.

She sighed softly. 'Unlike you were forced to do your duty?'

She felt Rampton draw back in surprise. His expression was quizzical. And uncertain. He must have felt her reserve.

'My duty?' he began. His hands dropped from her shoulders and he took a step backwards. 'My duty, my dear?' he repeated, his head cocked on one side. 'Do you consider this a duty?'

Shaking her head, she exhaled on a sob. 'Of course not. But please, Rampton, I'm very tired tonight . . . '

She knew she should say more. Rampton had been so understanding and used every opportunity to reassure her that her place in his heart was secure. Good lord, it was more than a bride who'd married for love could have expected.

Married for love? As she lay in bed, alone, that night the phrase kept returning, until she finally acknowledged the truth of them.

Love was the basis for her union with Rampton, not deceit, and she was only harming herself and what they had if she kept harking back to it.

She shivered beneath the counterpane of her large, empty four-poster in the private apartments she'd been assigned. How foolish of her to have elected to 'give him his privacy', thinking space apart would be good for them, and how much she wanted to go to him.

But she didn't think she'd know how to find his quarters in the dark.

Berating herself for thinking no further than her foolish insecurities she tossed and turned until daylight, when she would have sought him out immediately had sleep not finally claimed her.

11

Rose's guilt compounded her unhappiness when she found that her husband had left on an unscheduled trip at dawn the following morning.

'A man needs his freedom,' her mother-in-law said, looking up from her tatting. Rose had seen the malicious gleam in her eye as she informed her that Rampton had ridden to town and she had no idea when he might be back.

'It must be at least four hours on horseback. Perhaps longer. He must mean to spend the night. And you only just married. Still, it cannot be said he has not done his duty by you when all's said and done.'

Duty. That was what Rampton had talked of last night, before he had kissed her cheek and left her. She had clung to him for a moment. She wanted to rest her cheek against his chest and cry her heart out; she wanted him to reassure her — again, in view of Geoffrey's unkindness — that he had married her not out of duty but plain desire. She had been too self-absorbed to see that he had wanted the same reassurance. And now he was gone, before she could tell him so.

A gentleman's club was a refuge from domesticity, a sanctuary for beleaguered husbands. But not when every second member wanted to talk to one about one's wife.

Not that Rampton had left Larchfield strictly on account of Rose. Since he was not revelling in his wife's warm embrace that morning he had decided on his usual dawn ride. It was only as he was dressing that the remembering of a neglected piece of business had prompted him into changing his plans and making a day trip to London.

It had been a piece of perversity not to slide into bed beside Rose and inform her, he knew. The truth was that he was chagrined. Last night Rose had clearly not desired him.

It had been less than two weeks since they had wed and they had shared a bed every night. He had thought his desire would run its course, but its trajectory was ever upward.

But last night Rose insinuated that duty lay at the heart of their marriage, just as it did every marriage. At least, that was how he had taken it when she had not run after him, begging to explain a misunderstanding. No, she had insinuated that having been compromised she, like he, had had to pay the price by making their union legally binding.

Well, that was how his touchy male pride had taken it before common sense had told him he was being a fool. Last night he'd wanted to feel himself the object of Rose's slavish devotion to the same degree as he had on every night since they had wed.

Restlessly, Rampton turned the page of the periodical on the table before him. No, he decided, with a surge of almost self righteous pleasure, he had married a good woman whose only crime was taking on her sister-in-law's identity in order to help her family. She'd certainly not set out to entrap.

But she'd come to love him. She might have entered into a charade to repay a debt but she could not fool him that she did not love him. No woman could smile at him as if he radiated all that could be pleasing to her. No woman who was merely play-acting could drive him to such exalted frenzies of lustful pleasure and then make it plain she'd be quite happy to repeat the exercise five minutes later.

Turning another page of the periodical in front of him, realising he hadn't taken in a word, Rampton felt a real cad. Just when Rose needed reassuring over her role as his wife and hostess he had disappeared. That blackguard, Geoffrey, playing on her vulnerabilities, probably to spite Rampton, was largely to blame for her downcast spirits, but Rampton had been too absorbed in himself that he'd been unable to see what was right in front of his nose.

At this point Rampton's thoughts were interrupted by a heavy-set elderly gentleman stumbling against his chair.

As he stopped to apologize Rampton could not but be struck by his deeply tanned complexion. He was about to murmur that it was quite all right when the gentleman, obviously recognizing him, declared, 'It's Rampton, ain't I right? Lucky man who's just married the incomparable Miss Chesterfield. I'd not the nerve to approach you directly when you were pointed out to me before, but since I've literally stumbled upon you . . .'

He held out his hand, white teeth brilliant, like his snowy hair, a dazzling contrast with his leathery complexion.

'Sir Hector Stokes,' he introduced himself. 'Knew your wife back in the West Indies. Known her since she was born, in fact, and, what's more, had the dubious honour of being declined by her nigh on five years ago.' He chuckled. 'Thought that'd surprise ye. Yessir, I'd like to think she was in good, safe hands now. Couldn't be worse off than with that brother of hers whom she all but wet-nursed, and got little thanks for it. So . . . married last week, I hear.' He shook his head. 'And me only off the boat on Tuesday. Not that she'd have had me for all the fancy palaces I could have bought her, if she'd have let me. Ay, when I hear she set her cap at you it makes my blood fair boil. My Rose never set her cap at anyone. If ever there was a goddess of virtue, 'twas Miss Chesterfield.'

Rampton, as much astonished by the revelation of this character's identity as by his speech, was about to invite him to sit when they were accosted by Charles.

'Good Lord, Sir Hector, is it really you?' Sir Charles asked, a smile lighting up his normally hangdog expression. 'Why, it must be five years. Surely you've not been in England all this time?'

'Just stepped off the boat Tuesday last, as I was telling Lord Rampton. Been adventuring since I last saw you. Spice Islands, Americas. Nothing like travel to mend a heart and fire up the constitution.'

Rampton pressed his new acquaintance to take some brandy with him. He was disappointed when, instead, he found himself alone in the company of his brother-in-law.

'Back in town already, Rampton? Then perhaps you've heard the news. I don't know whether to be pleased for Rose or indignant.'

It was clear Charles was enjoying Rampton's suspense, however as Rampton responded with merely a slight raising of one eyebrow, Charles said, 'She's just been left a sizeable legacy from a great-aunt. Or half-great-aunt. Fact is, I didn't even know Aunt Gwendolyn existed until I heard that Rose had struck up an acquaintanceship with her a month or two ago.' The smile left his face as she stared moodily into his whisky glass while Rampton congratulated him.

'Oh, I won't see a penny of it for her house and an annuity has been willed to Rose, so of course you'll benefit, Rampton.' He grunted, shifting uncomfortably when he seemed to become aware of the churlishness of his tone. 'Fact is, Rose was counting on this some weeks ago, so she could repay you without obligation. Not that she didn't want to marry you, of course,' he added, hastily. 'Still,' he shrugged, 'life works in mysterious ways and you've been very generous to us, don't think I don't appreciate it. Now all that's needed is a marriage offer from Yarrowby to settle Arabella and then I can take Helena back to the plantation where I know she'd be so much happier.'

Rampton raised one eyebrow. 'Has Rose not passed on my cautions to you regarding Yarrowby?' he asked.

224

'Cautions?' Charles looked blank before he went, 'Not that it matters, I daresay, since Yarrowby who looked set to offer last week in fact has suddenly disappeared without a word. So if it's cautions regarding the fellow's address, I'd say he could learn some manners about what it is to let down a hopeful young maiden. I found Arabella in tears twice yesterday and I can't tell you how wearisome it is to live in a household of discontented women.'

Rampton stood up, bowing his intention to depart. 'I can't say I'm sorry Yarrowby has departed but you might like to quiz Rose on what I have to say about his suitability as a suitor. Good evening, Charles.'

★ ★ ★

Rose had left her mother-in-law's company to restore her spirits, so the last thing she needed as she rode out and inhaled the crisp morning air, gazing out over the beautiful hills and valleys which her husband owned, was to see Mr Albright, also on horseback, hailing her.

'Morning, Mr Albright,' she said, with a decided lack of pleasure as he brought his mount abreast of hers.

'Surveying your newly acquired estates,

madam?' he remarked in that outrageously direct way of his; so insulting.

'I had no idea it was so beautiful.'

'Then I hope you will remain in the country to enjoy it rather than rushing back to town at the first opportunity.' His tone was insinuating. 'I was looking forward to furthering our acquaintance . . . now that we are such close neighbours.'

Rose tried to look as unwelcoming as she could. He was sticking by her side like a leech.

'Your husband and I used to fish off that stone bridge over there whenever we could get out of our lessons early,' Geoffrey said, pointing. 'Not that that was often, for our tutor took fiendish delight in setting us Latin translation which took forever to finish.'

'You had lessons together?'

'Evidently Lady Rampton felt her son wanted in the way of play-mates. As we were both roughly the same age and had no siblings she proposed to my mother that I should take my lessons with Rampton. I daresay I can thank him for opportunities which might not otherwise have come my way.'

'And what use have you made of them, Mr Albright?'

At her arch look and tone he roared with

226

laughter and then responded, as if he genuinely thought she'd been making a joke, 'Absolutely right, Lady Rampton, I've never done a scrap of good since the day I was born. I am the despair of my poor parents. They even sent me off to the West Indies for a short time, you know. Alas, our paths did not cross, Lady Rampton. Perhaps you'd have seen that the wayward youth I once was needed the strictest of overseers, not some indulgent — and somewhat drink-sodden — brother of my mother.' His eyes gleamed at Rose as he assessed the effect his words had on her.

Rose frowned, recalling her father mentioning some lazy ne'er-do-well relative of some acquaintance. Perhaps it had been Geoffrey.

When at last she was rid of him she stopped in at the kitchens to supervise dinner. Little matter that the dowager would consider it a gross violation, but Rose wanted not only to see the way things were run and, if possible, make improvements. She knew how to run an estate and, after all, she was the new Lady Rampton and her husband had given her carte blanche. Following a heated but, she hoped, profitable exchange with the cook, she spent the rest of the afternoon exploring the house. She was determined to acquit herself more than creditably as wife and hostess and was not afraid of hard work.

If honour had, despite his efforts to prove to the contrary, forced Rampton to marry her, then she intended that respect, spiced with desire, would keep him true.

Just before retiring to her apartments to change she was handed two letters: one from her Aunt Alice and one from a man of the law of whom she'd never heard.

★ ★ ★

Rampton had barely drawn breath, changed his coat and sponged the dust from his face before going in search of Rose. He'd behaved like an immature schoolboy, misinterpreting her strained behaviour after her first dinner party in her new home. Then he'd rushed off without a word, giving his mother more ammunition against his new wife. The last thing he wanted!

He found her in her private sitting room, white-faced and trembling.

'My great-aunt Gwendolyn has died,' she told him.

He looked at the cream wafer she waved distractedly before her, and then at her face. Her eyes were blank with shock.

Having galloped as if the devil was after him he'd hoped for a warmer welcome than this. The rapid beating of his heart was not due to exertion only and he ached to enfold her as he murmured the tender rapprochements he'd been rehearsing during most of the journey home.

But she barely acknowledged either him or his honeyed words. He was unsure whether she expected sympathy. Great-aunt Gwendolyn had been a tartar, from all reports. Charles had said that Rose had barely known her.

'My commiserations,' he said, feeling unaccountably awkward as he put a comforting arm around Rose who was standing in the centre of the room. She seemed so distant. 'When is her funeral? I daresay you're obliged to attend?'

'It would be the least I can do, considering she has just left me a rather fine address in Mayfair, and an annuity for its upkeep.'

It was more, much more, than he had expected. He also had expected Rose to be delighted. He led her to the window seat and sat beside her. Clearly she was in shock. This woman must have meant a great deal to her, after all. He murmured, 'That was magnanimous of her.'

'No!' Rose shook off his arm and buried her face in her hands. 'Why did she choose to die now? Everyone said she was a vindictive old woman. And so she was. To die now . . . not three weeks ago!' The wafer which had conveyed the news, now a crushed ball, was flung across the room. Rose stood up and began to pace, hands at her throat, her breathing laboured. 'Don't you see?' she continued. 'If she had given some indication of her intentions earlier I would never have been forced to continue my deception. I could have paid our debt to you — honourably.'

She stopped and turned an appealing look towards Rampton and he, who'd returned from London in such anticipation of making good after his poor response the night before, felt only the deepest sense of disappointment. He frowned, trying to make full sense of her outburst.

'And thus neither of us would have been trapped into this marriage?' He rose and put his hands on her shoulders, bringing her face close to hers as she began to protest. Meanwhile, regardless of what his heart was telling him, the fires of lust were as ever being stoked by her mere proximity.

She looked confused. And hurt. Though why that should be, Rampton had no idea.

'I'll sell it, Rampton. The property might be willed to me, but the proceeds are yours, by rights. The debt — '

He waved a hand dismissively through the air. 'Does everything hark back to that goddamned debt? Do what you wish with your new address, my dear. Give it to the orphans' asylum for all I care. The house and whatever proceeds it may reap you are yours and of no interest to me.'

Of course, his mother had a different view. Smiling grimly, she said, 'This will go down well with those neighbours who might have attributed baser motives to the way in which you went about persuading Rampton into marriage.'

'Mother!' Rampton rose to his feet, fiercely protective of Rose, who extended her arm towards him saying in mollifying terms, 'If it's the truth, as I'm sure it is, you must not blame your mother for saying what I need to guard myself again. Yes,' she smiled at the dowager, 'my inheritance will help to redress many of the wrongs for which I must take responsibility.'

'It seems you have a more sensible head on your shoulders than I'd thought,' said the other woman. 'But now, tell me, I'm curious as to why you said nothing about knowing Mr Albright in the West Indies all those years ago.'

Rampton, surprised, jerked his head around at Rose who was looking blank. Then she shook her head. 'I've never met him before, though he seemed to think he knew me,' she said, slowly.

The dowager frowned. 'You say you don't know Geoffrey?'

'She certainly has no reason to like him,' Rampton muttered.

★　★　★

An uncharacteristic confusion of spirits made Rampton restless as Fanshawe, his valet, brushed his russet superfine coat in preparation for dinner.

Was it true that if Rose had received her bequest from her late Great-Aunt Gwendolyn she'd have continued to resist Rampton? The question chased itself round his brain.

Had the old woman died a few weeks earlier, as Rose had stated so plainly, she'd have had financial independence.

Freedom to choose her husband?

'Are you satisfied with the construction of your cravat, sir?'

Rampton studied his reflection and then the anxious expression of his valet. 'Perfectly satisfied.'

Fanshawe stood back to admire his handiwork while Rampton focused on dismissing the notion she'd developed a tendre for another gentleman in the short time she had been in England. A tendre which had been denied expression purely on account of her need to insinuate her way into Rampton's affections. Ridiculous! Catherine had smoothly planted the kernel of doubt in his mind after he'd proudly told her to what lengths Rose had gone in order *not* to tie him to what he believed were now his matrimonial obligations. It merely demonstrated what a fool Rampton was to believe something for which he had no direct evidence.

He went down to find Rose so he could speak plainly to her, but found only his mother in the darkened drawing room. The light gave her a headache, she said. He could not remember a time she she'd embraced the sunlight and the outdoors. Or when she'd truly smiled.

'Your new wife has taken herself off for a walk,' she greeted him, detaining him when he would have gone after her, with, 'Sit, Rampton, we need to talk.'

Stifling a groan, Rampton lowered himself onto a leather armchair far from the fire and looked enquiringly at her. 'I trust you have not inveigled me into conversation merely to bring to light some other defect of my new wife,' he muttered.

His mother shook her head. 'To be truthful, she is not the woman I'd have chosen for you but she is agreeable enough. I find I'm not so disposed to dislike her as I'd supposed.'

Rampton chuckled, despite himself. 'You are so lavish with your praise, mother. Small wonder I've grown up so accepting and forgiving of the foibles of those around me.'

She ignored his sarcasm. 'I took tea with Mrs Albright this morning and she told me something quite extraordinary.'

Rampton cocked an eyebrow, ready to pounce in defence of Rose, if necessary. Mrs Albright was a gossip. Still, he was glad his mother chose to share the rumours that might be circulating about his wife if only to be in a better position to quash them.

'Rampton, you remember five years ago when Geoffrey returned home after a year in the West Indies helping his uncle — Mrs Albright's brother — manage the sugar plantation?'

Rampton nodded.

'Do you recall that his mother was at her wits' end because he was so changed? So wild?'

'That's right. I believe I suggested he might be a poppy-eater. And barely had he been here a month than he got that poor simpleton into trouble and was forced to do the honourable thing. He's been nursing a grudge ever since.' He wondered what relevance any of this had to Rose. Perhaps it didn't.

His mother clicked her tongue. 'It turns out that Mrs Albright believes Geoffrey's anguish was on account of a young woman in the West Indies. A very beautiful young woman who captured Geoffrey's heart. He was very bitter over the affair. Of course, Geoffrey won't talk about it other than to say that this young woman returned his love but refused his marriage offer because he hadn't sufficient funds to keep her in the style to which she intended to become accustomed.'

Rampton had an inkling as to where this was going. 'You're suggesting it might be Rose?' He shook his head, groaning inwardly. More false rumours to have to counter. 'Nonsense, it could have been anyone. And Rose denied ever meeting him.'

His mother picked up her tatting with a sigh. 'Yes, she did deny it. Yet Mrs Albright says Geoffrey described Sir Charles and Arabella to her when he returned. And,' she levelled an incisive look upon her son, 'Rose did seem very uncomfortable about being in his company.'

Smiling, Rampton rose. 'Well, I'll just have

to ask my darling wife myself — in case her memory has subsequently returned,' he said, brightly. 'Then, when the truth of the matter is ascertained, mother, I trust you'll do everything possible to ensure Rose's reputation remains unsullied. She is a woman of substance in her own right now, you'd do well to remind everyone.'

He already had his hand on the doorknob when Rose in fact appeared upon the threshold. The faint scent of the orange blossom water she liked to wear seemed to power directly from his olfactory senses through to his loins and it was all he could do not to run his hands all over her. Instead, he stepped back to allow her to pass by then followed her into the room, asking, 'Rose, mother is curious to know if you perhaps recall having met Mr Albright since you were distant neighbours at roughly the same time in the West Indies.'

She gasped. 'I've never met him,' she said quickly. 'And if you'll pardon my rudeness, I'm glad of it. He seems a most unpleasant young man and I make no apology for saying so.'

Rampton put his hand on her shoulder to calm her. 'I'm sorry if he upset you, my dear. And that's quite all right. Mama was just curious, that's all.' Over the top of Rose's head he levelled an 'I told you so' look and was about to suggest they take a turn around the roses when the dowager called Rose to her side, asking, 'Since you must be worn out after your walk, Rose, I wonder if you'd be good enough to help me untangle these skeins of thread.'

★　★　★

Rose tossed and turned in bed that night as she went over the events of the past twenty-four hours. She realized she'd made a grave miscalculation in the way she had delivered the news of her bequest and that this had been compounded by her lack of interest in her husband that afternoon. But the ominous presence of Rampton's mother was a great inhibitor, especially when she strongly suspected Beth was furnishing the dowager with intimate details of Rose's conduct.

Eleven o' clock. Rampton should have come to her by now if he was going to at all. He'd been kept up attending to business affairs and had promised to join her later.

With thundering heart Rose slipped out of bed and wrapped a shawl around her shoulders. If Rampton had misinterpreted her distress then he needed reassuring as to exactly where her affections lay.

Her tumultuous emotions had certainly not abated by the time she reached his bedchamber where the sound of his even breathing indicated that he was not being kept awake by the same pangs of doubt and worry that besieged her.

She wasn't sure whether coming here was a mistake or not, but she had to show him honestly what was in her heart. Perhaps a distant approach might have been better, but wasn't that a device a scheming huntress employed prior to the wedding vows? No, Rose was determined to show Rampton that she found him the most irresistible gentleman she'd ever encountered.

'Rose, is everything all right?'

His voice was thick with sleep and surprise as he struggled onto his elbows, but she snuggled into the crook of his arm and, wrapping her ankle round his while nibbling his earlobe, made it quite clear her intentions had nothing to do with needing his assistance.

'I only want to show how much I love you,' she whispered, nuzzling his neck, 'and that I'm sorry if it seemed, before, that I didn't.'

'Oh, Rose.' All the relief for which she could have hoped was invested in those two words as he crushed her against his breast.

'And I'm sorry for being a cad and not realising how difficult it must be for you to enter a new life where everything is so strange. I was going to come to you earlier but it was so late I feared you'd consider me selfish.'

His touch was reworking the familiar magic that she was coming to desire with ever — greater intensity. Her heart skittered and sensation prickled the surface of her skin. Oh, what joy it was to see him similarly affected.

'Do you understand that I feel, keenly, the loss of pride and dignity in being foisted upon you as a dowerless, indebted damsel mired in scandal? An independent fortune would have changed all that. It would have given me social standing and respect. Everyone would have congratulated you on a fine match, including your mother, no doubt.'

'You don't need anyone's congratulations but mine, dear heart,' he muttered huskily. In the dim light of the candle she'd placed upon the chest of drawers beside the bed he could see her eyes glaze over with the heady sensations that were fast engulfing him. His last coherent thought was that Rose could come and apologise to him any time.

★　★　★

They didn't discuss Rose's inheritance before Rose left for London, though he'd made clear the asset was hers. Rose wished he'd relented in his decision to go on horseback, if only to save her having to endure the next few hours with the lacklustre Beth, but he'd said he had some business to attend to and would join her later.

Beth's sickly pallor and sour expression advertised her disgust at repeating the tiresome journey so soon as eloquently as words. It was clear she had no love for her mistress and as the hours stretched Rose determined she'd find a way to give the girl her notice, hopefully without offending the dowager.

Rose's only entertainment was in imparting the information that the recent rains had raised the level of the river so high that only yesterday morning the mail coach, while trying to ford it, had been overturned and several passengers swept away to their deaths.

'I fear, also, that the house is in some disrepair,' she informed Beth, smiling. 'I'm told the servants' quarters leak. And, regrettably, there's been a rat plague. However, with your able assistance we'll soon put matters to rights, won't we, Beth?'

She settled back into the squabs with a satisfied smile. Beth rarely showed pleasure or enthusiasm, but she certainly didn't disappoint when it came to exhibiting fear and distaste.

At last they arrived in London. Rose was thrilled at the opportunity to be once again reunited with Arabella. Unfortunately that necessarily entailed Helena's company, but the barely contained outrage with which Helena congratulated her on her inheritance was almost worth it. Goodness, but she could be a spiteful piece of goods, Rose berated herself, as she took a seat opposite her sister-in-law and began to regale her with an account of the wondrous size, location and fixtures and fittings of her new Mayfair residence which she had just returned from viewing for the first time.

Of course Helena was doing her best to hide her true feelings, though her politely enquiring tone gave her away. Helena was never politely enquiring when she was addressing Rose. And her eyes glittered as she marvelled, 'So, Rose, barely a moment after gaining a rich and titled husband, fortune smiles upon you yet again. If you didn't so obviously deserve it we'd all feel positively spiteful.'

Rose was not surprised when, later, Arabella deluged her with a torrent of tears.

'I can't endure another moment of Helena's company,' she wept, throwing herself upon Rose's shoulder when they were alone in Arabella's bedchamber.

Rose soothed her. 'There's still plenty more entertainment to be had before Helena and Charles take the ship back.'

'But then I'll have to go with them.'

Rose held her at arm's length and surveyed her sister. 'You'll be snapped up before then, my pretty,' she reassured her.

Arabella hiccuped and threw herself on her bed. 'Helena says no man of any consequence would look at me with less than six hundred a year.'

'Your nice Lord Yarrowby did.'

The words were immediately regretted. Rose knew Arabella was nursing a broken heart, although neither had spoken about Arabella's previous admirer's defection. Guiltily, Rose realised she'd taken the coward's path when she'd failed to address the conflict between their views regarding Yarrowby's potential as a suitable husband and Rampton's low opinion of the man.

'Perhaps it's for the best,' she now said, taking a seat on the bed beside her and stroking her sister's disordered hair. 'To tell you the truth, Rampton doesn't care for the fellow and in fact positively warned me to ensure you had nothing to do with him.'

Arabella turned her wide-eyed look upon

her sister before biting her lip. 'Oh, Rose, I know I shouldn't say anything, but Lord Yarrowby has told me all about Lord Rampton's jealousy of him.'

'Indeed?' Rose didn't try to hide her scepticism.

Innocently, Arabella went on, 'There was a lady they both were very fond of, only she preferred Lord Yarrowby.'

'Is that so?' Rose decided it was time to change the subject, but regretted bringing up Helena's name for it almost caused Arabella another bout of tears.

'Helena says he was only toying with me and that he left because I had no dowry and — '

The guilty way she bit off the last word made Rose suspect what other soothing reassurances Helena must have had for Arabella.

'Because your sister scandalized respectable society?' With heavy heart Rose pulled Arabella to her feet, saying in a falsely jolly tone, 'What do you say to our shopping for some new gloves to go with your pink sarsanet? You know I can afford it, now. Come. It'll take your mind off your troubles.'

A shopping expedition would be a tonic and help to while away the hours until Rampton arrived to fetch her, as arranged.

Her guilt over her role in damaging Arabella's prospects had led her to come up with what she believed would be a grand plan regarding the disposal of her house, but she wasn't sure if Rampton would share her enthusiasm.

Several hours later the young ladies were back with their booty: two pairs of gloves and a shawl each. Clearly, Arabella was just as miserable as she'd been before.

At last Rampton arrived. Rose caught her breath as he entered the room, marvelling at the fact he was her husband and at his power to make her heart miss a beat. Each time he entered her orbit she had to pinch herself to remind herself she was the woman he'd chosen to ally himself with. And that he seemed more than simply resigned to the fact. Supressing a thrill as her thoughts strayed to the previous night, she jerked her head round to Helena who had risen gracefully from her seat by the window.

'My lord — I mean, Rampton,' purred Helena as she clasped Rampton's hands between her own.

Despite every attempt to keep it at bay, jealousy rose in Rose's throat like bile, although she managed, cheerfully, 'Good afternoon, Rampton. The house isn't in nearly as much disrepair as I had been led to believe. I'm told it'll fetch quite a sum.'

Rampton smiled. 'Good fortune has certainly smiled upon you, my dear. What does Helena think of it?'

'The house, Rampton . . . or Rose's good fortune?' With a coy smile, Helena answered the question herself. 'She has been fortunate in her marriage to you, my lord, but it would appear you are not the only slave to her charms. Aunt Gwendolyn must have loved Rose very much to have made such a generous bequest. I believe they met only once. Before we arrived in England we never knew that dear Great-Aunt Gwendolyn existed. But Rose worked very hard to find favour with the old lady. Darling Rose is not all she appears, as you've discovered only too well.'

★ ★ ★

'But Rampton, you said I could do what I wished regarding the house.' With clenched fists Rose stared at him across the few feet of Aubusson carpet in her sitting room as she persisted with her argument. 'Now that I have been so fortunate in marrying such a wonderful, generous husband, I want to provide Arabella with a dowry.' She glanced from her husband's stony face to her clasped fingers and realised they were on the edges of

245

an argument. It wasn't a pleasant thought.

'So that Yarrowby will come sniffing around her ankles again?'

'Well, yes. Arabella's broken-hearted.'

'She'll be more than that if he weds her.'

Rose was unexpectedly spurred to anger. 'You have no right to interfere with her happiness.'

'You have no right to ruin it.'

'I've heard nothing to discount Yarrowby as entirely suitable, eminently eligible.'

Rose was not expecting the thunderous look in her husband's eye as he said, quietly, 'Except my warnings.'

She looked appealingly at him, but he had turned away. His voice sounded very distant as he stared across the gardens. 'I understand Arabella must be provided for and, as you know, I am not an ungenerous man. What does disappoint me, however, is that you appear to have completely disregarded all the cautions I've voiced regarding my aversion to Yarrowby. Quite simply, I will not countenance a match between your sister and that man.' She saw his fingers clench as he added, 'I really do not feel it necessary to elaborate. My strictures on the matter should be sufficient.'

Riled, Rose turned with a whoosh of skirts, muttering under her breath, 'Your injured pride, more like it. I know you hate Yarrowby because . . . '

The expression on his face as he swung round to face her made the words die on her lips. 'Take care, my dear.' His voice was low. Dangerous.

Rose had not thought it possible. Was he warning her that his altercation with Yarrowby over the opera dancer who had been snatched from him was forbidden territory?

Anger made her incautious. 'I will not be dictated to like this.'

'Then you should have been more careful in who you led to the altar,' came the viperish rejoinder.

Rose gasped. 'Do not blame me, my lord, for forcing your hand. You virtually dragged me off the gangplank.'

'Honour dictates that a gentleman offers marriage to the lady whose virtue he has stolen.'

'My virtue was not stolen.'

'Your brother put it about that it was. Facts count for little when gossip will tear a reputation to shreds. Yours for allowing yourself to slip into a compromising situation, mine for not doing the honourable thing.'

Rose was seething. 'You were adamant that honour was not your motive. Now, during our first argument, you say it was? What kind of a marriage does that make it?'

He drew a laboured breath and muttered, 'Society would have turned on you like a pack of baying hounds.'

'I was on my way back to the West Indies where such consequences did not matter.'

Miserably, Rose watched her husband fasten the cufflinks with slow, deliberate movements.

He was only partly dressed. Tight-fitting breeches moulded his well-muscled legs. He stood more than a head taller than she in his stockinged feet. His shirt was undone to the waist and his dark hair was tousled, as if he had spent the day in manual labour and had not yet attended to his appearance.

To Rose he had never appeared more desirable. Or more unattainable. This was their first real argument and she wasn't sure how they'd reached this point. Because she'd accused him of dictating to her without offering a reason for his seemingly unreasonable strictures?

Her feathers were severely ruffled, but more, she wanted to reach out to him, to bridge the gulf with an olive branch.

But he was not looking at her. Did not see the softening of her features as these thoughts flitted through her mind. As she was on the verge of moving forward he gave a grunt of irritation as the second stud continued to fight his best efforts. Then he said, crisply, meeting her eye, 'Of course, I should not be surprised — or allow myself to feel disappointed — that you completely misinterpret my concern over Yarrowby's suitability for your sister. Like my reasons for marrying you, you attributed the basest of motivations.'

She gasped, before defending herself. 'Likewise, my lord, I'd thank you not to attribute the basest of motives to my actions. Entrapment was not my plan.'

Confrontation did not come easily to Rose. She did not want to risk angering the man she loved; but in the desire to elicit more than coldness, she squared her shoulders. 'Whatever the truth, the fact is that we're bound to one another — *for life.*'

'I had no idea I was quite so repugnant to you, madam.'

She saw that he had conquered the cufflink.

But what further attempts would he make to conquer her, she thought despairingly, as he turned to leave. Was this really a man for whom excitement was lifeblood? Fired by the thrill of the chase and her supposed unavailability, had desire evaporated within a month of the marriage he believed she had tricked him into?

No, they were simply having a silly argument over the fact that he was not used to being defied — only she could not put it into such words.

'Stop.' She was clutching at straws. Anything to prevent him from leaving her. Achieving marriage to him at the cost of his love was the cruellest punishment of all. She would have preferred to have been his mistress to a wife he discarded with such impunity.

Hearing the hysteria in the single word Rose struggled to compose herself, even as she told herself she was over-reacting. 'You are too harsh, my lord. We have argued and I am sorry. I am not ignorant of my duties.'

He looked at her strangely. 'You are angry with me because you think me unreasonable yet you would entice me with your body?' He shook his head. 'I have no desire to force my attentions upon a wife who refuses to accept my judgement.'

She felt her mouth drop open but before she could rail at his arrogance he had bowed curtly and exited the room.

12

'Lady Jane has just broken a chandelier.' Helena hiccupped with laughter, and Rose turned to see how such a thing had happened. Lady Jane was now the centre of attention, sitting amidst the ruins of a smoking chandelier in a somewhat awry heap. A bevy of swains, one of whom had just tossed her high in the air as a finale to a very lively polka, were swatting the singe marks.

'Geoffrey, see if you can toss Rose into a chandelier and make her laugh,' cried Helena, welcoming a newcomer into their midst. 'You must lead her in the next dance. Poor Rose is having a fit of the dismals, as you can see.'

Geoffrey bowed. His full mouth curved into an apologetic smile, which he directed first at Rose, then at Helena, as he answered, 'I don't think Lady Rampton cares for my company.'

Rose's expression revealed the embarrassment the truth of this remark caused her but before she could reply Geoffrey said, 'If I promise to be on my best behaviour and don't throw you into the chandelier would you partner me in the next waltz?'

Despite her aversion, Rose had no choice but to accept his offer, and several minutes later Geoffrey led her on to the floor as the orchestra began to play. Almost at once she noticed her husband on the other side of the room. She had not expected him at Lady Jeffrey's ball. She faltered and immediately Geoffrey was all solicitousness.

'Are you well, Lady Rampton?' he asked, pausing while she regained her balance and her composure.

He would think she had had too much to drink.

But she had not had enough. Certainly not enough to dull the pain of the memory of parting from Rampton the previous night on such poor terms. He'd not been at breakfast this morning and when they'd crossed paths earlier this afternoon he'd told her, curtly, he'd be dining at his club.

She'd tried to tell him she was sorry for clashing with him but he'd simply bowed and said he was sorrier that she believed she'd married such an unreasonable man.

Now her misery, which she'd been unable to chase away with champagne, was made all the more excruciating as she watched him lead another woman on to the dance floor.

When she saw who the woman was she averted her head quickly, and in the process gripped Geoffrey a little more tightly than she meant to. She had no desire to meet Lady Barbery face to face.

'It's all right, I'll hold you,' Geoffrey murmured. 'I know how quickly the bubbles in champagne go to one's head.' The words sounded frighteningly intimate as his breath tickled her ear. Rose tried to pull away, apologizing as she trod on his foot.

'Relax, my dear Lady Rampton, and I'll steer you in the right direction.'

Again Rose tried to push him away but the champagne must have made greater inroads into her coordination than she had thought. She stumbled again and this time he had to clasp her tightly to him to prevent her from sprawling across the floor.

She gasped and flushed as he laughed, 'I beg your pardon, madam. Pray, I am not trying to take liberties, I assure you.'

'No, of course not . . . I'm being very foolish, I realize,' she managed to say as he executed a few more surprisingly graceful turns with her around the room.

'Not at all,' he murmured, reassuringly.

She found that if she just relaxed and let him hold her then she was coordinated enough not to make too much of a fool of herself and thus become the focus of critical attention.

Soon Geoffrey was leading her off the dance floor, his arm about her waist.

He murmured in her ear, 'Lady Rampton, permit me to escort you home.'

Rose pulled away from him, but he clasped her all the more tightly as Helena swept up to them, saying, 'You must go with him, Rose. There's no need to worry about appearances. He's your neighbour and Rampton's friend.' She tucked a straggling curl behind Rose's ear. 'I think you should go with Geoffrey now . . . unless you wish to continue making a fool of yourself.'

'I think I should see my husband,' she protested weakly, but Helena merely steered her, with Geoffrey, towards the door saying, 'You are hardly in a fit state to speak to your husband, believe me.'

★　★　★

With Rose taken care of for the meantime, Helena was ready to tackle Charles, fixing a smile upon her face as she turned at the sound of his concerned voice, and reassuring him, 'My dear, Rose is in perfectly good hands. You know that Rampton and Mr Albright are neighbours and boyhood friends.

It's hardly as if Rose will be accused of cuckolding her husband within a month of snatching London's most desirable catch from beneath the noses of every designing debutante.'

It was Rose who posed the greatest problem, Helena decided as she pondered her means of achieving the happiness she deserved. She forced herself to sink deeper into Charles's embrace on the dance floor. He could refuse her nothing — and would refrain from asking difficult questions — if she was sweet and plaint with him.

Yes, all Helena wanted was the same degree of happiness Rose had gained through Helena's machinations. And, later, as she twined herself in Geoffrey's arms while he rained passionate kisses upon her in a small antechamber they'd discovered once he'd returned, Helena was even more determined upon it.

★   ★   ★

With a headache fit to split like an overripe melon Rose was in no mood for Helena's excessive good cheer the following morning.

Nor for her suggestion for riding in Rotten Row. 'Arabella is very keen to be seen, you know, and she has made an assignation with her young man.' She looked at Rose meaningfully. 'You don't want to be accused of nipping that little romance in the bud. It would be a fine catch.'

At that moment Arabella appeared on the threshold looking exceptionally modish in a rust-coloured riding-habit and a dashing hat adorned with a single curling feather.

'I've no intention of nipping any little romance in the bud, but don't expect me to accompany you,' said Rose, cradling her head in her arms with eyes closed as she sagged into the corner of the chaise longue.

'Oh Rose, darling Rose, does that mean you'll agree . . . ? I mean, that you'll make sure Charles will agree?' With a whoop of joy Arabella swooped upon her sister and began showering her with childish kisses. 'Why, he was so cast down telling me that he was sure it was no good even offering, because of some silly argument he and Rampton once had — ' She broke off, blushing at the realization they were no longer alone.

'Helena and I were just leaving,' she said, hurriedly, as they went out through the door Rampton had just entered.

'I have the most ghastly head, Rampton,' Rose muttered, feeling at a distinct disadvantage as she found herself staring once more at the stern face of her husband. His look was inscrutable. One thing was for certain, his mood was not any gentler than it had been when they'd last parted. Rose tried to sharpen her wits. Eventually she gave up. It was painful even to focus. She closed her eyes and asked, 'Sorry, Rampton — did you ask a question?'

Rampton sighed and looked disapproving as he folded his arms and leaned against the mantelpiece. 'My dear, I have no objection to you enjoying yourself. However, would it be too much to ask that you comport yourself with the decorum your position demands?'

He was still smarting at the image of his lovely wife in the arms of no less a vagabond than his erstwhile schoolfellow Geoffrey Albright. If he had not had Catherine whining in his ear as he'd watched Geoffrey lead his wife outside, presumably to escort her home in her carriage, he would have flung down the gauntlet. Of course there was nothing scandalous, nor even improper in his wife being alone with their close neighbour. But Rampton did not like it one bit.

Rose glared at him. How dare he speak to her like that? 'I had one glass of champagne too many,' she said, in clipped tones, adding with heavy sarcasm, 'Pray forgive me.'

Ignoring her, he asked, 'And what is it that Arabella fears I may not agree to? The moment she realized I might have overheard her she scuttled out of the room like a frightened rabbit. It was most unlike her.'

Rose twiddled with the tassel on the cushion. She had been unsure how Rampton would take the news and realized she had been somewhat compromised by her sister this morning. Her wits had not been responding as sharply as they should.

'Arabella is very much in love, and apparently the object of her affections approached her last night to ask if she would object if he applied to Charles for her hand.'

Rampton raised his eyebrows superciliously and Rose's heart sank. She could tell he already suspected who it was and that he was not happy.

'So Yarrowby has come back, just as I predicted, now that there's a handsome dowry in the offing?'

'Apparently his uncle was very ill and he had no time to leave a message, and then his cousin from France was over and he was required to dance attendance on her . . . ' Rose realized that she didn't sound very convincing. She finished angrily, 'Rampton, you have given me no good reason to warn her off Yarrowby. You say he's a brute but you've hardly behaved like a gentleman in this matter, either. Arabella is very much in love. It will break her heart — '

'He'll do worse than that.'

Rose sat up straight and glared at him. 'You're so unforgiving! What happened between you was years ago. Why, it's a great opportunity for Arabella . . . and Arabella's sweet nature will tame him, if that's your concern. Besides, it's not for you to give or withhold your consent.' She took a deep breath, ready to field his anger.

Instead, he looked at her strangely. 'My dear, I had not realized quite how ambitious you really were.'

'A fine marriage for Arabella will set her up for life.'

'And bring her untold misery for the rest of it. Do you wish that for her?'

'You don't know that!'

Quietly Rampton set down the tinder box he had been toying with and looked at his wife through narrowed eyes. 'Yarrowby is an inveterate philanderer. He only wants Arabella because she's an ingenuous debutante with a pretty face who won't make a scene when he strays — and who now suddenly has a respectable fortune to tide him over when the cards don't go his way.'

Rose closed her eyes, haunted by the image of Arabella pleading with her to say a good word to Charles on Yarrowby's behalf.

Rampton called him a philanderer but her investigations suggested that Rampton had had more mistresses than Yarrowby.

'Do you think he'd offer if she had nothing in the way of dowry?' Rampton went on.

Rose bridled. 'So now you're suggesting that if Lord Yarrowby's suit is accepted I'll be responsible for delivering my own sister to the wolves, since I'm the one providing the dowry.'

'In effect, yes.'

'Yarrowby's quarrel with you was a long time ago. I'm sure he's changed . . . grown up.' Rose persisted with her argument, more out of pique at her husband's dogged disapproval than anything else.

'Men such as Yarrowby don't change just because they marry a good woman . . . or because they've grown up.' Rampton put down the box and took a few steps. 'You'll be doing Arabella no favours if you allow this match to go ahead.'

Rose sighed. She wished her head would stop throbbing so that she could form coherent thought and discuss this properly with Rampton. All she was conscious of just now was that he was being unreasonably obstinate and taking the matter personally.

'Rose.' The tone of his voice made her raise her head to look at him. His beautiful blue eyes kindled with anger. 'For once, just trust me.' He paused. 'It will be a marriage made in hell. Believe me, I know what I'm talking about.'

Rose opened her mouth to speak but Rampton shook his head. 'If you trust me, Rose, you'll make sure this marriage does not go ahead.'

When Arabella rushed into her bedchamber later that day, dragging aside the thick curtains and letting in the offensive summer glare whilst declaring in effervescent tones, 'Oh, Rose, I had the most marvellous morning,' Rose had not the heart to check her high spirits.

'I'm so pleased to hear it, dearest,' she said, dragging herself up to rest against the pillows. Her headache should have long since abated but her exchange with Rampton had done nothing to hasten her recovery. The image of his smouldering eyes and his warning regarding the purgatory of an unhappy marriage were not the sort of thing to send one into an easy sleep.

Now Arabella was babbling on about Yarrowby and how he intended to call on Charles the following morning, and had Rose had a chance to speak to their brother?

'Not yet.'

'You don't think there'll be any difficulty,

do you?' Arabella settled herself on the end of the bed, her look so troubled that Rose couldn't help but say reassuringly, 'No, dear,' before adding dutifully, 'but we do want to make sure that Lord Yarrowby is the kind of man who would make you happy. I mean . . . ' She hesitated, before adding, 'I mean, he has only become so attached of late since . . . since — '

'Oh Rose, you're not going to suggest he's a fortune hunter are you?' Arabella's laugh was light with relief. 'Why, Yarrowby was afraid that others might accuse him so. But that's not the reason he's returned, at all. You remember how attentive he was at the beginning of the season? And then his uncle was so ill and he thought his sister had delivered his letter, only — '

'Yes, yes, I know,' Rose interrupted. She ran the back of her hand across her eyes, swung her legs over the side of the bed and stood rather shakily. 'I'm sure you're right, dear. Now, if you don't mind, I'll just call Beth to help me ready myself for this evening.'

In answer to the concern she read in her sister's eyes she explained shamefacedly, 'I'm afraid I still have a touch of the headache from last night.'

Having summarily dismissed Arabella,

whose high spirits refused to be dampened even by her sister's cautionary tone, Rose suffered herself to be ministered to by Beth's less than deft fingers while she pondered her dilemma.

What could she do? She did not want to anger her husband. Yet he had not made a case compelling enough against Yarrowby to disqualify him as a desirable suitor.

She sighed. She must sound out Aunt Alice and see if she could dredge up further details about the quarrel between the two men.

★ ★ ★

The season was winding down. In another month Helena would board the *Sara Jane* with Charles. In the meantime Rose observed her desperate pursuit of pleasure. Her sister-in-law had formed her own coterie of admirers and, while her behaviour was not exactly scandalous, neither was she a model of decorum.

Rose had decided to delay her return to Larchwood, feeling that her presence in London was necessary for Arabella's benefit. Any day now Yarrowby would offer for her, and then Rose would have a gargantuan task ahead of her in seeing to the wedding preparations.

Aunt Alice had obligingly found out all she could from various acquaintances what she could about Lord Yarrowby. And to Rose's relief — and disappointment — the worst that could be dug up was that fisticuffs session with her own husband in Hyde Park . . . over a common opera singer.

The distant way Rampton spoke to her these last couple of days seemed to preclude the possibility of him ever being spurred to such dramatic action over her, Rose reflected with a surge of pique. And disappointment. In addition to the raging lust he'd inspired within her, he'd also exuded charm and magnetism and a masterful quality that reassured Rose that he could make everything right. She'd needed that when for so long the cares of her family and their financial situation had weighed her down. Now she'd discovered Rampton also did not like to be crossed. And that he was not above harbouring grudges and putting his personal animosity ahead of the potential happiness of others.

He'd behaved like a petulant school boy when she'd had the 'temerity' to ask him to give her one good reason as to why Yarrowby was not a suitable husband for Arabella.

Now, as Rampton put his head into her dressing-room and quizzed her directly as to whether she'd warned Arabella off or whether Charles had told his youngest sister he'd not sanction the match, Rose was mutinous.

'I had not thought you to be the kind of man to be put out by a wife of independent means?' she said angrily. 'That's what this is about, isn't it? Before I had the means to provide Arabella with a dowry you merely made clear your poor opinion of Yarrowby. Why wait until now to be so . . . forceful in your desires that your strictures should be obeyed? Without any substantive grounds?'

'Rose,' he said seriously, crossing the floor to grip her by the shoulders. 'When Arabella had no dowry Yarrowby was not a serious suitor. I know exactly the kind of man he is. Arrogant. Brutish. Give me a few days in which to furnish proof, if you won't believe me. But do not do this to your sister, I beg you.'

'So you're begging me now?'

'I'm being serious, Rose.'

'Yes, I know,' Rose said tightly, shrugging out of his arms to study her reflection in the looking-glass. 'You're begging me because you can't stand Yarrowby because of some schoolboy's quarrel, for I have asked around and there is nothing worse to be uncovered, it would appear.'

'How little you must think of me if that is

what you believe.' His voice was cold.

Fear that he would simply walk out prompted Rose to say, 'And how little you must think of me to accuse me of treating my little sister like a sacrificial lamb. Yarrowby has asked to speak to Charles tomorrow at noon.'

His look was grim. A nerve twitched at the side of his mouth. Rose was not a gamester but a thrill of anticipation ran through her as she watched him master his anger. No, she could not let it abate. She had to say something more. Something so outrageous that not all the willpower in the world could prevent him from laying his hands on her. Her body stirred at the thought. How she wanted him; to reassure herself that she could still stir up the desire which had led to their marriage. Yes, she was angry and upset with him but she still desired him, and if they couldn't sort out their problems in her dressing room, perhaps it would happen in the bedroom.

'So you would openly defy me?' He spoke the words quietly, but they resonated with danger. 'I have asked you for time in which to furnish you with proof, but you are so decided that the cause is nothing but my injured pride that you would defy me?'

Rose turned from her seat at the dressing-table and levelled her contemplative stare upon him. Finally she said, 'Rampton, you've had plenty of time to furnish me with the truth. Weeks, in fact.'

'I had no idea Yarrowby was still a contender,' he muttered, beginning to pace.

Rose bit her lip, torn between apology despite the suspicion she harboured as to the reasons behind his dislike of Yarrowby, and her desire to whip up some feeling within him that went deeper than his current frustration with her.

She'd not felt his arms around her in days. Without physical contact, they were drifting further and further apart.

'Well, Rampton, why don't you speak to Charles so he's fully cognisant of Lord Yarrowby's black nature, instead of telling me what I must do and not *why* I must do it? It seems you like putting me in my place.'

He stopped and glared, as if he couldn't believe what she'd said. 'Putting you in your place? I'm accusing Yarrowby of being such a man. It's rich to hear it from you, Rose.'

She'd really angered him now, when that hadn't been her intention. Trying to keep her voice light, she said, 'Well, I'm sure that you'd like to put me in my place for tricking you into marriage, just as you're trying to put me in my place the moment I oppose you.'

She turned back to the looking-glass and her task of combing out her long, rippling hair. Out of the corner of her eye she saw her husband freeze.

'You accuse me of being puffed up with pride and nursing grudges?' His voice was low and dangerous. 'What of *your* true nature, Rose? What do I really know of you?'

Shame burned her upon the instant and she had to hold back the tears, instead rising to face him as she countered, 'So, it is as I feared. Not one month since we are wed and you accuse me of false pretences to . . .' she almost choked on the words, 'trick you into this marriage.' She heaved in a shaking breath. 'Well, I am your wife, Rampton, and for all your insinuations as regards my character I will endeavour to be a dutiful one. Clearly your interest in me took no account of my character. No, you were looking for a mistress who would conveniently set sail from English shores when your natural ardour was waning.' She took a step towards him, her breath catching. 'Am I to take it that your displeasure with me will lead you to look elsewhere when it comes to satisfying your carnal nature?'

His eyes blazed in response. She saw the way his gaze flickered from her face to her breasts, which were heaving with anger and

— yes — fear, for the thought he may be enticed back to the scheming Catherine Barbery's bed was unendurable. So unendurable that when he gripped her shoulders and pulled her against him she welcomed the touch, even with the knowledge that he felt no tenderness for her at that moment.

Well, she felt no tenderness for him right now, either, but she wanted him. More than she'd ever wanted a man . . . or ever would.

She yielded, slackening in his arms, her breath leaving her in a soft sigh as she arched against him.

She needed proof that he still harboured feelings for her. Anything to affirm that she had the power to move him to something more than contempt or anger.

It was a lust-driven coupling, intense, physically satisfying, but quickly over and emotionally draining.

And Rampton, as he lay above her, exhausted, met her cool gaze and wondered if it saw contempt or triumph there. He could bear it no longer. This was not the woman he thought he'd married. Shutting out the sight he rolled over, slid to the floor and quickly retied his banyan. With a last, cold backwards look at her lying upon the tumbled bed, he left the room.

Only when he had regained the sanctuary

of his own bedchamber did he let out his breath in one long ragged sigh, sagging against the door frame of his dressing-room. This was not how he had imagined marriage. He rubbed his eyes. He had never felt so weary, so despairing. Was this his punishment for marrying the woman he'd thought to make his mistress?

13

Like gilded peacocks the guests at Lord Yarrowby's lavish entertainment promenaded across the lawns of the grand house in which he would soon ensconce his intended. His unexpected offer was the subject on the lips of many of his guests that night, although Charles had only given his consent that morning. Lord Yarrowby's long-planned fireworks spectacle coincided well with the news of his impending nuptials.

Helena, watching the setting sun from the balcony, felt it was setting upon her dreams. Time was running out. Charles would remove her from England within the fortnight and she had not yet discovered a way to stay, though she was closer than she had been since Rose's wedding. Rose had married money and Rampton had been generous to his new wife's impecunious relatives, though not yet generous enough.

Irritation bubbled within her as her mind roamed over the few avenues open to her.

'Any glittering baubles you see here with which you'd like to adorn your swanlike neck?'

Flinching at the familiar voice, she cast a baleful eye over the crowd. 'Even if you were clever enough to do it so that no one could lay the crime at my door you'd probably mistake the real thing for paste.'

'I hear that it was not paste that adorned your lovely sister-in-law's neck when she ventured out wearing the stolen necklace belonging to her intended's erstwhile lover.' Oswald looked enquiring. 'I also heard Lady Barbery's ire only brought our star-crossed lovers closer. Very close. Does that please you, Helena?' Gripping the balcony railing so their hands nearly touched, he asked, 'Perhaps you know more than I do. You look like you do. What's more, you don't look terribly pleased.'

She only realised she'd stamped her foot when he laughed at her childish display. Helena heaved in a breath. 'Rose has me to thank for her marriage but how have I been rewarded?' she demanded. 'I came to England, Charles' wife and as poor as a church mouse. It appears I shall leave the same way while Rose and Arabella remain here, drowning in wealth and admiration.'

Oswald scratched his nose. 'That hardly answers my question. Since you love to claim credit, were you behind the strange affair of Lady Barbery's necklace?'

'Rose received the necklace from an

anonymous admirer, only Edith, who works for the family, declared it would be scandalous to wear it. I recognised it as that belonging to Lady Barbery. I'd seen her wearing it the week before, in fact — '

'Indeed, you would notice what the rest of us would consider trifles.'

Helena sent him a disdainful look before continuing. 'A diamond necklace is hardly a trifle. Nor were Lady Barbery's actions. As you may or may not know, Lady Barbery was Rampton's mistress before he married Rose and it occurred to me that the anonymous giver was the lady herself. So I insisted Rose wear the necklace . . . and you know the rest.'

Her irritation increased when his gloating laugh at the flash of anger she was unable to hide revealed her plight only amused him. 'Do not laugh at me,' she demanded. 'Rose thought marrying Rampton was the culmination of her dreams. She will soon understand that the greater one's happiness and attainment of one's desires, the greater the despair when it all ends in tragedy.'

She was surprised by the fascination on his fox-like face. He stroked his chin as if he were contemplating a rare specimen and she snapped, 'It's rude to stare.'

He grinned. 'I had no idea you hated your sister-in-law quite so much. Why, I believe you despise her more than I despise my addle-headed step-mother.'

Helena felt the bitterness rise up her gullet. She feared she might drown in it. 'Rose condemned me to this life I despise,' she hissed. 'For five years I have lived in penury in a barren prison with a feeble husband whose attentions I must at least pretend to endure if he's not to sulk like the pathetic child he is and make my existence even more hateful.'

Oswald clicked his tongue. 'Poor Helena. And you at the height of your beauty. Is there nothing I can do to ease this terrible burden of yours?'

Angrily, she slapped away his hand while she narrowed her eyes, gazing into the distance at Rose who appeared the picture of self satisfied smugness as she fingered the handsome diamond necklace Rampton had given her for her wedding. A Rampton heirloom. Meanwhile, the best Helena had received from Charles was an all but worthless gold chain.

Following the direction of Helena's disconsolate gaze, Oswald chuckled. 'Nothing so desirable as the unobtainable, is there?'

'Unobtainable?'

Her tone should have warned him to tread warily, but Oswald clearly thrived on danger.

'Well, word is that Rampton is unfashionably mad for his wife. I hardly think he'll slip between the sheets at a crook of your little finger.'

'Mad for his wife?' Helena repeated, ignoring his other insinuation, for though she'd once desired it her interests had been very definitely swayed in a different direction. 'It might interest you to learn that the charming Lord Rampton has promised to appear enslaved in public only until such time as his wife is enceinte.'

'Listening at keyholes, dearest?'

It was Helena's turn to feel smug. 'Not on this occasion. Her maid told me. Or words to that effect. Behind closed doors all is not smelling of roses as their outward display of felicity would suggest.'

Indeed, as they watched, the pair looked the very picture of marital harmony.

'That's a very lovely necklace your sister-in-law is wearing,' Oswald remarked. When Helena did not reply he went on, 'So, has your husband graced your lovely neck with a precious memento of your London tour? You're due to draw anchor soon, aren't you?'

'A gentleman would have observed by now that I am surely dying of thirst,' Helena said, rapidly tiring of the conversation. 'You have not even offered me refreshment.'

'I had thought to offer you something else.' His voice was suggestive as his thin mouth stretched into a smile. His pewter eyes darted over her, lizard-like, assessing. Keeping her in suspense.

'Tell me,' she demanded.

'I am offering you any jewel your heart desires.'

She snorted. 'Much good that would do me when I could never wear it.'

Oswald gave an exasperated sigh. 'I'm in thrall to your beauty and your cunning, Helena, but you're not being terribly clever right now. I could procure diamonds you could take back to your little island home. Or . . . ' he paused. 'You could sell it. You'd like a necklace like Lady Barbery's, wouldn't you, Helena, since your lily-livered husband hasn't provided you with the promised diamond choker?' When he brought his head so close she could feel his breath on his cheek, she did not move away. Her heart was hammering as he went on, softly, his voice full of promise. 'Like the diamond necklace Lady Barbery pretended was stolen and which she sent to Lady Chesterfield. A little plan in which your intervention had the opposite effect, perhaps, of what was desired. Is that what happened?' He gave a crack of laughter as he caressed her arm and Helena swung round.

'Do it, if you think you're so clever. I want one for me to keep, and one which Rampton will find in his wife's possession.' Her body crackled with the delicious idea of it all.

'I have nothing against Cousin Rose.'

'I do.' Impatiently, she swung back to Oswald. 'Rose leads a charmed life. Look at her tonight, dripping with jewels while I have only this.' It had become a compulsive gesture to finger the gold chain around her neck when she watched others parade their jewels as if such wealth were nothing. 'My husband will never have the funds to do justice to my beauty. But Rose,' she pointed to her sister-in-law weaving leisurely through the crowd, smiling at her husband beside her, 'Rose has her heart's desire, all thanks to me . . . and I can't bear it.'

When Oswald took her hand between both of his and brought it up to kiss, she did not pull it away. Oswald wanted to perform some act that would please her. No doubt he wanted to be rewarded but she could deal with that another time. Right now, she sensed her opportunity. Her heart had never thundered with such passion. 'My dear Oswald,' she whispered, keenly aware of his desire which she must nurture while holding him at bay. 'Just think how grateful I would be with a diamond collar . . . or two.'

'Very grateful? I would hope so for the risks are great.'

She allowed him a few seconds in which to soak in the promise of her warm, fragrant cheek which she pressed briefly against his neck. She sighed, twining one hand up behind the back of his head while the other trailed from his breastbone to his thigh. 'I would think you the cleverest man in all England.'

★　★　★

With pleasant smiles glued in place there was nothing to indicate to the casual observer that Lord and Lady Rampton were anything but the most content of newlyweds. While they did not always attend the same parties they were seen sufficiently in one another's company, their manner suggesting a most harmonious union. Yet reproach dripped from every utterance.

'Have you seen how happy Arabella has been since his offer?' Rose bit her lip, anxiously, despite her question. It had all been so sudden.

'She didn't look very happy yesterday,' Rampton remarked mildly. 'I found her in tears in the drawing room.'

'Yes, because Edith wants to return to the West Indies with Helena. They were both torn. Edith has been with us since before Arabella was born. But Edith's family is there . . . '

'Arabella says you've promised to find someone to attend her?'

Rose nodded.

'Who? Beth?'

Rose rolled her eyes and Rampton chuckled at her obvious aversion. 'Dismiss her if you dislike her. You'll not offend Mama. But haven't any of the other girls volunteered to attend Arabella? Weren't you going to ask them?'

Rose sighed. 'I spoke to them this afternoon. No one wants to go. Arabella is such a sweet-tempered girl. And for some of them it would have constituted a very real elevation in position.'

After a moment's silence Rampton said, 'Don't lose too much sleep over it, my dear. This wedding will never take place.'

Rose gritted her teeth as they passed a throng of revellers. 'Your arrogance astonishes me. You might hate him but my sister happens to love him. And to me, that counts for much, much more.'

Rampton gripped her none too gently by the upper arm as he steered her along a more private path. 'You shall have your proof. As for your remark regarding my arrogance, I find it wounding. I had warned you on several occasions that he was an undesirable suitor. Little did I know matters were proceeding behind my back until the betrothal was all but announced. Since, however, you need proof I am arranging it.' He frowned down at her. 'Do you remember the very first time I warned you against him? I hardly even knew you then!'

'That was simply an excuse to entice me to be alone with you.'

Rampton gave a wry smile at the memory. 'That may have been part of the reason,' he admitted. 'But do you think even I would besmirch the good name of an acquaintance for such ulterior motives?'

Rose, who was feeling increasingly uncomfortable and beleaguered for her part in Arabella's impending nuptials, could only whisper, 'Your reasons for hating him are personal.'

One eyebrow lifted disdainfully. 'Give me credit for some finer feelings, Rose.'

'I do,' she whispered, her voice heavy with irony.

She felt she was in the wrong. But so was he.

Fireworks lit the dark sky. The crowd

murmured their anticipation for the next burst but Rose had no heart for the entertainment. She raised her head and said, 'I've been told Celia Baxter was the opera dancer who was your mistress before Yarrowby took her over.'

Rampton's mouth dropped open. 'Good God, Rose, do you seriously think I would stand in the way of your sister's happiness because of personal animosity?'

He seemed to withdraw, though he had not moved. 'You insinuated something to the effect that personal dislike was at the heart of my objections but you've clearly been digging deep.' His dark eyes smouldered as he gripped her shoulders. 'The reason for our altercation, I assure you, went far deeper than *Celia Baxter*.'

'That's not what everyone believes.'

'Including you, it would appear. How terribly sad, Rose,' his eyes were dark, his voice husky with anger, 'that you would honestly have so little respect for my integrity that you believe me capable of such pettiness.'

Rose shrank away. 'What else was I to believe? You gave me no other explanation.'

Rampton released her so suddenly that she stumbled backwards and nearly fell. He did not see her. He was already striding away and once she had regained her balance she had to run to catch up with him. She could not let this argument go unresolved.

'What was I supposed to think, Rampton?' she demanded, moving in front to block his path. 'You simply told me he was unsuitable. You made insinuations without hard evidence. Either I had to accept your edict or find out for myself.'

Rampton barely allowed his progress to be checked. As he walked around her he said, 'I had assumed I'd found myself a wife who would value the judgement of her husband.'

'So you are now suggesting that the real reasons are so terrible they could not be revealed to my innocent little ears.' Rose's tone dripped scorn as she added, 'And now poor Arabella is to pay for my lack of faith in you? Is this a lesson in morality, Rampton? That a good wife will simply obey her husband without question because he tells her she should?'

'Arabella will pay no price, my love.' Rampton's tone matched Rose's scorn with irony. 'I've told you. She will not wed Yarrowby.'

Rose gave a strangled laugh. 'I see. Then why are we here?' Struggling to keep up with him she indicated Yarrowby's great mansion and the peacock-and-guest-strewn lawns with a sweep of her arm.

'Because my plan has not yet come to fruition. Come, my love.' He took Rose's hand and laid it upon his arm. 'Your sister is beckoning to us.'

Rose glanced across the lawn and saw, to her dismay, that Arabella, radiant with happiness and flanked by Charles and Helena, was waiting for them.

'I see. Ever the knight to the rescue,' Rose murmured, stifling her anger, her misery. 'You know best . . . you have a plan . . . '

'Yes,' Rampton said, conversationally, smiling as the distance between them and Arabella closed. 'I predict that very soon Arabella will lose her heart to another.'

'Oh, you do, do you? And who might this be?'

'My brother. Good evening, Arabella.' He greeted her with an extravagant bow. 'I believe Felix is to paint your portrait.' With an indulgent look at Rose, he added, 'It seems that painting your beautiful sister has whetted his appetite.'

Arabella dimpled. 'I will be the envy of the ton and, like Rose's portrait, I hope it will be a happy reminder to my husband of his good choice in a wife.'

14

Rose paced the carpet and pondered her dilemma. Arabella had left not two minutes before — breezed out would have been the more appropriate description — on her way to Mayfair to sit to Felix. Clearly she was thoroughly enjoying the sessions and, while Rose had wanted to warn Arabella against Felix, Rampton's caution carried weight. Arabella was old enough to make up her own mind, he'd said. Unless Rose had a very strong case for Arabella marrying Yarrowby, rather than for Arabella making a match to please herself, Rose could rest assured that Felix was not a young man to undermine Rose's good work merely for the pleasure of it.

Now the reason for Rose's diminished spirits stood before her: a downcast girl whose enthusiasm and dedication to her work, good humour and surprising skill in arranging a complex coiffure had deeply impressed Rose. She had thought of employing Polly for herself and to find Beth some other employment, however Polly appeared to have formed a fondness for Arabella. Rose had thought the girl would be delighted to attend Arabella after her wedding but was now surprised by her obvious aversion to the idea.

'But Polly, not only would your wages be greatly increased, your position would be far superior. If you stayed here it might take years before you became a personal dresser.'

'That's as may be, ma'am, but I don't wish to leave.'

Rose had always thought Polly mild to the point of timidity. Frustrated, she demanded, 'Why is it that no one wishes to accompany my sister? Has Arabella been unkind? Is she not as sweet and mild-mannered to the servants as she is to her family?'

Polly had dropped her chin on to her chest. This unusually sharp demand from her mistress caused her to jerk her head up and bite her lip.

'It ain't Miss Arabella, my lady. Lord knows, she's the sweetest mistress and I'd have danced for joy at the prospect o' accompanying her anywhere else.' She took a deep breath, struggling. Then at last she blurted out, 'But it's the master I ain't so fond of.'

For a moment Rose thought she was alluding to Rampton. Then realization dawned. 'You mean Viscount Yarrowby?'

Polly nodded.

There was silence. Rose stared out of the window miserably as comprehension dawned. At last she asked, 'And why has no one said anything?'

'Weren't our place, ma'am. And Miss Arabella's been so 'appy in love.'

Deep dismay was now replacing Rose's misery. It seeped through her bones. More insinuations. This time she had to discover something substantial.

'Did it not occur to anyone that Arabella might be saved heartache herself — considering you all felt Lord Yarrowby was not an employer whom any of you would wish to work for?'

Polly didn't answer. Her narrow shoulders slumped even further. At last, as the silence stretched into seeming eternity, she said in a small voice, 'We talked about it, ma'am but . . . but then we decided that what great lords do to servants and what they do to fine-bred ladies surely ain't the same thing. So we decided that, since Miss Arabella found him so to her liking, and her being a great lady and no common serving lass, he'd most likely be good to her.'

Rose digested this in silence for some moments. After a while she said, 'So Lord Yarrowby chooses to take his pleasures in the servants' attic?' Distractedly she nibbled the tip of her forefinger. It was not a good reflection on the man's character. Unfortunately, so many men did indeed take advantage of their staff. It was not as if Lord Yarrowby were the only one.

When Polly still did not answer Rose said, more sharply this time, 'So you're telling me that Lord Yarrowby made advances to the servants?' She sighed. What should she do?

She moved to the window, her tone half apologetic as she turned, saying, 'I'm afraid, Polly, that it is not only in Lord Yarrowby's residence that such things happen — '

'Well, it don't 'appen here!' Polly interrupted fiercely.

'I am relieved to hear that,' said Rose with a wry smile. 'Nevertheless, it is, sadly, a well-established double standard that the way gentlemen cavort with obliging kitchen maids is not the way they deal with womenfolk of their own class.'

'Well, it ain't as if Jenny were that obliging,' Polly muttered under her breath.

Rose, about to continue her exoneration of Lord Yarrowby, stopped short. 'What did you say?'

Colour flooded the girl's peaky little face. Eventually Polly raised a pair of defiant eyes. 'I'm trustin' you 'eard me first time, ma'am, as I don't care to repeat it.' Gone was the timid little creature with whom Rose was so familiar. 'Jenny was my friend. I knew 'er 'cause we came from the same village and she's sister to the master's man, Fanshawe. Anyway, Jenny were a good, honest girl and, what's more, about to be married. But she were too pretty by 'alf and my lord Yarrowby didn't like that she objected when he tried to kiss her.' The slumped shoulders rose and the voice became more resolute. 'One day he chanced upon her, alone, in the scullery. It were late at night and she 'ad just one or two more things to finish up. Everyone else was abed 'cause otherwise we'd 'ave 'eard her screamin'.' There was a long, uncomfortable pause. 'Well, 'course, once she was . . . spoiled . . . and, what's more, 'aving a baby, she couldn't marry Johnny. Oh, he wanted to, but she were set on that point.'

Rose's chill deepened as Polly recounted her story. Of course, there was no proof that Jenny had been telling the truth, she told herself. She didn't even know what kind of a girl Jenny really was. She asked, 'Was Lord Yarrowby accused of the crime? I mean . . . it's only Jenny's word . . . '

Polly looked first confused, then affronted and Rose, despite the fact that she could not accept slander with no evidence, felt deeply ashamed. 'No, it ain't! Anyway, 'sides from the fact that Jenny ain't no liar, there was bruises on her arms, and blood on her dress, and, what's more, Rafferty, the butler, saw Lord Yarrowby sneakin' up the back stairs minutes before he came down and found Jenny all hurt and cryin'.'

Rose didn't need any more convincing. Added to her distress at Polly's tale was the fact that Rampton had known of Yarrowby's crime all along.

'I'm sorry, Polly,' she said, truly humble. 'I had no idea of this. I think . . . perhaps . . . my husband knew something.' Then, realizing that this sounded more like an accusation, she was about to rephrase her sentence when Polly broke in, ' 'Course he did. Fanshawe's been valet to my lord since the master came back from Eton, and Jenny's 'is sister. The master's bin supporting Jenny and the young 'un nigh on three years.'

'But . . . but why was Lord Yarrowby able to get away with such a crime?'

Polly's look made Rose squirm with embarrassment as the inequality of their respective situations was brought home to her. Great men like Lord Yarrowby were not brought to justice for raping mere kitchen maids.

Not three minutes after Rose had dismissed Polly, Rampton strode, unannounced, into the drawing room.

The pale and drawn countenance his wife raised to his face, coupled with the fact that he had passed Polly in the corridor, left Rampton in no doubt that Rose was now in complete possession of the facts. It had not been a certainty that one of the girls would volunteer the story. In fact, Rampton would not have been surprised if shame had kept their lips sealed.

'Did you mean to make a fool of me, Rampton?' Rose's tone was bitter. 'Or should I be apologizing for having misjudged you?'

Rampton shot her an ironic smile as he leant against the mantelpiece. 'When I explain, you can rest easy that I am indeed the base scoundrel your miscalculations forced you to wed.'

Before Rose could raise an objection he went on, 'First of all, my dear, how would you have explained to Arabella that the man she professes herself to be madly in love with is, in fact, not just a philanderer, but a brute of the first order?'

She was silent.

'Could you have found the right words to explain it to her? Would Arabella in fact have understood? It is my understanding that the mysteries of life are a somewhat neglected part of the education of a young, unmarried female.'

'Yarrowby should have been brought to justice,' Rose declared, hotly. 'Then Arabella would never have found herself in such a situation.'

'Of course, my dear,' Rampton agreed, admiring the gold-and-enamel snuffbox he withdrew from his coat pocket. 'Unfortunately, justice is not always served — most often not served in such situations. I think you know that.'

'But how could Yarrowby have the audacity to offer for Arabella, your own sister-in-law, when he knew you were acquainted with his crime?'

'Yarrowby is a conceited villain. But he didn't know — ' He stopped abruptly before adding, 'He has a child, you know. But he doesn't know that I know that. He doesn't in fact believe that what he did was a crime, much less that it'll ever be laid at his door. He thought he was quite safe in offering for Arabella.'

'She'll be heartbroken when she discovers the truth. Why did you allow the romance to progress . . . when you knew all along? It'll be so much harder for her, now.'

Rampton hid his discomfort, saying in a careless tone, 'Not when she is the object of so much flattering attention from other quarters.'

'I perceive you have as much faith in her constancy as you do in mine.'

He ignored this, saying, 'Arabella is so unworldly and ingenuous and this is only her first season out.' Nevertheless, he was feeling decidedly guilty as he put his hands on Rose's shoulders and looked deeply into her face. 'Rose, I made it quite clear, several times, that I had good reason for warning you off Yarrowby. For a long time he withdrew his interest and it was only when you generously provided your sister with a portion that he returned.'

He was glad to see that her eyelids flickered as she silently acknowledged that she wasn't guiltless. He went on, 'I admit that when I spoke to you of it again, I should have furnished you with specific reasons. I don't feel proud of the fact that I felt aggrieved and so instead of speaking plainly — though I wonder if you would have believed me — I decided to offer irrefutable evidence, such as has just been given you by young Polly.'

Rose shook off his hand and went to the window. 'So what do you plan to do now? Confront Yarrowby and make him withdraw his offer? If you never intended Arabella to make a match with Lord Yarrowby, don't you think it would have been more prudent to have acted earlier?'

'You forget, Rose, I did try to prevail upon you to trust me in this.' She was turning the screws upon his guilt and he didn't like it. Yes, he was in the wrong — but so was she. Before she could answer he went on, 'A man cannot withdraw his offer without risking a breach of contract. Not that I see Arabella driven by vengeance to such extremes. But Yarrowby is a cad. Arabella will soon discover this. Yarrowby thinks he is untouchable. He will soon find out he is not.'

Rose stared at him, as if the truth were only just now dawning. 'You've played hard and fast with Arabella's happiness in order to settle a score, haven't you? What were you trying to prove? That where justice could not serve Yarrowby his just deserts, then you could?'

Had there been, unconsciously, an element of this? Rampton squared his shoulders. To hear it put like that made him distinctly uncomfortable but he said, smoothly, 'That was not my first motivation.' He studied the snuffbox in his hands. 'Catherine gave me this,' he said, opening the lid and trailing a finger over the engraving. He did not look at Rose to see her reaction. 'You may be surprised to learn that lust is not the only motivation for taking a mistress. There is companionship . . . often mutual benefits in a wide range of matters. I was instrumental in her husband's promotion, incidentally.' Rampton closed the lid, pocketed the gilt box and directed his wife a level look. 'And, of course, there has to be trust. That,' he finished pointedly, 'as much as anything else, is what this was all about.'

He looked at his watch. 'My dear, we must get ready for Lady Gunther's alfresco party.'

Rose could only stare. The flint in his deep blue eyes belied the easy tone before he delivered his coup de grâce, 'And I was genuinely curious as to what kind of a husband you thought you had married.' His eyes bored into hers with disarming intensity. 'Quite obviously, you assumed you had married a petty tyrant.'

'Naturally I shall withdraw the offer of the house,' murmured Rose.

'So now you wish us both to appear tyrants.' He gave a mirthless laugh. 'Do you really want to deprive poor Arabella of any shoulders to cry on? Now, when is the contract to be signed? Tomorrow?' Rampton appeared to be thinking. 'You must remind Charles that you meant merely to offer the newlyweds the loan of the Mayfair house but that Arabella won't come into possession of any proceeds until she's twenty-one.' He chuckled. 'That should get Yarrowby's back up.'

'Arabella will be crushed. It's not what was promised.' Though Rose had no wish, now, to see the marriage go ahead, she felt unbearably compromised.

'Of course it is! Besides, Yarrowby is a man of great fortune.'

Rose, still sickened by her interview with Polly and the fact Rampton had not disclosed, earlier, the real reason for his objection to Yarrowby, felt close to tears. 'How shall I explain it to Arabella? She's just out of the schoolroom. I don't think she'd even understand what . . . what Yarrowby is actually guilty of.'

Rose suspected by Rampton's look that he too deeply regretted not having been more forthcoming, though to be fair, she had to accept it was not entirely his fault. Yarrowby had appeared to have withdrawn his interest in Arabella weeks ago and had only re-emerged as a serious suitor once the Mayfair house was incorporated into her sister's dowry. 'I cannot see Arabella reneging on this marriage, even though she's the only one who can cry off.'

Rampton put his hand on Rose's shoulder. The gesture, no doubt meant to be consoling, made her want to pull him down to the sofa beside her and curl into his arms. She felt ill, both in body and spirit. As she reached up a hand to stroke his, he pulled away and began to pace, muttering, 'Far better to show Arabella Yarrowby's less pleasant side: the real reason, in fact, behind his interest.'

Staring into the grate, he went on, 'If Yarrowby is after Arabella because he loves her, why should it concern him whether the pecuniary benefits brought by this chit of a girl land in his lap next month, or in three years' time? He'll be devilish put out' — thoughtfully he rubbed his chin with his forefinger — 'while Arabella will have no choice but to alter her mind and feelings when her erstwhile adoring swain turns ticklish over a few pence.'

★ ★ ★

Following the scandal caused by their hasty nuptials and the revelations of Rose's deception, it had been Rampton's great wish to show that he'd not only made a love match but that he was not a man who made hasty decisions he soon regretted. And nor was he.

As he watched Rose make her way through the crowd towards him, a guileless smile upon her lovely face, his jaded reflections fell away.

Male pride must answer for much of his current turmoil, he decided. Rose had been speaking from the heart when she said she wished she'd been a financially desirable marriage proposition. The scandal surrounding her deception would have been mitigated had she been an heiress. No one could have branded her the scheming fortune hunter his mother, among others, did.

And he should have told her the truth about Yarrowby much earlier.

As for the necklace . . . ? No, he did not believe Rose guilty of anything . . . other than trying to do her best for her family.

As she reached his side a great weight seemed to fall from his shoulders.

As Rampton would not want gossip that suggested disharmony between them, Rose decided that this evening was a wonderful opportunity to flirt with her handsome husband. They had both acknowledged their culpability, though not in so many words. She should have trusted Rampton and he should not have allowed the situation to get out of hand, as it assuredly had.

But it was not too late. With the situation regarding Arabella clarified, if not resolved, Rose was desperate to rekindle the happiness she'd briefly shared with Rampton.

It started as a game; and she was surprised

at the alacrity with which he joined in.

Soon she was dimpling when he made a remark, laughing at his witticisms, and on one occasion pretending to brush a crumb from the corner of his mouth.

The more she threw herself into her role the easier she found it to be in charity with him, her heart soaring at his unreserved responses.

'I thought you were doing such a good job play-acting in front of the guests here tonight that I'd set you a more difficult task,' he said, smiling through narrowed eyes as he set her away from him after their passionate trysting.

'Did I pass?'

He chuckled. 'I'm not registering any complaints.'

'That was not the whole-hearted endorsement I was hoping for.' Rose insinuated herself into his arms once more and tilted her face up to his. 'Am I allowed to try again?'

'Rose!'

Rose stiffened in his arms as she heard her brother's voice.

'Ignore it,' whispered Rampton, his arms tightening.

'I think he's seen us. Perhaps Arabella is in trouble.'

With a grunt of irritation Rampton

released her and within a moment Charles was beside them.

'Have you seen Helena?'

Sounding distinctly acidic, Rampton replied, 'Being fêted by her admirers. She's certainly not here.'

Helena gave the lie to his statement by appearing at that moment, effervescent with excitement and too much champagne punch.

'What a dreadful squeeze!' She hiccuped, then laughed unashamedly. 'My husband doesn't know how to keep me in good order, does he?' she asked, looking directly at Rampton. 'Not the way you manage to keep Rose in good order.'

Rose was about to retort when she was addressed by Yarrowby bringing up the rear, a radiant Arabella clinging to his arm.

'Where's Oswald?' Helena asked abruptly. 'He assured me he was going to be here.'

She pouted when Rose said she had no idea, then immediately berated her husband. 'It's a poor escort who can't even see that his wife's glass is empty!'

'Do you really think — ' Charles began, before her answering look obviously decided him against arguing. The moment he'd gone, Helena made her excuses — something about a torn dress — and dashed off in the opposite direction.

'The picture of marital harmony,' remarked Rampton, drily.

Arabella blushed and Yarrowby, bending over her hand, murmured, 'Your connection is by marriage only, my dear. Your virtue shines like a halo.'

Rose, nauseated by this remark, murmured to Rampton, 'I'm going to find Helena. It's unwise to leave her like this in such a mood.'

He nodded and Rose left the group, sick at the thought of what she was going to have to eventually tell Arabella.

$\star$　$\star$　$\star$

'Not the prettiest,' Oswald told Helena, relaxing against the back of a wooden bench in a secluded rose arbour. 'It's not as if you're choosing it to keep . . . It'll be keeping you.' He laughed at his own poor joke.

'Surely I could wear it just once.' Wistfully, Helena fingered the simple chain around her neck.

'Good God, no!' Oswald exclaimed. 'It'll be out of your hands by mid morning or else I'm for Newgate. And I don't intend going alone.' He watched as Helena unconsciously caressed her own neck, her eyes glittering in the darkness.

'What do you intend doing with your

newfound fortune?' He smiled slyly. 'Improving the slaves' quarters?'

'You don't suppose I'll be going home with Charles, do you?' she asked scornfully, not realizing he was teasing her.

'The proceeds from just one, or rather, two, diamond necklaces won't keep you in style for long, you know,' he reminded her. 'Certainly not in the style to which you'll quickly become accustomed.'

After a split second's hesitation Helena turned her feline gaze upon him and said, without any attempt at cajolement, 'Why, then you'll get me another.'

Oswald laughed. 'No, I won't. You don't suppose I'm prepared to risk my neck out of habit, just to please you.'

'I'm paying you handsomely for it,' she reminded him, sharply.

'Ah, yes, I was just meditating as to whether your barely controlled anticipation was for owning the necklace, or the reward you were contemplating for my benefit.' Slyly he extended his arm around her neck and dipped his hand into her bodice. 'Perhaps I should ask for a down payment immediately. I'm about to take a great risk for you, after all.'

She swatted him away. 'Next time I'll slap your face,' she retorted. She struggled free, glaring. 'The bargain is definitely weighted in your favour.' She shuddered. 'Procure me three necklaces. I need five thousand pounds' worth, Oswald, or this is as close to me as you'll ever get.'

Effectively checked, it was his turn to glare. Then he said smoothly, 'It makes no difference. Two are as easy to obtain as one. But my dear, surely I deserve to know what you intend? Do you really mean to leave your husband?'

Helena snapped a thin twig beneath her fingers. 'He's broken all his promises. He said that as soon as he got his baronetcy we'd return to England and he'd buy back the old family estate, and we'd come to Town every season and he'd buy me all the jewels and clothes I desired.' She sniffed. 'But it was all lies.'

Oswald stood up. 'Since you've made it clear that you have no interest in how I procure your heart's desire, I think it's time to offer you my apologies, madam, and ascertain the whereabouts of our hostess's quarters. My guess is that the ladies flaunt paste while the real thing languishes under lock and key.'

15

Rose closed her eyes and sank back into the pillows with a deep sigh. At least there had been no tearful recriminations. Arabella had simply bowed her pretty head and whispered that of course she understood her sister must obey her husband. And no, of course she didn't resent Rampton, either, since he had obviously compelling financial commitments himself which she did not understand. After all, it wasn't as if the promise of a great house in one of London's most fashionable quarters were being withdrawn. What was three years, after all? There had been a slight misunderstanding; however she was certain — quite confident — that Yarrowby would be perfectly obliging when he visited Charles that afternoon with regard to drawing up what had hitherto been only a verbal agreement.

In her usual good-natured fashion Arabella had tripped out of Rose's bedroom on her way to her sitting for Felix, turning with a smile to announce her excitement at presenting her finished portrait to her husband-to-be, then adding after a thoughtful pause, 'Why Rose, I do believe Felix is almost as charming as Rampton.'

After she had washed and dressed in a lace-edged morning gown of twilled lemon silk she was halfway down the stairs to the breakfast room when a sound on the landing above made her glance up. The door to Helena's room clicked shut but Rose had seen enough of the peaked white face with its large, staring eyes above purple smudges to realize that something was amiss.

Laudanum, again? she wondered, and her previous high spirits drained away.

Quickly Rose retraced her footsteps. After a cursory knock she let herself into Helena's bedchamber. There was a scrambling noise.

'Helena?'

The room was in shocking disorder. Clothes lay scattered over the bed, across chairs, and Helena was nowhere to be seen.

A daintily shod foot stirred beneath the silk dressing-screen.

Rose advanced, her heart thumping, imagining Helena collapsed on the floor, but when she put her head around the screen Rose merely saw her sister-in-law on her knees, bundling a green silk dress into a bag.

Helena looked up and focused blearily on Rose. Rose glanced around for the tell-tale little blue bottle.

'Helena?' She crouched down, not at all

sure of her reception. 'You don't seem at all the thing. Are you unwell?'

Helena's dark hair hung lankly down the sides of her face; and although she slurred her words her explanation was coherent enough for Rose to deduce that she had done something last night of which Charles would definitely not approve.

Surprisingly, too, Helena seemed frightened. The last time her sister-in-law had behaved so abominably she had carried it off with bravado. Never once had she apologized, even though she had put their very existence in peril.

Anger replaced Rose's sympathy. 'What was it this time, Helena? Loo? Vingt-et-un? Whist?' Her voice was harsh.

'What does it matter?' sighed Helena. 'All I know is that I've lost a lot of money, which somehow I must repay if Charles isn't to discover it.'

'Well, I'm glad you're concerned enough this time to worry about doing the right thing.'

The irony was lost on Helena who continued bundling another lovely gown into the drawstring bag.

Rose reached forward. It was Helena's diaphanous gown which had outraged Charles when Rose had worn it to meet Lord Rampton for the first time. Following the dress went Helena's small jewellery case, rattling with the meagre contents that Rose knew she scorned so much.

'You're not . . . ' Rose clasped her sister-in-law by the shoulder and drew face close. 'Helena, whatever you've done Charles will forgive you. Stop it. Come downstairs with me. We'll have a soothing restorative and you can tell me your troubles.'

Helena's expression made clear what small comfort that would be. With calm deliberation she packed another gown into the bag.

'Where will you go? Where were you planning to go?' Rose amended. As long as she was able to do anything about it Helena was not going anywhere. Rose was fond enough of her brother to realize his devastation — not to mention how injured he would be by the ensuing scandal — should Helena abandon him.

'Nothing would give me greater pleasure than to leave Charles, and you know it.' There was a feverish flush to Helena's cheeks and the pupils of her eyes were like pinpricks. 'But I have nowhere to go . . . except home with him to the West Indies. Nevertheless,' she added, stuffing one last shawl into the bag and pulling the draw-string tight, 'my immediate mission is to the pawnbroker's.'

'The pawnbroker's?'

'Unless you have a hundred guineas you'd like to advance me before tomorrow.'

Rose was checked. To begin with, she did not have anything like that sum. Rampton did not keep her short of pin money, but a hundred guineas was a different matter. Secondly, she had little doubt that that would be the last she would ever see of it if she lent it to Helena. And besides, it would do Helena good to settle her own debts.

'You've not done this before, have you, Helena?'

'I heard of a pawnbroker's in conversation. It's not far. I mean to go there' — she looked at Rose as if daring her to challenge her as she stood up — 'this very minute.'

Rose was torn between persuading her to make a clean breast of things to Charles, and allowing her to continue her mission. She decided upon the latter course.

If Helena were forced to give up some of her most precious possessions which could, of course, be redeemed at a later date, she might be less inclined in future to make wagers she couldn't afford to lose.

'Arabella's taken the carriage.'

'I think a hackney might be a little more discreet, Rose.' After jamming a black bonnet into the bag, Helena headed for the stairs.

Rose wondered what to do. Tell Charles? No, Charles had put up with enough. They all had. It was only right that Helena should atone for her misdemeanours.

Once in the street Rose hailed a passing hackney. Snatching the bag from Helena, she withdrew the veiled black bonnet and stuffed it on her sister-in-law's head.

'So devious,' marvelled Helena as the vehicle drew up. 'I always thought that was where I excelled. But then . . . ' she sighed, 'you are the illustrious Lady Rampton and I am merely impoverished Lady Chesterfield.'

Rose uttered a mirthless laugh. 'Such loyalty, Helena,' she said as she helped her sister-in-law onto the lowered steps. For some reason her high spirits had returned. Rampton loved her and Helena was doing the right thing by Charles.

The door slammed and Helena leant out, reaching out her hands. 'Bear me company, Rose,' she pleaded. 'I know you're not dressed for it, but you can stay in the carriage. Please!'

Rose began to protest.

'It's only round the corner. We'll be back in ten minutes and no one will be any the wiser.'

No, thought Rose, just as she was weakening. Helena could do this on her own. She needed to. For all their sakes.

'Please, Rose!' Helena began to cry as she fumbled for the door to try and let herself out. 'I cannot do it alone. I don't have your courage, Rose. Come . . . please? You may scold me all you like during the journey.'

'That's a rare treat hard to pass up.' Relenting at last, Rose settled herself opposite.

'You're always scolding me, anyway,' said Helena, sourly.

'Only because you've not shown my brother the loyalty he deserves from his wife. Anyway, what have you done this time that you must resort to all this cloak and dagger?'

'I'm not telling you. But as for Charles, I have not one ounce of guilt. He promised me the moon and anything else I desired if I'd marry him.' Helena tossed her head.

'You knew Charles had been in love with you since you were in short skirts. And you knew he wasn't in funds. It's only because Sir Hector wouldn't have you that you crooked your little finger at my brother. Though I can't imagine why, since clearly a great fortune was your chief requirement.' Rose remembered the whispers that were circulating at the time. She'd been astonished when Helena accepted Charles with such alacrity.

'Well Sir Hector made it brutally clear you were the only woman for him. And, Rose, you hardly advanced my case after you rejected him when it would have meant so little to you, and so much to me.' Helena's look was black. 'You couldn't have done better than Sir Hector. He was so rich! Richer even, than Rampton.' She glowered out of the window.

'But not nearly as charming.' Rose smiled.

A faint twitch of the shoulder and turn of the head indicated Helena's scorn. 'What does that signify? You can't tell me you love him.' Before Rose could open her mouth to deny this, she added, 'Well, you can't tell me you love him any more than you loved poor jilted Sir Hector.'

Forcing herself to remain calm, Rose asked, levelly. 'What makes you say that?'

'Why, you and Sir Hector seemed as thick as thieves — until he asked you to marry him. You were always together. I've never seen you laugh with Rampton like you used to laugh with Sir Hector.'

Helena had obviously been too wrapped up in herself to have noticed that last night Rose and Rampton had laughed like lovers. Poor Sir Hector. She'd felt terrible when she'd realised his feelings towards her were not paternal. Nevertheless, the truth was that now she was happier than she could remember. A warm glow suffused her.

Arabella's future bridegroom — whoever

that might be — was another hurdle to jump, but at least Rose and Rampton had apologized to one another and were of one mind in ensuring the marriage to Yarrowby would not go ahead.

Returning to Helena's remark she defended herself, 'You know very well the reason was because I had known Sir Hector such a long time and had supposed him Papa's friend — and mine.' What a shock it had been to realize that he had misconstrued her friendliness. She thought of his unexpected kiss, and shivered.

Not long afterwards Helena and Charles had married and everyone had said how lucky Charles was. Helena was famed for her beauty . . . and her numerous admirers, too many to recall.

There had been one, though, who lodged in her mind. Rose frowned, trying to remember the man Helena had alluded to on several occasions. She had never met him but word was that he had swept Helena off her feet . . . before sweeping suddenly out of her life.

She gave Helena an appraising look. 'Had I married Sir Hector the material gains would have made me as content as you are now with Charles. You were too impatient, Helena. You should have waited for your heart to mend after you were jilted.'

Helena's green eyes glittered. 'I jilted *him*. Granted he was dashing, but with few prospects. His pay wouldn't have kept me in silk stockings. We quarrelled and when I realized my mistake he had gone.' She muttered, 'Lord knows why I imagined I could live with Charles.'

'Well, you'll just have to make the best of it,' said Rose, adding, as the hackney drew up in a most insalubrious-looking neighbourhood, 'and I'm glad to see you've started.'

Helena stared, horrified, out of the window. 'Perhaps we don't need to go through with this. I think just fifty would do.'

Rose laughed. 'What, you think I have that my reticule at this moment?' She shook her head. 'You must think Rampton even more generous than he is.'

'And is he?' asked Helena, a greedy light in her eye.

'Generous?' Rose gave a soft, husky laugh. 'Very!' As Helena looked on the verge of tears, Rose relented. 'Wait . . . ' Helena, rising from the seat, turned.

'The white gown is a favourite and I know you'd planned to wear it on Friday. Don't give that one to the pawnbroker. I'll pay the equivalent of what he would.'

Helena clutched the bag more tightly to

her bosom and said in a strangled voice, 'Thank you, Rose, but no! Now wait here, I won't be but two minutes.' She glanced with distaste at the street urchins who had gathered, shooing them away as she held her handkerchief to her nose.

Wearing a look of utter tragedy, Helena put a dainty foot upon the step. One hand went shakily to her chest while the other gripped the door frame. She turned to Rose as she stepped down, saying proudly, 'Charles will not be disgraced by his wife on this occasion.'

It was a performance worthy of Shakespeare, thought Rose, before leaping forward as Helena's speech was cut short by her strangled cry. Relieved, she saw that her sister-in-law's fall had been arrested by the attentive jarvey.

'Got any burnt fevvers?' he asked, smirking as he cradled Helena in his arms.

'Put her in the carriage!' Rose snapped. 'That's right. Let her lie across the back seat.' Tossing off her own bonnet she replaced it with Helena's black veiled piece and seized the bag.

'Stay here,' she commanded the jarvey as she arranged the veil over her face. 'I daresay I can trust you with the lady. Here,' she rummaged in her reticule for her smelling salts, 'wave this under her nose. I shan't be

313

long. Oh, and here's something for your trouble.' The man's eyes glittered at the sight of the coin; even more as she added, 'There'll be another of those if you stay here . . . and remain discreet about this.'

Although what was indiscreet about a lady swapping bonnets and taking a stuffed bag into a pawnshop? Many ladies of quality found themselves under the hatches and resorted to such temporary means of delivering themselves from pecuniary embarrassment.

When Rose saw how the eyes of the wizened old man who emerged from the musty shop interior lit up she nearly turned on her heel and fled, but the thought of Helena languishing in the carriage, unable to complete the necessary errand herself, spurred her on.

'Just tell me what sum you are prepared to advance me,' Rose uttered, as the old man fingered the contents of the bag lovingly.

'No stains or damage. A dress of the first stare, as you young ladies would say, eh?' He gave another wheezy laugh, setting aside the dress and opening the clasp of the jewel box with shaking fingers. 'Not much 'ere,' he said. His tone was accusing as he held up first a pair of paste earrings, then a thin gold chain.

Bargaining complete, Rose was relieved to be out of there. Perhaps Helena had been expecting more, but Rose had done her best.

16

The satisfaction Rose gained from her endeavours on Helena's behalf were short-lived. Helena had retired to bed to nurse a nervous headache and Rose was about to change when Rampton entered her dressing-room after a cursory knock.

'What's the matter?'

'As expected, Charles isn't very happy at the new state of affairs . . . ' He broke off, eyeing with distaste the black bonnet she was removing. 'Not one of your most becoming, I must say,' he said before resuming, 'for of course he will bear the brunt of Yarrowby's displeasure. I told him new information had come to light which suggested the fellow might not make an ideal husband.'

Rose sat down at her dressing-table and ran a hand across her forehead. She wanted to unburden herself of the events of this morning but had promised Helena to keep the visit to the pawnbroker secret.

'He'll only judge me harshly,' Helena had said. 'And I intend to approach Charles first and then redeem what I can so that no one will be the wiser.'

So Rose made no remark upon the bonnet and listened as Rampton said, 'Arabella will probably want to retreat to the country for a little to nurse her wounded heart while this whole business blows over.'

'For goodness' sake, keep your voice down,' urged Rose. He had paused by the door which he had left half-open.

He looked at her for a moment before shaking his head as if to clear it. 'Sorry, my dear. Of course it would not do for the servants to hear of Arabella's disappointment before she does.'

'Rampton . . . ' Rose stopped him as he was about to leave. He levelled such an enquiring look at her that she almost did not have the courage to ask, 'Is something else the matter? Apart from Arabella, I mean?'

There was a pause before a flicker of warmth returned to his expression.

'Just the pressure of business which, after all, is why I'm in town — and to facilitate the pleasure of my new wife,' he added, with a brief caress of her cheek. But there was not sufficient humour in his tone to reassure Rose.

★　★　★

Rampton had been passing St Paul's Cathedral, returning from his unpleasant meeting with Charles, when he'd been hailed by the stepson of Rose's Aunt Alice, a man Rampton knew only vaguely.

'What brings you to these parts? Business, or the need to repent?' the young blood asked, bounding down the steps, brushing his dark hair back from his high brow.

There was something so out of place and unacceptably familiar about the question and its delivery that Rampton could not help but repulse him with a frown.

'My apologies, sir, but I'm late for an appointment,' he said, continuing to walk.

Despite Rampton's lack of encouragement the young man took no offence. 'How did you enjoy last night's squeeze? Cousin Rose had the right idea, seeking the solitude of the bottom of the garden.' He matched his footsteps to Rampton's.

'I turn down here.' Abruptly, Rampton changed direction while his companion, limpet-like, turned with him, saying, 'Lady Biddle warned Rose she would take cold, for there is a pond, quite marshy, at the bottom of the garden. It is why the entertainment is held on higher ground. And of course Rose couldn't see a thing, it was so dark. At least, I couldn't.'

'Keeping a close eye on her, were you? I had no idea you held her in such affection.' Rampton's tone was dry. As was his throat. He knew some slander was about to issue from this uncousinly cousin's mouth, and he did not want to hear it.

Whatever Rose might be guilty of, such as Catherine's necklace, must be relegated to the past. Or dismissed altogether, for it defied logic to suppose that Rose would knowingly flaunt a stolen piece merely to win some extreme response from him, as Helena had suggested.

Oswald's speculative glances suggested it was only a matter of time before he would come to the point. Rampton steeled himself, not realizing until now how much he wanted Rose to be above suspicion, beyond slander.

'Your neighbour, Mr Albright — ' Undoubtedly Oswald's abrupt pause was designed to centre tension on the name. 'I believe you've been acquainted with Mr Albright since you were boys together, my lord?'

Silent, Rampton continued walking. The greasy looking fellow's manner suggested blackmail but there would be no proof. The necklace incident had taught him that. Rose had enemies. He was now very sure of it.

Nauseated, he had to stop and support himself against the half-timbered wall of the

318

house that abutted the narrow lane. Geoffrey Albright? Rose claimed she held him in the greatest aversion. She claimed she'd never met him before his mother's dinner and Rampton believed her.

Then why was he now experiencing the most stomach-churning discomfort of his life?

Oswald clapped a hand upon his shoulder, frowning with feigned concern before saying brightly, 'Mr Albright, I'm pleased to report, looked after Rose's interests when she became lost for quite some time at the bottom of the garden. Miss Arabella was distraught and you could not be found.' He cocked his head. 'Have no fear, my lord, for my cousin and Mr Albright knew one another in the West Indies, don't you know? They were once quite close. Or perhaps Rose neglected to mention that.' He clicked his tongue. 'A touch of the ague, perhaps, my lord? You don't look at all the thing. Perhaps we should step into this chophouse and partake of a nuncheon. It's past the hour but I've not eaten and — '

'I'd as leif dine with a toad as with you, sir.'

Rather than be offended Oswald grinned. Thumbs in his gaudy waistcoat pocket he looked as if he might even crow with triumph. 'No, well, now you mention it, I haven't the time to be dawdling, either. Pleasant chatting to you, Rampton. Oh yes, I forgot to mention . . . '

With his malicious lizard eyes flicking over Rampton Oswald had proceeded to spew forth an inventory of Rose's recent exploits such as would see her deported to the Colonies at the very least, before finishing with a cheerful, 'So sorry time was too pressing for you to partake of a pot of ale with me, Rampton, though if you'd care to put your head in at the Merry Mermaid about four . . . ?'

Now, as Rampton gazed appreciatively at his wife's pale, slender limbs and tried to concentrate on her chatter, he weighed up whether to pass on the nature of Oswald's insinuations before he departed to meet the villain who, her cousin maintained, was in possession of several diamond necklaces which had gone missing the previous night. Oswald's involvement, the odious creature claimed, was in the name of protecting the family reputation — albeit with handsome recompense from Rampton.

'So, Rampton, darling, I know Arabella is going to be heartbroken but if necessary . . . I mean, if Yarrowby doesn't withdraw his offer . . . I'll have Polly speak to her.' Rose smiled up at him, tracing the fleur de lys design of the counterpane with her fingertips while she shifted her hips. 'That way she can't say it was merely hearsay.'

Merely hearsay. Suddenly Rampton was decided. He would not quiz Rose about her cousin's allegations since that was merely hearsay, too. She might interpret his questions as doubt about her innocence and he had no desire to churn up the waters between them when he so badly wanted their union to continue on the passionate, satisfying path it had taken after the several false turns that had proved just how wretched disharmony with his wife made him.

★ ★ ★

'Rampton! Please, step up and explain to Arabella that it is all for the best.' Rampton, who'd decided to walk to his assignation rather than take a hackney, was startled to see Helena leaning out of his carriage. 'I couldn't take her to the house like this,' she went on, indicating the weeping Arabella beside her when he'd opened the carriage door.

Her tone was not characterized by the sensitivity and sympathy that Rampton felt was better suited to poor Arabella's plight.

'Your heart will mend,' he said gently, indicating with a nod to Helena to change places once he was inside so that he could sit beside the young girl. Arabella gave a wail and put her head on his shoulder.

'Never,' she wept. 'He was so cold!'

'Ah, Arabella . . . ' Rampton felt like a cad. How had it come to this?

Because he'd wanted Rose to accept his judgement on Yarrowby. 'If there was anything I could do . . . '

Arabella scanned his face with feverish hopefulness. Turning his head away, he muttered, 'You can do better than Yarrowby,' prompting the strangled response, 'I love him!'

The words came muffled from the shoulder of Rampton's coat. He wondered vaguely what Fanshawe would have to say about it. He would no doubt consider the sit of a coat's shoulders of more importance than a weeping damsel in distress. He certainly wouldn't have any sympathy should he know that the damsel was shedding tears over his own sister's violator.

'Well, it appears he does not reciprocate the intensity of your feelings, dearest,' said Helena, 'since he's done a complete turn-around, and all on account of a bit of petty accounting over an old house. Come, we've all suffered disappointments.'

This, as no sympathy could, finally elicited

a more robust response. 'Yes, but only when your calculations are disappointed. Not your heart, Helena, for you don't have one — so don't start prosing on to me.'

Even Helena looked startled for a second. She made a quick recovery. 'You underestimate me, darling. My heart beats every bit as passionately as yours, I assure you.' She exchanged a wry glance with Rampton.

Wiping her face with the back of her hand, Arabella removed herself from Rampton's shoulder. 'Yes, but you've only ever loved what you can't have. You've never loved Charles.'

After assisting Arabella from the carriage, feeling a complete cad as he watched the quiet dignity with which she suffered herself to be led by Helena up the steps to their lodgings, Rampton set his coachman in the direction of his unsavoury destination.

★ ★ ★

If Oswald intended to play on the vain hope that Rampton did not trust his wife, Rampton wondered if money was his only motive. Certainly he'd be disappointed on that score since Rampton would need irrefutable proof that Rose was behind whatever nefarious dealings he was about to become acquainted with. He was convinced he would find none. Mind churning, he ducked his head to enter the dim, musty shop.

It would not be a crime if Rose had pawned the several pieces of valuable jewellery he'd given her since their marriage, though he'd be surprised. He'd gained the impression she was mindful of expense and proud of her efforts in keeping the family's head above water amidst the financial difficulties created by her profligate father.

The woman had pride in spade-loads. She'd gone to extraordinary lengths to absolve herself of the debt she owed him — without forcing him to the altar. True, he wished she'd shown a little more unfettered delight at the prospect of snaring London's most desirable catch, but she was more than satisfied with her lot, now.

With pleasure he thought of their recent encounters and wished he had not been so surly with Rose this morning, but that damned black bonnet had unnerved him. Once he'd laid this matter to rest he would buy Rose something to reflect his true sentiments, in case his words sounded clumsy and inadequate. Diamonds, he thought, as he ventured further into the unsavoury premises, wrinkling his nose at the smell of mouldering goods.

He would buy her diamonds.

Brushing past a pole offering up layers of discoloured petticoats, Rampton looked with distaste at the rheumy-eyed old man behind the counter who nearly dropped the silver teapot he had been polishing.

'I ain't got nothing to 'ide,' the pawnbroker whined. 'Not every day that Quality graces my 'umble abode but if it's about the necklace I never cheated the young lady, not a penny of what 'twas worth. 'Pon my honour.'

Rampton stared. What on earth was the old man getting in such high dudgeon over? His hands were shaking and it wasn't because of his age.

'Which young lady?'

'Mighty fine looking woman in a yellow silk gown.' Scratching his head, the old man asked suspiciously, 'She weren't my lady's maid wot pinched your missus's necklace, were she?'

Beth sounding like Quality? 'May I see the necklace?' Rampton heard the curtness in his tone at the same time he told himself it was nonsense to be concerned.

'Indeed you may, sir.' The old man rummaged through a drawer, and then the treasure was produced: a magnificent emerald and diamond heirloom which, held up, cast its dingy surroundings into unappetizing relief.

Rampton studied it carefully. It was not paste. Nor was it a piece with which he was familiar, but its value could not be disputed. Lady Chawdrey's? Rumours had begun circulating of a series of daring thefts. A kernel of doubt spawned in his entrails.

'Was this all the young lady had to barter?'

'Some clothes also.'

Rampton still clung to the hope that Rose was nothing more than an innocent pawn in a plot to smear her. Somehow the devious cousin was behind this, though Rampton had no idea why, or what his motive was.

Except that his fears which he'd anticipated would prove groundless took on a different dimension the moment the old man produced the dress that Rose had worn to her first dinner with him.

He shook his head to clear it, forcing alternative solutions to the fore while he reached for the dress, the better to study it. Was it possible it could have been copied in order to lay the blame at Rose's door? Perhaps the same person who sought to blacken Rose's name through the incident of Lady Barbery's necklace was behind this?

For he was certain Rose was not. Certainly not until he asked the question, 'Could you describe in particular detail the young woman who pawned the necklace?' and received a precise description of his wife, right down to the tiny mole beneath her right eye.

★　★　★

He took a hackney home. He didn't want his shock and despair to be on display to the world but in the dim, musty interior he closed his eyes and rested his pounding head against the squabs while his mind screamed for answers.

Why?

What had possessed Rose to come to a place like this and pawn a valuable piece of jewellery that didn't belong to her? It wasn't as if she had no fine jewellery of her own. Or that she was married to a penny-pinching tyrant!

It was inexplicable. He felt his nerves tauten at the prospect of challenging her. She'd claimed Lady Barbery's necklace had come from an anonymous admirer — and he'd believed her. She'd claimed she'd never met Geoffrey Albright in the West Indies — and he'd believed her. Would she claim innocence once again? When there was irrefutable evidence of her involvement? He didn't think he could bear it. His heart seemed to lurch to his stomach as the jarvey opened the carriage door once they'd draw up up outside his townhouse. If she would only confess he would be able to hush up the incident and, just as importantly, he would help her.

If she would only confess.

Rampton had come to regret his generosity in housing all of Rose's relatives when he entered the drawing room to find Helena busy at her stitching.

'Was that Dr Horne's carriage I saw leaving just now?' he asked and was surprised when Helena replied, 'Charles called him on Rose's account.'

Rampton looked at her enquiringly. 'I hope she is not unwell.'

Helena shrugged. 'A megrim. Nothing serious,' she said lightly, as her needle stabbed at the tapestry. She glanced up. 'Arabella, however, is deeply upset, as you know and Rose thought a change of scene might be in order. She suggested that if business held you up in town Mr Albright might go as their escort. You remember they knew each other in the West Indies?'

'I do. However Mr Albright will not be escorting them.'

Helena inclined her head. 'Dr Horne also said that if you wished to see him he'd be at home this afternoon, but not to discuss Rose's condition with her for fear of upsetting her more than necessary.'

'Upsetting her? Is Rose upset?'

'Yes.' Helena sighed. 'Rampton, Dr Horne is concerned about Rose.' She struggled to choose her words. 'When Rose gets these terrible megrims she does strange things. Things she wouldn't normally do and which she either denies having done, or has genuinely forgotten about. I think I mentioned it once before, if you recall. At Lady Barbery's ball-assembly.'

Rampton watched a couple of children playing at fisticuffs in the park while his confusion deepened. He did not believe Helena's sympathy was genuine. Nor did he, in his heart of hearts, believe Rose capable of all the misdeeds of which she was accused. Something didn't add up.

He turned. 'If Rose is upset it must be over something other than her husband.' He sent Helena a studied look. 'She was very happy last night.' He paused, adding, 'And this afternoon. Perhaps you can shed some light on her state of mind.'

Helena shrugged. 'Rose has never been fond of me so I was hardly surprised when she rejected my offer to accompany her on a carriage ride this morning. What was surprising was that Arabella had wanted to go, only Rose was quite snappish to her, too.' Helena met his look, candidly. 'That's when I discussed the matter with Charles. He's obviously had to deal with his sister on occasions like this in the West Indies and so he summoned Dr Horne. He attended Rose several times just after we arrived. She seemed so much better for a while but she's been acting decided oddly, of late. Haven't you noticed?'

It was too much to take in. No, he did not believe Rose had stolen Lady Chawdrey's necklace. And no, he did not believe she had ulterior motives in suggesting Geoffrey Albright accompany her back to Larchfield.

'Perhaps the country air will do her good. Rose and Arabella can leave for Larchwood in the morning,' he muttered. 'Jeremy and Hobson can go as outriders. That'll be sufficient escort.'

Ignoring Helena's outstretched arm, her mouth pursed in false sympathy, he made for the door. He longed to hold Rose and quiz her himself about her activities, but right now he lacked the courage. He needed to go to his own quarters, mull over everything he had learned and try to deduce what the devil was really going on. If that failed to provide clarification, he'd talk to Rose.

17

'Yes, you'll leave tomorrow.'

He'd twisted his mind in knots trying to come up with a motive for her actions and then he'd visited Dr Horne who'd said 'in these cases' the motive was simply the attention, even if that were in the form of anger. He said the general recommendation was that patients be removed to a quiet location to calm their over-excited minds.

Rose was not one to get over-excited, Rampton had immediately thought.

Now, the sight of the yellow silk morning gown, the bonnet still lying at the end of the divan, hardened his heart, despite the latitude he was determined to show her.

Her languid, welcoming smile had almost undone him as he'd put his head around the door but he steeled himself to be business-like. Dr Horne had said that if Rose took responsibility for her actions it would be a great leap forward. Dr Horne had said a great many other things that had thrown his entire world into turmoil but he couldn't dwell on those right now.

'My dear.' He tried not to let his fondness

for her cloud his purpose. She looked so very lovely, draped upon the bed. How he wished to close the distance between them and have her rest her head upon his shoulder. Then he would gently ask her about the two necklaces: Lady Barbery's and Lady Chawdrey's. He'd also ask her about Geoffrey and why she'd lied when she insisted she'd never met him before his mother's dinner. Instead he said, with commendable self control, 'You are at liberty to petition me for funds if you find yourself short.'

She blanched. 'So you know about the visit to the pawnbroker? I promised Helena I wouldn't tell you.'

'Helena?'

'Yes, I went on her account.'

His heart tumbled to his boots in sheer relief. Sinking on to the bed he took her hand and brought it to his lips. 'Did you not think it prudent to ask her where such a valuable necklace came from? When it clearly did not belong to her?'

His voice was only as reproachful as was needed to remind her that she should be more careful in future. He watched the play of emotions across her delicate features while she struggled for an answer. God, she was beautiful. Once she had confessed he looked forward to a long and leisurely afternoon luxuriating in her arms. He'd forgive her anything.

Frowning slightly, she asked, 'What necklace?'

He stared. The silence stretched as he waited for her to see that lies did not sit well with him. Did she honestly think he'd be quizzing her about it if he did not know? Dropping her hand he rose and went to the window. Turning, he asked, carefully, 'You admit visiting a pawnbroker's this morning. Why? To redeem some worthless trinkets when you know I am not ungenerous?' He answered his own question. 'No, to pawn a valuable necklace that did not belong to you. I have the evidence.'

She continued to look blank. 'It was on Helena's behalf I went. I just took some clothes and jewellery. The sum total was less than five pounds.'

Turning away Rampton steeled himself to face the truth. Rose had pawned a necklace that did not belong to her, and now lied about it. His mind raced. Was she unhappy? Last night and today would suggest otherwise. But Rose was a good actress. No. He dismissed the idea. She'd not give herself to him if she were trying to obtain sufficient resources to get away. The idea was preposterous and certainly did not fit with all he knew of her.

He stopped, mid-thought. What, exactly, did he know of her? She'd deceived him into marriage, for a start.

Was her motive money? He thought of the Mayfair house and realized the difficulty of procuring immediate funds. However, the only reason she'd need money was if she intended to leave him. A bitter thought, indeed!

Rose and Geoffrey Albright? He could not countenance it. Rose actively disliked the man. But then, she'd not mentioned the fact they'd known one another before. His mind trawled for possibilities. If Rose had learned that Rampton was the close neighbour of the man she had loved in the West Indies, could she have . . . ?

No, she could not have been so calculating that she'd put out a lure to Rampton on the chance he'd bite just so she'd be closer to her old lover. He was reading conspiracies into everything.

He tried to calm his disordered thoughts with a deep breath. First he needed to ascertain whether the owner of the necklace he'd retrieved from the pawnbroker's was indeed Lady Chawdrey. Then he needed to discover what Rose was planning to do with the proceeds. He would have to hire someone very discreet to follow her every move for the next few weeks — if only to confirm that she was not guilty of any wrongdoing.

He did not know how he managed to say, so calmly, as he turned back to her, 'The doctor says your health would be much improved with some country air.'

'My health!' exclaimed Rose. 'Why, all I have is a slight megrim. Besides, Dr Horne said nothing to me about it.'

Her look of injured surprise nearly unbalanced him but he pressed on. 'I think it best to follow the doctor's orders, Rose. I've arranged for you to leave first thing in the morning.'

★   ★   ★

Surely, he couldn't dispatch her to the country so summarily without some explanation? Having made her excuses at dinner, Rose waited in her bedchamber.

Even the most hard-hearted man, believing his wife guilty of some dreadful crime, would want to confront her with it. All she could think of was that Helena had intimated she'd pawned a valuable necklace. Perhaps Charles had asked after one of her trinkets and Helena had balked at telling the truth.

Ten o' clock chimed. Rose changed into a

filmy nightgown, dabbed a little Olympian Dew beneath her eyes to make them sparkle and arranged her hair. One hour stretched into two. Cold forced her to cover the diaphanous nightgown with a shawl, but the effect she strove to achieve was still the same: a beautiful woman who, once her innocence was established, was too desirable to resist.

When she put her hand on the doorknob her heart was hammering. Foolish! she chided herself. Last night they had talked like old friends. Galvanized by the memory, she quietly turned the knob and pushed open the door to the library.

They had their backs to her. No wonder they did not notice her, she thought briefly and bitterly as she saw how entranced they were with one another. Helena, dressed in white like an exotic gardenia, the patina of her olive skin soft and dewy — just as Rose imagined her look — had her head tilted to one side as she gazed at Rampton. And Rampton? One hand lightly cradled one of hers; as if he were on the verge of clasping her round the waist and pulling her to him.

As he half-turned, Rose saw in his eyes a look she had never seen: hunger and yearning.

Fighting back the tears she turned away. How long had this been going on? Was he a man of such appetites that one woman wasn't enough for him? Had Helena finally worked her way under his guard and issued an ultimatum? Was that was why he was sending her to the country?

★ ★ ★

Rampton tore his troubled gaze from Helena. He thought he'd heard a footfall in the passage outside.

Helena recalled his attention. 'Did Rose confess?'

Taking a few steps back, he winced at Helena's brutal phraseology. The moment he'd entered the library with her he realized it had been a mistake. If Dr Horne's earnest advice regarding Rose's mental condition had not been bad enough, Helena's feigned concern was enough to tip him over the edge.

'I must go to bed,' he said, abruptly, turning.

She stopped him with a hand on his sleeve and yearning gripped him. If only it were Rose, detaining him with a heartfelt plea for forgiveness; even a cry for help at the demons that tormented her.

'I warned you at Lady Barbery's of Rose's dangerous impulses, if you recall, but love knows no reason.' She traced the contour of his arm before taking his hand. 'Rose was never quite the same after Geoffrey left so abruptly from the West Indies. But when I quizzed her about it she said the subject was closed and never to be reopened. I think seeing him in London was a very great shock. And I'm sure discovering he was your neighbour and old friend must have been an even greater one.'

'Good night, Helena,' he muttered, unclasping her fingers and making for the door. 'I've had quite enough sympathy for one day, thank you.'

★   ★   ★

'What took you so long?' The asperity of Helena's tone was at odds with the air of serenity she had projected for the benefit of her legion of admirers promenading in the park.

For an instant Oswald was checked. But then, laughing as he reached down to help her into the phaeton beside him, he said, 'I have what you want, dear heart, though I'd venture the bargain will be mine. At least I'll not be saddled with a shrew for a lifetime.' He winked salaciously. 'How charming to see you, too.'

Pulling from his pocket a roll of bank notes

he grinned at her gasp. 'Might I remind you it was no mean feat. Twice I thought I was in trouble and it was only luck that stymied the one factor I had not taken into account — Lady Hocking's puling pug. There it was, yapping at me, fit to burst just as I was sneaking out of my lady's dressing-room with her gems in my hands. Then suddenly it had a seizure or some such thing. The old dragon or chatelaine of the jewel box had been on the point of investigating more extensively and was sure to discover me hidden amongst my lady's dresses, but when she saw the animal in a swoon it was she who had an attack of the vapours before rushing off to find the hartshorn or burnt feathers with which to revive my lady's precious pug.'

Oswald grinned at the memory. The rush of adrenaline had made it fine sport — not that he hadn't been close to having a seizure himself at the time. But Helena had not the sense of humour that made her want to enjoy the details with him. She just wanted the money.

'What a wondrous clever plan it was,' she said, 'to have doubled my reward by blighting Rose into the bargain. So Rampton paid up for you to keep mum over his wife's grave misdemeanours and now my honest brother-in-law is anonymously posting back the goods to Lady Chawdrey. Poor Rampton will be feeling very pinched in the pocket. What did he say when you told him about Geoffrey?'

Oswald grinned. 'Not very much. It was lucky that his neighbour spent time in the West Indies and that you ran into Mr Albright, what's more. Still, it was an evil tale that I was loath to put about. It's one thing to thieve valuables from a fat old trout who'd lief as not realize they'd gone missing until the next season. But to destroy a man's faith in his wife's virtue? That's a grubby thing to do. It nearly broke my heart to see how easily Rampton swallowed the tale. Still, you don't think he'll find out, do you?'

Helena's smile was serene as she smoothed the skirts of her dashing coquelicot pelisse.

'Dr Horne was an absolute darling. He earnestly verified every little symptom I suggested.' She giggled. 'He blushes when I so much as look his way so it pleased him to corroborate my story that Rose has been suffering from a rare disorder of the mind. Indeed, he was assiduous in advising Rampton of various avenues he might pursue.' With a look of moral rectitude she skimmed the length of the feather that adorned her handsomely trimmed headdress, adding, 'Of course, it's Rampton's just deserts since he only made a play for Rose because he thought she was married.'

'Such fitting consequences to please one as virtuous as yourself.' Oswald, leaning back in the phaeton, was pleased this made her cross. 'Still, I'm sorry to see it end this way for them. Seems that old grudge of yours won't be satisfied until she's packed off to Bedlam.' He yawned as he studied his fingernails. 'And all on the basis of your lies completely swallowed by the husband who might have loved her.'

'Oh, very prosy,' sneered Helena. 'Anyway, you're up to your neck in manufacturing evidence. How did that fence of yours perform?'

'The hunchback?' Oswald's momentary sympathy for Rose was quickly replaced by his delight in the success of his little project. 'Worthy of Drury Lane from what I can gather. With magnificent conviction he identified the purveyor of stolen goods as none other than our good Lord Rampton's lovely, troubled wife and obligingly whipped out her gown that you packed at the very bottom of the bag. There was not the shadow of a doubt in poor Rampton's mind that would prompt him to question whether in fact it was a con job. Obviously you did fine work sewing the jewels into the bodice of your gown — '

'Yes, and she was on the verge of whisking it out of my hands and paying me for it as she knew it was a favourite!' Helena snorted.

'She's very much nicer than you are,' Oswald returned, reaching across to snatch the bank notes out of her hands and replying with raised eyebrows to her look of fury, 'You don't imagine I'm fool enough to hand them over before I've received my reward, do you, my dear Helena?'

The insinuating thigh that rubbed against hers caused Helena to look sidelong at him with distaste. 'You know very well you have not fulfilled your side of the bargain and that I need four thousand to set me up so I might leave Charles. The money from Rampton and three diamond necklaces which need to be disposed of are not enough.' She smiled. 'I think perhaps a few mementoes from Lady Rampton's armoury of gems will suffice, but as I can easily persuade Rose to hand those over I don't think you'll have done enough to enjoy my favours.'

Dimpling at the thunderous expression on his face she said lightly, 'Yes, I suspected you might be capable of violence if I tried to renege.' She tapped him playfully on his knee with her fan. 'I only dared suggest it because we're in a public place.' As she stroked the point of her fan slowly up his thigh, her smile cloying, the thunderous look on Oswald's face dissipated. 'Dearest Oswald,' she sighed, 'you're so predictable.'

★　★　★

Three days in the country with no word from her husband was as much as Rose needed to persuade herself that her deepest fears were confirmed.

Rampton's moods had been erratic since they'd returned to London.

Where Helena had been waiting.

Of course, the idea that Rampton's feelings did not reciprocate her own hadn't occurred to her until she'd wandered listlessly about for several days with nothing but her increasing fears and doubts for company. She'd returned to thinking of his change in attitude since she'd inherited Aunt Gwendolyn's house.

Perhaps this wasn't entirely due to the Yarrowby affair. His anger with her at failing to heed his warnings suggested a man who liked to exert his own authority.

If Rose had dissatisfied him how easy would it then be to succumb to one of Helena's lures?

Rose knew Helena had no wish to return to the West Indies. Was she therefore making a play for Rose's husband? Rampton was conveniently under the same roof while Rose was . . . three hours away in the country.

At whose instigation had the doctor been summoned before he'd suggested all manner of ailments from which Rose might be suffering. Helena's? Or, God forbid, Rampton's? This afternoon Rose had dismissed a clearly concerned Dr Marsh — her mother-in-law's physician — with bright and energetic denials of any symptoms of ill health . . . and a deep foreboding.

No, it didn't make sense. Rampton's banishment of her had occurred too suddenly.

The uncomfortable thought kept intruding on her perambulations as her mind cast about for some plausible reason behind Rampton's change of heart. Something had happened, she thought wearily, that had convinced her husband that she had deceived him again.

After her third walk that day, with no catharsis from the fresh tears she had shed, Rose opened the door of the drawing room to the unsettling spectacle of Arabella and Felix with their backs to her, standing surprisingly close to one another. For a second Rose imagined she had disturbed a lovers' tryst; but their faces were guileless and welcoming as they turned to greet her. Arabella moved forward to take Rose's hands, thus revealing two paintings leaning against the wall beneath the window.

'Felix, it's splendid!' cried Rose after a quick recovery. 'Arabella must be so pleased!' The sight of her own portrait beside it brought a pang of memory. It had not been many weeks since the fateful sitting which had precipitated her unexpected and hasty marriage. Yet had her husband already tired of her? A spurt of anger bolstered her reserves. Whatever the problem was, she'd get to the bottom of it. She had to or else she was condemned to the same misery Helena complained of and for which she'd perhaps sought Rampton's assistance to alleviate.

'It's much too good for Yarrowby, don't you think?' Arabella dimpled at Felix.

'I'll take it,' offered Felix, with a sly grin. 'It's a fine advertisement of my skills. When I've tired of the social whirligig, and my impatient brother has put me out to grass on a paltry allowance I'll have to find some means of keeping my future wife in silk stockings.'

'You must be nice to Rose because when she becomes a well-established society matron you might need her patronage,' Arabella teased.

Looking embarrassed as Rose mumbled some excuse about seeing to dinner before leaving, Arabella lowered her voice as she stepped closer to Felix. 'Surely the rumours aren't true?' Then, more robustly, 'How could Rose have anything to do with the missing diamond necklaces when she is languishing up here . . . while your brother does nothing to gainsay the gossips who like nothing better than to say the rift between Lord and Lady Rampton came even sooner than expected.' Arabella chewed her lip. 'I think Helena's got something to do with it,' she said. 'I think she's made up stories which your brother has wanted to believe.'

'Not without evidence,' said Felix. 'Rampton can be deuced vexing but he's not a nodcock and he wanted this marriage.' He shook his head, pulling Arabella closer as he stared thoughtfully at the two paintings. 'Something decidedly havey-cavey is going on, Bella, and it's time we found out what.'

★ ★ ★

'Felix!'

There was more surprise than warmth in the inflection of Rampton's voice. His brother, radiating his usual robust good health and general bonhomie, reminded Rampton — who felt both smug and wistful at the thought — of a reincarnation of a much younger version of himself. It seemed a long time since he had walked into a room and thrown himself down upon a chair with such abandonment and obvious satisfaction with life.

'Fanshawe said you weren't going out tonight.' Felix raked his fingers through his dark curls. 'And since I've just returned from discharging — most assiduously, I might add — your parting command, I thought you might like to hear how things are faring at home.'

There was a secretive smile on his face as he assessed the shine of his hessians, his long legs stretched out in front of the fire.

Rampton was glad he had his face averted. When he turned, bearing two glasses of brandy, one of which he offered his brother, he had schooled his features into more ordered lines.

Rampton took a swallow of the amber liquid. The burning sensation was welcome. 'And how is Arabella bearing up?' he asked. 'Not driving mother to distraction with her moping?'

'Moping? Oh, yes, of course, Yarrowby.' Felix took a gulp and wiped his mouth with the back of his hand. An even more wicked glint appeared in his eye. 'As I've been following your instructions to the letter I've not allowed Arabella to spare him a thought the past couple of days. Poor Rose is missing you, though.'

'I understand the doctor saw her yesterday.'

'Can't imagine why. She's the picture of good health, though she'll run herself into the ground if she's not careful. You'll be impressed with the changes she's made. New cook, for one thing.'

Rampton decided he didn't like this tack. Rose, in good spirits, when she ought to have more reason to be pining even than Arabella. But then, Geoffrey Albright was right next door.

He banished the thought. There was no substance to it. The odious Oswald had planted the idea in his head.

But then, so had Helena. And his thoughts kept returning to why Rose should lie about having met Geoffrey in the West Indies. Why deny that they have ever known one another when too many accounts corroborated the fact they had? For the week Rose had been at Larchwood Rampton had left no stone unturned in his attempts to prove Rose was entirely innocent of wrong-doing.

It weighed heavily on her shoulders that he could find nothing to exonerate her.

Faithlessness was one matter but then there was the felony. The theft of Lady Chawdrey's necklace lay conclusively at Rose's door and now that several other valuable baubles had been reported missing at events attended by Rose he'd been told that Catherine Barbery was running around dredging up the evening she'd discovered Rose wearing her own diamond collar.

Why, it smacked of lunacy. He ran the back of his hand across his eyes. If Rose had only trusted him with the truth. He recalled the guileless look in her eye as she denied knowing anything about the necklace she'd pawned when the evidence was irrefutable.

As for Geoffrey, he still couldn't reconcile the idea of Rose harbouring a secret tendre for the unworthy Geoffrey.

Flooded with resolve to visit Rose at Larchwood, he refilled his brandy.

Another thought intruded.

Oswald. The odious Oswald had been quicker than Helena to mire his wife in suspicion. Wasn't it equally possible Oswald was behind those suspicions? Did he have a secret motive for blackening Rose's name? He'd already gone over this avenue but somehow he must have missed something. Hearing Felix discuss Rose made his heart cleave with frustrated longing for her.

'What did you say, Felix?' He jerked his head round to attend to his brother while his spirits soared at the thought of seeing Rose again and going through everything that might exonerate her.

'I said, if you weren't the elder I'd be charging you with a similar mission to the one I've just undertaken.' He grinned. 'Different sister, though, if you take my drift. Anyway, I suggested Arabella come back to town which she thought that a jolly idea.' He hesitated. 'Told me some unbelievable *on dits*, though — ' His blue eyes bored into Rampton's. 'About the West Indies and Albright and — '

The ugly fears which had swamped Rampton earlier returned with a vengeance. He clenched his hands so tightly that his glass was in danger of splintering. Breathing heavily, he said, 'I don't wish to discuss it!'

Felix blinked. Rampton appeared surprisingly agitated. Could it possibly be true that his brother had decreed Rose's removal to the country to give him free rein in London with Helena — only to have Geoffrey Albright throw a spanner in the works, as suggested by Arabella, who was highly suspicious of Helena's involvement with their neighbour. Who'd have believed that Rampton's old friend had played fast and loose with Rampton's own scheming sister-in-law all those years before in the West Indies?

Disappointed, Felix returned to the safe contemplation of his boots and the merry fire beyond. He was sure Rose was innocent of any wrongdoing despite everything Lady Barbery and the gossips were saying, though what the devil Rampton was about in sending her away, he had no idea. Rampton should be championing Rose. Rampton's next remark, however, went some way towards restoring his faith. 'As you can imagine, I've been worried about Rose — '

'Can't imagine why,' said Felix. 'She's as hale and hearty as I've ever seen her.'

'What did the doctor say?' Rampton shot him a piercing look. How much did Felix know? he wondered. The gossips were apparently having a field day with Rose's propensity for bold risk-taking, if Catherine were to be believed.

'He was very encouraging about his patient's general good health.' Felix felt it necessary to sound heartening; Rampton was looking very long-mouthed about all this. 'I'm sure you'll find her blooming, and quite anxious to see you again.'

'You think so!' Rampton was embarrassed to hear the echo of his own hopefulness. He chewed his lip contemplatively. It was difficult to know what to feel at this. Rose had behaved so reprehensibly and refused to take

351

responsibility for her actions while she blithely deceived him on so many counts. Could she be suffering some disorder of the brain? Did he want this to be the case so he'd not have to suffer the pangs of wondering what deficiency there was in him that she'd resort to thievery and, God forbid, adultery? Adultery! He could forgive her anything but that.

He rose abruptly. 'I'm going to Larchfield,' he said in answer to Felix's look of surprise. If Rose wouldn't volunteer her role in Lady Chawdrey's stolen necklace he'd shame her into it.

18

'You have the money?' Helena's breath felt like the caress of a feather against Oswald's cheek as she leaned into him. A waltz was playing and couples milled nearby but Helena and Oswald were hidden from view in a small curtained alcove with a large, obtrusive pot plant placed near its entrance.

'Mmm,' he murmured, taking advantage of their seclusion to caress her breast. Let her think he wasn't on to her game, he thought, and take his rewards while he could.

'Where is it?

Did she not have the finesse to at least pretend? Or was he that repulsive to her?

'I have it,' he murmured reassuringly, dropping a line of kisses down her neck.

She pushed him away, irritated. 'You can't imagine I'd reward you before you prove you've discharged my request?'

The flint he recognized in her eye sent his senses into complete revolt. What was he? An errand boy? One so beneath contempt that she couldn't bear that he should even touch her? When the terms of their bargain went so far beyond that?

With an effort he reined in his uncertain temper. It would serve no purpose to draw attention to themselves. But as he faced her down he realized that Helena had as much intention of honouring their agreement as she did of returning to the West Indies with her husband.

He caught her to him, roughly covering her mouth with his.

'You're hurting me!'

His hands, filled with bank notes, thrust into her bodice.

'There's your money,' he grunted.

'Get away from me!' she hissed, finally freeing herself. Swinging back after she'd feverishly counted the bills, she burst out, 'That's not nearly the agreed sum.'

'And this is the closest I've got to being rewarded.' His eyes blazed. 'Do you take me for a fool, Helena?'

'You'll be rewarded when you've fulfilled the terms of our agreement — '

'Three times I have thieved for you. Granted, it was a lark the first time and the thought of my just reward creamed the deal. But,' he gripped her shoulder and shook her, 'do you really imagine I'll be satisfied with smouldering looks and empty promises?'

'You'll get your rewards when — '

'When what? I've set you up like the bloody

Queen of Sheba . . . only then you'll be far too good for me!'

'I just need — '

She was too stupid to see the signs. All she cared about was the money.

Helena's second intimate encounter was far more pleasing to her, although her reaction was just as fiery.

'How dare you act so indiscreetly!' she demanded after being whisked from the saloon on to a balcony and into a passionate embrace.

'Because you're irresistible,' came the smooth rejoinder. 'Virgin or virago, you're equally irresistible . . . says the only one who's in a position to judge.'

Helena snorted. 'Don't sound so smug. If you hadn't cast me a lure I couldn't resist I'd not be married to Charles. Do you know how many times I've damned you to hell?'

'As many times as I have you?'

Leaning with her back against the railing for support she covered her eyes with her hands.

'This is madness, Geoffrey,' she whispered. 'I should hate you for what you've done to me. Instead . . . ' She left the sentence hanging.

Geoffrey's low, mocking laughter came in place of the comfort for which she'd hoped.

'You're making the most of your revenge, Helena. After that — imagine it — domestic bliss!' He paused. 'Though I doubt domesticity will suit you.'

Helena shrugged. 'You and I are destined to be together.'

'Rather rich, coming from the woman who refused to run away with me?'

'I was seventeen and you were penniless!'

'I was a man on the make. You had no faith.'

'My father was pushing me to marry.' Helena's defence was spirited. 'I had not the luxury of refusing all offers while you got your life in order, but how long did you wait after we quarrelled? Why, the very next night I packed a bag and went to find you, only you had gone. Anyway, you quickly saddled yourself with a replacement.'

'No! You just set your cap at Sir Hector, probably the one man in the world who didn't find you as irresistible as I — '

He stopped abruptly as the door was pushed open several inches. There was loud chattering, then the conversation was broken by the intruder's abrupt suggestion of 'punch first'. The door closed.

'Enough of trysting! Champagne punch, my lovely?' Geoffrey proffered his arm and with a demure nod of acquiescence Helena placed her gloved hand upon it.

'Champagne punch to celebrate. Oswald was difficult. However, we will have enough . . . when the final cache of jewels is delivered to us,' she sniggered, 'by the ever-obliging Rose, thanks to her loyal little maid.'

'You're sure you trust the girl?'

'She's as avaricious a dollard as is required. Besides, Beth cannot read.' After outlining the plan that promised her freedom, Helena added, 'Beth is motivated by the sizeable bounty I've already advanced for merely delivering the missive. With the doubling of the amount upon completion, I doubt she'll disappoint. She's a greedy simpleton.'

Geoffrey laughed. 'Pity the woman who tries to thwart you, dearest,' he said. 'I'll warrant the wench is motivated much more by fear of you than by material gain.'

★　★　★

Dressing had not been such a time of tension for a long while. First Rose discarded the coquelicot that Beth had laid out for her. No, white was much more in keeping with the image she wished to present. Then the expectation that had sustained her drained away and she sagged over her dressing-table.

357

What was the point?

One glance at Rampton's cold look when he'd materialized so unexpectedly in the Larchfield drawing room told her she had no hope of rekindling the passion they'd once shared. Perhaps the purpose of his visit was to inform her of his liaison with Helena.

'Are you all right, my lady? Would you like a vinaigrette?' Beth was unusually solicitous but Rose waved her away saying, 'Just help me dress. I'll wear the primrose silk.'

Rampton was waiting to escort her in to dinner. Assiduous in his duties as husband, there was more concern than warmth in his smile. Nor was there opportunity for frank speech with his mother in attendance.

'Rampton, your wife has been busy,' the dowager told him tightly, as the first course was cleared away, 'showing us up. She's met all the tenants, inspected their living conditions, and plans to start a school so the girls can learn their letters and a little sewing.' She raised an eyebrow. 'Giving them ideas above their station and setting them up for disappointment.'

'It's only one morning a week,' protested Rose. 'Obviously the girls have to work, too. But for those who can set aside the time, and see value in it, well,' she blushed and looked defensive, 'I think it's helpful.'

'It would perhaps be more helpful if you kept your husband close.'

The clatter of a knife shifting position as it was carried away sounded in the tense silence. Rose stood abruptly. 'I have a headache,' she whispered.

Instantly Rampton was at her side. She felt his hand clasp her elbow, the touch sending a sharp pain of longing to her heart.

'Mama's words were unpardonable,' he muttered as he thrust open the door to her dressing-room, closing it behind them once Beth had scuttled through.

Her legs felt boneless as she sank on to the divan. Watching him carefully she could see the struggle it took him to face her, calmly.

'Why did you deceive me?'

His words lanced her. She swallowed, turning her head away as the old accusation returned to haunt her as she'd always known it would. She had trapped him into marriage.

'I never intended matters to get out of hand as they did.' The words rasped painfully through dry lips.

His expression seemed to contort with pain. Closing the distance between them he gripped her shoulders, bringing his face close to hers.

'Did you not trust me enough to tell me

the truth? You pawned a valuable necklace, Rose. I have the evidence.'

She gasped, rearing up, angrily. 'I might have trapped you into marriage, Rampton, but I swear I'm telling the truth when I assure you that is the extent of my crimes.' Foul play was afoot. Her name had been blackened by enemies; she saw exactly how it was. Rampton had been deceived — but this not time, not by her.

'Helena — '

'Enough!' His lip curled as he put her away from him and made for the door.

Rose could not believe it. He was ready to believe Helena above herself? Why, because she'd trapped him? Lured him with that extraordinarily potent allure of hers so that Rampton's enslavement made him insensible to what he surely must know in his heart of hearts: that Rose was innocent.

Already his hand was on the doorknob when Rose asked, her words sounding amazingly bold to her own ears, 'Rampton, why did you send me away to the country . . . without a word of explanation?'

There, let him crush her with an avowal of his passion for Helena. At least it would clear the air.

For a moment he said nothing. Rooted to the spot with his eyes fixed on a painting on the wall, it was a moment before he met her look.

She had expected contrition, sympathy and relief at this opportunity to unburden himself.

Instead his eyes smouldered; but not in the manner she wanted. She trembled. How frighteningly devoid of warmth they were. She was unaware she was holding her breath. Unaware of all but the slow, deliberate approach of her husband.

What would he do to her? What did he want to do to her? Certainly passion kindled in the depths of his eyes — but not passion of a loving nature. She held her ground, refusing to move as her fear grew. She would not put her arms out to ward him off. Or to hold him, which was her first instinct.

His eyes bored into hers. Lightly, he traced a line from her shoulder, down over her right breast. She caught her breath, desire making her light-headed. She dared not speak, much less breathe, lest she spoil it. He did desire her! She felt the joy physically expand her lungs.

And then disappointment sucked the air from them at his next words.

'Confess, Rose,' he whispered, his tone ominous as he gripped her wrists. 'Confess so that I might forgive you.'

She shook off his hands while her thoughts roiled angrily round her head. *Confess so you can be with Helena, conscience-free?* So this was what it had come to. She swallowed painfully. 'You will never make me,' she muttered.

19

In the morning the letter was waiting for her. He must have entered her bedroom while she was sleeping for there it was, propped up on her dressing-table, the beautiful, formal script a chilling foretaste, she knew, of its contents.

'Later, Beth.' Rose waved the maid out of the room. She had seen the letter the moment her maid woke her with a copper jug of warm water.

Hastily wrapping a Pomona green silk shawl about her shoulders, Rose sat down at her dressing-table and, with trembling hands, tore open the wafer.

Dear Madam . . .

She needed to read no further to understand that this was not a love letter.

In just a few sentences Rampton set out the proposed course of both their futures. Futures which held no place for them as a couple. Lust, he wrote, had obviously set the tone for their relationship which, following their marriage, had become poisoned by its descent into greater deception and disillusionment. The prevailing situation, characterized by lack of love and mutual respect, now made their union intolerable to him and so he was offering her an option that, he felt, promised greater future happiness to both. With the money contained in the wooden box beneath the letter, Rose could resume her life in the West Indies. Rampton would be free to spend his time unencumbered in England for the next few months or until such time as he could stomach the idea of joining her in order that she might produce the required heir.

If she left with Beth this morning there was just time for her to reach Southampton where her ship was to draw anchor. He'd procured her a passage and he would appreciate it if she were discreet about her departure.

'M'lady?'

When Rose did not respond, Beth obviously felt no compunction in imposing her presence upon her mistress, tidying the bottles on her dressing-table, collecting the pins from the floor.

Rose continued to stare unseeing over the top of the looking-glass and through the window. Only when Beth began laying out her primrose twilled silk morning gown was she galvanized into action.

'My blue travelling dress, if you please.'

'Are we going somewhere, my lady?'

Rose might have expected more concern in her tone, knowing how much her maid hated travelling, but her future yawned bleak and empty before her.

Once she was dressed she dragged herself to the door, fearful of coming across a member of the household, as if the shame of her eviction was written upon her face.

'Rose, you missed breakfast and Rampton left early this morning.' Arabella smiled her greeting from the bottom of the stairs. 'Urgent business. He said he didn't want to disturb you. What's happened?' She frowned as she took in Rose's travelling attire.

'I'm leaving,' Rose announced, brandishing Rampton's letter as Arabella followed her into her room. 'Rampton has decreed it.'

'You're over-reacting.' Arabella looked perplexed. 'You can't just go . . . without confronting Rampton.'

'How can I when he's made himself absent. Clearly, he intended me to receive this letter before he returned. He wants to speak to me as much as I want to speak to him.'

Arabella gasped. 'I don't believe you!'

'Oh, Bella, you're such a romantic.' Rose gave a short, pained laugh. 'You didn't really think this was a match made in heaven? That we both fell in love with one another, despite the inauspicious beginning?'

'Then you don't love him?'

Trailing over to the window Rose stared miserably across the sweeping lawns. 'Would it make you feel better if I said I didn't?' she asked. 'He gave me a thousand pounds to go away. With a thousand pounds I can make huge improvements to the plantation . . . and to tell you the truth, there is no other place that I would rather be just now.' Seeing that Beth was now securing her trunk she picked up her reticule and went to the doorway. 'Rawlings is waiting with the carriage. Rampton apparently ordered it so I'll at least go in comfort.'

Arabella tried to bar her way. 'This is nonsense, Rose. I don't believe it. You're acting with too much haste. You must at least challenge Rampton.'

Rose pushed past her. 'If Helena has decided Rampton is the only man who can make her happy I don't stand a chance.'

'No, Rose!'

'And if Rampton is so easily lured, then I don't want him, anyway!'

★   ★   ★

A deep scowl blackened Sir Hector's already bronzed complexion, causing the captain of the *Mariah* to wonder whether his esteemed client considered he'd been cheated.

'The goods arrived in prime condition, I assure you, Sir Hector — '

'Excuse me!' Elbowing his way out of the saloon of the Pelican with uncharacteristic lack of courtesy, Sir Hector bore his portly form down the front steps with the agility of a man half his age.

'Miss Rose! I say!'

Rose turned, quelling the urge to hurl herself into her old friend's arms.

Rising from his bow, Sir Hector cast a puzzled look at her trunk, which several porters had set down while they waited, then at the tall-masted ship towards which Rose was clearly headed.

'I'm sailing on the *Mariah*,' said Rose, swallowing past the lump in her throat.

'Since it will be some hours before the tides favour her departure, might I request the pleasure of your company, Miss Rose?'

It was indeed a pleasure to enjoy the company of a man not disposed to judge her harshly. After a bottle of Madeira had washed down a hearty meal of jugged hare and pigeon pie, Rose was ready to pour out her heart for a sympathetic hearing.

Sir Hector, however, was more sceptical than sympathetic.

'Dispatched you by letter?' Lacing his

hands over his stomach, he shook his head. 'Sounds deuced queer, if you ask me. Not at all Lord Rampton's usual modus operandi, surely?'

Rose wiped her eyes as the servant cleared the table.

'So you love this fellow you've led such a dance, eh?'

'As I've never loved anyone,' Rose replied with a sniff, before explaining the circumstances that had given rise to her scandalous behaviour, followed by her suspicions regarding Helena and Rampton.

'I might have known Helena was behind the trouble,' Sir Hector harrumphed. 'Always eyeing out the advantage.'

'And now she's cast Rampton a lure he couldn't resist and that's why he's sent me away.'

She looked indignant as Sir Hector chortled at the apparent ludicrousness of her deepest fears. 'Maybe she did, but it's Mr Albright she's carrying on with. I happened upon them by chance in the Serpentine Walk at Vauxhall Gardens on Thursday last and it would appear she's as susceptible to his charms now as she was when he swept her off her feet six years ago.'

Rose nearly fell out of her chair. 'Helena and Geoffrey Albright?!'

Nodding, Sir Hector rose. 'I'd be investigating this letter a little more closely before I did anything hasty, Miss Rose. Now, my dear,' he stooped to kiss her forehead, 'there's nothing more I'd love than to see you safely back to town, but I have urgent business to attend to and you have your maid. Besides which, I'd hate to intrude on the fond reconciliation.' With a heartening squeeze of her hand he sent her on her way, adding, 'If I wasn't so sure you'll find nothing more than a simple misunderstanding and a vengeful sister-in-law behind your troubles, I'd be first to step into the role of gallant hero. But Miss Rose, your gallant hero awaits. Go to him now and see what he thinks about what I've said.'

Emboldened by her resolve to confront Rampton directly, Rose, on Sir Hector's arm, swept out of the inn and commanded that her trunk be retrieved and her passage cancelled. What had she been thinking? A week in the country with Rampton's brooding, critical mother had sapped her of her normal fight. Without Rampton's belief in her she'd found herself longing for the familiarity of her island home. But was that where she wanted to be? She wanted Rampton to love her and knew that it was up to her to get him back.

Rampton poured himself another brandy and stared at his wife's portrait. Was that what she was doing now? Laughing at him as she sailed into the sunset with Geoffrey Albright? Crumpling the cold-hearted missive she'd sent him into a ball, he hurled it at the wall.

'Rampton, I thought at least you'd be with your wife if you hadn't the courtesy to dine with your mother.' The dowager looked grim. 'I dined alone since Arabella was indisposed, also.'

Rampton, who had left for a dawn ride, had come back to find the house in an uproar. One of the servants was tending to Arabella who had fallen gravely ill shortly after the warm milk Beth had brought her in her bedchamber.

Apparently she'd been distressed, though Rampton hadn't enquired. To be told she was still pining for Yarrowby would have been too galling, not to mention uncomfortable.

Rampton had immediately gone in search of Rose, only to be informed she was visiting a friend in the village. Fortunately Arabella's condition had improved but it was just before dinner than he'd found Rose's letter, tucked beneath the turn-down of his bed.

'Rose is . . . resting. What can I do for you,

Mother?' His tone was as frosty as hers.

'I'm looking for my emerald necklace. I lent it to Rose for Mr and Mrs Lake's dinner last week.'

'Have you asked her maid?'

'No one seems to have seen her. And if Rose is as indisposed as she would have one believe I felt it discourteous to knock and disturb her.'

'Well, I don't have it, Mother,' said Rampton irritably, while his thoughts revolved around Rose's no-doubt dreadful legacy. As he watched his mother depart he felt dismay spurt its poison into the fibres of his being.

Trying to compose an inventory of the family jewels, Rampton made his way to the dowager's dressing-room and set upon the task of uncovering the full extent of his runaway wife's misdemeanours.

★　★　★

The closer to London Rose travelled, the brighter her spirits. By contrast Beth looked increasingly long-mouthed until Rose asked in exasperation, 'Were you hoping to set sail with me to the West Indies, Beth, and never see your family again?'

'It's just I were to meet someone at the

docks, m'lady, and now I dunno how I'll be paid.'

Rose looked at her curiously. 'You'll be paid as you always are. By me, at the end of the month.'

'You're going back to London, m'lady?'

'That's right.' Rose envisaged, with a surprising degree of relish, the confrontation that lay in store. 'I'm very much looking forward to my chat with Lady Chesterfield.'

The way she said it appeared to frighten the girl. 'You're going to see Lady Chesterfield?' Beth gasped. 'Oh no, ma'am, you ain't takin' me with yer.'

Rose stared at her maid. Beth's normally dull brown eyes gleamed in her sallow face. Fear lent her bovine features rare animation. Like a mirage taking shape and substance, suddenly everything made sense.

For a moment shock rendered her silent. Helena had recruited Beth to help blacken Rose's reputation in her husband's eyes. All the time Beth had pretended to serve her she had in fact been acting for Helena.

Rose's hands shook and she tried to school her features into impassive lines as she sought for a motive.

Why?

Another insidious thought intruded. She'd believed Rampton had sent her away so he could be with Helena. If she'd believed he was being untrue, what other lies must he have been fed to think the same of her?

Oh, God, she thought, shivering with fear and dismay. The sooner she could be at her husband's side the sooner they could sort out this tangled web of lies.

But first she must find Helena.

The carriage bumped uncomfortably over the rutted roads. London would soon be reached. So, too, she desperately hoped, would a reconciliation between her and her husband, once Helena's part in the conspiracy to part Rose from Rampton had been explained. In the meantime she needed to find out from Beth as much as she could. She took a deep breath and strove for icy calm. 'So Lady Chesterfield paid you to place the letter on my dressing-table yesterday morning?'

Beth looked mutinous. 'I ain't saying nuffink.'

'And Lady Chesterfield intends running away with that ne'er do well, Mr Albright?'

'Dunno, ma'am, only I don't want to never see Lady Chesterfield again if she knows that you knows everyfink, now. Please,' begged the girl, 'if you're not going on that boat just take me back to Lord Rampton's 'ouse so I can get me fings and do a runner.'

Rose pounced. 'Lady Chesterfield is not at Bruton Street? Has she gone already?' Fear that Helena might have neatly slipped away without being called to account for the damage she had caused Rose made her grip Beth's arms and shake her. 'Where is Lady Chesterfield going? What do you know of her plans?'

'I dunno, m'lady.' Beth looked close to tears. 'Only that she's bin visiting Mr Albright at a 'ouse in Marylebone. Aitken Street — number nine, I reckon — so you go and sort it out wiv 'er but leave me out of it for I don't know nuffink!'

Before Rose could stop her Beth had thrust open the carriage door and thrown herself on to the road. They were not travelling fast and as Rose pulled back the curtain she saw that the girl had regained her footing without apparent injury and was covering the adjacent cornfield with surprising speed.

20

Rampton contemplated the unsavoury truth. Rose had known what she was about. Just like the necklace she'd pawned, the family heirlooms were valuable stones in unremarkable settings. Having dismissed Fanshawe, Rampton was dressed only in his silk banyan when Arabella and Felix burst in upon the briefest of knocks.

'Most men find more honourable methods of disposing of their wives when they tire of them!'

The angry blaze in his brother's eye was so at odds with his normally placid demeanour that Rampton was momentarily speechless. Felix advanced a few steps and, to Rampton's incredulity, put up his fists, saying, 'If you weren't my brother I'd have no compunction in dropping you this instant!'

'Welcome home, Felix. I'm glad that brotherly love prevails.' To his further surprise, Arabella, who looked pale and wan, appeared fully to endorse Felix's threat of violence. 'Would you mind,' he asked, 'explaining to me the reason for this uncharacteristic, and certainly unwarranted, attack?'

'Unwarranted?' Felix made a noise of disgust. 'Unwarranted? Because my sympathies lie with my sister-in-law rather than my brother?'

Rampton blinked. 'I'd have thought I was particularly deserving of your sympathies at this moment. You are, I assume, aware that my wife has left me?'

It was the first time he had said the words. How remote from reality they sounded.

'Left you! Why, you sent her away with as much compunction as you would discard an old coat that no longer pleased you. Like so many of your mistresses.'

'I would like you to find one of my former mistresses who considers herself discarded in such an uncaring fashion,' Rampton was stung into defending himself. 'But I find the charge as regards my wife a bit rich since she has just run off with Albright . . . taking, I might add, a king's ransom's worth of our mother's jewellery.'

He felt only transitory satisfaction at the shocked dismay and confusion that replaced their anger.

'It can't be true!' Arabella was the first to break the silence. 'She has left Larchwood yes, but only because you sent her away. Back to the West Indies!'

'I did no such thing!' Rampton glared at

Arabella. 'What else did Rose tell you? That I am an unfeeling, nay, violent husband? That she can no longer tolerate my mistresses? That I have refused her every comfort? Failed to indulge her at every turn?' With superhuman effort he reined in his temper. 'I have not so much as looked at another woman since I married your sister!'

He looked witheringly at each distraught face. 'I wrote a letter sending her away? Show me! She went of her own volition . . . to be with her lover. Here is the letter she wrote to me!' He thrust the crumpled piece of parchment covered in Rose's handwriting at Felix.

'I can't believe it,' Felix said, putting a comforting arm around the now weeping Arabella. 'Albright? They hardly know one another.'

'They never met in the West Indies?' Rampton barked the question at Arabella.

Arabella looked downcast. 'But it was Helena, not Rose, who caught Geoffrey's fancy.'

'How would you know? You were only a child, still in the schoolroom!'

'I know my sister!' Arabella cried. 'She's incapable of such deception.'

'She deceived me into making her my wife.'

They jumped as the clock on the landing

chimed the hour. Rampton went on, 'Are you now going to tell me she has never been seen in Geoffrey Albright's company during the past few weeks? Pray, cast your mind back to Lady Barbery's ball. And Lady Chawdrey's. A little too much champagne punch and she was throwing herself into his arms. If you don't believe me, then read it!'

Felix held the letter to the light and murmured Rose's words of shame and regret at her decision to elope with Geoffrey, adding that she was taking nothing from Rampton that was not due to her.

'Nothing, except the family jewels,' muttered Rampton.

Soberly, Felix handed his brother back the letter. 'It doesn't make sense. To everyone else you appeared the love match of the season.'

'It doesn't make sense, because why would Rose tell me she loved her husband, despite the fact he was sending her away?' asked Arabella, fiercely. 'I saw the letter you wrote her.'

'The letter *I* wrote her?' Rampton harrumphed. 'Did you read it?'

Arabella bit her lip as she shook her head. 'Why would Rose lie about that? And I refuse to believe she wrote that letter to you.'

'Well, my dear,' countered Rampton, 'what

do you propose? That I saddle Chestnut and ride post haste to the docks to fetch my runaway wife — who has probably already departed — and prove this is all a lie, and that she is somehow the wronged party?'

'Yes!' came the unanimous rejoinder.

'And I shall follow in the carriage!' declared Arabella.

'Before Mother discovers her jewels have gone,' suggested Felix.

★ ★ ★

A relentless drizzle made the roads slippery but they pressed on. Not to the docks but to London following information that a carriage bearing the Rampton family arms had been sighted on the London road.

It was not until they reached the first post house, where they procured fresh horses and stopped for a hurried breakfast, that Rampton and Felix were able to exchange a few words.

'That little maid of hers went with her. I'll wager anything it's she who's taken Mother's jewellery,' Felix asserted as the publican's daughter removed the lid from a platter of calf's liver and bacon. 'Probably wrote the letter, too, to hide her part in it. Which she has conveniently taken with her.'

Rampton raised his head from his pot of ale and levelled a long, hard look at his brother. 'You're really championing that sister-in-law of yours, aren't you?'

Felix met his stare, confidently. 'You don't have much faith in your wife, do you? Or her sister, since you don't give much credence to what Arabella says about the state Rose was in when she left.' He shrugged and added between mouthfuls, 'Why, she's mad for you!'

'Then why has she left?'

Felix shrugged. 'A woman used to taking charge of her own life might consider disgrace and ignominy a fair price for her freedom if the alternative were a loveless marriage.'

The knuckles which held Rampton's mug handle turned white. 'A loveless marriage,' he repeated in a whisper and Felix said hurriedly, 'I'm not pretending I know anything about your marriage but — '

'You obviously know nothing about it, otherwise you would sympathize with the number of times I've been deceived.' Waving away the hovering publican's daughter who had made to remove several finished dishes, he went on, 'I'm not talking about the kind of love that every greenhorn experiences half a dozen times in his life; I mean the anguish of loving one woman, one's wife . . . despite everything.'

★   ★   ★

'What do you mean, she was sighted on the London Road?'

Helena swung round, her skirts frothing at her ankles, her high-heeled shoes clicking across the floorboards of the shabbily furnished little room as she advanced towards the fireplace. Her voice shook.

Geoffrey snorted. 'I thought it a ridiculous plan in the first place and we couldn't trust that little maid of hers to carry it out properly.' His voice sounded bored, disembodied in the gloom of the wing chair in which he was ensconced.

'We needed the attention to be on her rather than on us,' Helena persisted in defence of the letter she had insisted Geoffrey should write, copying Rampton's hand. 'Rose might well have not questioned that it was written by her husband, taken the money and sailed away. By the time Rampton discovers the truth — if he does — we'll be long gone.' She forced a smile. 'And rich.'

'But we'd have been a great deal safer if we'd simply taken the jewels without going to such lengths to blacken your sister-in-law's

381

name into the bargain.' Geoffrey sighed. 'If Rose hasn't gone to the docks then she's coming to London to win back her husband.'

'Not even Rose is that stupid,' Helena spat, going to the window and wiping at the grimy pane for despite her bold words she felt a tendril of discomfort. 'We've covered every contingency.'

'Well, if she's smelled a rat and elicits Rampton's sympathies we're in trouble.' Geoffrey's head appeared from the wing of the chair. 'Jeremiah was to have met Beth at the docks to pay her off but if the girl's taken everything and fled we'll have to cut our losses and head for the coast.'

Helena closed the curtains at the window with a violent tug. 'The coast is where Rose should be at this moment. You're sure Jeremiah knew what he was looking for when he reported that she'd turned south on the London Road? Oh Geoffrey,' she burst out in sudden agitation, 'what can we do when we don't even know where Rose is headed?'

'I daresay we should leave.' Geoffrey rose, threateningly.

21

The cold sweat of fear made Rose shiver, despite her warm pelisse, as she looked up at the dark house in the afternoon light. She'd not taken Geoffrey into account when she'd conceived her plan to force Helena to confess all to Rampton. Yet surely he must be complicit in Helena's campaign against Rose? Or was Helena acting alone? It was possible.

For five years Rose had lived with Helena's volatile temper. She knew her sister-in-law's capacity for vengeance, her spitefulness and her devious nature, but surely forging the letter purportedly from her husband was worse than anything she'd done before. Now the time had come for Helena to be called to account.

Rose's nerve nearly failed as the hackney drew to a halt and she heard the jarvey prepare to descend. She closed her eyes while her heart hammered. How would she approach Helena? How would she make her not only confess, but come with her to confess to Rampton?

Her thoughts were interrupted when a panicked voice hissed, 'Rose! I don't believe it, but thank God you've come!'

Before Rose could protest, the carriage door was flung open and Helena had grasped her by the wrist and was hustling her up the steps and indoors, crying, 'Rose, you have to help me!'

In the gloomy passage, Rose took stock. The peeling wallpaper and dust lent the dwelling an unsavoury aspect and she wrinkled her nose at the smell of damp. This was not where Rose had expected to find Helena.

'Beth told you what we'd done, didn't she? Where is she?' Helena's voice was thick with fear. As she put aside the heavy veil of her black bonnet her eyes glittered in the small amount of light that filtered in from outside.

'Gone!' said Rose, harshly, gaining courage from the knowledge Helena had set out to ruin her life. 'And now you're coming with me to tell Rampton that you wrote that letter. I put the pieces together after I realised Beth's involvement and how you must have been using her to spy on me.'

This was greeted by a gasp, then silence. Snatching her wrist from Rose's grasp, Helena stepped backwards. A tinkling laugh escaped her. 'You really know nothing, do you?' She sounded incredulous. 'Beth isn't with you?'

In the gloom Helena's rapid breathing indicated her agitation. She sounded as if she were speaking her thoughts aloud. 'No, obviously Beth is cleverer than I thought. Or perhaps it's just her sense of self-preservation is more well-honed than I'd expected. As for me, if you don't help me get out of this house before Geoffrey — '

'Don't be ridiculous!' Rose snapped. 'You're lucky I've said nothing about this or you'd be so mired in scandal you'd never be received again. It's Charles I care about, not you.'

In the dim light Rose saw Helena's mouth drop open. 'You really came alone, Rose, without telling anyone?' Her surprise seemed genuine. Gathering her concealing black shawl more tightly around her, she shook her head. 'You really don't know what people are saying?' she asked, adding under her voice: 'Fortune favours me, after all. Now Rose, I know you don't want me to elope with Geoffrey though you've never thought me good enough for your brother.' Her smile was one that Rose knew well. She waited for the inevitable bargaining or wheedling and was not surprised when Helena said, 'What would you say if I told you I've realized the error of my ways and I need you to help me?'

'Help you!' Rose gave a strangled laugh.

'You're asking for my help after everything you've done to damn me in the eyes of my husband? If you'd had your way I'd be on a boat bound for the West Indies.'

Helena gave a dismissive wave as if this were of no account. 'Rampton would have intercepted you. You know he would have!'

'I don't know anything except you've been telling Rampton lies about me.'

'And when Rampton discovered the truth — which he would have in good time — he'd be so beside himself with remorse for doubting you that you'd want to shower me with gratitude . . . only I'd be long gone.' Helena laughed again, impulsively pulling Rose to her and saying with apparent sincerity, 'I'm so glad to see you, though. Now that you put it like that, I can't tell you how terribly guilty I feel about what I've done — '

'You don't know what remorse is, Helena! You wrote the letter and you were behind the stolen necklace, too, weren't you?'

'What stolen necklace?'

'Lady Barbery's.' Rose heaved in a breath as Helena dropped her hand. 'You made Rampton think I'd stolen it, didn't you?'

Helena's laugh was spontaneous. 'I thought you were clever enough to deduce the truth of that long ago.' She put her head on one side. 'You really are very credulous, Rose. Surely it was apparent Lady Barbery was behind that? Do you recall when the parcel first arrived addressed to Lady Chesterfield and I naturally assumed it was for me? Do you remember my surprise when you opened it?'

Rose nodded, her suspicions far from allayed.

'Well, I recognised it as Lady Barbery's and of course it made perfect sense that she would act so maliciously since she was Rampton's mistress until you entered the scene. But yes, I suppose I did play on Rampton's suspicions.'

Rose drew herself up. 'So much so that he sent me to Larchfield.'

'Well, you obviously didn't do a very good job defending yourself.'

Rose felt like throttling her. 'I didn't know what I was defending myself *against*. But worst of all was the letter. You forged his hand so that I would believe he was banishing me to the West Indies,' Rose finished, hotly. 'Meanwhile, everything you've done is so that you can run away with Geoffrey, isn't it?' She threw a glance at their insalubrious surroundings and added, 'Though what you think will sustain you both, when Geoffrey is clearly as impecunious as you, I don't know.'

Helena gave a supercilious sniff. 'Geoffrey's gone to fetch a hackney. He'll be returning any moment to pick me up, only the problem is,' she sounded remarkably calm as she went on, 'I've changed my mind about eloping with him since I greatly fear his intentions.'

Rose blinked. Curtailing the heated response she'd intended, she muttered, 'It's a shame you didn't consider his character before you embarked upon this bold and wicked course of action, then, isn't it?'

The blaze in Helena's eyes was at odds with the calm in her voice. 'You think me disloyal and inconstant, but the fact is this isn't the first time Geoffrey's asked me to elope. I refused him when I was seventeen and I've regretted it ever since. Well, until now, that is.'

Rose gripped Helena's shoulders and put her face close. 'Do you know that you will be forever barred from polite society if you go with Geoffrey? Not to mention that Charles will never get over it. Please, Helena, if you've no further wish to associate with Geoffrey then what choice do you have but to return with me to confess to Rampton? Charles would forgive you, for if you come with me now I swear I'll say nothing about Geoffrey.'

The sound of a hackney carriage pulling up in the street outside made Helena gasp and pull away. 'Oh God, I thought I had more time!' She sounded truly panicked. 'Now it's too late! What will we do? Where can we flee? He'll hunt me down.'

'Well, why didn't you think of that before?' Rose muttered, her own palms sweating as for the first time she wondered what involvement Geoffrey had in Helena's plans to discredit her. She felt a tug and turned to see Helena untying the ribbons of her bonnet.

'Rose! Please, change clothes with me. My cloak, my bonnet.' Already she was divesting herself of these garments, forcing them into Rose's resisting hands. 'Nobody wants to kill you, do they? You'll be safe. But hear me out.'

Untying the ribbons of Rose's bonnet and whipping it off her head, she hissed, 'The reason Geoffrey is after me is he believes I betrayed him. We were lovers, you see, only we argued and he left.'

The sound of Geoffrey's voice telling the jarvey to wait came clearly through the partly opened window. Helena was now dressed in Rose's hat and cloak, but Rose had refused to tie the ribbons of the bonnet Helena had placed on her head.

'Help me, I beg you!' whispered Helena before, to Rose's amazement, she flung herself at her feet to kiss the hem of her skirt.

'You had better be telling the truth,

Helena,' Rose muttered as her sister-in-law pushed her towards the door. 'Go to Rampton, now, and tell him everything. I won't be long after you. When Geoffrey realises it's me he's eloping with he'll quickly set me down.'

Geoffrey's low growl from the other side of the door drowned out Helena's reply. The grating sound as he fumbled with the lock echoed the fear that reverberated through Rose, though she was certain she could handle Geoffrey if she had to.

She pulled down the veil as Helena seized her by the wrist, calling out to Geoffrey in a falsely reassuring tone, 'I'm ready, my love.'

Thrusting a small drawstring bag into Rose's hand, she pushed her on to the front step.

⋆   ⋆   ⋆

It was mid-afternoon by the time Rampton arrived at his London townhouse, only to be told that her ladyship was not at home.

Disappointment choked him. He'd allowed himself to be swayed by Felix's determined assurance that this was where Rose would be waiting for him, together with a full accounting of all the misunderstandings and manufactured evidence his brother claimed lay at the heart of their estrangement.

'However, her maid came in a short while ago. When I questioned her she appeared greatly agitated and seemed to have no inkling as to her mistresses's whereabouts. Decidedly odd, my lord, and I'm only telling you since I thought your lordship might be interested.'

'Very interested, Whibble. I want Beth brought to me immediately.'

'Very good, my lord.'

Rampton and Felix were in the library when the girl was delivered, clearly reluctant.

'Found her slipping out the back way, sir, and had to run to apprehend her when she failed to respond to orders.' Whibble looked with distaste at the sullen creature. Her mutinous gaze was fixed upon the floor.

'Where's Lady Rampton and why did you not obey Whibble when he called you?'

When Beth mumbled something about being turned off halfway between Larchfield and London, Rampton glanced at his brother. Felix looked smug, as if Beth's answer already exonerated Rose, before interjecting smoothly, 'Really, Beth, I can't believe her ladyship would be so unfeeling as to turn you off in a muddy field, no matter how great her distaste for your company.'

Beth said nothing, though she squirmed when Rampton said, 'You must tell us if there's anything you're owed. Fortunately you were able to collect your things.' He indicated the small bag she carried.

'Yes, sir. If that's all, sir?' Beth half-rose, clutching the drawstring bag from which protruded a grubby apron. Felix darted a horrified look at his brother as she sidled towards the door but Rampton had no intention of allowing her to leave yet.

'Just one thing, more, Beth.'

Like a frozen rabbit she hesitated on the threshold. 'Yes, sir?'

'I believe my wife entrusted you with some of her jewellery which may have escaped your attention. Please just ensure it's not in that bag of yours.'

Beth's eyes widened. Slack-jawed she whispered, 'Here?'

'You don't mind, surely?'

She reddened, gripped the door handle, hesitated, then said in strangled tones, ''Twere Lady Chesterfield wot said I must take the pieces. I never asked for nuffink only she said she'd slice me throat if I didn't do wot she said and I'd be well rewarded if I did. Wot could I do, sir?'

Felix sounded disarmingly sympathetic as he encouraged Beth to elaborate on what else

Lady Chesterfield had instructed her to do until his brother cut in.

'You could have informed Lady Rampton of the evil intended her. She'd have rewarded you for seeing to her best interests.' Drily, he added, 'I wonder what else you may have done to further her best interests. Delivered an important letter from me, perhaps?' His tone was at odds with the churning in his breast: the beginnings of a tremendous tide of self-recrimination. For the moment, though, he had to remain calm and discover everything he could.

Beth clearly decided she'd had enough. Clasping the bag to her chest she thrust her small frame through the door and bolted down the passageway.

She collided with Whibble, who was bringing refreshment, so it wasn't long before she was back in the library and facing a far less sympathetic hearing.

'I think the most pressing questions we need answered are Lady Rampton's where-abouts and Miss Helena's motive in soliciting your help, Beth.' Rampton looked up from studying the instep of his shoe. 'If you've stolen Lady Rampton's jewellery, Beth,' he went on, acidly, 'you could be looking at the end of a noose. However, if you were coerced by somebody you could expect a great deal of leniency.'

Beth dropped the bag, which made a dull thud as it landed at her feet. She looked terrified. 'When Lady Chesterfield told me there were things that she was happy to pay me to keep an eye out for, there seemed no harm in it,' she whispered, staring at the bag. 'Lady Chesterfield wanted to know Lady Rampton's habits and where she liked to go, so what 'arm was there in tellin' her that? 'Twere only at the end when that other gennulman got involved that me nerves started to jitter.'

With a triumphant look at his brother, Felix asked, 'Which gentleman was that?'

'Only met 'im once, and it were enough, handsome and nice though he seemed at first. Don't rightly know 'is real name except that maybe Lady Chesterfield called him Geoffrey Allnight once, if I recall rightly. It were 'im wot said if I failed to do me job right and see that Lady Rampton got the letter, an' if I didn't get the jewels, he'd slice me neck from the rest o' me.' Beth took a step back from the bag and said on a dramatic sob, 'So there you 'ave the truth, me lord. If you don't send me to Newgate it'll be just the same if I meet this other feller.'

Rampton scratched his chin in an attempt to cover the extent of his agitation. How could he have been so blind? God, how utterly he had failed Rose by believing all these manufactured lies about her. Overlaying his remorse was his desperation to find her and hold her as he begged her forgiveness. She must feel utterly abandoned by him.

But where was she? This was his most pressing question, but when he asked it, Beth's answer was terrifying.

'Gone to Mr Allnight's to find Lady Chesterfield and try and make her 'splain to you that it were Lady Chesterfield wot wrote that letter.'

Rampton leapt to his feet and raked his fingers through his hair. 'Does she not know the danger? Why did she not come here first?' he asked, though uncomfortably aware he'd hardly behaved in a manner conducive to Rose believing she'd receive a sympathetic hearing since he'd sent her away.

'Her ladyship don't know about any of them jewels that were stole or that it were her name put about as being in on it.' Beth sounded as though she was recounting nothing more than a matter of fact. 'I s'pose she thought it safe enough to visit Lady Chesterfield and her gennelmun.'

Felix rephrased Beth's words slowly, as if his brother were an imbecile. 'Rose has no idea of the lengths Helena and Geoffrey have gone to in order to blacken her name?'

'Or to what lengths they are likely to go in order to keep her quiet and the rest of the world ignorant,' muttered Rampton, struck with fresh horror as he contemplated the peril his wife faced.

22

Aunt Alice put her hands to the lace trimming of her voluminous gown and repeated in accents of horror, 'Helena . . . ? Eloping with Geoffrey Albright? Oh my! Poor Charles!'

'It's Rose I'm worried about.' Arabella strove for calmness, clinging to the newel post in her aunt's lobby and wishing she didn't have to raise her voice about such a sensitive matter since her aunt appeared dumbstruck on the landing a few steps above her. 'Helena has done some very wicked things in Rose's name and is no doubt attempting to flee the country as we speak, but we have no idea where to find Rose.'

'Geoffrey Albright?'

Arabella turned as Oswald sloped into the room. 'Geoffrey Albright?' He repeated the name in disgusted tones.

Arabella was about to make some dismissive remark in the hopes he'd go away when she was struck by his growing fury as he muttered, 'God in Heaven, so she's planned everything in order to elope with *Geoffrey Albright!*'

Arabella stepped back, frightened, as in a

blinding flash, it all made sense. How often had she seen her cousin conversing with Helena, usually in dark corners? She'd thought nothing of it at the time but . . . She drew in a sharp breath. Dear Lord, if Oswald had something to do with the plot in which her sister was mired, he needed to tell them now.

'Cousin Rose is not the only one in danger,' Oswald snarled as he headed towards the door, reluctantly turning as his step-mother cried out, ineffectually, and Arabella pushed in front of him, saying urgently, 'Wait for me! You'll have a much greater chance of getting Geoffrey to talk to you if you take me!'

★　★　★

There was nothing Rose could do, if she did have second thoughts. Pushed out of the door by Helena, Geoffrey quickly hustled her into the hackney and it didn't take long to see he was in a black mood.

Squeezing herself into the corner, she told herself she was in no danger. What could Geoffrey do when he found he'd been duped? He'd hardly hurl Rose through the door to risk death beneath the wheels in the middle of a London street!

'Still angry with me?' Moving forward, he touched her face through the veil. 'Vanity, Helena. Or is this your silent reproach?' His sigh was not feigned as he leant back into the squabs, his breathing heavy and his voice filled with emotion. 'Ironic, isn't it?' he went on when he received no response, 'Now that we are on the point of fulfilling our childish dreams we find that the love we once pledged would last forever has leg-shackled us to one another until death.'

Rose prayed for some opportunity she could seize for flight, as Beth had done hours earlier. Helena had not been lying when she said she feared Geoffrey. Oh, dear Lord, how had she allowed herself to be here and what good would it achieve?

'For God's sake, Helena, answer me!' Lunging forward, he grasped her forearms. 'Don't you realize we're tied to one another, more surely than if we were married? We have thieved and deceived . . . you have blackened your sister-in-law in the eyes of her husband to achieve all this. If we are caught we face the noose for our misdemeanours.'

Rose gasped, struggling in his grip as his hands felt their way insinuatingly over her body.

'My God,' he whispered, drawing back in shock before reaching over and wrenching the hat and veil from her head. 'Lady Rampton!' Cupping her chin he dragged her face to within an inch of his, which was black with rage.

Rose flinched, fearing he was going to strike her.

'What the devil? Where's Helena?' His voice was a terrifying whisper. Before she could reply he pounced on the bag at her feet and snatched it up, fumbling with the drawstring.

The discovery of its contents did nothing to improve his temper. With a blood-curdling howl he dashed it against the window and turned on Rose.

'Rocks, by God!' he screamed. 'So you were a party to Helena's deception all the time!' He shook her so hard her brain rattled. 'Where is she? Are you both so stupid you thought you could hoodwink me? Did you plan to jump out of the carriage before I discovered?'

Rose cowered into the corner while the old carriage rocked and lumbered over the uneven cobblestones. She whispered, 'I knew nothing until I arrived at the house less than an hour ago and Helena pushed me out of the front door so that she could escape because you'd threatened her.'

'Innocent Rose,' he sneered. 'Doing what was best to help Helena. Why come to my house if you were looking for an ally?'

'Beth said you and Helena were eloping.' Rose clasped her hands to stop them trembling. 'That's all I knew. I was suspicious about the letter and wanted the truth from Helena.'

'Where is Beth?'

'She jumped out of the carriage before I reached your house.'

Geoffrey let out a crack of laughter. Shaking his head at Rose he muttered, 'Aren't we the fools in this madcap charade for allowing Helena to manipulate us into achieving exactly what she wants, while we wear the consequences? It's a good thing you're not Helena at this moment for I can't answer for what I'd do to you.'

Rose drew in her breath on a sob. Slowly she tried to reach for the door handle but Geoffrey dashed it away.

'Not so fast, Lady Rampton. You've not yet paid your dues.' He chuckled. 'You're going to help me find some valuable trinkets that are going to fund my escape — and retirement — and hopefully my revenge.'

Rose bit her lip. In the last couple of minutes she'd realised there was far more going on than she'd understood before she'd blithely confronted Helena. Clearly Helena and Geoffrey were complicit in some dangerous game involving thievery and who knew what other skulduggery. And now she was alone in a carriage with a vengeful Geoffrey Albright who had never liked her.

'What have you done?' she whispered.

After a considered look, he said, 'You do know that Beth stole a quantity of jewellery from Rampton's mother's dressing-room to coincide with your departure?'

Rose stifled the gasp that would only amuse Geoffrey as he went on, 'And that she sewed Lady Chawdrey's missing diamond necklace into the lining of the gown you obligingly pawned on her behalf so that when Rampton redeemed it he had overwhelming proof of your thievery and deception?'

This time Rose did gasp. 'Helena cannot get away with this! I went to your house to find her so she'd confess to Rampton that she'd written that letter.'

'Actually, I wrote that letter, and the one he received purportedly from you, but I confess, I was not happy about doing it.'

'A letter from *me*? Why did you do it?' Rose challenged.

Geoffrey pushed back his carefully coiffed curls. His nostrils flared. 'To make Helena happy. She was determined to have her little revenge upon you for wrecking her liaison with Sir Hector after I'd sailed out of her life not weeks before.'

Rose, who had been slumped against the window, jerked upright in anger. 'Would she see me hang?' she hissed. Shaking her head, she added, 'Sir Hector saw through her from the start. It's a pity Charles never did.'

'Or you,' Geoffrey added. 'Come to that, neither did I.' He seemed to rally. 'It's time to find Helena and I think I know where she's headed, for all she was so cunning in trying to keep her own little insurance policy secret from me.'

'I want to find my husband first.'

Geoffrey shook his head. 'Rampton can wait. We must reach Hampstead Heath before Helena slips out of the country, laughing, while you and I contemplate the hangman's noose.'

★ ★ ★

Rampton balked at the unappetizing smell of boiled cabbage as he entered Geoffrey's house.

'Where would they have taken her?' Felix asked, looking blankly at his brother.

'God only knows,' snapped Rampton, crouching to pick up Rose's bonnet, squashed and battered, from the floor by the sofa. What a fool he'd been. Rose's guilt had seemed incontrovertible, yet he had been duped. And

403

not just once. He considered himself an intelligent man, yet he'd blindly accepted what was presented to him. Now, as he took in the dank, gloomy house he gathered Geoffrey had leased for his romantic trysts with Helena, he cursed himself for a fool. Remorse and pain tore through him. If Rose had been harmed he would never forgive himself.

He opened his mouth to speak then stilled as Felix raised his hand for silence. A stealthy tread sounded in the passageway. Rampton straightened and slid into the shadows as the doorknob turned, and the door opened slowly.

A figure appeared upon the threshold. Seizing his arm and twisting it up behind his back, Rampton thrust him into the room while Felix leapt from behind.

Arabella, following in the wake of the now apprehended Oswald, screamed before letting out her breath in a relieved gasp. 'Rampton! Have you found Rose?'

'I'm more interested in whether you've found Helena,' growled Oswald, casting a black look at Rampton as he rubbed his mauled arm.

Rampton regarded him contemptuously while waiting for his heart rate to steady. He'd been ready to give Geoffrey Albright everything he deserved. 'Helena seems to have acquired a multitude of enemies, for good reason, but at this moment my wife's safety is of greatest concern.'

Oswald exhaled on a hiss. 'Arabella tells me Helena formed an inappropriate alliance with your neighbour, Albright, six years ago in the West Indies. Now they have vanished with more than four thousand pounds' worth of the baubles I was foolish enough to be inveigled into procuring for Helena. Do you think I'm more concerned for your wife, or for my neck?'

Rampton contemplated the slimy character. 'So your role was in the thefts and placing the evidence so it implicated Rose. What else are you guilty of? Forging those letters?'

The righteous anger in Oswald's eyes pierced the gloom. 'I know nothing of any letters,' he muttered as his gaze traversed the room. With quivering nostrils, he suggested, 'Forged letters are a useful device for facilitating a lovers' flight, are they not? Well, Helena's not going to get away with her evil deeds. I have as much to charge her with as you do, my lord.' He laughed, a bitter sound though tinged with pride. 'Ah, but it was devious. She was devious. Helena, that is. A woman after my own heart and now she's *gone.* Gone with that scoundrel Geoffrey, who just sat back, waiting to reap the rewards of *my* labour.'

How Rampton wished he did not have to ask the question, for it painted him as the credulous fool he so keenly felt himself at that moment. Ah, but when he was reunited with his darling girl he'd make it clear he'd spend the rest of his days atoning for his lack of faith. Fear sliced through these thoughts. He had to find her first.

'Tell me what Helena did for her ill-gotten gains. It might help piece together where Rose actually is.'

Oswald chuckled. 'The clothes Rose pawned on Helena's behalf . . . ? Rose did not know Lady Chawdrey's necklace was sewn into the lining. The pawnbroker was paid handsomely for his well-rehearsed act.'

Arabella gasped and rushed forward to shake Oswald, crying, 'How have you the effrontery to confess such crimes which could send you to Newgate, Cousin Oswald?'

He put her away from him and Felix moved in, smoothly, to hold her against his side.

Oswald glared. 'Only Helena could send me there for only she knows the energies I expended on her behalf.' His cocky banter was replaced by a menacing energy. 'She has all the fruits of my labours and my only reward is telling you just how black her heart really is.'

Impatiently, Rampton moved to the door. His guilt and shame were compounded by the minute. 'I'm more concerned with Rose's safety than Helena's black heart. Where in God's name could she be?'

'Have you asked that little maid of hers?'

'Beth is locked up at Bruton Street,' muttered Rampton, 'she'd have told us anything to lessen the sentence she's facing.' He opened the door but Felix blocked his way, saying with sudden excitement, 'Not if she knows other secrets and there were any chance of escape. Remember, Beth was in league with Helena. Helena used many avenues to gain the funds she needed — '

'Poor Charles doesn't even know she's gone!' interrupted Arabella. 'We must return to the house to tell him, gently.'

'We must return to the house,' said Rampton, pursuing his brother's line of thought, 'to discover from Beth what it is she has neglected to tell us.'

★   ★   ★

Rose struggled to keep up the relentless pace Geoffrey had set. The length of cord that attached her wrist to his waist chafed painfully.

Her energy was flagging and her slippers

were wet through and torn. 'You can't have trusted each other very much,' she managed between gasps as they toiled through a thicket of gorse, 'if Helena hid from you the ill-gotten gains that were supposed to buy your freedom.'

She felt the chill through to her bones and glanced fearfully at her surroundings, deserted in the gathering twilight. What was Geoffrey planning? She'd felt frightened in the carriage but had believed she would be freed eventually. Geoffrey had no use for her, after all, she'd reassured herself. He'd be leaving England on the next packet. He had no choice but to flee, but he'd not harm Rose, surely.

And then he'd bound her wrists with rope and dragged her out of the carriage to this deserted expanse of countryside.

'About as much as Rampton trusted you after you deceived him into marriage,' muttered Geoffrey.

Rose turned her head from his unkind grin as he went on, 'Desire and trust don't go hand in hand, surely you know that? Cousin Oswald was thieving for Helena on both our accounts, though of course Oswald didn't know it. If it made Helena feel safer to store some of the booty where no one would find it, why should I care when what we each know binds us to one another as surely as marriage binds man and wife?'

Pausing to catch their breaths in a clearing, Rose glanced at Geoffrey's hard profile. She supposed some would consider him a handsome man, but loose living was taking its toll while Helena, ten years his junior, was still an exquisite creature.

Bitterly, Rose contemplated how easily Helena had persuaded her to go with Geoffrey so that she could skip away, free from the men who desired and had thieved for her, while she claimed the booty.

Would Helena seek greener pastures with the jewels Geoffrey was convinced she'd hidden somewhere near by? Choking down her rage at the sister-in-law who'd gone to such lengths to ruin her life, she whispered, 'If you find her, what will you do?'

'I shall remind Helena that she needs my protection.' Geoffrey's look was ugly.

'When my husband finds *me* all the wickedness you and Helena perpetrated in my name will be revealed.'

'Which is why you're such a threat, my dear Lady Rampton,' growled Geoffrey, swinging round, 'since we need time to leave this country without you revealing all.'

Cursing her stupid bravado as Geoffrey gripped her chin and tilted her face upwards, Rose gulped, 'I'll keep your secret.' She was shaking so much she could barely get the words out. Geoffrey was volatile. She knew him only enough to be certain he'd have little compunction in doing what was required to save his own skin.

'You'll have to, but the only way to ensure that,' said Geoffrey, contouring her face without tenderness, before tapping her nose lightly as if she were a child, 'is to bind you securely to a tree in the midst of the thicket we've just come through and leave a note which, we must hope, will be delivered at the appropriate time.' His lip curled. 'While I have no particular wish to see harm come to you, my safety is more important to me than yours.'

Panic charged through her as she glanced at the trees and thick gorse behind them. How would anyone ever find her, if Geoffrey bound her as he threatened? Rampton would believe she had left him. Why should he send out a search party, much less look for her here? With Geoffrey and Helena neatly executing their evil plot he would forever think her guilty of their crimes.

Weakly, she began, 'Rampton will — ' but Geoffrey cut her off. 'Rampton believes you a liar and a thief, my dear.' He stroked her hair. 'You're a pretty thing that caught his fancy but your allure quickly palled when he discovered the depths of your wicked soul.' He laughed. 'Poor Rose. Even Dr Horne innocently gave credence to Helena's diagnosis of your illness of the mind . . . of the lapses where a pretty jewel was too hard to resist, and telling the truth beyond your capacity.'

Rose sucked in her breath sharply and twisted her head away from his loathsome touch. Dear Lord, what had they *not* stooped to? And at her expense. She'd had no idea Helena hated her quite so much. All these years she must have bottled it up, waiting for a chance to have her wicked revenge on the sister-in-law she held responsible for her own blighted happiness.

Her breath misted in front of her. A bird startled into flight made her cry out but there was not another soul upon the heath to hear her. In the faint mist the trees looked like ghostly spectres of doom. If Geoffrey bound her, leaving her helpless in such a remote spot, Rampton might never learn the truth. The forlorn desperation that her life not be cut short here was like a flickering flame, faint but strong enough to sustain her; but more than her safety, Rose wanted her husband to believe in her honesty.

She felt the rope tug as Geoffrey turned back to the thicket but she stood her ground.

New strength surged through her. She'd not give in without a fight. Someone might help her. Someone could possibly be round the next tree, out of sight. Opening her mouth, she was about to utter a shriek when, from the corner of her eye, a slight movement caught her attention. She drew in her breath, hope giving her the strength to remain calm as she extended her arm and pointed down the hill.

'I think,' she managed crisply, 'you might want to attend to other matters, first.'

She watched the play of emotions cross Geoffrey's face as he looked in the direction she indicated.

In the far distance, near a copse of trees, Helena was wielding a large shovel with surprising expertise. A small pile of dirt rose from beside the hole she was creating.

Geoffrey measured his response. 'How observant, Lady Rampton, though congratulations are due to me, also, for my hunch has paid off. You see, I followed her one night after a particularly heated argument.' He pushed back his handsome curls from his sweating forehead, his delight apparent as he added, 'Let's discover Helena's intentions and who's included in her little plan, shall we?'

Stealthily, Geoffrey bore Rose along with

him as he descended the hill, approaching Helena from behind. The pain from Rose's cold, torn feet was nothing compared with her fears for her own future. Helena was ruthless. Rose doubted she'd countenance anything that might jeopardize her escape with the jewels.

And Rose was the greatest threat of all.

Above the horizon Rose could see the moon, as if caught in the treetops. Soon darkness would be upon them. Geoffrey and Helena would have their booty and Rose would be the inconvenient witness. She drew in a shuddering breath and cast about for some means of escape as Geoffrey bore her relentlessly onwards.

'Not a word,' he hissed, 'or you'll be sorry.'

Rose wasn't about to do anything to try his already ragged temper. Obediently she followed, despite her fear and the pain of every footstep. In the distance she could see Helena, the folds of her coquelicot pelisse spread about her as she knelt with her back to them.

Stealthily they continued, halting a few feet away. Geoffrey regarded his erstwhile lover with a mixture of amusement and anger and Rose stiffened in anticipation of the response as Geoffrey's clipped tones sheared the silence. 'Well-prepared as ever, my love, and just in time to make the evening's tide.'

It was clear that Helena had not expected to see him. Stifling her gasp as she swung round, she assumed the air of having intended Geoffrey to be a party to her escape plan as she straightened, indicating Rose and saying, 'What possessed you to bring her along? Couldn't you have dispatched her?'

Geoffrey shrugged. 'Couldn't find an opportunity. I thought we could tie her up hidden in the trees so we'd be unhindered.'

Helena's small white teeth glinted in a parody of a smile. She put her head to one side, as if contemplating the matter, and with sinking heart, Rose knew that in Helena's mind there was nothing to contemplate. Helena would go to almost any lengths to ensure her silence, for her crimes were sufficient to send her to Newgate.

Gulping down her terror Rose squared her shoulders and said, with an assurance she was far from feeling, 'Rampton will come before you can harm me.' In truth, Rampton had never felt further from her.

'Rampton! Little loyalty he's shown you when you were mad for him from the start, which is so unlike you, my dear.' With a toss of her head, Helena sliced the shovel she'd retrieved from a clump of bushes into the damp earth as she went on, 'Now you're learning what pain really is; the pain of separation and of love gone wrong. I hope you're suffering!'

She looked beautiful, her dark eyes glittering with a mixture of malice and self-pity, her raven hair half tumbling from its coiffure. Rose could understand Geoffrey's enslavement. She'd lived with Charles and Helena long enough to have observed the pattern Helena used to exert her power. It had been like living with an unrelenting tide of cloying sweetness interspersed with cutting scorn and wheedling requests.

'Not as much as you will be when Rampton learns of your villainy and that I was never once untrue,' Rose bit back, trying to block from her mind the very great threat that she faced. Her heart cried out to Rampton. He'd been so cold the last few times she'd seen him, but if he only knew the truth, would he not love her again?

Memories of the closeness they'd shared descended upon her like a comforting caress before the chill of fear tore away the warmth.

'So confident, Rose, but I am always one step ahead. Granted, Rampton may learn of my villainy if I have not time to dispose properly of your remains, but when he does it will be too late.' She swung round to Geoffrey, her voice hard. 'We must get rid of her.'

It was small consolation that Geoffrey visibly blanched. 'Theft is one thing, Helena, but murder — '

'Both carry a death sentence.'

Rose closed her eyes as she forced strength into her legs to prevent them buckling. Geoffrey's arguments would carry no weight when Helena was the stronger force.

'Tie me to a tree,' pleaded Rose. 'You only need a few hours before you're on a boat bound for France. No one will find you. You'll have all the money you need.'

Helena drew herself up like a cobra about to strike. 'For as long as I can remember, Rose, you've been my nemesis, for all that I've been the daring one, the beautiful one.'

Rose flinched at the venom in her hissed judgement, blinking with disbelief as Helena went on, 'You hated me enough to condemn me to the worst fate imaginable, damning me in Sir Hector's eyes after Geoffrey left me.'

'Leave it, Helena!' The note of warning in Geoffrey's voice gave Rose hope. He was just behind her and though he was not about to release her, Rose knew he could at least see reason. 'We had a bitter fight, if you recall, and you told me never to show my face again. You have only yourself to blame.'

Helena dismissed this with a snort of

derision before warming to her theme of highlighting Rose's role in her own downfall. 'Because of you, Rose, I was forced to marry Charles. Charles!' She spat her husband's name with more hatred than Rose had ever heard. 'He had not the means to support a wife when he could barely feed his sisters, but did you warn me?' Helena's grip on the shovel tightened while her eyes narrowed. 'Even when you were dowdy Miss Chesterfield in your drab clothes with your hair pulled back I heard the men whisper their interest, but you were too stupid to see how you could benefit us all. Why should I show you any clemency when your inaction ensured that we all remained stuck on that island, condemned to a poverty-stricken existence? When I was destined for so much more?'

'You blame me for all that?' Rose gasped. 'So much so that you would see me die?'

'It's what you deserve for killing my hopes and dreams!' Helena's voice rose as she took a step back, readying herself. Poison and vitriol radiated from every pore as she raised the shovel, its steel edge as well-honed as a fine blade, deadly and merciless when wielded with the force of so much hatred.

Rose jerked back but the ropes that bound her hands tautened as Geoffrey pulled her in the other direction. To save her? Or better position her? She was imprisoned regardless as her vision wavered and her legs buckled, the sound of fear thundering in her ears.

So this was how it would end. Here, on a remote part of Hampstead Heath with her grave already half-dug. A great sob rose in her throat and she tensed in anticipation of the blow, closing her eyes to Helena's face, twisted with malice, as the blade, sharp and deadly, swished through the air in line with her neck. Her shriek seemed not to come from her as her mind raced through all that had led to this: Helena's determination that Rose should pay for her perceived sins by sacrificing her happiness, and when that was not enough, her life.

There was not even the consolation that Rampton knew the truth; that Rose was blameless in all but assuming the role of a married woman. For that, though, he had long ago forgiven her; embraced it, in fact.

Helena and Geoffrey were about to make off with the family jewels, which Rampton and the rest of the world assumed she had stolen. Not only was she now condemned to death, she was condemned to being a party to a multitude of crimes of which she was innocent, yet Rampton would forever consider her a thief and a sinner. The fear thundered in her ears like cannon-fire.

'No!'

All the desperation and despair at the injustice of such a brutal, heinous act resonated from the one word. The anguished plea for clemency echoed in the void left by the flight of rational thought as she was reduced to a cornered animal facing slaughter. She didn't want to die. Where was Rampton? Where was her husband? He'd forsaken her, believing every vile lie that had been disseminated, yet she still loved him. Perhaps if he knew the truth he'd love her too.

'No!'

The cry continued to resonate in the chill evening air, its desperate hollow timbre sounding eerily like it belonged to a creature from another world. Going to another world, she thought as she was pushed to the ground, the air knocked from her lungs, her last conscious thought that she'd accept even a loveless existence only life was too precious to be condemned to eternity with a reputation she didn't deserve burnt into the memories of all those who spoke her name.

Shock, blackness. She thought she was dead. She thought she was still screaming but she was trapped beneath a body in a coquelicot gown and the scream had taken on a different dimension: shrieks of pain interspersed with disbelieving howls of rage.

Choking on the acrid smell of gunpowder, Rose struggled beneath the weight of a body slumped over her own.

Helena?

'In God's name!'

She turned her bewildered face to Geoffrey, raising her hands to see them sticky with blood. Not hers? Geoffrey must have . . .

But Geoffrey's face was a mask of horror as he bent over Rose to reach Helena, now writhing beside her. Helena had uttered the cry. It came in staccato gasps of horror as she held her hands to her wounded head.

'What has happened to me?' Her hysteria grew as her bloodied hands revealed part of the answer.

'Rose!'

A masculine voice sounded from a short distance away. Familiar and comforting. Filled with heartfelt emotion.

Rose transferred her shocked gaze from the grisly sight of Helena's mutilated face, to the direction in which Geoffrey now stared as he rose, rapidly fumbling with the knot that bound him to Rose; preparing for his own flight, though Rose in that moment had eyes only for her husband.

And all the fear, shock and horror of the past few hours was replaced by joy at seeing him bounding down the hill, tucking his pistol inside his coat before opening his arms to claim his wife.

23

Rose awoke to the sounds of birds singing and a lively chorus of frogs and insects. Stretching luxuriously on the blanket her husband had laid out for their picnic beside the river, she rolled against his side. Although she could not see his face she knew he still slept. His breathing was deep and even, yet even in sleep, in the middle of an innocent afternoon, he held her as though he'd never let her go. As he had every night since he'd eliminated the greatest threat to Rose's health and happiness. It was as if he couldn't keep her close enough.

Tremors of comforting warmth crept over her as he stirred, turning to stroke her hair.

'It'll be the last time we can do this,' she murmured, gazing at the hazy blue sky, conscious that the season was changing and their long rambles by the riverside would come to an end. Rampton, too, would inevitably become less attached to her as familiarity reduced the novelty of their reborn love, she acknowledged in the deepest recesses of her mind.

'What do you mean, 'the last time'?'

He was instantly awake now. Leaning over her so he could look into her face he demanded, 'How can you say anything will be 'for the last time'?' His voice was a low, demanding growl while his hands caressed the contours of her cheeks, nose and eyes as if committing them to memory. 'Has everything we've been through not proved how tenuous happiness is . . . how careful we must be to safeguard it?' His breathing was heavy, as if he'd been offended by her suggestion.

'I was talking about the weather making this sort of thing no longer possible.' Rose laughed and reached up to kiss him, pulling him back down beside her. She felt him relax with a slow, satisfied sigh as they both stared up at the sky, holding hands like the lovers they were.

There was gentle amusement in his voice, overlaid with conviction as he warmed to his theme. 'If we feel like trysting amidst the pouring rain, we should do it. Time is too short to allow convention to prevent us squeezing every last drop of enjoyment from life.'

Bringing his hand to her cheek, Rose sighed. 'That was obviously Helena's philosophy, but look where it landed her.'

With great reluctance Rampton helped her to her feet. 'Exactly where she deserves,' he said, plucking the leaves from Rose's hair before wrapping his arms about her from behind. 'And she should consider herself lucky to escape the hangman's noose.'

'I'm not sure that life with Charles in the West Indies bearing those terrible scars would have been her preferred option.' Rose shivered, remembering the horror of seeing the blade slice the air in line with her neck.

'It was your life, or Helena's,' he reminded her as he began to wind her hair back into some semblance of respectability. 'Thank God Beth was induced to reveal the exact point where Helena had buried the jewels, and that I got there in time. Now, stay still.' As he laced her gown, Rose was aware of his shudder as he performed the task of her lady's maid. Briefly he pressed his cheek to the hollow between her shoulder and cheek. 'I don't know how I could have lived with myself if something had happened to you, my darling.'

Hearing the catch in his voice, Rose reached up her arm to caress his soft, springy curls and closed her eyes. This was by no means the first of such avowals but they still had the power to stir her in ways she'd not believed possible. How sweet love was. And she and Rampton had a lifetime together in which to enjoy it.

Edith now fulfilled Beth's role, except when Rose and Rampton slipped away for afternoon pleasure jaunts like this one. It seemed they could not get enough of one another.

She thought he'd straighten and resume the task at hand, which was to prepare themselves to return to Larchfield for the vicar's visit, which the dowager had organised. Instead, shivers of longing radiated through her as his soft murmur tickled her cheek. 'You think it won't always be like this?' The gentle pressure of his hand, which had grasped one of hers, increased. 'It won't, my darling, I promise you. It will only get better. I shall only grow to love you more. You must believe it.'

Rose turned in his embrace and twined her arms about his neck. She stared into his face. 'Then I will believe it,' she whispered, with a surge of that now-familiar emotion, joy. 'I'm sorry Charles could not have found similar happiness.' She thought of him with sadness, bearing his grievously disfigured wife back to their island home aboard the the *Emily*.

'If Charles had shown her a firm hand from the outset, I doubt her behaviour would have got so out of hand.'

Rose ignored the criticism. 'Poor Charles. He'll forgive Helena anything. But it will be a life sentence for Helena.'

Rampton's arms tightened about her and she saw the fervour in his eyes as they locked gazes. 'My life sentence is one I have yet to earn, my sweeting.' Briefly, he caressed her cheek, his look tinged with remorse. 'I needed forgiveness for believing what was offered to me as irrefutable proof . . . though I wasn't sure whether you would grant it to me.' He sent her a meaningful look and Rose blushed. She could not deny the thrill of power she had felt when Rampton had gone down on bended knee and kissed the hem of her skirt, pledging his love and begging her forgiveness while Helena lay screaming in Geoffrey's arms. For all his faults, Geoffrey had not left her, although that was probably more due to the fact he'd been unable to slip the cord that bound him to Rose before Rampton had arrived.

Of course Rose had given her forgiveness without reserve. She knew that her husband, having already been deceived by Rose, was not to know she was blameless when all the evidence pointed to her.

They strolled back in leisurely fashion to Larchfield, pausing at the edge of the park to gaze at the beautiful stone house with its mullioned windows peeping through its cloak of ivy as the sun dipped behind the hill.

A nightingale began its evening tune and Rose shivered with pleasure.

Rampton squeezed her hand. 'Mother has offered you her diamond and ruby choker to wear to Felix and Arabella's wedding.' There was amusement in his tone, for Rose had declared that her mother-in-law would never fully trust her until Rose had supplied the nursery with at least half a dozen sons. 'Perhaps you should wear it when you pay your last respects to Geoffrey and Oswald in prison.'

Rose shuddered. 'I never want to see Geoffrey Albright again. The person I feel saddest for is Aunt Alice.'

Rampton's response was robust. 'Aunt Alice has never slept so peacefully since Oswald was incarcerated. She told me so.'

As Rose's mouth dropped open Rampton seized the advantage, stooping to brush her lips with his own. As always the familiar sensations of earthy satisfaction and all-consuming happiness swamped Rose as her wonderful husband murmured, 'I'd say we've all been given our just rewards. Wouldn't you?'

We do hope that you have enjoyed reading this large print book.

Did you know that all of our titles are available for purchase?

We publish a wide range of high quality large print books including:
Romances, Mysteries, Classics
General Fiction
Non Fiction and Westerns

Special interest titles available in large print are:
The Little Oxford Dictionary
Music Book
Song Book
Hymn Book
Service Book

Also available from us courtesy of Oxford University Press:
Young Readers' Dictionary
(large print edition)
Young Readers' Thesaurus
(large print edition)

For further information or a free brochure, please contact us at:
Ulverscroft Large Print Books Ltd.,
The Green, Bradgate Road, Anstey,
Leicester, LE7 7FU, England.
Tel: (00 44) 0116 236 4325
Fax: (00 44) 0116 234 0205

Other titles published by
The House of Ulverscroft:

LADY SARAH'S REDEMPTION

Beverley Eikli

When Lady Sarah Miles becomes the sole survivor of a shipwreck, she assumes the identity of her ill-fated travelling companion to avoid an arranged marriage. Masquerading as governess to the daughter of dashing Roland Hawthorne, the mutual attraction between Sarah and her employer quickly turns to love. But Sarah's past returns to haunt her, revealing more secrets than just her false identity. Determined to redeem herself in Roland's eyes, she unwittingly plays into the hands of an unexpected adversary. With Sarah's honour at stake, can Roland's daring plan succeed? Or will the woman he loves be lost to him forever?

LADY FARQUHAR'S BUTTERFLY

Beverley Eikli

Falsely branded an adulteress and separated from her child by her vengeful late husband, Lady Olivia Farquhar unexpectedly discovers a deep and mutual love for her son's guardian, Max Atherton. But happiness with Max can never be possible when Olivia is blackmailed into a union with her late husband's religious confessor. Unaware of the sinister motives behind the reverend's desire to make her his wife, or of Max's efforts to clear her sullied name, Olivia is bereft of hope. Can Max turn things around in time?

AS THE CARDS FALL

Christina Green

1891. Bella Reed, orphaned and working in Exeter, receives a letter from someone claiming to be her uncle. Travelling to an ancient farm in remote Dartmoor, Bella meets members of her hitherto unknown family and is astonished to discover she is to be her uncle's heir. But Bella is accustomed to city life and quickly finds the comfortless farmhouse, and its hard rural life, difficult to accept. Then a wise woman tells Bella tales of her late parents and advises her that life must be lived as the cards fall. Only when a violent act puts everything into perspective can Bella finally decide on her future . . .

BARBARA'S WAR

Fenella J. Miller

As war rages over Europe, Barbara Sinclair
is desperate to escape from her unhappy
home, which is a target of the German
Luftwaffe. Caught up by the emotion of
the moment, she agrees to marry John, her
childhood friend, who is leaving to join the
RAF — but a meeting with Simon Farley,
the son of a local industrialist, and an
encounter with Alex Everton, a Spitfire
pilot, complicate matters. With rationing,
bombing and the constant threat of death
all around her, Barbara must unravel the
complexities of her home life and the
difficulties of her emotional relationships
in this gripping coming-of-age wartime
drama.